The Widow's Confession

The Widow's Confession

Sophia Tobin

**SIMON &
SCHUSTER**

London · New York · Sydney · Toronto · New Delhi

A CBS COMPANY

First published in Great Britain by Simon & Schuster UK Ltd, 2015
A CBS COMPANY

1 3 5 7 9 10 8 6 4 2

Simon & Schuster UK Ltd
1st Floor
222 Gray's Inn Road
London WC1X 8HB

www.simonandschuster.co.uk

Simon & Schuster Australia, Sydney
Simon & Schuster India, New Delhi

A CIP catalogue record for this book is available
from the British Library

HB ISBN: 978-1-47112-812-7
TPB ISBN: 978-1-47112-814-1
EBOOK ISBN: 978-1-47112-815-8

Printed a ... Typeset by M Rules ... UK) Ltd, Croydon, CR0 4YY

To A.T.

PROLOGUE

Delphine's letter, April, 1852

I still remember the face of the first girl we found on the sands. I think of her name, and she is there.

Her features have the softness of youth, marred only by the frown remaining on her brow, even in death. She lies on her back, a bright shape on dark sand, the folds of her white gown made translucent by the sea. That sea is coming to claim her, each wave easing forwards, then retreating, each retreat a little less than the one before. The water deepens around her almost imperceptibly; gently, it floats a few of her golden curls.

I sometimes wonder whether my mind is playing tricks on me with this vividness. Perhaps, in reality, when we found her the hungry tide had already retreated from her, and the morning sun had begun to dry the sand. I suspect it is so.

I could not paint her, if you asked me to. Even though I see her face so clearly, I could not describe a single line of it with charcoal or watercolour. The memory of her is stored in some other place; at the thought of her there is a jolt of emotion, but I cannot reproduce the memory of her. I can only feel it.

My reaction to her and to the other dead girls surprised me. I thought that I had hardened myself and packed my emotions away; folded neatly, like the ballgowns of my youth, with dried lavender pressed in paper between them. Yet that summer, with its sea mists and storms, unlocked something in me. A thing I had not killed; just denied.

I write to you now as Delphine Beck, and I write only because you have asked me to. Hitherto, if we are truthful, we have been little more than strangers. To write to you seems dangerously intimate somehow. The paper is passive; it accepts my words as you may not. But I believe you when you tell me that you have to know everything. If we are to begin our lives together, all concealment must be put aside, and sunlight let into a room which has been dark and cold for so long.

My love, I promised you my confession.

Here it is.

CHAPTER ONE

Edmund Steele went to Broadstairs to escape a love affair. It was the first dishonourable act of his life towards a woman. As the train crawled its way through a countryside deep in the lushness of late spring, he pictured the shape of Mrs Craven's white neck when her face was turned away from him; remembered the sheen of the reddish-brown gown she had worn at their last meeting. And, knowing that she had expected him to propose to her, he felt the painful burn of shame, as though he had held his hand too close to a candle flame. I made her no promises, he thought, as the train neared the coast, and he watched the stuttering shadow of its outline on the ground as it moved on: I made her no promises. But he felt no better.

At Margate Sands, Edmund hired a man with a cart to take him to Broadstairs, the horse sweating in the sun and switching its tail. They travelled through the deep narrow lanes of the countryside between the two towns. When they emerged from the green darkness of the last hedgerowed lane, onto the coast road near Kingsgate Bay, Edmund put his head back; felt the sunlight, warm and harsh, slick across his city-worn face. 'Will you pull up for a moment?' he asked the man. 'I'll pay you extra for the lost time.'

The carrier found a stopping place near the edge of the cliff. There was a sharpness to the air, bitterly cold, but welcome to Edmund. He hoped the clean air would reach the depths of his lungs. He had wanted to see the sea: the distant breakers, the vast sky, and the curve of the tan-coloured sands beneath the bone-grey, crumbling cliffs.

'Is it far to Holy Trinity?' he said.

'Less than half a mile. Past the North Foreland light-house over yonder, then we're on the road to Stone, and near enough to the town. Come for a holiday, sir?'

'I think so,' said Edmund.

The church of Holy Trinity and its parsonage were mere steps away from the town, at a point where the road narrowed to a single carriage width. Edmund said he would take his own trunk to the house, and sent the carrier off, but the driveway was long and the exertion tired him swiftly and without warning. He was breathing heavily as he knocked on the door of the parsonage.

When the door opened, he blinked at the darkness, his gaze suddenly clouded by the contrast with the sunlight, as he peered at the young man who was saying his name.

He saw immediately that his host's face had once been marked by illness, and exposed to the scourges of the most brutal heat. Now only the signs were left behind – fading freckles on a face pocked with scars. Yet, it was still a handsome face in its way, its disfigurements giving its underlying beauty a certain power. Its owner hung back, in the shadows of the hallway.

'Do come out of the sun, Mr Steele,' he said. 'It is merciless today. The sea breeze takes the edge off the heat, which means you do not feel it as it beats down on you, but it will punish you if you stay out in it.'

Edmund wondered whether he really did look so bad that he needed to be sheltered from the sun like some delicate maiden, and it pinched his pride. The penalties of easy London living, he thought; too much claret, too much meat. 'You must be Mr Hallam,' he said. 'I admit I did not expect you to be answering your own door.'

Theo Hallam laughed; it suited him. 'I should be working on a sermon. But my housekeeper Martha is fretting over our supper in the kitchen, and as she is sadly overstretched at the moment, it would have been unfair to expect her to look out for you as well.'

'Well, I am pleased to meet you,' said Edmund, holding out his hand.

Theo shook it briskly. 'And I you. But do come out of the heat, Mr Steele, I beg of you.'

The coolness of the tiled hallway was a relief to Edmund, as was the tea Theo ordered from Martha, who looked with frank curiosity at Edmund as she loudly unloaded the tray. They took tea in the drawing room, an immaculate room, uncluttered but tastefully decorated with paintings and ceramics. Its austere beauty surprised Edmund, for he knew the clergyman lived alone, and he did not link such clean serenity with the habits of a bachelor.

'I must thank you for allowing a perfect stranger a room for the season,' he said, trying to take in the details of the room without his eyes lingering too much.

'A friend of Mr Venning is a friend of mine,' said Theo. 'He has known my family since I was a boy, and went to Oriel College, as I did. And I admit that what he told me of your work piqued my interest. I understand you have medical connections, and that you are interested in the study of the mind.'

'I fear Charles has overrated me,' said Edmund, with an uneasy laugh. 'It is true that I count many medical men as my friends, but I do not practise myself. I am comfortable enough – I worked in a City counting-house in my youth, and invested in railways at the right time – so I have the leisure to study what interests me. I have been concerned in one or two cases.'

'And the mind is your area of interest?' said Theo.

Edmund swallowed. 'Yes – that is, it was. I think it is a subject which is in its infancy.'

A warmth had crept over Theo's previously neutral expression. 'You speak of healing the mind, and I the soul. Perhaps we may discuss the way in which these areas overlap.' There was a faint glow in the young man's blue eyes; an enthusiasm which Edmund moved quickly to quash.

'If you would be so kind, I am glad to take a rest from it. Do not mention my interest to any of the sea-bathers, I beg you. I wish to be nothing but a tourist here.' He thought of his study at home – the labelled drawers and cabinets of papers, the neatly written indices. 'I am of robust health, but my friends tell me that I have over-exerted myself recently. I do not feel it myself – I am quite merry – but I trust their opinions. Mr Venning has instructed me to rest,' he smiled, 'and I am sure you can imagine his firmness on the matter.'

Theo nodded, without any offence. 'Very well. You are here before most of the incomers – forgive me, the tourists, I should say. "Incomers" sounds so bare and unwelcoming. Well, you are among the first, so you will be settled in before the rest arrive. My aunt, Mrs Quillian, will be here in a few days or so. She comes every season to the town, and always stays at the Albion. She does not care to dwell with her poor parson nephew; she prefers to be surrounded by people.'

'I thought this was a quiet place,' said Edmund, feeling slightly alarmed.

Theo laughed. 'It is not always so. And any increase in numbers is doubly noticeable to its inhabitants. Many of the local people claim to prefer the rough seas and empty streets of January, but we would be ruined without our guests. We are to have gaslight soon, you know, so the modern age has reached us. You may read of the London arrivals in the newspaper – we have the occasional Duke and Marquis, and Mr Dickens, of course.' He offered Edmund a slice of bread and butter. Edmund took it. The butter was spread thinly, as though it had been spread on, then scraped off, then scraped again.

'Empty streets are unknown to me,' said Edmund, biting into the bread and discovering it was stale. 'Perhaps I should have come in January – I would have liked to see that.' He chewed, slowly. 'Mr Venning says clean air and pleasant company will restore me to my normal ways.'

'Have you been truly unwell?' said Theo. The beauty of the question was all in the way he said it: without the sharpness of gossiping curiosity, but with enough steadiness to assure Edmund he had an interested listener.

Edmund took a gulp of tea to wash down the bread, then put his teacup down, gently, on the small table beside him. 'Well asked,' he said. 'Charles sent me here with good reason. I can see you will be drawing my confessions from me like poison from a wound.'

'Any gifts I have are given me by the Lord, Mr Steele. I will not press you – I do not seek to force confidences – but I am here if there is some burden you wish to discuss. And if we only talk of trivial things, that is welcome too.'

'Do you find it lonely, living in such a small town, without many diversions?' said Edmund. He caught the slight flinch Theo gave, an almost imperceptible movement.

'I would never say that.' Theo folded his hands in his lap and sat up, straight-backed. 'I am where I have been called to be, to serve God's purpose. I am following my faith. But your company is welcome.'

8

It was only later that Edmund realized he had not answered the question.

It was many years since Edmund had attended Evening Prayer on a weekday, but when his host asked him to, he agreed in a moment. The church of Holy Trinity stood a few steps from the parsonage; built as a chapel-of-ease to the Parish of St Peter-in-Thanet, it had been dedicated only twenty years, Theo informed him. It was a flint construction, black and glittering in the summer light, but within, it changed character from brooding to serene. The interior was a large open space, with white walls. The only division was an elaborately carved rood screen. The sweetish stale scent of incense hung in the air.

Edmund took his place quietly in the front pew Theo had pointed out, fearing that, fatigued as he was, he might doze off in the warmth of the summer evening. He could not help but think that he would normally have been in his club at this time, but reminded himself of his resolve to be open to new impressions and new places. London had been his whole life since his teens, which was a good while ago, for he was in his late fifties now. With the exception of his intermittent visits to his parents in Cheshire, which had ceased on their deaths, he had known few other places. It was true he had travelled abroad, but those experiences were like mere framed prints on the wall; distant, separate, as though they had happened to other people. Nothing had touched or changed him. Now, suddenly aware of his advancing years, he felt a little ashamed of it.

He rubbed his eyes. Despite his distance from London, there was much to think of, not least the pressing matter of Mrs Craven and her happiness. He had written a thousand letters to her in his mind, but the outcome was never definite; to ask her for her hand in marriage, or not. Just as he decided on one course, he would think, *and yet* . . .

He heard the church door open and close behind him. Theo looked up from his prayer book. Edmund glanced over his shoulder. A lady had entered the church and was standing a few steps from the door, her gaze sweeping over the church and the few worshippers there without any embarrassment. Slim and tall, she was dressed entirely in black. A widow. Edmund thought her striking, but did not want to stare. He turned back to see that Theo had paused in the deep hush. He gazed long at her, before he returned his eyes to the page and continued reading, his voice moving fluidly over the elements of the service.

The last Amen woke Edmund from his reverie, and he heard the cries of seagulls seeping through the stone walls of the church. When he glanced back, the widow had gone.

Prayers; supper; bed. These would be the things, Edmund thought, which would soothe his troubled mind. He retired as ten chimed on the grandfather clock at the turn of the stairs, and inspected his room by the light of a candle. It was pristine. There was a neat four-poster bed, with heavy hangings drawn back for him; a wardrobe; a washstand with clean towels, soap, a basin and a ewer filled with cold water. A table had been set out in the bay window with writing equipment, and beside his bed was a chair on which sat, neatly placed, a box of matches and another two candles. There was no dust, no cobwebs; knowing that Martha was Theo's only servant made Edmund wonder. Already, Theo had struck him as the kind of man who was concerned with details, and he thought he saw the priest's own hand in the careful preparation of the writing desk, and provision of candles. For a moment he wondered if his host had even made the bed with his own hands. He pulled back the top cover and saw that four blankets had been layered on the bed; but then he had been warned about the fierce sea breezes.

His host's room was situated at the other end of the hall. Edmund heard his feet travelling the length of the corridor, the boards squeaking with every light step.

He settled down at the writing desk, where everything had been prepared for him, dipped the pen into the inkwell and began to write:

My dear Venning,

I have arrived, and find the young man very much as you told me he would be: warm, and hospitable. But there are depths to him, Charles, as you said. This evening we passed his study door and I glimpsed within a portrait of Saint Sebastian. It was a mournful sight, that saintly face full of suffering, his sides pierced with many arrows. Mr Hallam closed the door as soon as he saw my eyes upon it. It is clear that he has not taken a role in the church for the sake of a profession, or convenience; but I will not complain of his intensity. His fireside is warm, his port and brandy good, and, for now, he is short on lectures for a clergyman. I see nothing to trouble me yet.

Did you really only send me here to 'recover my spirits' as you so charmingly put it? I blame myself for confiding in you that, as a bachelor, long past fifty, I look dully at my life and am weighed down by the burden of my accumulated wisdom. Are you giving me a rest cure, as you claimed, or another diversion?

I doubt I will receive a full explanation by return. I will breathe in the sea air and smile benignly, and pray that I get through this 'holiday' of mine alive.

Your good friend, Edmund Steele

Edmund left the letter open so that the black ink, glossy in the candlelight, would sink into the paper. Then he got up and walked around the room, not worrying too much about the creaking boards, for his host was way down the corridor. He had shied away from mentioning Mrs Craven in the letter, though Charles Venning and his wife had encouraged the match. He thought of his father, as he often did these last months, and wondered if he had disappointed Alban Steele by not being as pure in intention as him. It was in his recent studies that he had sought to close this gap, and to add some seriousness to a life that had been full of trivialities. He had also wished to examine the darkness which had haunted his father; the shadow which, despite Alban's happiness, had yet come over him sometimes.

'Too late, too late,' Edmund said, under his breath. Amusement and diversion; these were the things that made his life bearable. If his father, a silversmith and an artist in his way, had bequeathed him something, it was exactness: a precision which had served him well in the building and keeping of his fortune, and was at odds with his otherwise relaxed nature.

Fretfully, he went over to the window and lifted the drape. Dense, blue-black darkness greeted him: it was perfect night in this seaside town, deeper and darker than any city night. He could not hear a sound, not even the cry of a gull. He wondered if it was the trees, waving in the growing breeze, that swathed the parsonage in such complete darkness; but after a minute or two he saw there was a gap in them, a line of sight intermittently blocked by their movement.

He saw a light.

He tilted his head and took a step to the right. Across the narrow road at the end of the driveway, someone was standing on the step of one of the cottages. He narrowed his eyes at the pale column and made out the figure of a woman, holding a candle, shielded from the sea breeze by a glass shade; he caught the glint of it. He raised his hand, but the pale shape showed no sign that she was aware of his presence. She stayed still, seeming to stare straight ahead. He had no idea what she was looking at; the building he was in was surely cloaked in leaves, a mass of darkness to her eyes.

He waved a little more, until he felt foolish, and

dropped the drape. He took a turn around the room and closed his letter. Then he could not help himself; he went to the window and looked out again. But the figure was gone. There was no light behind the shutters of the cottage, no sign that anyone was within.

He undressed and got into bed. The balminess of the day had quite gone; the bed was cool, and he was aware that his heart was beating hard, and that he wanted to know who had been watching the parsonage. 'It is a quaint little place,' Venning had told him, 'but do not listen to the local people: they can talk only of wrecks, and they try to scare the ladies, speaking of sea-monsters and ghosts.'

Ghosts, thought Edmund. Foolish, so foolish. He closed his eyes and thought of his childhood, imagining that he was in his parents' cottage again, his mother stirring a pot on the range. He thought of the London streets, the chaos and energy, the messenger boy running to him, bringing news of the money he had made through no labour of his own. He heard the chink of Mrs Craven's wine glass as she set it down on the silver salver bought by her first husband. And at last, as he fell asleep, he saw the pale shape of a woman on a step, and the dark and glittering sea.

CHAPTER TWO

The summer of 1851 seems as distant to me now as my child-hood. It is as though a different Delphine Beck lived through that time. My cousin Julia and I began the year in London, but as the world flocked there to visit the Great Exhibition and see its nov-elties, we knew it was time for us to leave. Just as the world opened up, we went to Broadstairs because it seemed to be the perfect place to hide. A place for invalids, for those who hoped to convalesce, and those that never would. The town was known for its retired nature, and we thought that if we stepped quietly amongst its residents they would never notice us.

Broadstairs was one more resting-place on the ceaseless jour-ney Julia and I had taken since the autumn of 1841, when we left New York for England on the Great Western. We had spent ten years touring Europe, travelling as much as our small income would allow. We thought this quiet sea-bathing resort would be no different from the spa-towns or the lakeside villages we had seen, where we kept to ourselves, careful not to make connections.

We arrived in May, before the season had begun. The days were long and bright; the light hard and clear, sometimes even cruel in its merciless exposure of every flaw. Going to sketch on the beach in the early mornings, I thought that I had never seen such light before.

Night fell differently there, too. Raised in New York, I was surprised by the swift way in which it descended: the sharpening air, the total darkness, only broken by the sweep of the lighthouse's lantern at North Foreland and the flashing signals of the lightships marking the Goodwin Sands out at sea. Coming out of our cottage, I would never know which way to turn: towards the darkness of the foreland, or towards the town, where the locals sat in the taverns and conversed by the light of flickering candles.

I often wonder what that summer would have been, without the deaths. Would we – a group of strangers – have been thrown together with such intensity? Our loves, our hatreds, focusing in the presence of death, giving every word, every touch, a sense of urgency. It seems so strange when observed at a distance, now that time has passed. We could have been like any other group of travellers, passing and grazing each other lightly, with polite conversation and the occasional cutting remark. Instead, we were a conflagration, or perhaps that conflagration was only within me.

Delphine went to sketch on the sands at Main Bay, going early, before anyone else was there apart from one or two fishermen on the pier. She was seated with her back to the town, and the bathing machines were not yet drawn to the water's edge, so she saw only the sea, the clouds and the sun. When the first walkers came, she closed her sketch-book and left the beach.

Harbour Street and the clifftop promenade were still quiet. Delphine walked for some way until the path verged upon a cornfield, which went right up to the cliff's edge. On its most far-out point, she looked down upon the whole bay; the perfect view for a painter. But already, more people were out, and she knew it was time to go back to Victory Cottage, her home for the season.

Her route back took her through the town and past the Albion Hotel. It was a large square building, solid as a dowager and with the same pretensions to stateliness, despite evidently having been battered by the sea winds that winter. It was the foremost of the town's hotels and associated with Charles Dickens, though he had long since decamped to Fort House, a private residence, for his summer seasons in the town. She paused to look at the hotel with the interest of a stranger's eye – the lantern over the large entrance and the little ornamentation cut into the stones – to consider whether she wished to sketch it.

In the back of her mind she had noted the swift approach of a carriage from the distance, but it was only when the growing noise of hooves and wheels intruded into her thoughts that she became truly aware of the danger she was in. The horse and carriage had come from the top of the town; it was downhill all the way, with the

Albion at the bottom. The horse had bolted. It was hurtling forwards, head high, eyes rolled back as its driver struggled with it. As she turned, the sudden vision of it arrested her where she stood; frozen, one hand against the wall of the hotel.

So this is how it ends, she thought, after a journey of a thousand miles. And in that single, endless moment, she closed her eyes.

In the blackness she heard the carriage draw up with a fearful, skidding sharpness, scattering grit so that some hit the windowpane of the hotel past her head, and the horse gave a painful whinny. She waited for the sound of splintering wood, the scream of the animal.

The sounds did not come.

She opened her eyes and saw the proprietor of the Albion, Mr Gorsey, come running out of the front door, a young woman in drab clothes on his heels, wiping her hands on her apron.

'Michael!' Gorsey shouted. His voice quietened as he came nearer; it would be foolish to scare the horse more. 'Damned idiot!' He caught sight of Delphine. 'Forgive me, madam – Polly, see to the lady.' He reached for the horse's head, as its driver jerked viciously at the reins.

The girl who had followed him turned to Delphine, straightening her hair as she did so. The triviality of the gesture almost made Delphine laugh out loud. 'I am unharmed, thank you,' she said.

The door of the carriage opened. 'Madam – are you hurt?'

It was the first man who climbed out of the carriage. He was at her side in two steps. Her shocked mind took in every detail of his appearance: a pallid wide face, black eyes, and lank black shoulder-length hair. He was dressed in the finest of the London fashions, but in a dishevelled way, as though his clothes had been flung on rather than arranged. On his lapel a pin glittered: a white enamelled skull, with ruby eyes. Delphine knew the price of many things, and she certainly knew Parisian jewels when she saw them. Before she could draw away, he had taken her gloved hand in his.

'Mr Dean lost control of his horses. Mr Ralph Benedict RA, at your service,' he said, with a bow. She looked down; he was still holding her hand. 'Madam, do speak to us, and tell us you are not harmed. This young lady will find you some tea.' He smiled briefly over Delphine's shoulder at the young woman who worked in the hotel.

His touch had violated the space that Delphine normally kept around her, and she felt his gesture to be a mark of disrespect, an advantage taken of her shock. There was something else, too: a fleeting irritation at his confidence. She withdrew her hand, saying coolly, 'I am well,' and turned to walk away.

'And your name, so I may enquire after you?' he said, with a quickness that irritated her further. She wondered how he could say it in such an unperturbed way, when she had her back to him.

'As I said, I am quite well,' she replied, turning back. 'There is no need to enquire.'

'Will you come into the hotel, and rest for a moment?' he said. But she merely curtseyed, and moved off.

She heard the uproar of Mr Gorsey's rage begin again; the sounds of trunks being pulled down. She walked away as swiftly as was decent, keeping her head up, trying to quell the strange emptiness of shock which was rising in her.

'I know who she is,' said Michael Dean, who had finally climbed down and seen off the admonishments of the hotel-keeper with a few swift curses. 'Her name's Mrs Beck. I unloaded her trunks when she arrived the other day. She's come here with another lady.'

'I thank you,' said Mr Benedict, with a glance at his ashen-faced servant, who had finally emerged from the carriage interior. 'But that's not quite enough to earn my forgiveness for the ride you've just given us.'

As the others unloaded the carriage, he kept his eyes on the lady who was walking away from him, until she finally disappeared around a turn in the road. Then, and only then, did he turn and smile at the young woman who was ushering him into the hotel.

Victory Cottage stood opposite Holy Trinity Church. It had been renamed forty-six years before, after the *Victory* at the Battle of Trafalgar, but was that indeterminate age known as old, at least a hundred years, but probably more. It was built of the local flint; courses of circular stones hewn in two to reveal smooth dark grey or black with the restrained, occasional glitter of polished jet. There was a naïve quality to the building. Three small panes of glass at the side of the front window were white, green and red for no apparent reason, and the front wall was decorated with a square section of blue and white Delft tiles depicting ships at sea, in stark contrast to the dark flint around them. It had, unusually, a lantern turret; a small watchtower piled on top of the cottage, as though it had been built to watch the sea.

Victory Cottage was dumb witness to Delphine's distress as she hurried through its gate and opened the front door. She had believed the carriage would hit her, and was still shaking, despite her resolution to be calm.

As she walked into the small hallway, she almost tripped over a large girl on her hands and knees, who was scrubbing the tiled floor.

'I'm glad to see you again, Martha,' said Delphine, putting her sketchbook on the hallstand and unpinning her cloak. With relief, she heard the timbre of her own voice: low and firm, as though everything was normal.

The girl smiled broadly. 'Of course, madam. I said I'd come, did I not? I'm happy to be of use to you for the season, or until my sister is well again. I have to go to the parsonage first in the mornings, but they finished breakfast early this morning. Even if I can't be here much, I'll be sure to make you something cold for supper every day.'

'Don't exhaust your strength,' said Delphine. 'We are quite independent, you know; if you cannot cook for us, we can make other arrangements.'

'There'll be no problem, madam,' said Martha, with the serious, direct stare Delphine had come to associate with her. 'I'm as strong as an ox, that's what Pa says, and if you do not mind that I am not here often, I will char as best I can for you. My sister may be well again in a week or two, and then she will come and do it.'

'As you wish,' said Delphine. She walked into the back parlour, where her cousin was eating breakfast.

Julia said tightly, 'I thought we agreed that I would go out with you in the mornings. I hardly need to point out to you how improper it is for you to be wandering around on your own.' Her blue eyes flashed as she poured the milk.

Delphine shuffled into a little space next to her. The round gate-leg table took up most of the room. They had fallen in love with the cottage and its small rooms, smelling of the sea, but they had not yet adjusted to the lack of accommodation for their clothes and their belongings. Their trunks lay largely unpacked. The two ladies travelled alone and were used to hotels, so when Martha, a local girl, had turned up on their first evening and said she had been sent to lay the fire in place of her sister, who normally cared for the cottage, they had engaged her for the season without a moment's hesitation. Delphine wondered whether she would have cause to regret it: the girl had proved to be far from the average servant, with her irregular attendance and cheerful inquisitiveness.

'Delphine?' Julia put her cup down. 'You are trembling. What has happened?'

'Nothing of any consequence,' said Delphine, with a laugh that sounded false, even to her own ears. 'I was nearly run down on Albion Street by a carriage and a bolting horse. I fancied for a moment that the estate agent might have hired someone to end my life.'

'You poor thing.' Julia put her hand over Delphine's. She raised her voice. 'Martha, fetch Mrs Beck a glass of Madeira – quickly, please.'

Martha did so, and Delphine drank it back swiftly under the concerned gaze of the two women.

'It was nothing of consequence,' she said.

'If you don't mind me asking, madam, did you say you had trouble with Mr Aiden?' said Martha.

'A little,' said Delphine, ignoring Julia's warning glance. 'He struggled with the idea of renting a cottage to a lady. It mattered not that I had a letter in my hand written by Mr Lock, my agent in London. I suspect also he did not like my accent; he mentioned an accident – I believe the word "lugger" was used?'

'The *Mystery*,' said Martha, pouring a second, healthy amount of Madeira into Delphine's glass without asking. 'One of our luggers, run down by a London-bound schooner which was American.'

'Ah,' said Delphine, resisting the urge to light a cigarette. Julia had made her promise to smoke only when they were alone.

'It's hardly your fault what some other Americans did,' said Martha. 'Where in America do you come from, if you don't mind me asking? I've been itching to know.'

Delphine stared at the tablecloth, and the delicate sea knots worked into it in white embroidery silk. She wondered why she had not engaged a proper maid: silent, and discreet.

'New York,' she said.

'New York!' said Martha. 'How I should wish to go there! And why would you choose to come here?'

'By accident,' said Julia, a little too quickly, though there was no sign of suspicion on Martha's good-natured face. 'We considered Margate first, and then thought better of it.'

'Margate is fine enough,' said Martha.

'I suppose it is,' said Julia, 'if you do not care whether you catch cholera or not.'

At that moment a gust of wind buffeted the house, setting the slates rattling, for it was as though the house, sturdy as it was, lived and breathed with the weather. Martha smiled at the look on Delphine's face. 'No need to worry,' she said. 'This cottage has been here longer than you and me.'

'Mrs Beck is not used to the elements,' said Julia. 'And I admit, last night, the sound of the sea seemed close to me, and the whisper of the wind almost ghostly. I even thought I heard someone out there, and went to look.'

Julia's remark lit a spark in Martha's eye. 'We are good at ghost stories, round here,' she said. 'But you must not go out, madam. When I was a girl my mother always told me never to look from the window if I heard a horse and cart passing by in the early hours; that it would be the ghost of old Joss Snelling, the smuggler, bringing his contraband into the town.'

'And we thought this would be a sleepy place,' said Julia.

'This Joss Snelling interests me,' Delphine said. 'I have heard there are wild tales of smuggling on this coast. And we must have more ghost stories, please – are there no wailing women, dressed in grey? Pale little wraiths, haunting the coastal caves?'

All of a sudden, all the cheerful pleasure Martha had taken in the conversation drained from her face. She looked suddenly sad, and stilled. Mutely, she shook her head. Julia raised her eyebrows at Delphine, questioningly, but Delphine decided not to ask more, for she knew not to press a person in sorrow. She had spent years fending off questions from interested strangers, and had no desire to inflict the same on this young woman.

'I'd best be off, ma'am,' said Martha. She went without a curtsey, suddenly preoccupied, and they let her go. When Delphine went out into the hall, she saw the girl had left her straw bonnet behind.

CHAPTER THREE

The other visitors came slowly at first, like the warning drops of rain in a summer storm. And, like blotches of rain on a hot New York pavement, Julia and I noticed them all the more.

Mr Benedict was the first. Our previous meeting, when his carriage nearly ran me down, seemed to convince him that we were somehow friends. One morning I found him at the place on the cliff I had wished to use as my viewpoint, his easel set up. He sought to charm me, and asked to see my pictures. I held them close to me, and was blunt when he tried to insist. He woke a violent anger in me; his unceasing persistence reminding me of that last meeting with the man I refer to as my husband. That persistence is a kind of violence, in its way; it pushes through everything and tires its victim, forcing one to either surrender or angrily break away.

You will wish to know of that man Benedict reminded me of.

The so-called husband I hide behind. I use the ugly remembrance of him to shield me. When creating a protective legend, it is best to stick to the truth as much as possible. So I use his first name, and when occasionally someone has asked me to describe his looks, I use his looks. It is risky to do so, for I have never yet learned to really control my features, and I cannot help the shadow of disgust which moves across my face at the thought of him. It is a puzzle to the asker, who thinks I have spent so many years in mourning for that man.

I do not use his surname. I thought of Beck myself: a mountain stream, running clear and pure.

Edmund soon found that Broadstairs in daylight was not the mysterious place it had seemed to be on his first night in the parsonage. In the sunshine it appeared peaceful, benign and a little old-fashioned, with no hint of danger. The dark thoughts which had troubled him on the evening of his arrival began to drift away in the purity of the sea air.

A few days after his arrival he went with his host to meet Mrs Quillian, Theo's aunt, who had just arrived at the Albion Hotel. As they entered the coffee room, Edmund observed with interest the world-weary grandeur of the place: the deep red carpet, the dark walls and the hundreds of knick-knacks which, Theo told him, the late Mrs Gorsey had put on the mantelpiece before she had died. 'Poor Polly, Gorsey's daughter, is tasked with dusting them,' said Theo. 'At least I do not give Martha that burden, though the current fashion is for such clutter.'

He looked around the room, acknowledging acquaintances here and there. 'Let us go out into the gallery and take our tea there,' he said. 'You may look at the sea, and it is much lighter and airier there.'

They passed out of the coffee room and crossed the dining room to reach the gallery. Polly was setting the tables, a sulky look on her pretty face, and the only other occupant of the room was a young gentleman, seated in the far corner, looking out at the sea.

Theo and Edmund had settled on a table, and Mr Gorsey had delivered them a tray of tea, when Edmund observed the entrance of a man whose marine garb and weather-beaten face immediately interested him. He was rather surprised to see him walking across the reception rooms of the hotel, and his presence awoke the disapproval of more than one grand lady he passed. Yet at the sight of him Gorsey raised his hand in greeting and went to speak to the gentleman in the far corner with some urgency. The mariner paused near Theo and Edmund; Edmund had the sense of being watched by keen, observant eyes.

'Good morning, Solomon,' Theo said. 'Mr Steele, will you allow me to introduce you to Solomon Holbourn, the Harbour Master? Mr Steele is visiting from London, Solomon, and we are attending my aunt.' He gave a weak smile. 'She is late, as usual, but that is her right.'

'A fine lady, Mrs Quillian. We shall be glad to see her again,' said Solomon. 'After the *Mary White* she sent me the finest letter I ever received – I have it still. Along with a bottle of brandy.' His eyes glittered appreciatively.

'Well-deserved,' said Mr Hallam, turning to Edmund. 'Solomon here is a hero – you may have read of him. He was instrumental in saving seven souls from the Goodwin Sands in March in our new lifeboat. His health is toasted in taverns all over Kent, and even Her Majesty knows his name.'

'I read about it in the London paper. You went into the water yourself, did you not? That must have been a fearful venture,' said Edmund.

The man nodded, only a twitch of his lips indicating that he was glad at the words. 'It was our duty,' he said. 'That is all. And Captain White has gifted us a fine lifeboat, so we have him, as well as God, to thank for our lives.'

Behind him, Gorsey was approaching with the young man who had been sitting in the far corner. The landlord was flushed and cleared his throat repeatedly as he approached, in a kind of rehearsal of what he was about to say.

'I am sorry to interrupt.' Against all expectations, the young man spoke first. He was a well-dressed pup, thought Edmund, a little rough-looking to suit his manners, with long, unkempt black hair but fine clothes and a stance that indicated a good deal of confidence. He bowed low. 'Will you allow me to introduce myself? Ralph Benedict – call me Benedict, that is all. I am here for the summer.'

Uncertain introductions ensued. After a moment's polite conversation, Benedict took a seat at their table without being offered it and leaned back in a relaxed way, flinging his legs out and crossing them at the ankle. He declined tea.

'Mr Benedict is a painter,' said Mr Gorsey. 'He's the gentleman I told you of, Solomon.'

'Here for the whole season?' said Solomon in Benedict's general direction. He had remained on his feet, and his expression indicated that he was no respecter of artists or gentlemen, other than those who impressed him through their actions. His cool gaze surprised and amused Edmund; it was obvious that the mariner had seen men like Benedict before, in great quantities.

'I am,' said Benedict. 'My wife and children will be taking a villa at Ramsgate for the summer, but I will be spending much time here at Broadstairs. I have to work; I am lucky that there is a great demand for my work at present. I must make hay, you know, Solomon. And for my current painting, I need your assistance.'

Solomon said nothing.

'Our Sol is being reticent with you,' said Gorsey, 'because there's already a favoured personage who likes to paint here in the mornings – isn't that so? Your Widow of the Sands?' He gave a pleased little giggle.

Edmund saw Theo's eyes flicker to Gorsey's face, before he looked back down and stirred his tea.

Solomon seemed annoyed at Gorsey's words, as though a confidence had been betrayed. 'There is a lady who comes to paint on the beach in the morning,' he said, 'but I have nought to do with it. Nor do I care to meddle in other people's business – unlike you, Gorsey.'

'How do you know she is a lady?' asked Benedict, with a smile that won a sharp look from Theo.

'She is,' said Solomon, his voice low and firm. 'There's many a bad woman dressed in good clothes – I know that – but she is a true lady in her manners and her expression. Not old, but with a gaze that's as deep as the sea. Wise. The kind of woman you'd carve on the front of a boat to keep you safe from the waves.' He said this without embarrassment, as though it was a matter of fact, plain and simple.

'You can tell he is smitten,' said Gorsey. Edmund was glad to see that he was not winning points; Benedict was watching the boatman, his expression softened and interested, and he was not responding to the mocking tone of the hotelkeeper. Gorsey ploughed on. 'Oh, I have seen her myself – elegant, but unconventional, and Solomon loves that sweet American voice, do you not?'

'American?' said Benedict. 'I think I have met her, the day I arrived. She was on the pavement when Dean nearly drove into your parlour, if you remember. Is she really a painter?'

'What do you need me for, sir?' said Solomon, and Edmund saw Benedict put away his curiosity; for all of his roughness, he was a sensitive reader of the expression on the man's face.

'I would like you to take me to the Goodwin Sands,' said Benedict. 'I've heard much of their horrors, but I also happen to know that it is possible to be taken there. I would pay a handsome amount to see the view from that swirling island of quicksand – and Gorsey tells me you are the man to take me there.'

'A ridiculous idea,' said Theo. Benedict glanced at him, bemused.

'I'm a hoveller and a shipwright, sir,' said Solomon. 'But I don't go to the Sands unless necessity takes me there. As Mr Hallam indicates, it's not a place for picnics and sketching. I treat it with respect, and I suggest you do the same.'

Amused outrage permeated the young man's expression. 'What makes you think I would not treat it with respect?' he said, glancing at Gorsey, whose face was reddening at the thought of his lost commission.

'The fact that you can name it with a smile on your face, as though it means nothing to you,' said Solomon. 'You may find someone to take you out there, but I am not the man. No, Gorsey – be silent on the matter; you've said quite enough already. Mr Benedict, if you take my advice, you will spend your money on donkey rides for your children. Those that go to the Goodwin Sands – whether willingly or otherwise – most often have cause to regret it.' He nodded, and went to turn away.

'What time does your widow come to paint?' said Benedict, to his back. 'I am planning to go out there in the mornings myself, and I wouldn't wish to disturb her.'

'I hardly know,' said Solomon. 'And you are free to do what you wish, sir. It's nought to me who walks on the beach. Mr Hallam, Mr Steele, I'll wish you good day.' He nodded at Gorsey, and strode out of the room.

*

To Theo's evident irritation, Benedict stayed with them after Solomon's departure, and even managed to wrestle an introduction to Mrs Quillian, who came to join them not long afterwards. Having charmed her with several compliments, the painter departed with little ceremony, saying that he should be working. Edmund was relaxed about the young man's lack of manners, but he could tell Theo was not sanguine.

Edmund found Theo's aunt to be an agreeable presence, enlivening his conversation with Theo like a shot of rum in water. It was clear she was past sixty, but despite her widowhood she dressed in bright colours, and confided immediately in Edmund that Mr Quillian would not have wished her to wear black for longer than was necessary. She was wide-eyed, rosy-cheeked, and had the kind of nimble movements which showed that she had long enjoyed climbing mountains, making tours and arranging excursions, and was not the kind of woman to make a fuss over small things. She had already canvassed Mr Gorsey for the most interesting arrivals to Broadstairs and, she told Edmund, made firm friends with a certain Miss Waring, a woman near her own age, who had come down from London with her beautiful niece. She looked at Edmund with frank interest and admiration. 'You may even wish to marry the young girl!' she suggested, a wicked glint in her eye. 'She is as pretty as a picture, you know.'

'Aunt,' said Theo, with a sigh. He had been out of sorts since the conversation with Benedict, and was listening to

Mrs Quillian with a resigned expression, toying with the knife on the tablecloth.

'Mr Steele is not offended, Theo,' said Mrs Quillian stoutly. 'And I'm told that gentlemen often come down to the seaside to find a bride, even a distinguished man such as Mr Steele, who I am sure could marry whoever he wishes.'

'I am sorry to tell you I am not looking for a bride,' said Edmund, with a smile. 'And I am practically in my dotage, so if you have found a beautiful young lady, she is not for me.'

'In your dotage?' cried Mrs Quillian. 'Nonsense. You can't be more than five and forty.'

'I will ask for more tea,' said Theo, getting up and squaring his shoulders, as though he might shake off his aunt's words like a dog shaking off dust.

Mrs Quillian watched her nephew cross the red carpet and speak to Polly. The brightness faded a little from her face, and the smile she gave Edmund was one of such intense sadness that he hardly knew what to do or say.

'I am so very glad you are here with my nephew,' she said. 'So very, very glad. He has long needed company. He has long needed a friend.'

CHAPTER FOUR

I accept my own agency in all that happened. I strongly believe there is no other way to live. Those who cast everything into God's hands – how comforting that must be. I have never been able to surrender control in that way. You must tell me, one day, how you do it. As when I had recovered from the first wave of bitterness after we left New York, I accepted that I had played my part in shaping my fate, so I will not blame others for any suffering I underwent that summer in Broadstairs.

When the first girl's body was found on the beach, I need not have been there. The gentlemen actively tried to stop me from accompanying them, but with what would have been considered indecent firmness, I insisted on going. Despite what I said, my decision to go was mostly informed by curiosity for, parched by my sterile travels, I thirsted for experience.

I did not know my decision would haunt me. I can hardly

believe I hurried towards it, towards her, *as though seeing her dead would be another experience, another sketch for my portfolio. How foolish and heartless that seems. My only excuse is that perhaps I feared that I myself was dead in some way, and wished to compare a living death with a real one.*

When Delphine opened her eyes, she could not hear the sea or the wind, and the window showed a clear sky, the light merciless. It was the perfect morning for painting, and she rushed to dress and gather her drawing materials. Despite her cousin's warnings that she should not go out alone, she cherished such mornings. In London she had asked her dressmaker to produce a drawing dress – one that could be fastened at the front, by her own hands, and did not require her to have help dressing on a day such as this. She put it on. Then she swathed herself in her voluminous, hooded cloak, pinned up her hair, and tied her black bonnet on.

She went outside, into the small garden before the cottage. As she had guessed, the light was perfect, every shadow hard-edged. So it was that she saw Mr Benedict's servant. He was hurrying from the direction of York Gate and the beach, and carrying an easel under his arm. He paused and looked in her direction, but with unseeing eyes, it seemed, for without any acknowledgement of her presence he turned away, to his left, and began to stride up Albion Street, towards the hotel. The combination of his looks – a shocked expression with an extreme pallor – and the urgency of his movement made Delphine leave her sketchbook in the hall and follow him.

There was no one on the street but them, and the man's pace did not slacken, so Delphine had to hasten to keep up with him. As she expected, he turned into the Albion. When she reached the reception she saw signs of his hurried entrance – the easel left leaning haphazardly against the counter. The hotelkeeper would not like it, she thought, scraping the wood. The room was empty and the sound of raised voices drew her on to the coffee room, where the servant was talking in an agitated manner to Mr Benedict and Mr Gorsey. His back was to Delphine, but the tone of his voice as he said, 'We must go there, quickly,' indicated extreme distress.

Along with Gorsey, Mr Benedict saw her immediately, and despite the look of grave concern on his face, his eyes sparked at the sight of her as the hotelkeeper held up his hand commandingly to silence the servant.

'Not in front of the lady,' said Mr Gorsey.

'Oh, I wouldn't worry about Mrs Beck,' said Benedict. 'I am sure she is unshockable.' His eyes roamed her face, as though he was savouring her expression. 'My fellow artist,' he said, 'were you out roaming on this fine morning?'

'What has happened?' she asked, ignoring the insolence of the question. The servant's shoulders bowed a little more, as though he was attempting to fold himself away.

Benedict patted him on the back. 'Go up to the room,' he said. 'You have had a shock, and will be no use to us. Gorsey and I will sort all this out.' He turned back to Delphine. 'Nothing to alarm you unduly, as an American.

In your nation of shotgun-bearers, life is cheap, is it not?
Poor old Edward went to construct my easel and found a
body on the beach.'

His eyes met hers.

'How terrible,' she said.

'Yes,' said Mr Benedict, 'a young girl, apparently.' And
the look of curiosity that had been painted so large across
his face at the sight of her was replaced completely with an
expression of distress. The sudden change did not suit
him; his was a face that was suited to a smile, for it gave
his pale complexion and rough dark features the glitter of
energy and health. In his sudden sorrow he looked
drained and ill. He gazed at Delphine for a moment, then
turned back to the hotelkeeper.

'We have spent too much time talking,' he said. 'Let us
go. Edward said she was at the shoreline – well, she can't
be left there. Do you have a constabulary here?'

Mr Gorsey looked amazed. 'Why, this is not London,' he
said. 'They tried to bring one in for Kent, but it was
rejected.' He looked obscurely proud of this. 'There's the
parish constable, but he won't thank us for fetching him at
this hour, if she's nought but a drowning.' He shifted awkwardly on his feet. 'Are you sure you wish to be involved
with this, sir?' he asked. 'The only medical man is Dr
Crisp, and we won't raise him at this time. He's never up
before noon, and he's been getting worse recently. He'll
downright refuse to come, even if we knock him up.'

'Not even for a body?' said Delphine.

'Especially not for a body – for a corpse won't pay.

Forgive me,' said Mr Gorsey with a glance towards Delphine. In his agitation he had forgotten his obsequiousness. He pondered the problem. 'I can fetch Mr Hallam, the parson – he may know what to do. Or . . .' he hesitated. 'We could leave her. She is hardly our responsibility.'

'That is not possible,' said Benedict. 'Let us fetch Mr Hallam. We will go together. But not you, madam,' he said to Delphine. 'It is not right that you should come with us.'

'I think it absolutely right that I should,' she said, and saw Mr Gorsey look sharply at her. 'I am hardly a green young girl, and I have seen much of illness and death in my own family. We do not know what the circumstances are, but it would sit better with me if I could be there. This poor woman should have one of her own sex at her side, for the sake of decency.' She looked at each of them in turn, and waited for their objections. 'Let us not lose any more time,' she said.

They found the clergyman and his guest at breakfast; the meal was hastily abandoned and Mr Hallam asked Mr Steele to attend also. 'Your medical knowledge may be of use to us,' he said. Edmund thought it would be ungracious to remind him of the fact that he was on holiday, and noted with interest that there was a lady in their midst – the fine lady he had seen at church.

'She is the painter Solomon mentioned,' Benedict said in a low voice to Edmund as they left the house. 'Fine-looking, is she not? But headstrong. Short of forcibly bundling

her back to her house we cannot get her to quit the situation.' He looked as though he would have relished the
prospect of putting such a plan into action.

'She seems determined,' said Theo, who was walking
on Edmund's other side. 'If she is so wilful that she will
not listen to reason then she must take what comes.'

Walking behind them, Delphine heard everything but
said nothing. She had seen the displeasure in the priest's
face at the sight of her. Yet the same impulse which had
urged her to follow the servant to the hotel pushed her on.
She knew it was dangerous to involve herself in local
affairs, to attract attention, when the safest course was to
remain anonymous and away from prying eyes. Despite
this, the gentlemen's desire to stop her from going with
them intensified her need to continue; it was an instinctive
battle.

The group hurried on, turning the corner and passing
downhill, walking under York Gate, a gateway that had
once had a portcullis as a defence against raiders from the
sea.

The bay was empty except for gulls; the blue sky and
pale sand giving an impression of serenity, with the sea
lapping at the shore and barely a cloud in the sky. There
were no hovellers or mariners on the pier; the only breaks
in its dark silhouette were the capstans, and a few gulls.
The strong smell of seaweed, entangled in the legs of the
wooden pier, hung in the air, and a dense green line along
the beach showed where the outline of the sea had been
earlier.

As soon as they came to the sand Mr Benedict began to walk faster, and as he passed her Delphine saw a kind of desperation on his face – as though he knew that if he did not press on, at speed, he would turn away and not come back. Mr Gorsey came to a halt on the road, as if some invisible barrier had been reached. 'I will stay here,' he said. Then, defensively, 'I did not ask to be part of this business.'

Mr Benedict hurried along the water's edge for some way. He reached what Delphine saw as a small mound, then raised his hand to signal to them.

Mr Steele reached him next. Delphine sensed Mr Hallam come alongside her, then saw that he was offering her his arm.

'If you must see this,' he said.

She remembered the flicker of harshness in his eyes when he had caught sight of her.

'I thank you, but I do not need your assistance,' she said.

He dropped his arm. 'Very well.'

Mr Steele was crouching down beside the girl, so at first Delphine only saw her bare feet and her legs. She was wearing a flowing white gown – an underdress. Mr Steele was examining her; he looked up at them and shook his head. 'There's no hope,' he said, 'no hope at all. She has been dead several hours at least.' He stood up and dusted the sand from his trousers, and the girl's face and torso came into view.

Delphine could not look away. Her eyes were fixed on the dead child before her, and her heart was beating hard.

She forced herself to keep her composure, but she felt suddenly, desperately sick. The girl looked to be in her early teens, but there was nothing of adulthood about her at all; her features still had the softness of childhood, and the tiny number of freckles across the bridge of her nose shone out against the now purplish-white hue of her face. Her hair was long and a pale blonde, and there were pieces of seaweed and shells entangled with the loose curls. She looked as though she was sleeping, but it was a troubled sleep; a slight frown seemed to lie across her beautiful, childish face, and her right arm lay curved above her head, as though she had flung it there. Her dress was saturated with water.

'I can see no mark of violence upon her,' said Mr Steele. He knelt down again, and raised the body slightly. Delphine wondered at the wiry strength in his arms as he did so. 'I cannot be sure, of course,' he said, 'but it would be logical to think that she has drowned.'

'It seems the sea has carried her in,' said Mr Hallam. He crouched beside the body, holding one hand up in a gesture of blessing as Mr Steele placed her back down. 'Bless this child of Yours, O Lord, that she may find eternal rest in You.' And his voice sank low, as he murmured in Latin.

Mr Gorsey had, at last, joined them. He had made his way across the sand and now stood a little way from the body, his lower lip trembling. 'Poor little thing,' he said hoarsely. 'I do not recognize her.'

Delphine flinched at the sound of his voice, and realized that she was standing, staring at the girl and the praying Theo, her arms limply at her sides.

Mr Steele came towards her. 'Forgive me,' he said, wiping his hands free of wet sand, awkwardly, on his coat. 'I know we have only just met, but you do not look well. Do you think you may faint?'

'I will not faint,' said Delphine sharply, and he raised his chin and nodded.

'Look here.' Mr Benedict was staring at the ground a small way from the macabre discovery, trying to keep his gaze averted from the body. 'Writing,' he said. 'It doesn't make sense.'

Delphine walked over to him, as did Mr Steele. Hallam had stood up, and was looking down on the girl, his features softened in a kind of mourning protectiveness. He took his coat off, and laid it over the girl's body.

Delphine, Benedict and Edmund stood together, looking down, bonded in their mutual incomprehension. Drawn in the sand, in capital letters, was the word: WHITE. Beneath it, in smaller letters, drawn falteringly: *White as snow*.

CHAPTER FIVE

I did not understand Mr Benedict. His emotions would emerge suddenly, violently, and were as changeable as the weather on that coast. One moment he would weep for the dead child; the next I would see him watching me with a coldly observant eye. I had no idea why I was the particular subject of his interest, though already I noticed his eyes linger on every woman he passed.

They put the shell of that poor little girl on a table. The writing on the sand had changed the mood of the group from one of mere sadness: there was an amorphous fear in the room, at least that was what I felt. Was it I alone who thought that a man had snatched her, perhaps violated her, and drowned her? No one said it; I think we all had the desire to turn away and suppress the thought, for surely who would wish to hurt such innocence? Now, I know it was because of that innocence that she died. Her very purity was an invitation to darkness.

Mr Gorsey quailed at the idea of the girl being taken to the Albion Hotel. He went immediately to the Tartar Frigate, the inn which sat almost on a level with the beach, looking out onto the bay – an inn which often had sandbags at its door in the winter, he informed Delphine conversationally. There he hammered on the door and hallooed up, for he knew the landlord well.

In the end it was the landlord who picked the girl up from the beach, the water now fully retreated from her, and the sun beginning to dry the wet sand near the tide, so it was turning from a dark brown to that lighter multifaceted golden colour, the colour which, beneath the sun, showed every grain. The innkeeper was a short, broad man with huge, muscular shoulders and arms covered with tattoos that told of a seafaring past, but he lifted the girl so tenderly that emotion caught Delphine unawares; she had to turn away, to hide the tears stinging her eyes. She had not wept for many years and she had no idea, not then, and not later at her fireside, why it had caught her so, that emotion, and blindsided her. Only that, as she tried to gather her composure and harden herself, she saw the painter, Mr Benedict, who had dropped all pretences along with his hat and was wiping tears from his face with his handkerchief.

As the innkeeper trudged away with the mermaid in his arms, Mr Hallam bent down, picked up the hat, and presented it to Mr Benedict.

'Ah,' said Mr Benedict, his voice trembling, 'that is good of you, Hallam. Thank you.'

The Tartar Frigate was dark inside. There were aged bare boards on the floor and at the bar; the walls were of black flint, and there were thickly varnished wooden benches and booths. It was a place of ancient lineage, Delphine could tell, of nooks and crannies. A place for local lovers, mariners, fighters and conversers: not for tourists. The innkeeper laid the girl down on one long trestle table, still ringed with the remnants of the drinks taken the night before.

'I've seen others like her,' he said, his voice low. 'Plenty are taken by the sea. But she's a young 'un. A baby.' He put his hand out and Delphine saw that, instinctively, he was set to brush the girl's pale curls from her forehead, as one might do to a sleeping child. But his hand stopped halfway through the action: it froze in mid-air and he drew back, glancing at a woman who had just arrived behind the bar: hard-faced, commanding. Sure enough, he went towards her and placed his hand upon the bar; and the woman laid her hand over his. Delphine was fascinated by the gesture: it seemed to combine protectiveness, strength and ownership, all in one brief movement.

'Gorsey,' said the woman, in a rich, deep voice. 'What the bloody hell have you brought to our door?' Then she caught sight of Theo. 'Sorry, sir. A good morning to you.'

Mr Steele sprang into action with an apologetic smile. 'Madam, please forgive us. May I introduce myself?'

In moments, they found a mutual respect borne of plain speaking.

'We're not open for a while yet,' the woman ended, 'but get Dr Crisp here, and then take her out.'

Mr Benedict decided it would be he who would fetch the doctor; he seemed to feel that action was preferable to waiting in the darkness of the inn. He looked so severely distressed that Delphine worried that he might begin to sob or collapse. As he bolted out, she knew that time was moving on, and that Julia would be wondering where she was. If only she had had the foresight to leave a note, or wake her cousin – but how was she to know what would develop?

Within fifteen minutes Dr Crisp had arrived. He was a fine-looking, if pasty fellow, not more than thirty-five but with an air of respectability which comforted Delphine. Nevertheless, he had purplish bags under his eyes and looked as though he had enjoyed a heavy night. He was still rubbing his eyes when he came to the Tartar Frigate, and at the sight of the body, he did not flinch nor let his eyes dart away; there was no sign of distress. Mr Benedict, who had apparently almost beaten down his door in summoning him, had gone to the bar, where the landlady was pouring him a generous whisky. He drank it then put his hat on, pulling it down so low it was almost over his eyes.

Crisp sighed. 'A sad case. I see nothing unusual here, at all. She has gone into the water.'

'Nothing unusual?' shouted Benedict, from the bar. 'My God, what a hardened soul you must be.'

'Do you recognize her?' asked Edmund.

'No,' said Crisp glumly. 'She will be reported soon enough, I'm sure. Pretty little thing.'

Delphine swallowed hard, and looked away. A headache was building behind her eyes, and she suddenly realized she was holding herself in tension, as though she might be struck. Mr Hallam came over to her quietly. 'You are not well,' he said, his steady gaze taking in her face. 'You must allow me to escort you back to your house. You should not have come.' His voice was icy, but his gaze showed no emotion at all.

'I am quite well,' she said. 'I will go home in a moment.'

He checked his pocket-watch. 'I must go to Morning Prayer,' he said. 'Mr Steele – will you see that this lady is taken back to her house?'

Edmund came forwards, his face showing his puzzlement at Theo's abruptness.

'Dr Crisp, it's good to see you,' called the landlady, refilling Mr Benedict's glass as he handed over some money to her. 'Do you care for a porter?'

Crisp brightened visibly. 'Don't mind if I do, ma'am.'

'On the house, sir,' she said merrily. 'But you'd better move things along.'

Edmund walked Delphine back to Victory Cottage. Mr Gorsey had marched back to the Albion Hotel, with the distinct air of someone who hoped to completely disentangle himself from what he had just seen, whilst they'd left Mr Benedict drinking with Dr Crisp. It had been agreed that the body would be moved to the undertaker's, and Mr Benedict was insisting that an inquest should be held. Dr Crisp, however, had made it clear that in his mind, the girl had merely wandered into the water and been drowned.

'Well,' said Edmund, after several moments of silence. 'What terrible things we have seen this morning.'

'There is no need to deliver me to my doorstep,' said Delphine. 'I am quite well, and I promise not to faint in the road.'

He smiled. 'I have no doubt of it,' he said. 'I am sure you have a stronger stomach than some of the men we have just left behind. But I, leave a lady alone to make her way? It is not possible for me, I am afraid. Besides, you live opposite the parsonage, do you not, where I am staying? I am glad Mr Hallam said some words of blessing over that poor child. I know not why, but sometimes one cannot explain the benefit of such things.'

'You seem to have some expertise in medical matters,' said Delphine, remembering the careful way in which he had lifted the corpse and examined the body.

'A little,' he said. 'I have friends who are doctors in London; I am interested in medical matters, and have been for many years. But my main subject of study recently,' she noticed a hesitation as he took a breath, 'has been the mind.' He gave her a fleeting smile. 'You could say, the anatomy of melancholy.'

'How fascinating,' she said.

'It does not help us with this case, however,' he said. 'The writing in the sand is peculiar, though the doctor says

49

it could have been written by anyone, perhaps even a child the day before.'

'But the tide would have dissolved it,' said Delphine.

'I know that,' said Edmund, 'and so do you. But Dr Crisp will not listen. I hope that he is right; that the girl died naturally. It is possible that she went to the beach, and a sudden illness took her. You know, as I do, that death often comes swiftly and mysteriously. Perhaps she even wrote it herself.' He glanced at Delphine and saw the doubt in her eyes. 'When I asked Crisp if he had considered foul play, he shut me down immediately. It is the beginning of the season,' he sighed, 'and they do not wish for even a hint of scandal. Did you see Benedict's servant? The man who found her?'

'I did,' she said. 'But he did not seem guilty, only shocked.'

'Let us hope that is the case.' Edmund paused. 'Mrs Beck, I am sorry, I should not speak to you so openly on the basis of an hour's acquaintance. It is early morning.' He rubbed one hand across his eyes as they stopped at the gateway to the cottage. 'I am not thinking clearly. Forgive me. It is the fresh air, perhaps – it acts like a drug on my system.'

'Do not be concerned for me,' said Delphine. 'None of us are thinking clearly, and I value plain speaking.' They bade each other goodbye, and Edmund turned to walk up the driveway to the parsonage.

'Mr Steele?' said Delphine. He turned back. She wanted to ask about Mr Hallam, and why he had seemed angry with her. Then she realized that their sudden fellowship was illusory, and that such a question would seem ill-mannered. 'Forgive me,' she said, 'I wish you good day.'

That Sunday morning, Edmund waited in the drawing room for Theo to appear from his study. The clergyman was preparing for the service of Holy Communion with meditation and prayer. They had spoken of the dead girl, and Theo said he would touch upon her in his sermon.

Edmund was troubled. He found that when he had come to speak to Theo of the girl's death, he could not talk openly. Though he thought Theo was good, he could not feel it; whatever saintliness was in this boy – for although he knew Theo was in his early thirties, he still had the innocence of youth in his face and expression, and Edmund could not help but think of him as a boy – his particular type of goodness pushed Edmund away. His intensity was a barrier, not an opening; every time Edmund thought he knew him a little more, the next morning the same Theo would appear who had opened the front door on that first day: polite, measured, with an acreage of calm. The surface, Edmund thought; the surface went so far. It reminded him of Mrs Quillian's words about her nephew's loneliness, but he had no idea how to be a true friend to the clergyman.

He dared not begin a discussion of religion, and of the questioning he had seen amongst his circles in London. Theo cleaved to the Catholic past of the Church of

England; it was clear from his choice of music, the ritual he used in worship and the air of monasticism which Edmund sensed in his words and manner. He had studied at Oriel, the heart of the Oxford Movement, and Edmund wondered whether he might convert to Catholicism. Although he was not anti-Catholic like so many Englishmen, he did not wish to pursue the subject, and he wondered if it was this tendency which so disturbed Mrs Quillian.

Edmund had long observed that the quiet faith of his parents' generation – practical, convenient and unobtrusive – had been dissolved, harsh fault lines developing between men of faith and men of science. He was grieved at such division, yet he identified more with the latter than the former, so he supposed his friendship with Theo would have to remain only so deep – at the first strata, the scrubby grass on top of the chalk cliffs.

The church this Sunday did not seem shrouded in the holy mystery that the priest cherished. It was decked with the yellow and purple of spring flowers, and the sound in the air was that of the polite, genial chatter of those who were preparing to meet socially. Edmund even sensed the thrill of sensation in the air, for the news of the body on the beach had spread. The church was full – all free and paid pews taken. Here and there, he saw heads bow in acknowledgement, gentlemen greet each other, and ladies' hands play over silk and satin as they smoothed their best Sunday dresses. He took his seat at the front, alongside Mrs Quillian, and looked around, trying to pick out who was local and who was not, and hopeful that he would see Mrs Beck again.

The crashing chords of the organ called the congregation to attention. There was the rustle of fabric, the soft bump of the occasional prayer book dropped as the congregation rose to its feet and the priest, acolytes and choir processed in. Theo's face was solemn, contemplative, as though he was hardly aware of the people around him. He was dressed in a green cope, embroidered finely in gold thread. When he moved into a pool of light, the sun's rays danced and glittered over the gold on his back, like sunlight on green water. There was a chill to the glitter, however, and Edmund had a sudden sense of the deep and leaden sea that had carried the girl's body round the bay. He tried to suppress the thought.

It was the moment when Theo sang Psalm 130 that awoke Edmund to the man's gifts. His voice had an astonishing beauty; there was something of the cloister in its focused purity.

> 'Out of the depths have I cried unto Thee, O Lord;
> Lord, hear my voice: let Thine ears be attentive to the voice
>   of my supplications.
> If Thou, Lord, shouldest mark iniquities, O Lord, who shall
>   stand? . . .'

Edmund looked around and saw rapt faces; as the incense began to billow, clouding the clear air of the church, one woman fainted and had to be carried out.

Mrs Quillian shook her head. 'Incense,' she whispered to Edmund. 'Is it really necessary?'

Before the service, Delphine had stood outside for some time, feeling the prickly veil of cold sweat on her back, the threat of rain in the air. At the sight of the young girl's body, she felt everything had changed; the shadow of fear, and threat, had made the ordinary seem alien.

As the service commenced, the church was suddenly illuminated by a burst of sunlight through the windows that lined the length of the building near the ceiling. The slanting columns of light pierced the mist of incense as though through treetops in a wood, breaking the darkness of the canopy's shade. It was an effect the artist in her longed to capture; she wished she had a pencil and paper in her hand, for she knew that memory would not be enough to capture its beauty. Had he not been sitting behind her, she would have glanced at Mr Benedict, to see if the artist was watching it, the contrast of light and smoke, the sudden piercing of shadow. If so, she knew he must be tempted to take out his sketchpad, to make some recording of the event – unless, she thought with envy, he held it all in his mind.

Delphine and Julia had paid for places in pew 18, sharing with an amenable family down from London, only just recently arrived. It was the mother of the family – a fine, strong-looking woman – who had fainted the moment the incense had reached her, so that she descended with a clatter and a thump onto the floor and had to be scooped up by her husband, who muttered something about popery as he raised her up. They were gently ushered out into the fresh air, their children, white-faced but silent, tiptoeing behind. Delphine honoured Mr Hallam's composure; he had not ceased, only continued to sing the psalm, his voice soaring. There was nothing showy about the voice, though it was beautiful; it was pure, without any affectation, note-perfect, so that it seemed to meld with, and belong completely to, the beams of light falling through the incense.

Delphine closed her eyes. She thought that, surely, if she was to feel any revelation, it would be at a moment like this. As a child she had stared at the colours in stained-glass windows; had repeated the words of a single prayer, to find something like peace. Much as she knew that revelation could not be forced, still she tried to force it. She had not felt it in years, not since before she had left New York. She could go for months without even seeking it, imagining that she was reconciled to the fact that her heart had hardened. Now she opened her eyes, and found Julia looking at her sadly.

She did not, in truth, listen to the sermon. She concentrated on looking at the details of the church, with its sense of cautious, provincial lavishness. It was a strange thing, this church; it seemed to have a mixed sense of its identity. For all the incense and the stained glass, there were vast stretches of plain, light wall, as though it was trying to play two parts at once. Protestant and Catholic; plain and ornamented; uncomplicated and mysterious. Delphine looked around at the other worshippers, some local, some clearly visitors.

Then, someone turned and looked at her.

It was a young woman; Delphine thought she could not have been more than eighteen years old. The girl caught Delphine's gaze and held it, with no discernible emotion, neither curiosity, hostility nor warmth. Her beauty contracted Delphine's heart as the sunlight had done. Her skin was luminous and dewy, like that of a baby; even from this distance, her eyes were a deep, piercing violet, and her face was surrounded by a silky mass of coppery-gold hair. But there was something else in her; something beyond her features. In that open gaze, there was innocence – and the protectiveness that had sprung up in Delphine as she had looked at the girl on the beach transferred itself to the beautiful face, as easily as releasing a breath. As the girl turned back to listen to the sermon, Delphine found that her gloved hands were clutching the prayer book tightly.

It was then that she glanced over her shoulder, and immediately caught the eye of Mr Benedict, sitting two pews behind her. His eyes were bright, and she was sure that he, too, had seen the girl. He raised his eyebrows, as though he thought himself in silent communion with her thoughts, and with a slight smile curling on his lips, inclined his head to Delphine.

As usual, she chose not to take communion. She was removed from God. She did not wish to do it for the sake of convention, and let Julia pass her and join the lines snaking up the nave to the brass communion rail.

'A life has been lost on our beach and our hearts are full of sorrow, but we must rejoice for her sake, for she is with the Lord, and she will nevermore know suffering.'

These were the sole words spoken by Theo about the dead girl. There was a palpable ripple of excitement through the church. Then he continued, with no further mention of her. Edmund could not help but feel disappointment, as though the child had not been honoured sufficiently.

The moment the procession, led by a silver cross on a wooden staff, had left the church, the atmosphere returned to its pre-service state, the chattering voices rising as the organ continued to play. The instrument increased in volume, as though the organist was valiantly trying to outdo the collective voice of the congregation. At the final crashing of chords, Delphine rose, but when she looked for the young woman who had met her gaze, she could not see her.

Delphine slipped away from Julia. From one of the arches leading into a side chapel she watched her cousin speaking to the clergyman, who was waiting at the door to greet the congregation. From observation of her cousin's back, Delphine knew Julia would be complimenting him warmly on the service, but in Mr Hallam's face she saw only the studied politeness of duty. When Julia moved away he greeted the next person – a person he evidently knew – with deliberate enthusiasm and, knowing that Julia would notice and feel this, Delphine felt a pang of sorrow for her cousin, a kind of tenderness which Julia had recently drawn from her. Still, she did not move; she watched Julia looking at her prayer book, then turning to greet their maid Martha, who had been sitting at the back of the church with her own family.

Delphine was looking at the details of a crucifix in the side chapel nearby, when she heard movement behind her. She anticipated seeing Mr Benedict and braced herself, but the voice she heard made her turn and smile.

'It's a fine piece of work, isn't it?' said Edmund Steele. 'Mrs Beck, may I introduce you to Mrs Quillian? Like you, Mrs Quillian is here for the summer. I am afraid that I made the assumption you would not object to an informal introduction.'

'Forgive him; I begged to be introduced,' said Mrs Quillian, shaking Delphine's hand. Her bright eyes searched Delphine's expression, glittering in her strongly wrinkled face. 'I said to Mr Steele: "Do you know that fine-looking woman?" I am most glad to make your acquaintance.'

'And I yours,' said Delphine. In the past, she would have withdrawn at that moment, but she found herself signalling to Julia to come over. 'May I introduce my cousin, Miss Julia Mardell?'

Introductions were made and acknowledged; it was only later that a detail occurred to Delphine – that on meeting Julia, Edmund Steele had bitten his lip, and let his eyes rest on her face for a moment too long. She wondered if he had noticed the red stain on her pale skin, even beneath her veil.

'I did not expect to see something like this crucifix here,' Delphine said, trying to deflect any questions about their plans or background. The piece she gestured to was wood, the carving naïve, and more brutal than any of the other furnishings in the church.

'I am told it was made by a local man, from timber from a shipwreck,' said Mr Steele. 'But I don't know whether to believe that. It has a certain power, though.'

'The local people must feel in need of protection,' said Julia suddenly. 'The sea can be cruel, as we have discovered this week.'

'Oh, let us not speak of disagreeable things!' said Mrs Quillian, in a brusque tone which made the phrase sound like a reprimand. 'I am afraid that is my rule: we must speak of summer warmth and sunlight only. There are many interesting diversions in this part of the world. I always arrange excursions during my stay in Broadstairs – I am quite established here, you know – and I hope I may rely on you both, such interesting ladies as you are, to attend at least some of them?'

Delphine felt Julia's eyes on her. In all of their travels they had made every effort to remain friendless. It had not been difficult – but this old woman, with her wrinkled face and the Georgian jolliness which seemed thirty years out of date, seemed suddenly to have insinuated herself into their company.

'I am sure we can attend at least one,' said Delphine. 'We are at Victory Cottage, if you wish to call.'

Mrs Quillian seemed pleased with this; goodbyes were said, and they moved apart. Julia tucked her hand in the crook of Delphine's arm and steered her swiftly towards the door.

'What on earth were you thinking of?' she said in a severe whisper.

The vicar was conversing in an animated way with an elderly couple. Delphine was glad to be able to leave without speaking to him. She did not want to have to face down his disapproval of her, nor be troubled by trying to decipher its source. On the church steps they passed Martha and her family, who were evidently arguing about dinner. Martha's family were all tall and stocky, like her, so that they made others look stunted; and Martha, dressed in her Sunday best, looked splendid, a lavender ribbon in her bonnet, her face relaxed and bright with pleasure.

As Delphine and Julia passed the group, a small child, who was evidently one of their number, slipped away in parallel. She was about seven years of age, dressed in a dark blue dress and a white apron, and holding her straw bonnet in her hand.

'Martha's niece,' said Julia. 'They seem to adore her. She did not wish to go to Sunday school today, so came with the family.'

As she spoke, the little girl descended the steps in front of them and seemed about to cross the street, transfixed by the sight of an unruly gull that was pecking at a piece of rubbish. As she came near, it stopped, and regarded her with its angry, yellow gaze.

Delphine glanced back towards the church; none of Martha's family were watching. 'Wait there,' she said, running down the steps and taking the child's arm. 'Wait for your family.' The little girl turned and stared at her, round-eyed, as though she didn't know what to do next.

'Sarah! What have you been doing?' It was Martha, looking more flushed than usual as she came quickly out of the church and down to the roadside. Her family filtered out onto the steps and stood there, awkwardly gathered as though grouped together ready for a daguerreotype to be taken, their faces set. Delphine felt their eyes on her: curious, and not without hostility.

'Sorry, madam,' said Martha, taking the little girl's hand. 'She is so very particular about going here and there on her own, a little like me.' She swallowed hard. 'She is my sister's girl, and my sister is ill, very often. Sarah can be a little wild.'

'I was not thinking that,' Delphine said. 'I simply did not wish her to wander into the street and be crushed by something. I know from experience that the carts and horses come round that turn at a lick sometimes.'

'Yes, they do,' said Martha. Then, gravely, 'Did you hear that, Sarah? Did you hear what the lady is saying? Does it remind you of anything, Sarah? It's what we say to you, all the time, isn't it? You must not wander off. It is not safe.' There was a throb in her voice which surprised Delphine.

Sarah said nothing, clearly feeling that her words would have no bearing here; she merely nodded.

61

Martha curtseyed and said goodbye, and Julia came down the steps to Delphine. As Martha led Sarah away, they heard the little girl's piping voice. 'I am quick,' she said. 'I could have got out of the way of any hoss. That's not why you always make such a fuss.'

CHAPTER SIX

Now I write of that sore spot, deep in the cleft of my heart.
Touching on it shoots pain through every limb and every faculty.
So I must write of it in a sideways way. I cannot face it head on;
and I cannot show my enemy all my cards at once.

Forgive me, I should not call you my enemy – do not put the
letter down at the sight of those words. You are the most beloved
of foes, forcing me to face the past and relive what has caused us
both such pain. I both love you and hate you for causing me to
do this; if I could become your wife, without doing it, I would.
But I fear if I did so, I would only be wrapping my wounds in so
many cloths, and they would not heal, kept from the light and
air.

Shall I tell you of Mr Theo Hallam? The first evening in
Broadstairs, when I walked late into evening prayer and my
eyes met his – I knew there would be something between us. The

following Sunday, I felt relieved when I could escape speaking to him at the church door. That voice of his – as he sang the psalm – changed everything. I loved that voice, and feared it, as I feared anything that had power over me.

It was a strange thing; I felt both drawn to him, and repelled by him, and when I came to know him, I could sense he felt the same. I have heard talk of magnetic fields; I have heard of repulsion and attraction, and we were – it seemed – unnatural: one moment drawn together, one moment repelling each other; one meeting brought coldness and the next, heat. I did not know why – not then.

'There are no marks of violence on the girl's body,' said Dr Crisp. 'None whatsoever. And you yourself heard – she was often one to go off somewhere, dreaming. If she was cut off by the tide and could not escape, then it is a tragedy, but not a crime. Often, drownings are not even reported; the bodies are simply buried.'

The Red Lion was emptying out, but Edmund could not find the inclination to leave. He sat at the table and saw Dr Crisp check his pocket-watch. The inquest had been brief; it had hardly been worth the coroner attending, he thought, and the coroner had made it clear that normally one would not have been held. It seemed that Mr Benedict had sent him several letters, and pestered the parish constable, so it had happened under duress.

Edmund had spoken of finding the body, as had Benedict's servant; it had not been thought worthwhile to call the others who had been at the beach. They wished to trouble the sea-bathers as little as possible, Crisp said. No medical witnesses had been called; there would be no post-mortem. Edmund understood the practical reasons. The coroner would have to pay for the expense of it, and it was likely the justices at the next quarter session would not refund him if they found insufficient reason to do so – which they often did.

'She would have to have had her skull caved in and the murderer's name written on her in blood for it to be worth going to the length of a post-mortem,' said Crisp. 'I, and the coroner, cannot go chasing after doubtful cases; I am not encouraged to do so. There must be certainty.' He lowered his voice. 'The coroner is hale and hearty enough, but he doesn't wish to be called to Broadstairs for a drowning at a rate of only nine pence per mile. Mr Benedict has made no friends by causing such trouble, and he didn't even bother to come here tonight.'

'I accept all that you say,' said Edmund wearily. He did not wish to argue, pointlessly, and he knew the case seemed to be a simple one. However, he could not help the unease he felt at the verdict of Natural Death.

'Still, the strain shows on your face,' said Crisp. 'I am grieved that you, as an outsider, have been involved in this matter. You must believe me when I say that the constable questioned the young man most thoroughly.'

It had emerged that the victim was a girl from London who had come to Broadstairs to be apprenticed as a servant. She was young, but old enough that she had a local man interested in her: Davy Holland, eighteen, and bad-tempered, had quarrelled with her when she said she wished to take up a post as a servant at Northdown House. On being questioned, he had broken down and sobbed that he had not hurt her; he had witnesses to vouch for his whereabouts that evening and the morning after.

She had gone wandering – gone dreaming, they thought. Perhaps she had been taken ill, or fainted. 'We all know how emotional and excessive young women can be,' the coroner had said, and there were nods and murmurs of approval which caused Edmund to down his drink even more quickly. It was agreed: the tide had cut her off, she had drowned, and her body had been carried round to Main Bay by the sea.

It was past ten o'clock when Edmund heard Theo come in from attending an invalid's bedside. The parson went upstairs and changed into fresh clothes before he appeared, perfectly neat and his hair oiled, in the drawing room. Edmund had been aware of Martha speaking in the passageway, and when he looked up he saw concern in his host's eyes. The lamplight gave his pale blue eyes a shimmer and warmth that Edmund did not think of when he remembered him; it made him like the boy better.

'My dear Mr Steele, is all well?' said Theo. 'I wish I had disobeyed you and come to the inquest. Martha says she was quite worried about you.'

Martha, who was standing behind him, mumbled something. Edmund just caught the words 'many hours', before she gave a brisk nod and went off to the kitchen.

'I am perfectly well, thank you, but I was shaken by the process,' said Edmund, rising, until Theo took the seat opposite him and he sank down again, amazed at how weak his legs felt. 'The girl was called Amy Phelps. She had been in Broadstairs for a couple of weeks.'

'I have not heard of her,' said Theo.

'She was a Nonconformist, I understand – not one of your flock,' said Edmund. 'She was fourteen, but was being courted by one of the young mariners. He had a bad temper and they quarrelled the day before she was found. There are no marks of violence upon her, and yet I am uncomfortable with the idea that she simply got cut off by the tide, and drowned.'

'It does happen,' said Theo. 'Even those that live by the sea may be misled, and trust it when it should be guarded against.'

'I cannot get the child's face out of my mind,' said Edmund. 'Her swain was there. He sobbed and said he wished he had made her his wife.'

Silence fell between them. He heard the soft clattering of Martha, making the kitchen her own.

'How terrible.' Even in the softness of lamp and fire-light, Theo looked pale and anguished; his right hand, formed in a fist, pressed against his lips, and he brought it away only to speak. 'It seems he had good intentions towards the girl.'

Edmund shook his head. 'He seemed hot-headed and vindictive to me, for all of his tears.'

'Marriage,' said Theo, 'is a blessed state, ordained by

God. It is at least to his credit that he sought to cool his ardour in the righteous protection of marriage.'

'My father would say that marriage was a furnace: capable of forging bonds, but also of destroying both with its heat.' Edmund wished he could speak with more authority on it. He was also aware that his father would never have envisaged his words being shared with a clergyman, but he was out of sorts. Another case had occurred to him. 'I remember a boy who worked for me once. He married a girl and I thought it would be the making of him. But how they fought! They fought until they parted. I have seen such unhappiness. It has served as a warning to me.' He thought of Mrs Craven – of her laughter, a little forced. 'Perhaps too much of a warning,' he said. 'I wonder now, if I should have married when the chance presented itself. I was wary of being unhappy. I still am.'

'The only salve for an unhappy marriage is prayer,' said Theo. 'Though I accept it is difficult. A difference in temper may seem small at a distance, but the reality of life with someone who is ill-suited to one can be harsh; a piece of grit in the eye felt every morning on waking.' There was a slight tremble in his voice which made Edmund examine him more closely. Theo caught his eye and lifted his chin, regaining his composure. 'I see it, sometimes, in my work,' he said. 'It is my role, to remind persons of the mutual comfort which God urges upon us.'

'I have been, perhaps, too careful,' said Edmund. 'But I have never felt myself prepared for marriage. So often I have worshipped a face, with no knowledge of the heart;

and I pity the women too. They are encouraged to be weak, silly creatures these days.' He passed a hand over his eyes. 'This Amy Phelps was just a child. She should not have had to worry about the ardour of a boatman, yet it seems she encouraged him. Still – we will not speak of it any more. I will not cloud your evening with my own sorrows. How is your patient?'

'Coming through the worst, I am glad to report. Ah, Martha, thank you. You read my mind.' Martha handed them each a glass of red wine, then stomped back to the kitchen. Theo leaned forwards. 'It will just be a chop each again, I'm afraid,' he murmured. 'I hope you do not mind our simple fare. Poor Martha is overstretched in her duties.' They raised their glasses.

'In this sleepy place, I'm sure you have no truck with suspicious deaths,' said Edmund.

Theo took a large gulp of wine. 'Wherever there is human life, there is mayhem. But you are right – our losses are often made by the sea, by accident and illness, or occasionally by melancholy, particularly in the winter months. Some years before I came here there was a mysterious case, though. You may have seen Martha's sister, Anna, with her at church? She was once the char for the cottages in Nelson Place, but she is often unwell, and poor Martha runs herself ragged trying to do everything rather than lose the income.'

Edmund nodded, the wine warming his numbed faculties.

'There was a terrible tragedy involving Anna's daughter, ten years ago. It was before my time here, but Martha told me of it; it was as if she could not rest until she had told me, as though by repeating it, the girl could not be forgotten. On the beach one day, at Kingsgate, Anna was busy talking with some other women, and the girl went ahead, round the curve of the cliff. When Anna went to find her, she did not see her at first. Someone had drowned her – held her face into a full rock pool. She had put up a struggle, I was told. As I say, it was ten years ago, but the family still bears the scars. At the time, Anna did not have other children. Two years after the little one's death, she had Sarah, and now they are,' he paused, and looked into his glass, 'protective. Very protective of her.'

'Did they never find who had done this?' said Edmund.

The priest shook his head. 'No. Anna did not see anyone on the beach. But it would have been easy for the person to hide, and the woman was, of course, hysterical with shock. There is always talk, of course – troubles bring out the worst in human nature as well as the best – but there was no question that the child was adored. Besides, two of the women Anna had been talking to went with her and found the child.'

'How is she now?' asked Edmund, struck to his core with the image of a mother finding her daughter's body.

'Poorly,' said Theo. 'Now and then she rallies, and manages to do some of her work, but Martha mostly carries the burden. I sit with Anna sometimes, but she says she has no need for prayers. Poor soul. Her husband is a hoveller; you will see him down on the pier most days, like Solomon, whom you met. They watch the weather, and keep their eye out for vessels in trouble. They will help where they can – pilot a boat home, for example. In the case of a wreck,' his voice dipped, 'they have the right of salvage. It is only fair to repay the risks that they take. They are hard, brave men, and they have the correct respect for the Goodwin Sands.'

'Do you know much of the Sands?' asked Edmund, intrigued by the dark look that had fallen over Theo's face. For a moment, he thought that Theo would not answer. He became very still, fixed, his face frozen and stiff. Then he caught Edmund's eye, and moved as though waking from a reverie.

'Living here, you are forced to know of it,' he said. 'Go out on a clear night, Mr Steele, and you will see the light-ships marking its place, warning ships. On stormy nights, I wonder how the men who tend those lightships cope with them, for even with their anchors forty fathoms deep, they must fear for themselves. They know – and accept, I suppose, as the hovellers do – that it would be possible for day to dawn and them never to be seen again.'

Something in Edmund's face must have shown a hint that he thought this was over-dramatic, for Theo looked at him with a sudden intensity.

'They call it "the ship swallower" – you know that, don't you?'

'I did not,' said Edmund. 'Why is it so dangerous? Can craft just not avoid the area?'

'If only it was that simple,' said Theo. 'The sands change, and shift. The place seems solid at times, like an island – and in a way it is, but it is also an illusion. The sand is of a quality that it will claim a ship and take it whole; suck it down and swallow it, once it is in its grip. A steamer with two hundred souls is as much in danger as a skiff with two. Can you imagine being taken by the sea and the sand, in such a way?'

'No,' said Edmund. He had a strong imagination, and Theo's words were chilling him, adding a fear to the emptiness he had already felt at the inquest. He saw from the look on his face that Theo was lost in thoughts of the shifting sands of the Goodwins. His eyes were blank, fixed on the middle distance, when he next spoke.

'Do you know the term they use? They say a boat is "swaddled down" into the sands. It always makes me think of a baby. A huge ship, wrapped and coddled and shrouded in liquid sand, until it is gone, along with every living creature on board. So often a ship sets its course, and does not allow for the beam tide when sailing down the Channel, so heads on confidently into catastrophe. With the Goodwin Sands, as with much else in life, to pre-sume you are safe is the most dangerous thing.'

CHAPTER SEVEN

We did not hear from Mrs Quillian for ten days after our first meeting. Julia thought we were safe, again. We were alone with our secrets, free to walk and to watch the sea. Did the serenity of the place melt some part of my defence? No. I had experienced the picturesque before, and remained impervious.

Alba was the key. She was the reason why Julia and I came to be part of Mrs Quillian's circle.

She had the kind of beauty that pierces the heart of whatever man, woman or beast it shines upon. When you experience such beauty, there is no help for you. You are lost to it, and to look upon that face is almost painful, for when you see it, you feel that original wound in your heart. And that wound opens you to others.

I have been accused of trying to corrupt Alba. I think those words even passed your lips, as though the interest of an older woman in a younger one can only be malign. But it is not true. I was never jealous of her. I pitied her. I saw that she was living through my own predicament; I recognized in her struggles the very things that had burned up my own youth. My interest in her was totally innocent; I have nothing to confess there.

One afternoon, Delphine and Julia decided to walk towards the Foreland, to see Kingsgate, the bay named in honour of the arrival of Charles II there two centuries before. Walking was an occupation they both enjoyed, for as pampered girls in New York they had barely walked at all.

'Do you remember?' said Delphine, as they set out. Julia knew she spoke of New York; that was the phrase they always used, when they ventured into their past lives. They could only speak of the past to each other, for they kept their secrets close to them. 'There was always a carriage, always a room where the drapes were let down and the light shut out.'

Their grandfather, the head of the family, had come to view the physicality of the outside world as a kind of corruption. He had held the common view that women should be protected from fatigue. So when they first left New York, Julia and Delphine were soft and plump, with delicate limbs and skin that looked as though it had never seen sunlight. Then they came to Europe, and found that walking was one occupation to fill the endless stretch of their days. To their amazement, their health improved, rather than declining. For weeks they compared their blisters and raw, tenderized feet. But Delphine felt a kind of triumph in enduring the pain. It was proof that she had broken free from the old world; that she was, now, different. Besides, she hardly cared then whether she lived or not.

One blister she had treasured – a long blood blister that ran down the outer length of the pad of her foot. The red blood beneath the skin at first looked so angry that it might fight its way out. Over time, it darkened to brown, and lay there for weeks, then months. She wanted to pierce the skin, but Julia warned her against worsening the wound and, though she heated a needle in a candle flame, she left it, and wondered if it would stay with her forever. But it did not, gradually fading and working itself away, until her foot was normal again, but harder.

Now, their boots meant nothing to them as they followed the coast road. They saw large, agreeable houses, then only fields, the sea always at their right hand. The road curved, and wandered gently up and down over barrow-like hills. At Stone they saw a large stuccoed house and estate behind high flint walls, and skirted farmland, seeing workers in the fields.

'How was your sketching today?' asked Julia.

'Well enough, but nothing worth seeing yet,' said Delphine. 'I am pleased with how our dresses are lasting – I told you this material would work well being packed and unpacked. Wearing mourning, it hardly matters if I look rich or poor, as long as I do not draw notice. But I could almost be tempted to cast off black and wear pale clothes, now we are free from the London soot.'

'I do not feel quite settled here yet,' said Julia, giving her a dark look. 'London seemed safer, somehow.'

'We need to be somewhere different. It does not pay to become too comfortable in one place.' Delphine breathed in the freshness of the air. 'Mrs Quillian seems harmless enough, but as for Mr Benedict ...' She paused, remembering the intensity of his gaze. 'He is an artist of some type, you know. A member of the Royal Academy, as he was careful to make clear to me. I am suspicious of him.'

'We are suspicious of everyone,' said Julia. 'Forgive me, I am sorry – that was meant to be in jest. If the town is not what you wish it to be, perhaps we should consider where we should go next?' She was wearing a thicker veil than usual over her face. Delphine, so accustomed to the sight of the red birthmark on her cousin's face, sometimes forgot that Julia was conscious of it.

'Let us decide that at the end of the season,' she said.

'Yes, but my dear,' said Julia, 'what does Mr Lock say, of money?'

'Let me think of that,' said Delphine. 'There is no need to worry. We have lasted this long.'

'But our income is not increasing, is it? And there is nothing of value left to sell.'

'Hush,' said Delphine. 'If things get bad for me, you can simply go home.'

'I won't leave you,' said Julia, and Delphine did not

bother to ask the question which always occurred to her, and which she had asked several times, in train carriages and hotel rooms across Europe: *why not*?

They reached the lighthouse at North Foreland. It had been worth the walk. The white octagonal building towered over them, arresting in its brilliance, its patented lantern at rest. Beside it stood the coastguard's handsome cottage, also painted a dazzling white.

'Knock for the keeper,' said Delphine.

'*You* knock for the keeper,' said Julia. 'It's quite possible that he hates Americans too.'

But before they could debate it, they saw the figure of a girl hurrying towards them from the direction of the bay. Her bonnet had fallen back, and as she waved at them, urgently, she dropped one side of her skirts and nearly fell head over heels.

Delphine and Julia were on one side of the road, and the girl arrived on the other. When Delphine looked at her properly, she realized the girl was the one she had seen in church. Violet eyes, aquiline nose and small and mysterious mouth were framed by the coppery-gold hair that had been tamed into a bun. She thought again it was a face she would have to paint.

'Can we help you?' Delphine called.

The girl spoke, but her voice was soft and high, and her words were carried away by the breeze.

'Speak again,' said Delphine.

'It's my aunt,' said the girl, shouting now, the flicker of

distress across her face indicating that she knew she was behaving with impropriety. 'She is down at the bay and is feeling unwell. I was wrong to make her walk so far. We were going to be met by a local man who said he would bring his cart for us, but he has not, and now she will not move, and the tide is coming in, and I tried at Holland House, but no one would come at my knocking, and after that body was found . . .' She began to cry. The serenity of her beauty was at odds with the tears which suddenly began to pour down her face.

'We must help this young lady,' said Delphine to Julia, who had said nothing. 'Come on.' She took her cousin's hand and pulled her along. The girl had taken off running, which was astonishing, unladylike. She was ploughing down the hill at some speed, holding her skirts up, and Delphine said a small prayer for her sake that a coachload of visitors did not appear around the turn in the road, to shame her. Julia cast Delphine a look of astonishment as they tried to follow her at a more decent pace.

'She is more child than lady,' said Delphine, unsure why but feeling the need to defend this young stranger from her cousin's censure. They hurried along, trying to look as though they were walking.

The girl scudded ahead of them, skimming down the length of the grassy slopes, then disappearing through a gap in the cliffs.

'Smugglers,' said Julia breathlessly. 'We are following smugglers' routes.'

'You have been listening too much to Martha,' said

Delphine, glad to see that the girl had finally stopped. As they got nearer they saw she was bent over a person sitting on the sand, holding her hand. The woman looked to be a matron of fifty or more, with a buxom, tightly-corseted figure.

'She is unharmed!' called the girl.

'Alba,' said the woman, as Delphine and Julia approached, seeming both frightened and glad. 'What has she said? Have we troubled you? There are no gentlemen, are there?'

'No,' said Delphine. 'It is just me and my cousin. I am Mrs Beck; this is Miss Mardell.'

'I am so sorry to be sitting on the sand,' said the woman. 'I could die of shame. But I cannot rise. I feel so weak. I am trembling – look.' Dramatically she held out one large hand, its fingers glittering with rings. After this demonstration, she opened and delved into a capacious bag which sat on the sand beside her. She produced a vial which she unscrewed, then sniffed.

'You must have something to eat,' said Delphine, trying not to laugh at the self-administration of smelling salts. She put her basket down and unwrapped the sandwiches they had planned to have for lunch, then produced an earthenware flask of ginger beer which Martha had provided for them. She glanced at Alba. 'The tide is not dangerously close yet; there is no need to panic.'

Alba turned away, as though she had been scolded.

The woman needed no further encouragement. She

began to eat – at first slowly, but soon quickly and heartily, barely managing to stifle a burp when she took a gulp of the beer. Julia had moved off to the water's edge, and Delphine thought she saw her turn away to hide a smile.

'Are you lodging nearby?' she asked.

'No,' said the woman. 'We are at the Albion Hotel, near Main Bay. We came too far – Alba wished so much to see the Foreland.'

'It is all my fault,' said Alba, turning back to them abruptly, obviously having been listening. 'I am so sorry, Aunt. And to think I could have placed you in danger.'

'I have forgotten my manners,' said the woman. 'My name is Miss Waring, and this is Miss Albertine Peters, my niece.'

'I am pleased to make your acquaintance,' said Delphine.

'Are you ... Americans?' Miss Waring said, having taken a mouthful of cheese.

'We are,' Delphine said, feeling her expression harden. 'How clever of you to know the accent.'

'I think it delightful,' Miss Waring said, and real pleasure seemed to light up her little hazel eyes. 'I knew an American man once, in London. He was a very jolly fellow. Entertaining. He went back there. It was a shame for all of us.'

'Oh, Aunt,' said Alba. Delphine could not work out if she was speaking in exasperation or affection. Having recovered from the shock of her aunt being ill, her face had returned to that neutral, expressionless beauty which had so struck Delphine. The perfect artist's model, she thought, an empty canvas, waiting for a story to be painted upon it.

Suddenly, the aunt's pleasure faded to fear. 'Alba, my dear,' she said. 'What if Mr Brown comes? He will expect to see us up on the cliffs.'

'He did not come when he was supposed to,' said Alba. 'Traitorous man. We sat there for a long time. He said he would be but half an hour.' Delphine had to suppress a smile at her dramatic tone.

'I am here to convalesce,' explained Miss Waring, addressing Delphine. 'I have a nervous complaint. The air has been doing me good, until the unfortunate events of the last few days, which have unsettled me. Well, we need not speak of it. Alba has come to join me and be my companion for the summer. She knows the place a little, and we have visited with our friends at Northdown House. You love that place, don't you, my dear? But I am afraid I am a wearisome companion, and being in the hotel suits me a little better. The young have such energy. My poor girl.'

'I am grateful to be here,' said Alba stiffly, and she kicked hard into the sand, like a recalcitrant child. Miss Waring tutted under her breath. Delphine noticed that Alba was wearing thin shoes, not the heavy strong boots needed for such walking.

'The tide is coming in,' said Julia, as Miss Waring

finished the sandwiches. 'We should think of making our way up to the cliffs. Someone should go and wait for this Mr Brown, just in case he comes.'

'Alba – that is, Miss Albertine – must stay with me,' said Miss Waring. There was something definite about the turn of her mouth when she said the words.

'I will go up,' said Delphine, rising and brushing off her skirts. 'What does this Mr Brown look like? I do not wish to stare and wave at every man I see.'

'Of course not,' said Miss Waring with a hint of severity. 'He is a rough-looking man, and wears a very old straw hat. He has thick black whiskers; is short, but stout and strong. His pony is a dappled grey.'

'That is quite enough to be going on with,' said Delphine, impressed by her powers of observation. And with a nod at Julia, she turned and made her way up the steep slope with its uneven footholds cut from the chalk, wondering how on earth they would get the woman up there.

Delphine stood waiting for some time.

Finally, coming from the opposite direction of town, she saw a black dot moving along the road, the shape of a horse and cart. It was approaching in a slow, almost leisurely fashion, and she had to fight the impulse to shout and wave. Impatience was always a sin of mine, she thought. It is what damned me, really. So by strength of will alone she stayed rooted to the spot, frowning, until she saw with grim satisfaction a stout man wearing a straw hat, driving a dappled grey pony.

'Mr Brown!' she said, as he pulled up.

'Yeah?' he grunted. 'Who's asking?'

'Your patroness, Miss Waring,' she said tartly. 'She has been waiting for you for several hours.'

He got down from his post, held his pony's head protectively. The pony laid her ears back. Delphine longed for the animal to butt at him, perhaps even give him a bite, for he fixed her with an insolent glare.

'I never promised anythin',' he said. 'I said I had business to do at Northdown, and then I'd be back.'

She hardly knew why, but Delphine hated him in that moment; and the feeling came upon her so suddenly and completely that it left her silent. Was it the confident sensuality in his gaze, she wondered later, that reminded her of the past, and sparked her hostility?

'Here they are,' he said. 'Just in time.'

They had made it up the cliff: Julia, Miss Waring and Alba, the two women supporting the matron. At the sight of the man, Alba's face transformed with dislike, and Delphine felt a bond with her.

'You naughty man!' Alba said. 'You did not come to collect us, so I took my aunt down to see if the coastal walk would be easier on the sand, and we could well have been stranded if these ladies had not come to help us.'

'Coastal walk easier on the sand?' said the man, with a snort of contempt. 'What a notion. Wherever did you get that from, miss? If you'd just stayed up here there would have been no problem at all. You're lucky you didn't get in trouble down there. That's the smugglers' bay, that is, and

I wonder you weren't chased by their ghosts. And now the bay has more ghosts . . .'

'Do not frighten her,' said Miss Waring rather stiffly, but with none of the displeasure Delphine had imagined she would unleash. 'You are here now, so help me up, if you please. We wish to go home and have a cup of tea.'

The man rolled his eyes but heaved the lady up, Julia supporting her elbow. Alba stayed below, watching anxiously, her arms wrapped around herself. When the man went to hand her up – with a lascivious glint in his eye – she turned her back on him and curtseyed to Delphine and Julia. 'Thank you for your assistance, Mrs Beck, Miss Mardell,' she said. 'We are staying at the Albion Hotel, and usually take tea there every morning and afternoon. I hope we meet in happier circumstances during your stay in Broadstairs.'

'As do we,' Delphine said. 'We are at Victory Cottage.'

But Alba was already leaping up into the cart, snatching her hand away from Mr Brown as she settled next to her aunt. 'Adieu,' she said. Mr Brown snapped his whip with a nasty smile and they set off.

Julia and Delphine stood on the clifftop and waited until the cart had rattled out of sight. Julia looked at Delphine. '*Adieu* indeed,' she said. 'And why on earth did you tell her our address?'

'Did you not think her extraordinary?' asked Delphine. 'I saw her at church. She will be fending off proposals as soon as the summer season begins.'

'I am no judge of what men think of as beautiful,' said

Julia. 'Everyone agreed that my life had been ruined by being born with such a face as this. But as a child, when I looked in the glass, I could never bring myself to be ashamed of it. Now, shall we go to Kingsgate – at last?'

CHAPTER EIGHT

After our meeting with Alba, the old fear and bitterness came upon me again, as though the past was on my heels. I kept myself from the fresh cool air of morning and stayed inside my parlour, trapped inside my tightly-laced corset and the layers of my dress, waiting for the heat of the day to reveal itself. As the days passed, the heat deepened into that kind of warmth which is held in rock and sand as afternoon passes into evening. It was so hot that Martha had to grate horseradish into the milk to keep it fresh, and leave saucers of beer on the floor at night to trap the cockroaches. And as the sun rose in the sky, I lay on the faded embroidery of the sofa in our parlour and thought of the past, in the hope that thinking of it might inure me to it, but it had never lost its grip on me, and the memory of it still made my heart beat hard in my chest.

Then came the first summons from Mrs Quillian.

Mrs Quillian showed her character the next week, in a
flurry of notes delivered to the people she had met, with
promises of an excursion and a picnic: 'cold hock, salty
ham, and fresh bread warm from the bakehouse', were the
words she used. Delphine smiled at that, liking the fact
that she – unlike so many women – did not keep her bread
until it was starting to stale. She supposed the old lady
was from that generation where pleasure was not so
frowned upon. *Dear ladies, bring shade from the sun*, she had
written, as if there was any doubt in the matter. The
group's rallying place was the Albion Hotel. Delphine
wrote and said they would go, surprising herself as well as
Julia with the wish to, but on the morning of the picnic her
enthusiasm faded. She dressed in her most stifling dress of
black stuff, and twined her hair choker around her white
neck.

They waited in the saloon of the Albion. Delphine saw
Mr Benedict across the room, and knew from his movements that he was trying to catch her eye, so she gazed
around her, as though absorbed in the décor. A large clock,
with crystal pillars either side of its ornate face, ticked on
a high shelf, and she pointed it out to Julia.

'A fine piece, don't you think?' Delphine said, nodding
towards it. Their grandfather had been a connoisseur of
such things; the family's Fifth Avenue house stuffed with
every kind of objet d'art. 'I wonder how much it cost.'

Julia glanced over her shoulder then turned back to
Delphine. 'You have a better eye than me,' she said. 'And
I wish you would not mention the price of everything, as

though we are in trade. You know how the English dislike it.'

'You must forgive me if money concerns me,' said Delphine tightly.

'We are in a fix, aren't we?' said Julia. 'I knew you were keeping something from me.'

'Hush,' said Delphine. Mr Benedict was striding towards them.

He bowed low. 'Mrs Beck. Will you permit me to join your carriage? I very much wish to discuss painting with you; our first stop will be a viewpoint I think you will like.'

'I would not wish to disrupt Mrs Quillian's plans,' said Delphine.

'Nor I, of course. Ah, see how poor Gorsey produces this fêted picnic.' Mr Gorsey and his daughter Polly were labouring with a heavy hamper. Benedict came closer to her, and Delphine was aware that Julia had stepped away to speak to Mrs Quillian, their words blending into the mêlée of the other voices in the room. 'Are you well?' he said, in a low voice, so close that she felt the warmth of his slightly sour breath. 'We have not had a moment to speak of what we both saw on the beach. I was unprepared for the shock of it. Strange, when death is all around us, to be so shocked by something.'

'Not strange,' said Delphine. 'Natural. But I do not see any reason to speak of what we saw. As Mr Hallam says, she is with God now. We should do our best to forget what we have seen.'

In truth, she did wish to speak, but not to Benedict. She could not bring herself to trust him, not even when his face, in the light, looked to be all goodness and openness. She felt no hint of the confidence she had felt even on her first meeting with Mr Steele. And yet – she knew that all confidence in a person was dangerous; trust was not a word she favoured. Mr Benedict, Mr Hallam, even Mr Steele – they were all enemies waiting to hatch. The dead girl's vulnerable body, lying on the sand, had woken some deep pain in her. Her normal calmness had not reasserted itself; instead she found, reawakened, her bitter distrust of the world which had sprung into life one distant week in New York. And, not for the first time, she wondered if Julia carried that in her too – a distrust so deep it felt like a wound.

'Forget it?' Mr Benedict was echoing her words, and even her tone, and in his sudden, quiet-voiced anger she knew that she was right not to trust him – for so quickly, wildness was returning to his eyes. 'How we can forget what we have seen? What we have experienced, together? Do you not feel fellowship between us, having been through that?'

'I do not know what game you are trying to play, sir,' she said, matching his low tone with her own. 'But if you attempt to use a dead child to establish some con-nection with me, then I will think it very poor of you. We are at Mrs Quillian's excursion; let us travel lightly, and leave off our thoughts of sorrow. But I beg of you, do not think me any more connected to you than,' she glanced at the grumpy landlord, 'Mr Gorsey, or Dr Crisp – or Mr Steele.'

She then stepped away, keeping her face averted so he would know not to speak to her again, and so she would not be forced to look at him. She began to speak to Julia and saw that Alba, standing next to her aunt, who appeared to be chattering to the air, was gazing at her: the same gaze she had seen at the church, but this time infused with a piercing curiosity.

'Mrs Beck?' It was Mr Steele, his smile one of unaffected pleasure. 'I am glad to see you have been able to join the excursion – and you, Miss Mardell, may I say what a pleasure it is to see you?' He sought a smile from Julia, and gained one, and Delphine saw that her cousin was both flattered and puzzled by his attention, a blush rising in her face.

There were two carriages and Delphine was relieved when she found that Mr Benedict had been placed in the second carriage, and she in the first. They travelled slowly, the clopping of the horses' hooves languorous, as though they were sleepy, and Delphine noted as they went that the small town was fuller than she had seen it. Many of those who walked were grandly dressed; now and then an invalid passed, pushed in a chair, or a little crowd of children with straw hats and raised voices, freed by the seaside. Marchesi's, the confectioners, was already busy. They passed a line of donkeys being led down towards the beach, a swinging little line with doleful eyes and twitching ears.

The carriages stopped first at the southern tip of Main Bay. The ladies got down, opening their parasols, and took a turn in the field at the edge of the cliff. Mrs Quillian told them that Mr Benedict had asked for the stop, for he often painted here, and considered it the perfect viewpoint of the town.

It was the spot Delphine had stood at on her second day in the town. It was the natural curve of the bay that she loved, as if it was carved out of the cliffs by the water. She tried to fix it in her mind: the sea, stretching out over the horizon to France, was formed from discrete layers of colour. Anyone would forgive the sweep of the water-colourist's brush in trying to portray it, but you would have to be here to really believe it: hold up the sketch and compare it to the skyline and its stripes of blue, and grey and green. The pattern of the waves could be seen even at this distance, the dance and sparkle of sunlight on water, the turning over of a wave, chasing away the golden sunlight temporarily as it smoothed out its place on the shore.

There was a scattering of people below, and some bathing machines parked near the water. All as if that dead girl was never there, thought Delphine. She heard the sound of children's voices, faint screams here and there of delight and rage, and the way in which the little ones seemed to be in cautious pursuit of the sea, daring to come up to the edge of it, then swiftly retreating, then returning in a game of which they never tired. But more than that, she was entranced by the constant movement of the sea, unchangeable, unceasing. From this distance it seemed gentle, yet she knew it was an unstoppable force, carrying everything in its wake. Carrying a body as easily as it carried pebbles and seaweed. She saw the churning of the water around the pier, its endless turning and overturning.

Julia had walked up alongside her, her veil draped over her face.

'I am trying to memorize it,' said Delphine. 'It's beautiful, but cruel.'

'What do you mean?'

'I can't help thinking – remove us all, and the sea would still be here. Its delicate shades of colour, the light playing on the water.' She did not add that in each wave she saw the merciless repetition of nature; that in every child's scream of delight, she imagined another kind of scream, and saw the still face of the dead girl.

'You seem troubled,' said Julia gently, then Delphine heard the smile in her voice as she added, 'Now, look at that. Surely that chases the melancholy away.'

She was pointing to a young seagull, its wings outstretched, riding the currents of air beside the cliff. It did not have the confidence of an older bird, but wavered a little now and then as it passed them. Despite its yellow eyes and long beak it was half-grown, its downy cream-coloured breast flecked through with baby grey. Delphine had been observing the seagulls, and she loved this stage most of all – its hesitant serenity, each day bringing a greater mastery of its skills. Julia herself preferred the bleating, terrified babies with their iron-grey plumage,

constantly berating their mothers with their wailing, grat-
ing calls.

'We shall be back in the carriages in a moment or two,'
said Julia. 'Mrs Quillian has decided this is no place for a
picnic. It is not quiet enough, and she does not wish us to
be disturbed by other sightseers, or musicians, or donkeys.' She could not help a tiny snort of laughter. 'We will
continue a little way up the coast, to Dumpton Gap, where
the air is apparently just as bracing but the beach less populated. There is talk of shell-collecting after our picnic.' She
glanced back over her shoulder. 'I know I wished to have
nothing to do with anyone, but I think we will find this
excursion amusing in its way. Poor Miss Waring is trying
hard to guard her niece from the men, as if they were rav-
aging beasts. No one is worried about us.'

'Thank you for giving me all the news,' said Delphine
wearily. 'I wish I had brought my paints and we could
settle here, and let them go on.'

'If you are unwell, we can go back,' said Julia. 'You look
a little pale. My dear? This is not like you.'

'I am perfectly well, darling, but thank you.'

Soon, Mr Steele came over and offered his arm to both
of them, seeing them into the carriage. He was quiet as he
did so, only saying their names and assisting them with
careful gallantry. Delphine noted that his gaze often
turned to Julia, but as the carriages rattled off up the coast,
she wondered if there was something amiss with him, for
she had caught a hint of sadness in his eyes.

Before long they came to Dumpton Gap which, as had

been predicted, was much quieter. There was a small gap in the cliffs, and a steep incline down to the beach, which looked slightly dangerous to Delphine's eyes. She had a vision of attempting to struggle down the slope in her slippery shoes, with the back of her dress catching as she stepped, and the idea that she might have to take a man's arm (in her mind, this was the incorrigible Mr Benedict), made her wonder if she might have to stay at the top. Still, it was a beautiful place, with a high rolling down of green, where they settled for the picnic.

The spread had been well put together by the reluctant Mr Gorsey. The men ate heartily, and poured out hock for themselves and the ladies. Miss Waring and Mrs Quillian, past the age of censure, ate heartily too, taking some of every dish with much enthusiasm. The burden of eating little lay on the younger ladies. As though by secret agreement, they each took a small piece of the bread, and some sliced cucumber to ornament the plate, and left them there, occasionally picking at what was there, in the elegant way they had been taught. Delphine felt sad as she watched them, Julia's veil fluttering in the breeze as she raised her glass to her lips, and she wondered if she even took in any of the sweet wine, or simply did so for effect, for none of them would allow themselves more than a single glass.

Alba looked around, for the new surroundings had animated her, and she giggled at any remark which seemed to require it, as though helplessly in the grip of her good spirits. Mr Benedict ate with relish, his teeth tearing at a chicken leg; he offered every dish to the young ladies, but seemed pleased when they all refused it and equally pleased to serve large helpings to the older ladies. 'May I compliment you on making such perfect arrangements, Mrs Quillian,' he said with a broad smile, starting a girlish flush in the lady's face.

When the blue cheese was unwrapped, Delphine decided she would take it no more; she requested a large slice, and ate it with an apple hungrily, as if she was showing her parents and grandparents her defiance of them. As the years had passed she had allowed herself to forget them for long periods of time, living their privileged lives in New York, but in the past day or so they had hovered in the corner of her sight, ghosts of her former life. The presence of these people, whose rejection had untethered her, made her deliberately defiant of the rules and conventions she had been raised by, even though they could not see her.

She knew that she would be noticed when she ate the cheese, but was surprised when the eyes that hovered on her with the most intensity were those of Mr Hallam. He allowed his gaze to rest on her as she ate, for a minute too long.

Mr Benedict evidently saw it too, and the way he caught Delphine's eye before he spoke indicated that he was ready to do battle on her behalf. 'Many of your parishioners are farming folk, is that correct, Mr Hallam?' he asked. He was chewing his chicken in a haphazard, almost gratuitous way, and took a large mouthful of wine.

'Yes,' said the priest. 'Visitors normally think only of the sea, but our farms and their produce are just as important.'

'Do you ever take meals with them in the field?' said Mr Benedict. 'Do you – shall we say – try to bring yourself to their level?'

There was an insult in what he was saying, Delphine was sure of it, though she didn't know what it was. She glanced at Julia, but her cousin's face was expressionless as she took another mock sip of white wine. Then she saw Mr Steele, and his expression confirmed it; there was a look of disquiet on his handsome face.

Mr Hallam sighed; a departure from his normal way, she was sure. 'Not on their working days. I bless their Harvest supper, and we eat soup and bread and cheese together.'

'Very rustic,' said Mr Benedict. 'I've been meaning to ask, having seen your church service – do you think we should all be Papists, Mr Hallam? Is England a little too Protestant for you?'

Alba gave an audible gasp. Before, Delphine had seen only studied politeness in the clergyman's features, but Benedict's words had put a light to a wick, and now a flame flared in his eyes.

'I hope you have not just seen the service,' he said. 'I hope you have been part of it. I have served you the blood and body of Christ; Our Saviour demands not just mere attendance, but faith, nurtured in the heart. It is not mere show, Mr Benedict. We must be truthful Christians, pre-pared for the Day of Judgement.'

'I wondered, though,' said Mr Benedict. 'You seem to embrace so many Catholic principles that I thought you might be a secret convert.'

'Really, gentlemen,' said Mrs Quillian, who was polishing off a large slice of pork pie. 'Is this a conversation for a picnic? Theo?' She put her hand out, and touched his arm. 'Where is all the joyful, light conversation I hoped for?'

'Forgive me, madam, forgive me,' said Benedict, with a pleading look, a little too intense to be genuine.

'Perhaps we could play word games,' said Alba.

'Alba,' said Miss Waring, in gentle warning. She was not touching her food, but sat straight, her hands clasped in her lap. Delphine saw that her eyes darted between the painter and the priest; and she guessed it was the priest whom Miss Waring supported.

Delphine roused herself. 'Shall we walk down to the Gap?' she said, her alto voice breaking through the tension. She raised a linen napkin to her lips. 'We were promised shell-collecting, were we not?'

'That was well done,' said Mr Steele. Delphine was staring down the steep incline of the Gap, wondering at her rash suggestion. 'May I assist you?' he said.

She shook her head. 'Take Miss Mardell.' She saw the flicker in his eyes as he bowed and turned away; she had noted his chivalry towards Julia, and the thought crossed her mind that he had a partiality for her cousin. She watched him go to her and offer his arm, and there was a kind of beauty in the way Julia placed her long white fingers on his sherry-coloured coat, and they went down the slope easily, their steps in time.

Delphine began to walk alone; she was graceful and upright, but as she had predicted, her boots were a problem, and in a few steps she began to slip and slide. She stopped, wondering how she would go forwards, and was settling in her mind that she did not care if she fell, but she would not ask for help, when she sensed someone come alongside her, and she prepared a rough retort for Mr Benedict.

But it was Mr Hallam. He said nothing, only put out his arm. She looked at it for a moment. Her hesitation was hard to overcome; not just because she had refused his help in the past, but because he was a puzzle to her. She had thought she could identify character and motivations as easily as she peeled one of her grandfather's hothouse oranges. Not him; there was a withholding in him, an opacity twinned with a certain purity – and she could not understand him. She was fearful of such mysteries and, unable to admit her fear, felt on the brink of dislike.

She put her hand on his arm and they started forwards. But they were on a poor section of the path, and when a little gravel gave way, they skidded down a few steps. It was only seconds, but it felt as though time had stopped to Delphine. As panic seized her, she thought they would fall. When they came to a stop, Mr Hallam's left hand was gripping her elbow, and his right hand her right hand, clasped tightly, his whole hand encompassing hers in a tight grip; he was holding her arm against his chest.

They looked at each other. In that brief moment, the look seemed to have a quality of its own that shocked both of them; it was as if their sudden physical closeness had opened up a realm of possibilities between them. Neither of them moved.

He released her.

'We are safe,' he said. 'Do not worry.'

'I am not worried,' she said.

As he placed his arm out, formally, and she put her hand on it and they continued to descend, she saw that his pale complexion had gained a tinge of red.

'The sun is hot,' she said.

'Yes,' he said. They continued in silence, and when they reached the bottom of the slope he drew his arm away even quicker than she could raise her hand from it. He raised his hat. 'I wish you a good afternoon, Mrs Beck,' he said. Confused, and wondering whether he might be leaving, she gave the briefest of curtseys. He had left her alone and she saw, below her on the beach, Mr Steele reaching down to pick up a shell and give it to Julia.

'Mrs Beck?'

It was Alba. Shielded by a bonnet, and in a pale cream dress, she held a parasol over her head, her eyes narrowed in the sun. She had seemed a vision of perfection in the church, and she remained so. Yet the sunlight also revealed her faults – that she was human, not a goddess, with a freckle here and there and, today, shadows beneath her eyes. But the light brought out the extraordinary cop-pery-gold of her hair, the slight slice you could see, for it was drawn back from her face, and mainly hidden beneath her bonnet. Some yards behind her, her aunt was talking animatedly with Mrs Quillian. The latter said something in response and Miss Waring laughed; a rich, warm sound.

'Good day, Miss Peters,' said Delphine. She hadn't noticed it before, but the girl's voice was not the perfectly pronounced, middle-class English of her aunt's. There was a tinge in it, of unfinished words, casually pronounced.

'Please,' said the girl, 'do call me Alba. That is what everyone in my home calls me, and I do miss them very much. It was how I said my name – Albertine – when I was little. It would make me feel better if you called me that.'

Delphine inclined her head. 'Then I shall.'

'I have been meaning to say,' said Alba, 'I was so fussed the other day, that I did not thank you sufficiently. I meant to write, but when I came to do it, I could not remember the name of the cottage where you said you lived. I am so silly about these things.' She gave a nervous little laugh. 'So, I am here to say thank you, thank you from the bottom of my heart, for the kindness you showed me. I am truly grateful.'

Delphine felt a trifle embarrassed. Alba seemed sincere enough, but there was too much intensity in her voice. She smiled, to indicate that the thanks had been accepted, and putting her hand to her brow to shield her eyes, watched the figures on the beach.

'I also wished to say,' said Alba, taking a breath, 'that I would very much like it, Mrs Beck, if you would be my friend.'

Delphine did not know what to say. She looked at the girl, but Alba was in earnest, and was watching her with the same hungry, eager look that she had fixed her with in the saloon of the Albion Hotel. She felt flattered, but also wary, before she told herself: She is just a child.

'What a sweet thing to ask,' she said. 'But I understand there are many girls your own age here at Broadstairs. I am sure you will not need to bother with a stuffy widow like me.'

Alba's violet eyes clouded. 'Oh, I do not like people my own age, Mrs Beck. But, if you will be my friend, then I am very glad.' She came closer. 'I heard you saw the body on the beach,' she said in a low voice, glancing back to check that her aunt was not listening. 'Was it very terrible?'

Delphine had to stop herself from drawing away. 'I do not wish to speak of it,' she said. 'Your aunt says you are easily frightened, and I would not wish to give you nightmares.'

Alba tempered her obvious disappointment with a small smile. 'You are so kind,' she said and, unperturbed, bobbed a curtsey and went back to her aunt.

They all went down to the sand. Julia was the best at collecting shells, moving easily over slippery rocks. Delphine saw that Mr Steele's eyes hardly ever left her cousin; he seemed delighted when she laughed, though he said only one or two words to her, and stood with his hands clasped behind his back.

Alba refused to go onto the rocks, and there was a general sense of approval that she was keeping away from undignified scrambling. Still she bent forwards, peering at shells and rocks in the sand, and picking up a pebble or two.

Delphine preferred watching them from a distance, this group, which now and then moved into the perfect composition, and she wished she had some way of capturing them and framing them in her mind just as she saw them now: the elegant ladies, bonneted, dressed in their summer dresses and ribbons; the gentlemen slim, curious, clad in white and black apart from Mr Steele in his burgundy coat; the crumbling white cliffs; the wet, muddy-brown sand; the slippery rocks, dense green with seaweed as though they were made of them. And she noticed that the painter was the same, though he was not at her distance. He had gone out onto the rocks, taken out a small sketchbook and was drawing them. When Mrs Quillian called and asked him what he was doing – 'for you know, Mr Benedict, as an old lady I have the licence to ask whatever I wish' – he had replied that he was making notes of the landscape, of this beautiful gap and its wide, rock-strewn beach. He said this with a broad smile. But Delphine knew he was lying.

She knew he was drawing the people.

The afternoon drew on, but the women's thirst for shells was inexhaustible. Hooked on Alba's arm was a basket, and the shells were piling up, a kind of central bank that she and Julia had agreed upon – although

Delphine suspected that in fact Julia did not really care about the shells, and would forget them the moment they returned home, whereas Alba was careful, inspecting each and every shell minutely, as though she was trying to decide whether they were beautiful or not. After a while, so as not to appear churlish, Delphine ventured closer to them. But she had no taste for pebbles, for she had banned any desire in herself to collect, on the principle that its pretended permanence was only another way of being cheated. Instead, she left Julia and Alba under the indulgent gaze of Miss Waring and Mrs Quillian, who were speaking to Mr Hallam. She found Mr Steele, at a decent distance, looking out to sea.

As she approached him, he glanced at her and smiled, a smile almost of familiarity. 'I think there is a sea mist coming,' he said. 'What do you think?'

Delphine looked. Sure enough, at the blue-green limits of the many-layered sea there was a faint, slim band where the air looked slightly milky; a ghost-line at the horizon.

'It's skilled of you to spot it,' she said. 'Are you an old cove, Mr Steele, like Solomon on the pier?'

He threw his head back and laughed with real pleasure, and Delphine could not help but laugh too. As she glanced back at the group, she saw Mr Hallam looking at them. To their left, Mr Benedict was sketching furiously.

'What a strange group we are,' she said. 'If you do not mind me saying it.'

'I do not mind, and I suspect you know that,' he said.

'I had to check,' she said. 'I know that being American

gives me some licence: I am able to say some things without them thinking that I know what I do. I don't think I
can get away with that with you.'

'Your cousin won't speak to me with such openness,' he
said, and she saw disappointment in his gaze.

'She is not as hard and battle-worn as I,' said Delphine.
'She still keeps the notions we were raised with – gentility,
delicacy and concealment. Give her some time, and she
will speak frankly.'

He looked back at the horizon, his expression not softening.

'Forgive me for asking,' she said, fixing her eyes on the
horizon too, 'but have you had a disappointment, Mr
Steele?'

She knew he was looking at her, and as he did so, she
thought she presented the perfect façade of hardness, the
brittle glitter that she had perfected in the looking glass.
What she did not realize was what he saw: a face wide open
to the light, and a fellow-traveller in disappointment. He had
opened his mouth to be bluff, for he had wavered between
bluffness and truthfulness his whole life. Then he decided to
speak to the face that he saw so clearly in the light.

'I left London quickly,' he said. 'I was hoping that being
here would make me see things anew. Yet I find I cannot
be certain about anything. I had hoped to be a family man,
Mrs Beck. But I have never been married, and I think I
may have left behind my last chance at life.'

Delphine felt a brief shock, and knew that he had
spoken the truth.

'What a sad thing to say.'

They both turned. It was Alba, standing several feet away from them, her basket of shells on her arm. Her voice – young, soft, a note or two too high – was full of expression, but her face was not: it was just its same, remorseless loveliness. Delphine felt chilled, the kind of chill one feels when a cloud moves across the sun – and it was apparent from the look on Mr Steele's face that he had not meant his words to be heard by anyone but Delphine.

'I do not believe it,' Alba went on, with perfect confidence. 'I think we all have a thousand chances – another and another and another.' She smiled. 'We have found the most perfect rock pool, with a hundred beautiful shells. Please come and see, before Miss Mardell pulls them all up and ruins the picture.'

'Al-baah!' It was Miss Waring, her deep voice reaching surprisingly far. Alba bobbed them a curtsey and walked off towards her aunt.

When he was sure she was at a safe distance, Edmund glanced at Delphine again. 'What do you think, Mrs Beck?' he said. 'Do we all have a thousand chances, as Miss Peters says?'

Delphine kept her eyes on the line of sea mist. It seemed to be getting closer.

'The American spirit in me will not reassure you,' she said. 'I trust the individual. If you think it was your last chance, perhaps it was. I am convinced of my fate, and no power on earth could convince me otherwise, unless I witnessed some miracle, and it changed me. If you can live, content with your situation, then that is what matters. We have, at least, the chance to live, unlike that poor young girl we saw the other morning, whose face will not leave my mind.'

The waves seemed to be moving steadily in one direction; now and then the white of a breaker showed itself, then was gone.

The excited voices of the women were growing in volume.

'We had best go and look in that rock pool,' said Edmund, 'lest we miss something spectacular.'

They walked, quietly together, and Mr Benedict, drawn too by the voices, was picking his way across the rocks. They found Julia, Delphine, Alba and Mrs Quillian staring at a particularly deep rock pool. Alba was now picking shells off, and naming them, with the kind of precocious pleasure that a young child repeating its times tables to the class would show.

'That is a cockleshell, and that is a – oh, look at that one!' she said. 'It is so beautiful. I would like that one. Aunt, I could decorate a box for you, and that would be the central shell.'

'Would it, my dear?' Miss Waring was standing several steps away, too far for her to see what Alba was talking about, but looking in her niece's direction with an indulgent yet tense glance that flitted about. Delphine wondered what was making her so nervous.

Alba held up the shell and Mr Hallam examined it. 'Ah,' he said, 'a fine specimen. The local people call it "the

beauty shell".' And he moved aside as the others came forwards to inspect it.

They were all peering over the girls' shoulders; it was
only Mr Hallam who noticed Miss Waring falter suddenly.
'Miss Waring?' he said. 'Are you well?'

'Oh,' she said. 'Oh, I am very sorry, but ... I am not.' She
swayed as though she would faint; Theo caught her.

'Aunt!' cried Alba.

Mr Steele went to Miss Waring's other side, and along
with Mr Hallam he helped her to a large rock, where she
could sit down.

'Silly me,' said Miss Waring. She sat, rod straight on the
rock; the only difference was the pallor of her face. 'I have
been standing up too long.' She rifled in the large bag she
carried with her – its size had caused Julia much hilarity
when she first saw it – and gave her niece a small silver-
mounted bottle which Delphine recognized from their first
meeting. Alba unscrewed it and held it under her nose; her
white face jerked up. 'Thank you – oh dear, oh dear.' They
all gathered around her, quiet and embarrassed, not sure
of what to do or say. There was a general feeling of relief
when, after a moment or two, Miss Waring pronounced
herself mended.

'My dear lady,' said Mrs Quillian. 'Please forgive me, we
have been too long in the sun. We must go now, for there
will be tea at the Albion Hotel. Tea for all of us – ladies,
gentlemen!' She walked on, speaking the words tea-tea-tea
as though it was a summoning bell, chiming out and gathering her followers.

'It is no wonder Aunt is feeling a little delicate,' said Alba, swinging the basket of shells as she passed Delphine and caught up with Mrs Quillian. Ahead of her, Miss Waring was leaning on Theo's arm as they approached the Gap. 'It was so shocking to hear of that young girl being found dead on the beach. What must it be like to drown?'

'Please, Miss Peters,' said Mrs Quillian. She spoke agreeably, but with firmness in her voice. 'This is not a subject to be pursued in company – or to be pursued at all by you. Let us have tea, and look at your shells.'

The group climbed the Gap again, this time Julia and Delphine walking together, their backs to the group, gripping each other's hands tightly as the slope steepened.

On arrival at the Albion Hotel, Mr Gorsey directed his tired visitors to the gallery which ran along the back of the building where, he said, tea would be served shortly. Delphine thought to herself that the summer had really started, for Gorsey's daughter Polly had put aside her drab clothes and was well-dressed and glossy, like a bird with freshly grown plumage, directing people with neat little gestures and smiles.

'You were industrious today,' said Edmund to Mr Benedict.

The painter's mood seem to catch on his words, and he brushed his black hair away from his face with a violent gesture. 'It is no good,' he said. 'My drawing today has been hopeless. I keep thinking about that poor girl on the beach. I cannot help but think it should have been looked into more. How petty our amusements seem in the shadow of death.'

Edmund put his cup down. His day, too, had been veiled over with sadness, Amy Phelps's face recurring to him every so often. 'It is natural that we should feel upset over what has happened,' he said. 'But we should do our best to protect our fellows from it, and to try and recover, for nothing can be done about it now.' He spoke carefully, not wanting to encourage drama in the other man, who seemed to be spoiling for it.

'I am only grateful that Mrs Beck was not out sketching that day; it freezes my blood, the thought that she might have found her, and been put through the ordeal of seeking help,' said Benedict. 'And it was the attitude of Crisp which so infuriated me. As though the girl was nothing, to be buried and forgotten as soon as possible.'

And yet, thought Edmund, you did not come to the inquest.

'Mr Benedict,' said Miss Waring, a little severely, for she was seated several feet from him, her fingers playing over the pretty cameo brooch she had pinned at her neck. 'Pray, we do not wish to converse about such a disagreeable thing.'

'My dear Miss Waring,' said Benedict, pushing his chair back and leaning forwards, as though he had something of urgency to say to the lady. 'Are we so divided from our fellow creatures that we can refer to their suffering as something merely disagreeable? She had a name; she may have been poor, but she was a person with a life that has been extinguished. Her name was Miss Amy Phelps, God rest her soul. Her name was – is, in the sight of heaven – Amy.'

Edmund saw movement in the corner of his eye before he heard the thump of a cup on the carpeted floor; he sprang to his feet and caught Julia as she stumbled. He thought she was about to faint, in the pattern of Miss Waring, but instead she righted herself against his arm.

'I am sorry,' she said. 'You must think all of us ladies poor creatures.' He could only shake his head gently at her words.

'It's the heat,' said Delphine. 'Sit down, my love. Thank you, Mr Steele.' She nodded at him as she carefully disentangled Julia's arm from his hands.

Julia sank onto a chair and Delphine's eyes met her cousin's with an understanding of the word that had weakened her.

Amy.

It was strange, she thought, how these things came at you. Out of the clear blue sky of a summer's afternoon, a storm. She could think of nothing to say.

'It has been a long day,' said Julia, and there seemed to be a note of pleading in her voice. Her eyes seemed to say: *forgive me for not being as strong as you.*

'We will go home now,' Delphine said quietly. 'Mrs Quillian, thank you for organizing this trip. What a very pleasant day it has been.'

Edmund sat at the desk for some time before he began to write. Had someone been in the room, watching him, they might have said that he was in a daze; he sat with his hands in his lap, staring out of the window before him at the innocuous view of green leaves and sky. Occasionally, he would lift his hands and run them over the smooth surface of the desk, wondering at the delicacy of the wood, which, pale and cinnamon brown, felt like fine woven cloth beneath his fingertips.

He blinked slowly as he thought, yet every time his eyelids closed he would see a flash of wet sand, a golden curl, or a hand, purplish-white, the fingers slightly curled, the nails bitten down.

Then he saw footprints in the sand, the corpse alive, walking away from him, to the water. In this vision, she alone sought her own death, creator of the final image he could not, despite his years, cast from his memory.

He knew he could not write of this to his friend; he knew also, that Charles Venning had sent him a question which he was honour-bound to answer, and so it was he sat for some time, summoning the bonhomie necessary to create a letter fit for its purpose, and trying to stow Amy Phelps into some distant corner of his mind. So he sought to remember London, but the bustling streets, the colour and noise, the smoky air seemed to exist in a different dimension. And because of the letter's subject, he thought of Mrs Craven too, of the jangle of the cut-glass drops around the candles in her drawing room; the colour of those full, deep glasses of red wine.

At last, he wrote; and the only trace of the dead girl's influence was the earnestness he fought until it seeped into his sentences, the keen sense of life, death and the desire not to waste time.

So, my dear Charles, you will get plenty of these letters from me, and it shall be your punishment – your penance – for sending me here. An old man like me needs a walk into town every day, and as there is only one post to London – at twenty past eight in the evening – no decision needs to be made about when.

You asked me what happened with Mrs Craven, Charles, and I will tell you now at last. She is a fine lady, and an opportune chance at matrimony for such a man as me. Being a widow, no surprises would have lain in her path with marriage, no light dreams such as young women have. And indeed she is a handsome woman. But I can write all of these things, Charles, without even a single twinge of regret. I think of her kindly. But our conversations always had something of effort about them; I always forced my cheer, and measured my words to please her.

Well, so? I hear you say. I am an honest man, Charles, and I simply knew, that last night I spoke to Mrs Craven, that I could not say those vows and make them true. My parents were not so. They had love wherein they could read each other's glance; their own kind of language, even in silence. So I have seen it; I know it can be true. But not for me and Mrs Craven. I am sorry if I have grieved the lady. I hope, my good friend, you will write and tell me that I have not.

I meant to write to you of this small town, for much has happened in the last few days; tragic things, which have no place in this cheerful letter. I meant to make pithy observations, like an insect collector pinning butterflies to a board (Theo collects

insects – *did you know?). But your query, perfectly understandable, deserved an answer. Now I will close this letter and
seal it up, and hope that you will comprehend my reasons, and
know them to be honourable.*

Your friend, Edmund Steele

CHAPTER NINE

I can hardly describe the terror that I felt at the sound of that name: Amy. I was insensible with it. I forgot myself for that moment, and existed only in fear. If my cousin had not dropped her cup, and brought me clear of it, I might have said anything.

For days, it was as much a haunting as a memory. I had never seen the dead girl's eyes, and yet she opened them for me and looked into my face. They were blue, flecked with violet. Then, as now, my mind could not allow an incomplete image; the picture had to be perfect and whole. But how she looked at me. Without defence, for she was a young girl with none of the fortifications I had built around me. It was as though she, from the world of the dead, could look into the furthest reaches of my own, dormant soul. Her name linked us; as a locket opened up to find some long-forgotten relic, pressed whole into it, so her name opened up my fear of the past, and of being discovered.

'It is from Mrs Quillian,' said Delphine, her gaze lingering on the small square of cream card, the neat, curving hand-writing in straight lines with small, restrained flourishes. It had been a fortnight since the shell-collecting. 'She is planning another excursion; this one to Yoakley's Almshouses.'

'We will not go, of course,' said Julia in a flat tone, lift-ing her teacup to her lips.

Delphine looked up from the card. 'I think we should accept,' she said.

Julia put down her cup, and the movement was full of grace, as though they still sat in their family's salon in New York. Julia always moved so, but the sight of it in this moment hit some nerve in Delphine and she felt a stabbing pain arc across her brow – a pain of the past like a trailing comet, which she had not felt for a long time.

'All these years,' said Julia, 'we have never gone out into society before. I was astonished enough that you granted us one trip with this group, but another? Why now? Is it something to do with that poor dead girl on the beach?'

'Do you think I have become unhinged by it?' said Delphine coolly. 'I thought you would welcome another excursion. I saw you speaking with Mr Steele on our last trip, and I see no reason why you should keep your dis-tance from him. He seems to be a good man, as well as a handsome one, and he seems to have a liking for you. Our financial position – yes, you may well look at me so if you wish – is not desperate, and I will not have you think that it is. But our old life is quite gone from us. You always had hopes of returning, whereas I . . . I knew, the first day, that we were leaving for good.'

'I do not believe that,' said Julia.

'It is the truth. Or, at least, it is the truth for me. They will never forgive me, Julia. I dishonoured our name and the most they could hope for is that, in time, I will be forgotten completely. I am dead to them.'

She saw Julia's usually smooth composure begin to crack; she could not bear to look upon the rawness breaking through her serenity. 'It is why I always urged you to return,' Delphine said. 'I had hoped you could live that life again even if I could not.'

'You forget,' said Julia, hardness entering her voice. 'My existence was not like yours.'

They saw in each other's eyes the world they had left behind. Delphine remembered music, champagne, balls, laughter and wit – however false. But she knew that Julia's life had been spent seated at the side of the sprung dancefloor, her head averted so that the red stain on her face could not be seen, expecting only disappointment, preparing herself to be a burden, no matter how loved she was by her parents.

'It is the past, for both of us,' said Delphine. 'Consider Mr Steele. You cannot stay with me forever. And I feel the old bitterness creeping upon me again – as it did when we first left America. I am not the person I was, and I will become more disagreeable as time passes; I know it.'

'You are frightening me now,' said Julia, casting her napkin on to the breakfast things, and rising. 'We will go, if you wish, to these almshouses, but do not speak any more of Mr Steele.' She made to leave, then turned back. 'I did not rebuff him; there is no need to. I would not cheapen myself by seeking to encourage a regard that does not exist. You are painting pictures, Cousin. And do not speak of me being settled upon him, like some faulty gift. Even you could not persuade a man to do that.'

She left the room, and Delphine heard her ascending the stairs. She put the card on to the white tablecloth, and let her eyes lie upon it for some time.

So it was, on a bright morning, at the unusually early hour of half past eight, before the roads and beach were filled, that Mrs Quillian's hired carriages rolled up the hill of Broadstairs' High Street, past the mill and on out across the fields towards Margate.

'Will you let me read from the guidebook to you all?' said Alba. She was holding the new book in her gloved hands. It was a small, ox-blood-red volume which, Mr Able in the High Street had assured her, told her every- thing she needed to know about Broadstairs and its environs.

'I am not sure, Alba,' said Miss Waring, glancing with concern at Julia, Delphine and Mrs Quillian. 'It might be tiresome for our new friends.'

'It would be a pleasure to hear you,' said Delphine,

and Alba cast her a look of particular warmth. Delphine had put away the sense of disquiet she had had when Alba had asked about Amy Phelps. She was growing to like Alba very much. The girl had intelligence, good spirits and a kind nature, and Delphine felt protective towards her. She sensed that Alba had not been educated to do well in life, and wondered whether she could use her influence to help shape her, and make her stronger, for such were Alba's unique talents and beauty that she knew the girl could shine in the world – shine where Delphine, cut off from society at such an early age by her loss, could not. It was also a balm to be with someone who took pleasure in her company, for Julia's affection had the quality of weariness which had become second nature, and which Delphine only now recognized.

The fields they passed were flat and planted with lines of vegetables, bordered with grass verges and the occasional tree. Now and then the suggestion of a shallow chalk pit could be glimpsed, a dip of shadow near the verges. Alba named the places they passed, her soft voice rushing through the paragraphs, sometimes running words together. They drove by the fine rectory of St Peter's behind its high flint walls, the parish which had once encompassed that of Holy Trinity; then, to their right, the fertile fields and livestock of Dane Court Farm, home of the Mockett family. It was at this point that Alba mentioned that the jolting of the carriage was making her feel unwell, so her aunt took the book away and pressed her hand against her niece's brow. 'It was as I thought,' she said. 'You have grown hot. It will not be long now, I'm sure.'

Delphine had taken pleasure in the reading, but it was clear that Julia had not. Her blue eyes had remained fixed on the views outside the window, even when Alba said she was unwell. Only once did she look back into the carriage, as it began to slow on the approach to the almshouses, and Delphine saw that her eyes were bright with dislike.

'An excursion like this is truly a balm to the soul,' said Miss Waring, taking up the conversation. 'It teaches humility, and shows the exercise of the Christian soul in charity.'

No one responded.

Yoakley's Almshouses were situated, conveniently for visitors, at the side of the road to Margate. The drivers were used to making the trip, and drew up alongside the neat, red-brick almshouses with their Dutch gables. They had been built in 1710 by Michael Yoakley, and now housed poor old women, who sold Tunbridge Ware donated to them by local ladies. They were accustomed to tourists, Mrs Quillian said, as she was handed down by Mr Benedict, who was in a chivalrous mood. 'Such did Mr Gorsey stress their popularity, I was worried they might not be able to accommodate us; it is why we have visited so early in the morning.'

Delphine noted the mud of the yard, dried up in the

heat, and she was glad it was not churned up, to spoil the ladies' dresses. Behind the almshouses lay a cultivated plot of land planted with vegetables, and a coop for chickens. A local man stood at the door, bowing to the new arrivals; he was the overseer, who lived in the central almshouse, and directed visitors. Just this little way from the coast, the air was still, and the heat of the day was gathering and building, the air heavy with the scents of grass and manure.

The almshouses were tiny within, the old women neat and glad to see them, with their fancy boxes set out before them on a table, the lids inlaid with different coloured woods. The visitors were offered, and accepted, tea. Theo spoke to each of the ladies, and their faces lit up at his approach; Delphine wondered how many times he had come here. Mr Benedict lodged himself in a dark corner and observed proceedings, occasionally attending to Mrs Quillian and Miss Waring. But it was Alba who the women really warmed to. Delphine watched her, speaking to the ladies and inspecting their wares. Carefully, the girl opened her reticule and exchanged money, selecting one piece after another. But it was not her money that the ladies cared about. For when Mrs Quillian, too, began piling wares in her own arms in order to buy them, she elicited only politeness and smiles. The women did far more than that for Alba: they seemed almost to worship her, thirstily drinking in every graceful gesture and every smile. Even in the dark, close room, her exceptional beauty, and the sweetness that laced it, shone through. One of the women even reached out, silently, and put her hand on Alba's face, fixing the girl with a toothless grin. Alba did not start away; she only smiled worriedly.

'Don't mind her, miss,' said another of the women. 'Nan cannot resist loveliness in anything. When I came, she wanted my locket. You are just the same; she would like to take you and keep you here.'

'So I would,' agreed Nan.

The other women laughed, and the visitors continued their transactions over the Tunbridge Wares. It was then that Delphine realized that Julia was missing. She moved unobtrusively around the room, checking that she had not lost her in the stuffy shadows, then went out into the passageway and asked the overseer if he had seen her cousin. He had not – but then he had been in the room until a moment before, helping to set out the wares.

Delphine walked out of the front door, a slight panic rising within her. Julia's gaze was always so steady, her serenity never challenged ... and yet Delphine had seen some nameless unhappiness rising in her cousin. Mr Steele had greeted her that morning with warmth in his eyes, and Julia had looked away, speaking only briefly. Did she truly believe he had no interest in her? Delphine longed to shake her into belief.

In the fresh air, the carriage drivers were affixing nosebags to their horses' bridles. Delphine went to question them, and they immediately pointed over her shoulder. She turned and saw Julia, pacing up and down in the shade of a tree a few yards away, her eyes fixed on the ground before her. Delphine saw the bemused look on the drivers' faces as they glanced at each other. She left them with thanks, pressing a coin into each of their hands, and walked to her cousin's sphere, following in the path she had worn with her steps through the deep grass.

'Do you not wish to buy something?' Delphine asked as Julia moved past her.

'I am excusing myself from watching the worshipping of Miss Peters,' said Julia, without even a flicker of embarrassment. Delphine wondered at her sudden wildness. Her cousin was always so serene, and so aware of her surroundings, that when she changed, her vehemence seemed all the more shocking.

'Come now, this is not worthy of you,' said Delphine. 'Alba is simply young, and you know how the old worship the young. Besides, she is very sweet-natured. I have just left her apologizing for buying too few knick-knacks, when she need only buy one. She has the endearing quality of confessing slight faults as though they are monstrous in scale.'

'It is because she knows the fault is slight,' said Julia. 'All her real sins she will keep to herself, and carry them tight, like a piece of lead strapped to her chest. I warrant there are many – and if you will not listen to me, then you are foolish. I would that they would sink her.'

'Julia, keep your voice down,' said Delphine. 'What if Mrs Quillian, or Miss Waring heard you?'

'What do I care for them? And what do *you* care?' cried Julia.

Delphine stopped her with a hand on her arm, held her gaze, pleadingly, and watched her cousin begin to calm down.

'We cannot dislike her because she is young and beautiful,' Delphine said, lowering her voice. 'I do not think she has any great fault, or sin. She is all innocence.'

'She is the *picture* of innocence,' said Julia. 'Which is not the same thing.'

Delphine sighed and shook her head.

Julia watched Delphine closely; her temper had faded and now she seemed hopeless more than angry. 'I know,' she said, 'you think I am bitter – that she reminds me of my own disfigurement. Have you ever seen me react so before?'

'I have not.'

Julia seemed mollified. 'Do not trust your connection with her. The death of that young woman has shaken you, and now you are – well, I hardly know – reaching out to people like Alba, whom you would not have gone near before. I have taken account of my bitterness, and I still see more clearly than you. That girl is all trouble: trouble through and through, but masked as goodness, and that is the most dangerous type of character. You make such a point of shunning Mr Benedict, but *she* is far more objectionable. For you not to have seen it – I would not have thought it of you.'

Delphine knew she would not be able to convince her

cousin otherwise. 'We cannot discuss this here,' she said, glancing at the men with their horses, who were making a show of not listening. 'If we must speak of this, let us do so at the cottage. Now, come back into the room and buy a wooden box. That is why we are here.'

Delphine had hoped the carriage occupants would be arranged differently on the journey back, but it was the same, with the gentlemen in one carriage and the ladies in the other. She felt Julia's silence keenly, for her eyes were dull, as though she had given up even the pretence of enjoyment.

'Mr Benedict is such a charming young man,' said Mrs Quillian, with roses in her cheeks. 'He gave the ladies a generous leaving present of money; the astonishment on their faces would have made a good addition to one of his paintings. I hope you all enjoyed seeing this place?'

The ladies murmured acquiescence.

'They had such pretty trifles for sale,' said Miss Waring, 'though you did not have to buy quite so many, Alba, my dear. You will fill my sister's mantelpiece with all those things, when you return to London.'

'They are very hard to resist though,' said Mrs Quillian. 'We must have such things to distract us.'

Alba looked hurt at her aunt's words, and Delphine was just thinking of something soothing to say, when the carriage jolted wildly. Delphine had her back to the horses, and for a moment it seemed as though they had quickened up, but then she saw that Miss Waring and Alba were being thrown towards her, clutching at each other, and Alba was screaming; and it occurred to Delphine in the midst of that empty feeling which precedes shock, that the driver was pulling them up, and as fast as he possibly could.

CHAPTER TEN

Perhaps it was due to my preoccupation with Amy, but the next girl we found seemed to me to resemble her, even though she was older, and it became clear that her innocence had been lost long ago. She too had golden hair; she too was a servant. It was enough to tie their deaths together in my mind, and in the minds of others.

I suppose we are all servants, women, in our way – does that shock you? Kept to be ornamental, social creatures; kept to order the dinner, and bring the man his pipe, and speak of only the things he wishes to hear. If you want that from me, you will not get it.

It is necessary for me to test your affection, you see. Your declaration of love lies on the page before me: pretty, but cold and untested, like a jewel that may change colour when held to a flame. As much as it thrilled me to read it, I cannot believe it yet. You must make me believe it, by loving me despite everything that is in me. So know the truth, and know then if you wish to be with me, or not. Whatever the law says, I will never be your servant.

Once the carriage had lurched to a halt, Delphine did not wait for anyone to come to the door, but opened it herself, even as she heard Mrs Quillian and Miss Waring protest after her. She jumped, and landed heavily on the road, almost falling. As she raised herself she glanced at the astonished face of the driver, who was calming his horse. The boy who had accompanied him clung on grimly as though they were still moving.

Ahead, the gentlemen's carriage was stationary, the doors all open where the occupants had clambered out. Mr Steele and Mr Benedict were climbing the grassy verge at the side of the road. Delphine recognized Dr Crisp, who was clearly angry and shouting at a huddle of men on the top of the bank.

Her steps were checked by Theo, who was walking towards her. 'Mrs Beck,' he said, and his voice had the quality of a warning. She glanced at him, but made to pass him, at which he reached out and took her arm to prevent her from going any further – a strangely intimate gesture. It was a gesture made out of desperation, she could tell, but when her eyes met his he released her, as though he had received a shock. 'Please do not go any further,' he said.

'Mr Hallam,' she said, 'whatever is happening here, you do not need to shield me from it. See to Mrs Quillian and

Miss Waring – they are the ones who need your attention.' She could hear their voices from the carriage, and the driver's mate looked too shocked to jump down and hand them out.

Theo looked at her as though she was a troublesome horse he could not control, then nodded and walked past her to the carriage. Delphine continued walking, swiftly, her skirts gathered in her hands. When Mr Benedict saw her, he came down the bank before she could climb it. He looked as though he had taken a hit; he bent over for a moment, as if to catch his breath, but straightened up as she approached.

'Are any of you harmed?' he asked, when she reached him. 'One of those men ran out in front of the carriage. It was lucky Mr Steele had seen Dr Crisp and was already banging on the side of the carriage for the driver to stop. Still, the driver did well to pull up; his poor mare was most affrighted. A London horse would have run him over.' He smiled ruefully, but his hand twitched at his collar, and Delphine could see that it was trembling.

'None of us is harmed,' said Delphine. She saw Benedict look over her shoulder, where Mr Hallam was presumably helping the shaken ladies down. 'What is going on?'

'I know better than to stop you,' said Mr Benedict. 'See for yourself if you must – they have found more bodies, Mrs Beck.' He held her gaze for a brief moment, then broke away. 'God save their souls,' he said. 'I must check on the ladies; it will not do to leave them to the parson. And I need to compose myself.'

Delphine climbed the bank in two steps, and came to a halt next to Mr Steele. They were on the edge of one of the small chalk pits, dug out of the earth in fields around there. At the bottom lay a man, face up, his long dark hair loose, his dead eyes wide with astonishment. At his side lay a woman in a pink dress and a straw bonnet. She was lying face down, her dress fanned out, her dust-covered boots clearly visible. Her left arm was flung over the man's body in a last embrace, and Delphine felt the sudden sting of tears in her eyes; unexpected again, this grief at the death of strangers. Beside the man's head she saw an edging of rusty brown: dried blood.

'Everyone move back,' said Dr Crisp. He had taken off his greatcoat and jacket, and his shirt was smudged with dust. 'And you, Mr Steele. The sides are unsteady. They may collapse, and we will end up,' he paused, 'down there – with those two.'

'Will you not bring her up?' said Edmund. 'There may be life in her yet.'

A spasm of exasperation crossed Dr Crisp's face. 'There is no life in either of them,' he said. 'I have been down there already.' He glanced at the group of four men, labourers from their clothing, huddled together a few feet away. 'It would be easy enough to raise them if those wretches helped, but they are squeamish around dead bodies, it seems. My housekeeper would be of more use. They have been drinking all night at the Red Lion in St Peter's, and Mark Bennet, who just so nearly stepped in front of your horses, cannot even walk straight. They found these two on their way home this morning, and one of them came to summon me from my home. I was just trying to work out the best course of action when your carriages pulled up. It is not the day I was planning to have.'

'Are they too poor for you to bother over, like Amy Phelps?' snapped Mr Benedict, who had rejoined them. 'I am astonished that you attended, as they are such an inconvenience to you. Good God, man, look at them!'

'I've done little else since I got here,' said Dr Crisp, wiping the dust from his forehead with one arm, and not concealing the violence in his tone, 'and your play-acting won't help them.'

'Play-acting?' shouted Benedict, and he took a step forwards, as though he might seek to strike the doctor, a step which took him near to the edge of the pit. It was Edmund who drew him back.

'You must keep hold of your temper,' he said quietly.

'I am sorry,' said Benedict. He spoke in a whisper, careful that Delphine and the doctor could not hear. 'I believe I met them, Steele, one evening when I took refreshment in the town. The man's face looks familiar to me. It has shocked me, that is all.'

Edmund slapped his back. 'Be still,' he said.

'Mr Hallam,' said the doctor, sounding relieved at the sight of the clergyman, who had joined them. 'Thank goodness. Will you keep these rowdy excursionists in order?' He pointed at Delphine, and his look had no ceremony in it. 'And take that lady away,' he said. He said 'lady' as if it were an insult. Theo glanced at Delphine, and his mouth twitched. He longs, she thought, to say 'I told you so.'

It was Edmund who offered Delphine his arm. She did not refuse; and they descended the verge together. 'What a sight,' he said.

She did not reply; Julia was walking towards them.

'Miss Waring is praying,' Julia said, as she reached them. 'She is under the impression that something *terribly immoral* has happened. I have given her my smelling salts. She is thinking well enough to find the flask of brandy in her capacious bag. Mrs Quillian is comforting poor Alba, who is weeping terribly.'

Edmund offered Julia his other arm. To Delphine's surprise, she took it, and she saw her hand close tightly over it. 'Thank you,' she said, so softly that Delphine realized the words were meant for him alone. Was that a suggestion of emotion in Mr Steele's face, a change in the line of his mouth?

When Edmund returned to the men on the verge, he found Dr Crisp instructing one of the labourers to go to St Peter's and fetch a cart. 'Run, then,' he shouted. As the man headed off, he glanced at Edmund. 'I would not trust them with my horse,' he said, indicating his own mount, which was tethered to a tree stump and munching grass contentedly.

'It's an uncommonly dark coincidence, to see you all here again at a scene of death,' Crisp continued, his hard gaze sweeping the group. 'You'd best not let word get around. You Londoners are good enough for your money in the season, but if you become associated with events like this, you'll be turned out of town.' Edmund wasn't sure if there was sarcasm in his tone, or real meaning.

'We should take the ladies back,' said Theo. 'They cannot stand at the side of the road forever.'

'Poor souls,' said Benedict, his eyes fixed on the bodies at the bottom of the pit.

'I think it's clear enough what happened,' said Dr Crisp, rolling up his shirtsleeves. He called two of the other men over and directed them down into the pit, with the idea of lifting the woman. They looked unhappy, but eventually obeyed him.

'And what is that?' said Benedict. His voice, quivering with anger, had a jarring note.

Dr Crisp gave him a withering glance. 'These two were out carousing, probably at Ranelagh Gardens – the pleasure gardens here, sir. I'm sure you're familiar with that particular place of entertainment. They came to walk home, he wished for some fun, pulled her aside, and in the darkness they tumbled into this pit. They have been dead some time.'

'Clear enough,' said Benedict. 'Neat, and convenient. That is what you said about that poor girl on the beach, when someone had written something in the sand beside her body.'

'You are embroidering the facts, sir,' said Crisp, with a sigh.

'Does your mind not recognize complexity?' said

Benedict. 'That girl's body; now these two. For all your sideways swipes at *us Londoners*, if there is evil in this town, it should be looked at head-on.'

The two labourers in the pit were gazing at Mr Benedict; they seemed terrified.

'There is no evil here,' said Crisp angrily. 'For God's sake, Mr Hallam and Mr Steele, please remove this man, who is making my job harder, before I have to ask these men to do so by force.'

Theo and Edmund did as they were told, and there was initially little resistance from Benedict. As they led him away, however, he snatched his arms free from their hands and twisted back to direct his words at the doctor. 'There is nothing clear about it,' he said, raising his voice to a shout. '*Nothing*, I say.'

CHAPTER ELEVEN

I know in the past you have considered me wilful; you say you wish for me to be myself now, but I must take that on trust. My desire to be free was born in me, but my life would have been simpler had I learned to repress it. I was raised in New York. After the fire of 1835 my grandfather built us a mansion on lower Fifth Avenue, with Corinthian columns at its front and a dome at its centre. He filled it with what he described as 'Greek-style' statues, and French works of art. I often think of those cool marble halls, even now, and I remember the conservatory that opened out from the drawing room, with its canaries and bullfinches.

It would be easy to imagine that time as a perpetual summer, but it was not. I was never free, for my family was new to money, having created a fortune selling pills and powders. The money gave them the glittering shell of outward confidence, but it was a veneer; they yearned for social acceptance, and for me to make a great marriage. My mother put all her hope in me, and I disappointed her.

I read in the newspapers there was another fire in New York, in 1845; it was ever a city plagued by fire. I broke the rules of my exile and wrote directly to the Fifth Avenue address. The reply came by the agent in London: your family are well, but it is requested that you do not write again.

The memory of Julia's touch on his arm kept Edmund awake late, that night. He reasoned that his mind had been disturbed by the discovery of the bodies, and that a sudden, intense affection was understandable, his mind seeking solace in destabilizing times. He had observed it many times in others, and knew that in time it would fade, like an illness, under the effect of rest and normality. Still, he recognized that he had felt a strange, instinctive tenderness the first time he had seen her, and that his affection was only the logical progression of those thoughts. Troubled, he rose in the middle of the night, having lain long watching the candle by his bedside burn, and went to the window, lifting the drapes, as though she might be standing on the front step of Victory Cottage. He thought it must have been her, that first night; there was an otherworldliness to her gaze which made him think she might do such a thing.

Mrs Quillian had sent a note to him that afternoon. It was brief, but clear in its request: Mr Steele would be so kind as to stay with Theo that evening; his very company seemed to be acting as a tonic on her dear nephew. For all her agreeable phrases, the letter was firm, and for a moment Edmund felt a little like a guard, or a prisoner. But he turned away from those dark thoughts, aware that they had come from the same place as his tenderness for Julia – uncertainty, and fear.

He did not wish to speak to Theo of religion any more. The clergyman, understandably, was continually bringing up the subject; he had blessed the bodies in the chalk pit before they had departed. But he would not stray from the personal or speak of the wider context. When Edmund mentioned rationalism – gently, experimentally – it was as though a shadow moved across Theo's face, and he put up one hand to his forehead, and pressed his fingers there. Edmund could not ascertain if the man was not beyond doubt, or whether the thought of the souls of the damned, who would not turn to Christ, simply overwhelmed him with distress. He felt, instinctively, it was a subject which should be best left alone.

For the next few days Edmund kept to himself, going out deliberately early or late, so that he would not meet any of the party who had gone to Yoakley's. He went back and forth in his mind about whether he should return to London. The trip was hardly making him more healthy or rested, and he thought the one sure way of escaping his sudden feelings for Julia would be by severing the connection entirely.

He did not manage to avoid everyone. On the second morning, he was out walking early when he spotted Mr

Benedict and his man coming up Harbour Street. The servant was carrying an easel, and Mr Benedict the paintbox. At the sight of him, Benedict cast his belongings into his companion's arms and declared himself ready to walk with Mr Steele. Edmund did not have the energy to deter him, and together they made their way along Albion Street.

'I am glad to have the chance to speak to you,' said Benedict. 'You must forgive me for the strength of my reaction the other day, at the chalk pit. My emotions run away with me sometimes, and I was so angry that Crisp seemed to treat those deaths as unworthy of his attention.'

'There is no need to apologize,' said Edmund. 'Such a sight is shocking, and brings many feelings to the surface.'

'But I wish you to understand,' said Benedict, stopping and turning to him, seeking to read Edmund's expression with his urgent gaze. 'I can trust you, Mr Steele, can I not? You see, I have been accustomed to being treated as though I am worth nothing, too. I was not born to this state. I am the son of an innkeeper. One of six. Without my talent – for which I thank God, every day – I might have been one of those poor souls myself, beneath the notice of men like Crisp.'

'We all have our tender places,' said Edmund. 'Do not think on it any more.'

'And I am absolved!' said Benedict brightly. 'I feel I could tell you everything, Mr Steele.' He smiled broadly.

'Have you managed to paint much in the last few days?'

asked Edmund, hoping to encourage him on to another topic. The painter's cheerful expression left his face, as suddenly as a curtain being dropped.

'Yes,' he said. 'I make studies every day, but I tend not to speak of my overall plan for the next painting. I find, if I do so, the inspiration dries up. Life is difficult enough, without chasing the muse away. The deaths have affected me greatly; I do not have enthusiasm for my subject.'

'There is much natural inspiration here,' said Edmund, thinking of the coastal paths, the bays and the sea. But his remark won, surprisingly, a sly smile from Benedict.

'Correct, correct. But in the current circumstances I must snatch at inspiration; it is a matter of minutes rather than hours. I have no difficulty persuading local girls to sit for me, and Polly, Gorsey's daughter, is a most stunning natural beauty. But look at the ladies in our own party. They are jealously guarded by elderly relatives, or by their own sense of propriety. I am fickle, I admit – my current favourite is Mrs Beck. "The Widow of the Sands", old Solomon on the pier calls her, and I admit she distracts me.'

He seemed to catch some disagreement in Edmund's expression. 'Do you not think so?' he said. 'I am not surprised. A gentleman, asked to guess, will never choose the right model. You have to see with a painter's eye, and the face has to have something apart from beauty. I am not, like some, seeking to paint only a dead beautiful face, lips parted, an object of brute desire – Polly Gorsey. The effect I am after is more nuanced. And Mrs Beck . . . it is not just her sensuality – for she is sensual, you know – but that she has a quality of raw hurt about her, as though cauterized in the midst of some early tenderness.'

The words shocked Edmund into silence, not least because Benedict had hit on some truth that Edmund had not, until now, perceived. Although experienced in matters of the mind, until that moment he had thought Mrs Beck enigmatic and strong, and he liked her; he did not wish to go deeper than that. His immediate response was revulsion at Benedict's words. He wanted only to ally himself with Delphine and Julia, and protect them from the artist's hungry gaze, the sense of hunter and prey in his words. 'I have not seen that at all,' he said. 'I might say that you are wrong.'

The artist seemed untroubled; he yawned and shrugged. 'As you wish,' he said, then: 'My wife will be arriving with the children soon. It will almost be a relief to see her, after the drama of the last few days. I have taken our normal house at Ramsgate for her, and though I will be able to spend some time here – for she understands that I must have peace to work – she will also expect my attendance on her sometimes. She is a good girl; I do not begrudge her her summer, as long as she never speaks of domestic troubles or the servants, or any other such tiresome thing. That is our agreement.' He smiled again, his eyes bright and glittering.

When they reached the section where the road branched into two, the painter turned and offered Edmund his hand. 'I'll bid you good day,' he said. 'I don't want any genteel tea parties for a good few days. It is too like a hothouse for me. If you wish to find me later I will be in one of these fine alehouses. The Dolphin shall be my favourite, I hazard.'

Even a good dinner could not cure Edmund of his malaise, and it was against his own will that he found himself mentioning Julia and Delphine in passing to Theo that evening.

'Miss Alba was talking of Mrs Beck and Miss Mardell when we were at the almshouses,' he began. 'She said that she admired "their faded grandeur", as though they were ancient monuments. I almost laughed out loud, for they are such vital presences in our group. I could not think of anything less appropriate.'

The dark expression which flashed across Theo's face lasted only a moment, but Edmund felt it as a knife, for Theo was normally so even that he thought the expression must be an indicator of a deep dislike.

'They are both most elegant and interesting ladies,' Edmund went on, beginning to feel uncomfortable. He was not used to justifying himself to anyone.

'I admit I do not see that,' said Theo. 'Martha has mentioned them to me, and says they are good to her, if a little strange in their ways – she is in awe that they have butter *and* jam on bread. As for my opinion: Miss Mardell is agreeable enough. But Mrs Beck – there is a certain hardness to her aspect, a wilfulness which I cannot admire.' He caught the look of discontent on Edmund's face. 'Perhaps I am being unfair,' he said. 'But they have forced me to become quite the housekeeper, by taking so much of Martha's time. I find myself filling in the order books for the tradesmen, and planning what we must have for dinner, when there are many other things I need to do.'

'Perhaps a wife is in order,' said Edmund. He had meant it as a joke, but his tone was harsher than he had intended, and the look on Theo's face showed that he had taken offence. Edmund had never seen before the painful turning-in of his gaze.

They parted for the evening with polite but distant words, and Edmund retired to his room – neatened again – washing his face in the basin of cold water left for him by Martha at his request, though he now wondered if Theo had been forced to fill it in her absence. He heard Theo's footsteps pass along the landing, heard the door close, and the house rest – but he could not. He was angry, very angry, and he had no idea why. For so long, he had prided himself on knowing his own mind, and being able to quietly examine his own thoughts. But the anger had him in its grip, and he had the unhappy conviction that he did not know himself at all.

He took his place at the writing desk, and thought that at least one irritant should be addressed.

My dear Charles,

You write warmly, and yet you mention nothing of Mrs Craven. You could hardly have thought I would not notice. I asked you for reassurance on the subject, and you send none.

Very well. If you will be silent on it all, so will I. I am not some fat old fish to be pulled out of the water by such a hook.

E.S.

He threw his pen down, and it took every effort for him not to go to the window and pull back the drape. Instead, he lay down on the bed, without undressing or even pulling a blanket over him, and blew the candle out, resolving that he would not see or speak of the American ladies again, until he could be said to be indifferent to them.

'Poor Mrs Quillian,' said Julia. 'She so wished to create a kind of salon by the sea, but the deaths have tainted all her plans and her favourites keep deserting her.' That morning, they had met the lady, who informed them that Mr Benedict would be spending the next two weeks in Ramsgate with his wife and children. They had passed Solomon on their way to the beach, and he had nodded to them, but other than that, the past few days had been free of any familiar faces.

Delphine and Julia were seated in a bathing machine: a contraption which resembled a slatted chalet on wheels, to be pulled by horse into the sea for the purposes of modest bathing. It was evidently not the first time the machine had ventured into the water that day; the women's feet were cold against the soaking wet carpet. Released from her corset, Delphine slumped luxuriously against the side of the machine. She was dressed in a long-sleeved flannel shift, and her hair lay in a plait down her back.

The bathing machine began to move, drawn by the old carthorse who had eyed them emotionlessly at their arrival, jolting them this way and that. Julia, who had been so busy looking around at the rather dirty interior as she knotted a scarf over her head, fell off the ledge she had been sitting on. This unlocked a wave of hilarity in Delphine, who laughed and laughed until she was crying, and she also fell off the ledge.

Another wave of hilarity struck them as the machine came to a halt, and it was a minute or two before they fell silent.

There was the sound of water all around them – the plash of waves against wheels and the sides of the machine. Delphine would have thought they were afloat, if not for the heavy stillness of the square room. They heard the creak of the modesty hood as the dipper – a large, strong woman who had not spoken since they paid her – let it down. Delphine jumped when there was a thud against the door.

'It's the waves,' she said. 'Come on.'

She opened the door and peered out from beneath the modesty hood, a wave rising and striking her as she did so, and she cried out at its fierce coldness. The horse stood impassively, held by its grim-faced attendant.

'We can go out a little further on our own,' said Delphine, feeling bold. 'I do not see anyone on the cliffs watching us; surely we will be safe from gentlemen's eyes.'

They treated it carefully, the grey-blue, alive water, so powerful in its swell even this close to the shore, the sand dissolving beneath their feet as they walked, until they were in the water up to their necks, encased by the cold of it.

'I feel so vital, as if I can feel every nerve in my body,' said Julia. But she could see that Delphine was unhappy; all the delight had faded from her face.

'Is this how Amy Phelps felt?' she said, and saw her cousin's face fall. 'I am sorry. I should learn to speak less. That was always my fault.' And for a moment she was in her mother's drawing room, being reprimanded for an unladylike remark.

She felt Julia take her hand, and squeeze it. In the distance, she saw a little girl playing by the edge of the sea.

They walked back up the beach, dressed and wrapped in their cloaks. The locals were out in the good weather, the hovellers smoking their pipes on the pier, some laughing and talking, others, like Solomon, bearing watchful, calm expressions. Some local girls were conversing with them. They looked strong and warm-fleshed; they were proud of any embellishments to their dress, and talked and laughed loudly. It struck Delphine that they all looked as though they could defend themselves, and would not be shy to do so.

'Is that Polly Gorsey?' said Delphine. The girl was

standing, talking to the men, laughing. 'She is usually in the Albion, working.' She watched the way in which the sunlight caught in the girl's coiled hair; the ideal silhouette of her figure beneath the elaborate dress she wore. Delphine wondered whether Polly had sewed all the little embellishments herself, for it was not a plain dress, but one decorated with hand-worked cloth roses and ribbons. She also wondered how much of a struggle it was for Mr Gorsey to get his daughter to wear the plain white apron over her clothes, and recalled how drab Polly had looked that first day she had seen her, when Mr Benedict's carriage had nearly run her down.

Julia was resting when Martha marched into the cottage, carrying a basket of bread and milk and eggs. Delphine let her pass through the house, heard her stamping about in the kitchen. It was only when she heard the crash of broken porcelain that Delphine went to see her.

'I have to pay for that,' she said, looking at the white fragments in Martha's hands.

'Sorry, madam,' Martha said.

'What is wrong?' Delphine asked. 'Are you over-tired? I fear you are working too hard, looking after us *and* Mr Hallam. We can hire someone else, you know. It might be for the best.'

Martha turned away, flushing as she always did when embarrassed. 'It's not that,' she said. Her large hands were trembling, and Delphine wondered if she might cry. There was something so deeply moving about this big, strong girl, normally so proud, suddenly wishing to hide, that Delphine felt her throat tighten in a mirror of her distress.

'It's nothing really,' she said gruffly, but her voice quivered. 'Just some of the girls. I grew up with them. You think they would be past their tittle-tattling, but it reminds me of being a little chick again, and all their spiteful words. Polly had the devil in her today, to speak to me so.'

Delphine waited, knowing that encouragement would not make her speak, but that silence might. She knew that Martha did not have the wherewithal of the girls on the pier: that tough shine, like sea pebbles tossed against each other until the surface is smooth and hard.

'It's a boy, ma'am,' she said eventually. 'I would say he is my sweetheart, but he is not. He was at least my friend, I thought. I was foolish, very foolish. I am not a girl who men favour. I could never be Polly, even if I tried, and I do not want to try. At least I shall never end up at the bottom of a chalk pit with some fool from the Ranelagh Gardens.'

She dug her fingers into an onion skin, and peeled it.

'I've seen those girls down by the harbour,' said Delphine, not wondering at the reference to the latest deaths, for word travelled faster here than it did in London. 'Did one of them take your beau? He is best forgotten, if so.'

'I did not say he was mine,' Martha said, without raising her voice. 'And if I ever had a hope of him – well, it was long ago, at least a year or two – but I find thoughts can get deep rooted sometimes, without you even noticing it. I told one of the girls in a weak moment, and now they use it to make fun of me. How I hate them.' She stabbed the onion with the knife.

'Our supper will be ruined if you insist on hacking up the vegetables,' Delphine said. 'Come now, dear Martha. I see the sense in what you say. But this boy was not worth it – you must believe me. Not worth it at all.'

'He would not even look at me, at the pier,' the girl said. Now she was slicing carefully, the tears from the onion pouring from her red eyes. 'He let them say their insults to me.'

'Then he is a coward too,' Delphine said, feeling hot anger rising in her. She remembered the icy restraint of her own mother, the serenity of her grandfather, and wondered if it was her father who had given her anger, and the doubtful gift of forgetting restraint. It was Delphine's turn to move away, but Martha had already seen her face. She put down her knife and wiped her eyes on her arm.

'Why, ma'am,' she said. 'Are you angry for me?'

Delphine half-turned back. 'Yes,' she said. 'I am.'

The words seemed to break over the girl, and her face was illuminated with joy. 'I am grateful,' she said. 'To have such a mistress! I could almost kiss your feet.'

'It is unjust, that is all,' said Delphine. 'There will be a husband for you, Martha, a good and kind and truthful husband.' She said it with a rush of fervour, though she did not quite believe it. The local population was limited; the girls at the harbour would take whatever men there were. Although there were villas on the cliffs ... villas with menservants.

'Would you like us to train you a little more?' she asked. 'You said you wished to learn to be fit for a larger household. Both my cousin and I have lived in such houses – we could educate you in their ways.'

Martha had stopped preparing the food. She bit her lip. 'It's a great honour,' she replied. 'It's very kind of you to offer such a thing. But I am not sure if I am made for a big house. It seems to me that I should be always bowing and scraping, and I am not sure if I could, madam, whether my pride could take it. For I should want to be thanked – the way you and Miss Julia, and Mr Hallam thank me – and I should want to go here and there when I pleased.'

'You must think on it, then,' Delphine said.

'I used to think I would never wish to leave here,' said Martha. 'But now I think I would go to somewhere bigger – like London.'

'There are certainly more men to choose from,' said Delphine. Martha's eyes widened, and Delphine sensed her disapproval, remembering her in her Sunday finery; the blank, straight-backed respectability of her family.

'What troubles you?' she said. Martha looked down, and there was something about her mute censure that made Delphine say, 'Answer me!'

'Nothing,' Martha said. 'I do not wish to offend you, ma'am. My mother's told me things are different in America.'

There was a prudishness in her face which enraged Delphine. She felt it, again: anger, too sudden and complete, as though a tight knot had been tied beneath her breastbone. 'If you do not wish for my help,' she said, 'you should stay quiet and do the cooking, as you are paid to do.'

Delphine left the room and ran upstairs, to her bedroom with its lantern turret. The conversation had taken an unexpected turn, and Martha's sudden disapproval had pressed on some sore point and hurt her savagely. She sat down on her bed, unable to take any pleasure from the view.

She knew if she closed her eyes she would be surrounded by the darkness of a New York night, by the lights of Fifth Avenue and Broadway. The taste of champagne was sour on her tongue. The knowledge that her life was over struck through her like a physical pain, making her bow her head with it. But no, it was not then that you knew, she thought: it was the morning afterwards. Breathe, she thought: only breathe. You must keep breathing. You must put one foot in front of the other. These memories are not real, now; they can no longer touch you.

She knew she would weather it, the terrible diffuse pain, the many strands of it. There were so many different details, so many different wounds, if you chose to remember them. She decided she would not think on them – not now, not ever – aware that she had made the same decision many times before. She must only weather it, and by teatime she would be able to eat scones, and talk of whether Mrs Quillian's salon by the sea would ever be reconstructed. But in that moment, she was only angry. Later, it would frighten her: how much she had wanted to take hold of Martha's hair, and smash her head against the wall.

CHAPTER TWELVE

What I remember most of that summer – if I take the people away, as I often try to do – is the weather, the air, the colour and smell of the place. The freshness of the air, so pure, so liquid as though it was a drug, made to knock you out each night at nine, made to make you sleep and forget. The smell of the salt wind, and the smell of the seaweed, that deep, dense, rotting vegetation, that was somehow part of it all. How quickly the weather would change: from heavy heat to thunder and lightning; from clear blue sky to a sea mist so dense it was best you should stay inside and not think of the ghosts of smugglers. We could hear the sea from Victory Cottage, hear the breaking of the waves, its roar and rush on stormy nights. It was the taker of lives, that sea. But how I loved it; how I loved to catch sight of its broken waves from the lantern turret.

The first Delphine and Julia knew of the storm that came to the town several days later was the gathering wind, the casements rattling throughout Victory Cottage.

It was the kind of day that made a jacket and stock seem unbearable, the air was so dense with heat. Edmund decided that he would stay in his room and rest. He did not wish to be out in the blistering heat nor fight the crowds who gathered near the house of Mr Dickens, nor even to speak with some of the old hovellers on the pier.

He slept. On waking, suddenly, he checked his pocket-watch; it was a quarter to six in the evening. Sitting up in bed, he became aware that the house was silent. The heat was still heavy and thick in the air. He went to his window and drew back the drapes. The white sunlight of the day was gone, its harshness softened in the early evening, but the light was luminous in such a startling way that it seemed unnatural, the sky more violet than grey.

At that moment he saw lightning shiver across the sky; it too had a violet tinge. Then the thunder came – low, primal, awakening fear in the depths of his belly.

He went downstairs. The house was empty – no Martha in the kitchen. He supposed she was seeing to the American ladies. From the drawing-room window he saw a faint glow from within the church; Evening Prayer. He decided not to go, and fought the urge to pour himself a strong drink. Instead, he stood before the window and watched as it began to rain. Heavy, sheeting, so thick it veiled everything: nothing could be seen from the window. Again the lightning came – a vein of light, ending in a scythe-like curve. The thunder was so loud that he felt it tremble through him, and he had to pretend to himself that he was not afraid. Then, similar but different – came a second boom. He had been warned of it: the signal that there was a wreck on the Goodwin Sands.

The heat of the day had been dispatched, cut through by the storm. He tried not to think of what was happening at sea. Instead, he made up the fire. As a bachelor, he had done it often. His mother had taught him how to do so as a child, with the same quiet persistence she had applied to teaching him to read. She had filled his young life with so many similar lessons, anxious that he should grasp the practicalities of living, as though she was afraid he would be alone in a room his whole life. She said once that she had learned early the habit of dependence, and that it was something she had had to unlearn, under the influence of love. As he watched the fire beginning to catch light, he thought of his parents. So often, his thoughts rested on them now. I am an old man, he thought, and I am falling in love, Father, as you promised – but not with the woman I *should* love.

The silence was broken when Theo entered the front door with a clatter and a crash. Edmund ran out into the tiled hallway. Martha was tucked under Theo's arm, limp as an injured animal. 'Mr Steele,' said Theo breathlessly, observing the proprieties even in this moment of emergency, 'a boat went out to the Goodwin Sands, to help some foolish excursionists; it has not come back. Martha's brother is on board. I must go to the pier where his wife waits. Please, will you look after Martha? She is too shocked to come with me.' He handed the woman over to him. The rain was dripping from his hat brim. He held Edmund's gaze, and for the first time – from that unblinking gaze – a confidence moved between them.

Edmund accepted Martha as he would accept a fragile package, half-carried her, heavy as she was, into the drawing room as he heard the front door bang shut. She didn't seem to feel his arms around her sodden sides, and against the conventions of all of her previous behaviour, she sat down on the sofa, her wet dress creating an aura of damp on the fine silken covering.

Time passed slowly that evening, as the storm raged outside. Out of decency, Edmund pulled the drapes closed, so that Martha did not have to see the ferocity of the lightning and the pouring rain, rain landing on water now as it flooded the gutters. He offered her food, and wine, but she would not accept them; in the end, he poured a large glass of wine and held it to her lips. She sipped from it, gazing at him with strained black eyes. Kept sipping, until the glass was drained.

'No more,' she said, when he stood to fetch some. He went anyway, poured it, and put it in front of her.

'God bless Mr Hallam for going out there,' she said, and the words seemed all the more poignant for being said in her rough voice. 'He does not have to, and I know it.'

'He is a good man,' said Edmund. Despite the closed drapes, there was a vibration through the room, a shiver of light which hinted at the lightning tearing at the sky, then, within moments, the thunder falling like an axe upon the land, and the very foundations of the house seemed to shake.

'He is called by God,' she said. 'That is how he does all that he does. It is what brought him here from Ceylon, what took him to Ceylon in his younger days.' Her gaze flashed to the ceiling, as though it might find something there, then down again. 'He is led by the Almighty.'

Ceylon, thought Edmund. A missionary life had been hinted at by Charles, but never explained or mentioned by Theo, only references to the heat which had once scarred him and occupied his mind. It did not seem the time to question Martha any further. Instead, he pushed the glass towards her, but she shook her head. Then, suddenly, she lowered her head into her hands, and the movement of her shoulders showed that she was weeping. He did not know what to do; only sat there. When she looked up, her eyes were red in the candlelight, her face wet with tears.

'He went out there on the boat,' she said, 'my brother, to help some foolish people out on the Goodwin Sands. Incomers.' She shook her head. 'My mother says the incomers bring bad luck. To you, the people that wait down on the pier are just strangers, but I know every one of them, have their stories up here.' She tapped her forehead. 'I know them in my bones. I like you, sir, I like the misses at the cottage, too, but my mother says you bring bad luck.'

*

It was past eight o'clock when Theo emerged from the storm. Edmund and Martha heard the bang of the door, then his footsteps moving quickly along the tiled floor. Martha raised her head, like a cowed animal waiting to be struck.

Theo's clothes were soaked through. He took off his hat and threw it on the table, with no thought for the rug he dripped upon. 'They are home safe,' he said. 'Safe, thank God.' And he laughed with an exhilaration Edmund had never seen before, light in his eyes.

'Safe?' said Martha.

'Yes,' said Theo, kneeling beside her and taking her hands. 'All of them. Go home, go and see him.'

For a moment Edmund thought she would say no; that she would gather herself and become dutiful Martha, and offer to make some tea. Instead, she burst into tears. 'I'll go,' she said. 'I quarrelled with him last week. I must see him.' And she ran from the room and they heard the front door shut, as she went out into the storm.

Theo rose to his feet. Edmund saw him gradually becoming more aware of his surroundings, a filtering awareness that made him uncomfortable with the emotion he had witnessed and participated in. He went to the window. 'She has gone without her bonnet,' he said. 'Into the rain.' And he shook his head.

'My dear boy,' said Edmund. 'You are shivering. You should go and change, lest you catch a chill.'

Theo went slowly upstairs and Edmund went to the kitchen. He found a chunk of cheese and cut some bread with the large knife. The size of it made him chuckle, imagining Martha sawing away with it, for it was as blunt as a butter-knife, though twenty times as large.

He took a blue and white plate from the dresser and carried the bread and cheese to the drawing room. In the dining room, by the light of his candle he found a full decanter of Madeira and took it, and two glasses, in. By the time he had arranged this feast Theo had come down. He stood awkwardly, near the door, rubbing his hands together. 'You must be chilled to the bone,' Edmund said. 'Please, sit down by the fire, and stay there until you feel you might melt, for you must be warmed through.'

Theo smiled weakly, and thanked him for the food. He had recovered his composure and ate like a church mouse, delicately, without seeming to savour the meal. He sipped his wine, and Edmund gulped it.

'We are in need of good news, after the past few weeks,' said Theo. 'I should not wish to associate this beautiful bay with death again so soon.'

Edmund nodded, and let him eat.

'You have seen the drama of life and death tonight,' he said eventually.

'There are such moments in all places,' Theo said. 'Suffering, joy. God is needed in every nook of human existence, and is wanted here as much as anywhere.' He chewed a mouthful of bread and cheese. 'When I heard the boat had not returned, I could imagine the women waiting for them, staring at the terrible, thrashing water – and it did not sit well with me to be safe and dry when they were

terrified and in trouble. I led them in prayer on the pier,'
he said. 'They are such strong women, yet the blessed
words reached them even in the midst of the storm. Some
sobbed, some were still, but I could see how it touched
them. It is grace. The prayer book gives us the poetry to
pierce their hearts, to peel back all those layers. They never
come to church, some of them. Ordinarily they would turn
away from it. But it is needed, and never so much as then,
and if they remember that God was here for them in their
hour of need, then it is a good thing.' He looked up from
the plate, and Edmund was struck by the unblinking
intensity of his gaze. 'The Virgin appeared here once, on
Harbour Street, in the twelfth century. And ever since, the
sailors lower their sails as they pass the headland, in
honour of the Blessed Virgin. And though they sometimes
forget it, the faith is always there really – they know its
worth.'

Edmund knocked back his wine, and filled the glass
again. He topped Theo's up, but the priest did not seem to
notice it.

'I was asking for God's mercy,' he said, 'when someone
said "I see them, I see a light". And they all let go of each
other's hands, in the cold and the rain, and ran to the edge,
and strained to see, and one of them shrieked. When the
first man came up, his wife clung to him like a mother
with a child. She would not let go of him.'

'It is holy, such love,' said Edmund. He did not know if
it was the wine, but he heard his own voice break on the
words. 'It is the best of us.'

Theo held his gaze for a moment, but he said nothing. When he began to speak, it was about the Sunday service – the choice of hymns. Their moment of honesty had passed.

Edmund felt sadness roll over him, submerge him, like the turning over of a wave on a beach. He felt homesick for London, and the friendship with Charles Venning, and sorry for writing so harshly to his friend a few days before.

My dear Charles, he wrote later, *I had begun to think myself Theo's friend – but now I know I am not. You would not have done such a thing. If you could not speak openly, we would have sat in the silence, listening to the rain outside, and draining the decanter as the clock ticked.* After he had written the words, he sat for some time, and thought of the unbending quality of Theo's gaze, the picture of St Sebastian hung on the wall in the study – the study he had never been allowed into since his first day in Broadstairs – of the saint's body all pierced with arrows, and his face the picture of suffering.

When Edmund rose the next morning, all was calm and verdant beyond his window, as if the storm had never been. He dressed quickly, and went down to find Theo sitting at the dining-room table, eating his breakfast. He wished him good morning cordially. Martha appeared to serve them. 'How is your brother?' asked Edmund, but she only bobbed him a curtsey and said, 'Very well, sir,' with a studied subservience. Theo continued reading the paper.

Edmund was toying with his eggs when there was a

sharp double knock at the front door. He saw Martha pass the doorway, hurriedly wiping her hands on her apron. A double knock had to be answered, for it might be a telegram. 'Message from the Albion Hotel, Mr Hallam,' she said, putting an envelope on the table.

'It is my aunt's handwriting,' said Theo, with a quick smile. 'Perhaps she is planning another excursion for us. There has been talk of the Shell Grotto in Margate.' He opened the envelope and as he began to read, all the pleasure drained from his face.

'What is wrong?' said Edmund. And when there was no response: 'Theo?'

Theo's eyes met Edmund's. He was pale.

'They have found another body,' he said.

CHAPTER THIRTEEN

Mr Steele has told me that every man admired me, that summer. If it is true – and my vanity does not seek it, believe me, for men's desire always was a poor amusement to me – I was not aware of it. I had moved invisibly through crowds for so long, that I still thought of myself as invisible, even as I spoke to people, even as I boarded Mrs Quillian's hired carriage. I thought I could step amongst the crowd, observe and withdraw, like a ghost. That is also why I identified with those little ghosts, that summer.

I had thought myself unobserved on my morning walks – apart from Solomon, who could be trusted, you knew from looking in his eyes – but now I know nothing passed unobserved in a place like Broadstairs. Politeness was the key, of course; we were visitors, we brought money, we were to be served, after a fashion. But they had seen us all before, and stripped us clean of our pretensions with their eyes.

I was different, though. I was the Widow of the Sands. And after the body of Catherine Walters was found, I became something else – not just a stranger, not just a widow, but a bringer of bad luck. I will never know who began that rumour. Was it a mutter of something, late night, in a tavern? Was it a charwoman on her doorstep, with her arms folded across her chest? Or was it someone I knew, a member of our group? But I will not enquire too deeply. I cannot bear to think of it.

'Did you come here to watch for corpses?' said the landlady of the Tartar Frigate, acidly. 'A fine holiday you're having.' And she glared at Edmund, as if he was in some way to blame. Her gaze softened a little at the sight of Theo, who had stood for a moment on the doorstep, looking out at Main Bay, so peaceful in the morning light, though the water was high, claiming most of the beach.

'Solomon found her,' she said, polishing a glass. 'I've put him over there with a tot of something to calm him. At least, I think he found her – he carried her here. Sol?' she called. 'Did you get sight of that widow today? Was she there too? Or anyone else?'

Solomon shook his head, knocked back his drink and rose to acknowledge Theo and Edmund. 'Just me found her,' he said. 'Poor little thing. Mr Gorsey came along when I was dragging her out, and helped me carry her here. But he has gone back to the Albion now – he has no stomach for this.'

'Understandably,' said Theo. 'My aunt is staying at the

Albion, and she had it at breakfast from Polly.' He glanced at Edmund. 'Word travels fast here.'

'Do you not think it strange,' said the landlady in a low voice to Edmund and Theo, 'how all these things have only started happening since that widow came here – that widow Solomon sees every morning? I watch her from my window sometimes, walking as slowly and deliberately across the beach as if she were in some procession of her own devising, and it chills me through and through.'

'I am sure Mrs Beck has nothing to do with this,' said Theo.

Edmund's gaze rested on the object of their discussion; for a few feet away, the body of the girl lay on the trestle table that Amy Phelps had occupied only a few weeks before. She was covered over, for decency's sake, but he saw, from beneath the cloak that shielded her from people's eyes, a few chestnut ringlets. He was of half a mind to ask the landlady for a drink, but wasn't sure that she would react kindly to such a request.

'I will bless her,' said Theo, and Solomon gave a grunt of approval. The landlady uncorked a bottle and poured the hoveller another drink.

Edmund felt he should support Theo in some way, so he stepped forwards, but kept a little way back. He saw Theo recoil when he lifted the cloak.

'She's bashed up, Mr Hallam,' said Solomon. 'I should have mentioned it – I am sorry, sir. I figure she must have gone into the water last night, and when the storm churned up all the water, so it did its worst to her, too.'

Over Theo's shoulder, Edmund saw her face. She looked to be around the same age as Amy Phelps; perhaps a little younger, twelve or thirteen. Her face was covered with dark smudges – storm clouds of bruises – and there was a bloody gash down one side of it. Her long chestnut ringlets were shot through with scraps of seaweed and fragments of shells. From the small section of her torso Edmund could see, her dress had been torn away.

'She must have gone into the water alive,' he said, 'for all those bruises to be so livid.'

'Is it anything to do with the Goodwin Sands?' said Theo suddenly, his hand lying on the table beside the girl's head.

'No,' said Solomon. 'Everyone is accounted for from the boats last night.'

'My husband's gone for the constable,' said the land-lady, with a sigh. 'If he comes, he'll be sure to put handbills out. We'll find out soon enough who she is.'

Theo began to pray, his hand raised in blessing.

That night, Edmund went into the town to escape the mournful atmosphere of the parsonage. Theo had gone to his study and was guarded by the terrier-like Martha, who told Edmund it was best to leave him alone, as she put on her cloak to go and check that the ladies in Victory Cottage had their supper. Thinking of Julia, he walked down Harbour Street a little way, then up the passageway on to the promenade. Here and there, the windows were lit by the softness of candlelight. A dance was being held, and he heard the stamp of feet and the scrape of a fiddle as he passed the assembly rooms. He went to the railings of the promenade; looked out at the sea. The smell of burnt sugar and frying potatoes was cut through by the salty air, and the competing smell of seaweed. The only trace of the storm were banks of sand built up against the cliffs, dug by the locals as a defence against what Solomon had referred to as 'more weather'. There were still people on the beach. He wondered if these last hangers-on, clinging to the scraps of the day's heat, were people on the last night of their holidays, breathing in the clean sea air, trying to set the horizon in their minds as they pointed and said, 'Can you see the cliffs of France?'

The light was fading. He passed one girl, walking alone, and she smiled broadly at him and let her shawl drop from one shoulder. The shawl, worked in a way that it was a criss-cross of strong cords, like a fisherman's net, the colour of the red brick of the parsonage in the setting sun, lay like a grille across her white skin. He smiled back, for he had seen her working at the Albion Hotel, but did not slow his step, and he was several feet along the promenade before he realized her intention. He was baffled by it, and slightly flattered; he thought himself too old to be worth a second look, but he knew that he bore his father's looks, a kind of youthfulness which played counterfeit to his actual age.

He found Solomon in the back bar of Neptune's Hall, a tavern whose polished woodwork resembled that of a ship's deck. The front bar was bare boards, but clean and wholesome, newly lit by gaslight; the back bar was carpeted in a dense dark pattern which swallowed up the light. Solomon was seated near the fire. Edmund ordered a beer from the landlady, then pulled up a chair and sat down beside the hoveller. 'I thought you might be at home tonight,' he said.

'My wife is the understanding kind,' said Solomon. 'She knows what happened this morning, and that I must be on my own for a while. What would I say? We are not allowed to speak to women of such things. Even if she gave me leave to, I do not think I could bring the words from my mouth, to tell her of that ugliness.'

Edmund shifted in his seat. 'I am sure your wife is a woman of good sense,' he said.

'I talk of my character as well as hers,' said Solomon.

They sat in silence for several minutes. Then Edmund took an extra large gulp of beer.

'She was just like the other girl, the one we found on the beach,' he said. 'Young, but not so young that she could have wandered into the sea without knowing what she was doing.'

'Her name is Catherine Walters,' said Solomon, his lips puckering as though he might weep. He took another mouthful of his drink. 'Someone came looking for her. She's not a local girl. An orphan. She'd been here two days, brought down with a group of other orphans by a wealthy lady staying near Stone, the charitable type. She had been unwell, and was told the sea air and bathing in the water would help her. She slipped out with two other girls, but went off without them. They returned when the storm came, but she did not.'

'She means nothing to Dr Crisp, I suppose?' said Edmund. 'Does he think there is a natural explanation?'

'The sea is hazardous, especially for those who are not used to it,' said Solomon. 'It is possible – nay, likely – that she was swept in last night if she was foolish enough to walk too near the edge. The waves came in high over the pier last night, sir – you should have seen it.'

Edmund leaned closer, and spoke low. 'I cannot help but suspect a pattern – Amy Phelps, now Catherine Walters, and a few years ago that young girl, drowned in a rock pool.' He did not wish to add that they were all poor, and unimportant to Crisp; nor venture that as long as no duke's daughter or baronet's wife was killed, the doctor would have no truck with the idea of foul play.

'Dr Crisp will do what he thinks is best,' said Solomon gently. 'He said your group gave him trouble about the couple at the chalk pit.' It had been proved, from conversations with family, that the man – a married labourer – and the girl – a young seamstress from Margate – had both gone to the Ranelagh Gardens and been seen there, drinking and dancing. The coroner's inquest had agreed that they had both sustained head injuries in their fall into the chalk pit, and died there in the night as a result. Edmund had read of it in the newspaper.

'Dr Crisp was right about that,' said Edmund. 'But still, do you not see there is something to be looked into?'

Solomon drained his glass. 'You're a good man, sir, and

I truly commend you for taking trouble over all of this. But all of these deaths are near enough to be accidental. People are often washed away, on nights like the last.'

'And Amy Phelps?' said Edmund.

Solomon shook his head. 'Let us pray it's over, this run of deaths. You will not convince Dr Crisp otherwise.'

'Just one more thing,' said Edmund, as Solomon rose and signalled to the barmaid. 'Was there any writing at the scene, this morning? Anything unusual?'

Solomon's expression was full of pity as he looked at him. 'There was a storm,' he said. 'I pulled the girl's body from the water, water which was almost up to the door of the Tartar Frigate. You know it, sir. There was no "scene", as you call it. Everything was washed away.'

Edmund went out onto Harbour Street, pulling his hat on, astonished by the severity of the chill in the air. Glancing behind him, he saw lights on the pier and wondered who he would find if he went there now. As he turned back, a couple passed him, and he recognized the woman he had seen on the promenade, the brick-red shawl huddled tight around her, her laughter ringing in the air. Mr Gorsey's daughter, he thought, and remembered a slighter version of her smile as she had handed him tea after the shell-collecting. Her male companion was swaddled against the cold night air, dressed in black, a scarf around half of his face, and his hat pulled low. With one glance at the man's eyes, Edmund felt sure it was the painter, Mr Benedict, though he had heard he was in Ramsgate with his wife and children. He opened his mouth to hail the man, but the couple were moving fast, and there was something about the way in which the man turned away and pulled his pretty young companion along which made Edmund decide to leave it.

He ascended Harbour Street with quick steps, passed Holy Trinity, which sat in stately flint-covered stillness and darkness, and was about to turn up the drive to the parsonage, when something made him stop and turn around. He was just a few steps away from Victory Cottage, and there was light behind the curtains of the front parlour. He knew the correct thing to do would be to return to the parsonage. But he longed to speak honestly to someone. Before he could change his mind, he crossed the road, opened the gate and rapped sharply on the door of Victory Cottage.

Delphine opened the door; she was carrying a candle in a glass shade, and the sight of it reminded Edmund of his first night in Broadstairs, and how seeing a light on this step had made him think of ghosts and spirits.

'Mr Steele! We haven't seen you for a good while,' Delphine said. She looked out at the evening. 'There is a sea mist drifting in again. Come inside.'

He was grateful that she had not blanched at the sight of him, nor hinted at the impropriety of him turning up at her door at this hour of the evening. Instead, she only opened the door wider for him to come in. He glanced behind him as he did so, and saw that she was right: the air was thickening, as though a light smoke had been breathed over the town, and he saw it in the beam of the new lamps that lit the road.

He was surprised at the smallness of the parlour. Delphine and Julia's singular elegance – an elegance which, to him, set them apart from all of the others in their party – had meant that he had pictured them in a larger house. Even though he had known they lived in the cottage, his mind had somehow created for them an elegant room within, large, well-appointed, with paintings and ornaments that went with the neatness of their clothes and deportment. He saw only the parlour of a furnished seaside house, a small clock, some books, a handful of cheap ornaments, and two faded sofas. Delphine settled on one, and he realized that she was no longer wearing her day dress, but a plainer gown without corseting, a dark blue silk robe over the top of it. Her hair was still up and dressed, but she looked tired, and after a moment's thought he recognized that the careful veneer of politeness and brightness which she wore in society had slipped from her face. She was alone with him in the room, and as he sat down he felt suddenly as though this was very intimate indeed. Except for the fact that he felt no attraction to her at all, he would have been embarrassed to look upon her.

'I did not mean to intrude,' he said to her.

'You have not,' she said, taking out a cigarette case, opening it and offering him one. 'They are Turkish,' she said, when he looked at her questioningly. 'I gained the habit in Paris, last year.'

He took one, lit it from the lamp beside them, then offered to light hers. She shook her head, and lit her own. 'You may look me in the eye,' she said. 'I think we are friends. I have trusted you from the first moment I saw you; or, at least, trusted you as far as I trust anyone. Julia is resting. She will be cross with me when she sees I have let you in, but I do not think you care whether I am respectable or not.'

Her words should have made him feel more awkward, but in fact Edmund felt his cares slipping away. He felt comfortable with her; a hundred times more comfortable than he did at the tea table of the parsonage. The smoky taste of the cigarette comforted him. He watched her tired gaze wander over the room.

'I have just been with Solomon,' he said. 'They pulled another girl from the sea.'

Delphine drew on her cigarette. 'I know,' she said. 'Martha told me today. Her distress is equal to the effort she inflicts on our house. Today she blackleaded the fireplace, polished all of our boots, and would have baked a fruitcake the size of Margate if we had not stopped her.' She looked down. 'Forgive me,' she said. 'I should not be flippant about such a terrible thing.'

'I have been at the tavern,' said Edmund. 'Solomon bids me to be sanguine, but I begin to suspect that foul play is involved.'

'At the tavern?' she said, with a knowing glint in her eye. 'I admire a man who can drink, and take comfort in it. I am not sure I ever could; it only makes me more restive,

171

and angry.' She saw that propriety stopped him from commenting. 'What troubles you so deeply?'

'The two girls are similar in age,' said Edmund. 'They are both of the labouring classes, and they have both been found in the sea. Then there is the writing we both saw, near the body of Amy Phelps: WHITE, and *White as snow*. What could it mean?'

He glanced at her; she shook her head.

'I admit,' he said, 'I would not be so worried about it if I did not have an older story lodged in my mind. Mr Hallam told me that some ten years ago, a young girl was drowned in a rock pool. She was Martha's niece.'

'Oh.' Delphine seemed shocked. 'Oh dear. I had wondered about their carefulness over Sarah – and I thought there was something.' She pressed her fingers into her brow. 'Poor, poor Martha. How terrible.'

'It was never solved,' said Edmund. 'And perhaps it is because I have too little to occupy me here, but it troubles me.'

Delphine looked at him steadily. 'Does this small town have a murderer in it?' she said.

'I do not know,' said Edmund. 'I hope not. I believe I am worried for you and Miss Julia, if so.'

Delphine put out her cigarette neatly before its time, folding it on to itself. 'How do you know I do not carry my own pistol in my trunk?' she said. 'I am not frightened, Mr Steele, though it is very worthy of you to think of us here. I have already endured death, in America; another will not pain me so very much.'

172

He thought she must be speaking of her widowhood. 'The loss of a husband must be a terrible thing to bear,' he said.

Delphine blinked, and looked at him for a moment with a lack of comprehension. 'Yes,' she said. Then she stopped, and said, 'No.' She looked him full in the eyes. 'I will not lie to you, Mr Steele.'

'Della?'

They both looked up to see that Julia was standing in the doorway of the parlour. She was dressed in a pale tea gown, and her blonde hair was loose down her back. Edmund was unused to seeing her without the veil across her face and encased within the layers of her elegant clothes. Like Delphine, she looked unmasked in this small room – pale, a little tired. Edmund did not even see the red stain across her face; to him it was another shadow in this room full of shadows. There was nothing extraordinary about her, this tired young woman, but the outline of her stillness in the doorway, her tallness, her grace, everything about her – took his breath away. But he also saw that she was afraid. She was looking at Delphine.

'My darling,' Delphine said. 'I told you, Mr Steele, she would be cross with me for letting you in here. All is well, my love.' There was a slight tremor in her voice. Julia stayed in the doorway; she did not move or come to join them. Edmund realized he was holding the cigarette out in his hand – he, like her, frozen, the cigarette gently disintegrating and ash dropping on the floor. He started, and more fell, and he put the cigarette out on the glass ashtray, moving to scoop some up from the floor.

'Do not worry,' said Delphine. 'Martha will be on that tomorrow, scrubbing it until the carpet has no pattern. The sea mist will be almost fully down now. You may wish to make your way back before your way is lost entirely to it.'

Edmund rose; he could hardly remember ever having felt so self-conscious before. He brushed the ash from his trousers, put his hand to his throat and realized his scarf was still tied there. Delphine did not rise; she lit another cigarette, acknowledged his bow with the inclination of her head. It was Julia who moved silently ahead of him and opened the door. The sea mist rolled in upon them, unfurled itself even into the hallway.

'Can you go out into this?' she said, and for the first time, his eyes met hers without her veil between them. There was barely half a foot between them.

Was it the spirits he had drunk, he wondered, or the coldness of the mist, but in that moment he wished to touch her, in a way he had not with Delphine. He did not let his eyes rest there, but he saw the outline of her face, of her neck, and he wished to brush his face against it, to place one, chaste kiss where the pulse beat in that pale skin.

'Yes,' he said. 'Yes.' And he pulled his hat on, and staggered out into the night. He did not hear the door close behind him. Groping in the thick air, he reached for the gate and pulled it shut.

He was on the roadside. He knew this only because of

experience; he was surrounded on all sides by the mist. To his right he saw the faint glow of a streetlamp; ahead of him a step or two of the road. He knew that the parsonage drive was just across the road, but he suddenly became aware of the silence, broken only by the distant call of the fog-horn. In the mist, any sound could be muffled or thrown; he was seized by the idea that a horse or carriage could come looming out of it. He recalled the smuggler's tale told by the locals, and for a moment he thought he heard the approach of hooves. He wondered how Solomon would make his way home. He hardly knew whether to take a step forwards or not, and felt like a fool, putting his hands forwards, groping in the mist, its purplish darkness. He took several steps forwards with no guide at all, until his hands met, with a gasp from him, the sharpness of the flint wall across the road from Victory Cottage. He guessed it was the parsonage's drive wall; he felt its curve, and then the waxen leaves of the first trees, and ahead of him there was a faint glow, and he knew it was the lantern above the front door. He walked slowly, steadily, knowing that he was disorientated and that he might trip. When he came to the front door he put his hands on it, and stood for a moment, feeling a surge of relief.

The door was pulled open. Theo stood, lamp in hand, his face full of amazement and relief. 'My dear Mr Steele, I was afraid something had happened,' he said. 'Come in, come in. Foolish of me, I know, and yet,' Edmund saw him smile in the darkness of the passageway, 'I cannot get used to these sea mists. I know they are glorious, these sudden changes in weather, but I cannot get used to the mists.'

'I did not come far,' said Edmund. He went into the drawing room and sat down. Theo brought him a woollen blanket and wrapped it round him.

'Your clothes are damp,' he said. 'I will fetch you some brandy. It does not take long for the sea mist to soak you through. I was wondering where you were. I had thought about bringing a lantern out to look for you, but I would have needed a beam as powerful as that of the lighthouse.'

Edmund nodded, huddling into the blanket. He felt, suddenly and powerfully, deeply vulnerable. He watched Theo bring in the brandy and pour out a healthy measure.

'How would you have looked for me?' he said.

'I do not know,' said Theo, handing him the glass. 'In truth, it would have been impossible to find you.'

CHAPTER FOURTEEN

Julia continued to be suspicious of Alba. It was true that sometimes, her exquisite looks attracted impatience or malice, but in every conversation I had with her, I glimpsed only innocence, and a desire to do good. She was full of high spirits, and often laughed in answer to questions, and although this earned her the censure of her aunt and the accusation of silliness from others, I felt sure that it stemmed from her nerves in social situations.

Unlike me, Alba wished only to please. Such an inclination leads sometimes to tragedy, and sometimes to triumph. I felt protective of her, and remembered how my life had turned on one poor decision: to walk with a man one evening on Broadway, alone, without recognizing the danger I was putting myself in. I told you men's desire was a poor amusement to me, and so was his. Yet I felt safe with him, for we moved in the same circles, and I had known him since childhood. I thought only to rile my *mother – but not of the destructive power of a man's desire, when thwarted.*

Two days after the night of sea mist, Theo Hallam rose early and left his sleeping house, having instructed Martha the night before to only make breakfast for Mr Steele.

There had been a high tide again. Passing the Tartar Frigate, he glanced at the scattered sand on the road, where the water had come almost up to the door of the inn. He had already noted, from way off, the familiar comforting silhouette of Solomon on the end of the pier, smoking his pipe and watching the weather as Tarney, Martha's brother, moved around him. Tarney was a man who had to be constantly doing things, even if it was only sweeping sand from the pier boards. In contrast, Solomon conveyed immense stillness, the stillness of a tree or a mountain. Theo could never imagine such a man being lost to the sea, this certain figure beneath the sun – for he was as weather beaten and bleached as a piece of driftwood. The sea had smoothed out all wrinkles in his character, had sanded him clean, and surely if he was ever cast into it, she would recognize him as one of her own, and bob him home on her surface.

Of course, Theo knew never to utter such notions out loud. The hovellers and fishermen would joke about many things, but never about their fate in the sea. She was to be respected, above all things – for, as Solomon had once told him, one sharp wave could wash you free of all your thoughts of mirth, and lick the soul right out of you.

As Theo walked along the pier towards Solomon and Tarney, he looked out at the perfect curve of the bay, at the handful of luggers as they gently swayed in their docks. It was how he had imagined Broadstairs would always be, when he had come here, seeking gentleness, retirement, purity of thought and good health. Every wave, soft and neat, had the gentility of the turning of a page in a book. But he had seen the other side to the place too, for it had its moods and its seasons, its sudden changes in weather, and this lack of certainty both excited and troubled him. He thought of mentioning it to Solomon, but he had no idea if the hoveller would agree and utter something sage, or look at him as if he had lost his mind.

As he walked, Theo saw, in the very breast of the bay – dead centre, as though it was measured – a figure standing. He thought of Delphine immediately, and put his hand up to shield his eyes as he looked. If it is her, he thought, I will go back and abandon my purpose for today. Every sight of her seemed to weaken him more, seemed to awaken some unshakeable shame in him. He no longer wanted to be seen by her; he wanted no questions in her eyes. But he could not see the swell of a lady's skirts beneath the cloak, nor was the figure wearing a hat that might identify them, but a hood. As he peered at the figure, Theo was annoyed by his short-sightedness, and wondered if it was worsening.

'Morning, Mr Hallam,' called Solomon, with easy respect. Tarney jiggled and muttered something also,

and Theo took the tone of his voice as a sign of awk-
wardness and anxious respect. He wished them both a
good morning.

'Wasn't sure if you'd come,' said Solomon, blowing out
the smoke from his pipe.

'I am grateful to you for doing this,' said Theo.

'I don't like it,' said Solomon, 'but you have seen us
through many a time, through loss, and grief – so if you
wish to go, you're the only man I'd take.'

'I'm obliged to you. We didn't speak of payment,' said
Theo.

'We'll worry about that later,' said Solomon, as though
money were the last thing he thought of on such a morning.

The journey in the *Susan* was easier than Theo thought it
would be. He felt strangely secure in the lugger, comforted
by the solid presence of the boatmen in their black oilskins.
Even the occasional high wave or roll of the boat did not
disturb him. But as the bay receded from him, and the air
grew fresher, he wrapped his cloak tight around him.
Tarney had turned quiet; Theo wondered whether he felt
more at peace in his natural habitat. Solomon was the same
as ever, his steady gaze fixed on the horizon, now and then
sweeping the surroundings with the detached serenity of
a lighthouse beam.

The water grew choppy; then the Sands came into view.
Before long Theo felt the drag of the boat against the
bottom.

'We're here, sir,' said Solomon, as Tarney hooked the

ladder over the side. 'You'll have to climb down and wade a step or two – you won't mind a little seawater?'

'No,' said Theo, swallowing hard.

'Ah, she's a proper island at the moment, on account of the Spring Tide,' said Solomon. 'Have no fear, sir, you've a while before we'll float again. But the weather can turn quick, and though the Spring Tide means the Sands are well-exposed ... well, it makes the current stronger too. If we need you back here, then we'll give you this sign.' He put his hands to his mouth and gave out a shrill, uncompromising call, half-whistle, half-owl's hoot, which shivered through Theo. He nodded, and climbed unsteadily down the ladder, descending into a few feet of water. It seemed to drag at him; he moved quickly, and in a moment was out of the water. With a wave at the men, he wrapped his cloak around him, and set off along the uneven banks of the Goodwin Sands.

He walked quickly, without looking back, drawing away from the men as the boat had drawn away from Broadstairs. He wanted to be solitary here. He had meditated on this moment, and the chill which even now was invading his flesh and bone seemed apposite.

He walked for some time, climbing then descending two sandbanks. He thought only of his privacy; the fear with which he had set out had almost evaporated. The distant lightships looked as innocuous as pleasure crafts, as though they should be populated with sightseers.

When he had walked a good way, he stopped and looked around.

Solomon was right, it did feel like an island: solid, and
safe from the waves, though the idea was ridiculous considering the place of dread it held in the minds of all who
knew it. There were all kinds of tales about the Goodwins;
there was even an innkeeper in Broadstairs who claimed
to have a table made of the last tree from the island it had
once been. But the one most ingrained in Theo was that of
the ship-swallower, and as the phrase rose in his mind he
swayed a little, as though the Sands moved beneath his
feet. What would one poor clergyman be, to this monster,
this deep, swelling graveyard?

He had meant to come here, many times over the years;
a thought it had been easy to put away, neatly. Until these
last weeks when, surrounded by death, he had felt the
desire to live waken in him. It had made each moment,
each sensation, more precious – and yet this sudden resur-
gence of the life-force had puzzled and tortured him.

He looked around at the innocuous Sands, pleated from
their last contact with the sea. The breeze against his face
was not foul, but as clean and health-giving as it ever was.
He looked desperately at the distant line of the cliffs on the
horizon – at his home. Despite the air, the sea, everything
was desolate on these Sands. A tomb. To his right, he
caught sight of something in his peripheral vision. He narrowed his eyes. It was a piece of mast, the end of a
structure; only God knew how much lay beneath. Theo
turned sharply away. To his left, he stared into a huge
gully, filled with clear water.

He had imagined he would hear the voices of people

screaming. But there was nothing, only the lapping of water and the cry of the gulls.

He unbuttoned a pocket in his coat and took out a small bottle. He fumbled in opening it: how fussy the container seemed now in this mortal place, its silver surface enamelled with green and blue gothic motifs, a pretty, ornate thing, from another world. Still, he opened it with reverence and scattered the holy water, saying, in a voice so low it was drowned out by the gulls: 'I am the resurrection and the life, saith the Lord: he that believeth in me, though he were dead, yet shall he live: and whosoever liveth and believeth in me shall never die.'

He screwed the lid back on the bottle, and put it back in his pocket. Then, from another pocket, he took out the thick piece of parchment he had put there this morning, on rising.

He remembered the small white Scottish church in Colombo, long ago. He had stood in the shade of its porch as she walked away from him – the woman he would come to know as Georgina – her ragged skirts fluttering, so that her ankles and calves were clearly visible. With every step she took away from him, a small wisp of sand would rise, so that every step had a ghost, and his beating heart had an echo. It was that image which was responsible for his persistence – he, so quiet, so timid, walking through the alleys of Colombo, searching for converts, for one particular convert, speaking to her parents, suggesting an English name. Driven on by holy fire, by conviction underlined with every prayer.

Even now, with the breeze cold against his face, he felt the heat of that distant day, and the sweat broke out on his face.

He had come out here, because in the past weeks that vision of the lost woman had returned to him again. But when she turned to look back over her shoulder, she had the face of Delphine Beck.

He hardly knew how it had come to life, this desire, but the death of those poor girls had done something to all of them – the presence of death seeping into them, making them want to live all the more. He saw it in Alba's frantic gaiety; in Edmund's gentle pursuit of Julia, and in his own, angry desire for Delphine. There were days when he hated her for it, her effortless dismantling of the serenity he had worked so hard, for so long, to build.

He thought the past was possessing him again, and turning his mind; making his thoughts swarm with heat and possibility, and the American widow was at the heart of it. He had believed himself strong, but he could not divert his thoughts away from Delphine, as they turned back to her, again and again in the long evenings: her dark, adamantine gaze, her coiled, ash-coloured hair, the way she always wore lace gloves, so that when she removed one it made him catch his breath at the intimacy of seeing her hands, so smooth and pale as though they had never seen the sun. Only once before had he been so obsessed with a woman, and he knew now that these thoughts were not to be encouraged. He felt lust; the same lust that had steered the first woman here – *here*.

The ship bringing her to him, at his request, wrecked on this site.

How would Georgina walk in this sand? There would be no small sand-ghosts here; with every step her feet would be suckered at by the sand, as though it sought to absorb the life-force from her.

But she was here. It had already taken her.

He unfolded the letter. He knew it off by heart. In it was wrapped the string of polished stones she had given him. *For counting prayers.* Of course, he had never used it. It had been banished to a drawer, together with the letter, signed *Your Georgie.*

'God bless you, in your innocence,' he said. 'He takes the blessed early, so that they may never know suffering.'

He thought he could hear the screaming. Hear the tearing of wood, the roar of the sea. See, as if he stood on deck, the distant, gazing beam of the North Foreland, as it sought to warn. *I told you*, it said. *I warned you. It is all as I said.*

He threw the letter and the beads into the clear water of the gully beside him. He wanted to say a prayer over them, but the words had gone from his head.

Then across the Sands, he heard Solomon's call, and it sounded desolate. The beads had already been swallowed up by the Sands; he still saw the white glow of the letter below as it floated down. He turned and began to walk, and as he topped the bank, he saw Solomon waiting for him.

Then, Theo stopped. The thought had come suddenly,

but with a right-feeling intensity, as though everything had fallen into place; it was stronger than the voice of God which counselled him in his prayers. *I must stay. I must be with her. It is my duty.* The thought had come as a surprise; for buried deep, he had had the idea that coming here might finally close up the wound within him. But he could feel no healing; his desire for Delphine had not been extinguished as he hoped. *If I go back,* he thought, *it will continue: and we will both be driven on to the rocks by it, and destroyed.* The sudden pull to stay surprised him with its strength. It was not an urge, but a duty, and the hidden desire he had always had for martyrdom suddenly opened up in him.

'Go without me,' he called, and he had no idea whether they heard him, or if his voice had been lost in the breeze. He saw Solomon start to walk, coming towards him, and he waved his arms, then placed them in a cross: do not come here. 'Go without me,' he shouted, louder.

He turned his back to the men, and heard a cry: his name. He began to walk away from them, saying to himself: *leave me, leave me, leave me. I will save myself from the flames.* He hoped they would understand. The sea was already growing louder; or was that in his mind?

He considered himself alone with the gulls and the sky, ready for the Sands to take him as they had taken her, when he heard the sodden thump of Solomon's feet behind him, and two strong hands grabbed his shoulders. As Solomon pulled him round, Theo saw the other man's face: saw his disbelief, and displeasure, and also with a sudden ache, the knowledge that the man would not let him go. He read the question that the mariner posed with his eyes: *will you let the Sands take me, too?* It was with that sudden humanity before his eyes that Theo felt fear silver his heart, like the edge of a sickle moon, and when Solomon grasped his hand and pulled him, bawling, 'It's flooding! Come *on!*' his feet responded, and he began to run.

He had not imagined the sound. The sea was rushing in on them fast, and this incoming tide was not like the gentle lapping at the bay in Broadstairs. His body responded: the strong thud of his heart, the sensation of the muscles in his legs stretching as he ran and jumped, all the time the Sands seeming to dissolve beneath his feet. And they *were* dissolving, brought alive by the sea, changing themselves, transmuting from solid to liquid, ready to reveal more wrecks, more secrets. He imagined the yawning of the sand beneath his feet, a pit of lost souls beneath, reaching for him. A kind of ecstatic panic overcame him as he neared the boat, which was already floating completely with the turn of the tide, and they waded through the water, waist-deep, Tarney leaning out to them as they reached for the ladder.

'Good,' said Solomon, once they were at sea again, the distant roar of the Sands surrendering to the water finally dulled. The word was ridiculous in its understatement. There was no hint of the previous moments, other than he was breathing hard, and that Tarney had fixed the clergyman with a hard stare. 'I don't mind your sermons, Vicar, but I didn't much fancy swimming back to the Sands to rescue you.' And he gave a hearty chuckle, the sound of which warmed Theo like hot liquor, as the boat shuddered and rose on a wave.

'I am grateful to you,' he said.

And Solomon thudded his hand onto the younger man's shoulder, a touch that seemed to tell of his understanding. 'You were out there for a long time,' he said. 'We called and called.'

As the boat moved through the water, Theo shaded his face with his hand. He wanted only to be back in the vicarage again, with the tick of the clock, and the sun beating down on the red bricks, and that drawer in his room – empty, empty, empty, as though the contents of it had never existed. As though Georgina had never lived.

CHAPTER FIFTEEN

*I told Julia that Mr Hallam was a puzzle I could not compre-
hend. I told her that he would often look away when I spoke, and
I interpreted it as impatience. 'Perhaps he dislikes Americans,'
she said. 'Perhaps he disapproves of your frankness. And yet,'
she said, her blue eyes so steady, 'he stands close to you. He looks
at you. When you look at him, what do you see?'*

*I thought long on her words before replying, on his gaze,
which had the heavy quality of the air when a storm is coming.
'His eyes are unfathomable,' I said, 'like the depths of the sea.'
It frightens me sometimes, what I feel when I look into those
eyes.*

Alba settled down happily in the deep grass at the side of
the cornfield, surrounded by the swell of her white dress,
holding her parasol up to protect her face from the

harshness of the morning light. Behind her lay the view Delphine had looked upon on the day of their first excursion, the first stop of the carriage: the basin of the bay, the pier at its far point. The natural beauty of the landscape seemed unnatural in its intensity to Delphine, so beautiful, like the features of the young girl before her, it was almost painful to look upon.

It had been a great surprise to her when, after a week of silence, she had received a note from Alba saying that Miss Waring was unwell and keeping to her room, but that she had granted Alba the opportunity of going out, as long as she had the protection of one of their party. Delphine guessed that Miss Waring had anticipated that Mrs Quillian would be that protector, but didn't question her any further.

Delphine sat a little way from her, also in the deep grass, and began to sketch. She did not ask Alba to be still, so now and then the girl turned to look at the bay, or twirled her parasol, or batted at a butterfly in the long grass, her small grasping hand reminding Delphine of a toddler, so that she almost laughed. She tried, but could not capture her in the way she wished; she had always had trouble with faces, and Alba kept appearing as a collection of features, but without the piquant beauty Delphine saw in her.

'Did you know,' said Delphine, 'I read in the London papers that some women in London were protesting about the clothes we must wear.'

The remark stilled Alba, as she had hoped it would. 'Clothes?' she said. 'What objection do they have?'

'They think it is a tyranny that we are forced to wear corsets, and so many layers in our dresses,' said Delphine. 'Some of them even wore pantaloons, on Piccadilly.' She couldn't help but smile at the thought, and wondered what her own mother would think of such an outrage. She probably would have fainted on the spot, at the very least.

'How strange, and ridiculous,' said Alba. 'I am glad we are here, rather than in London. Such a thing would distress my aunt greatly.' She glanced around, no longer staying still. 'Did you hear about the death of that poor young girl?' she said.

'Yes,' said Delphine, keeping her eyes on the drawing. 'I understand the inquest has found it was accidental.'

'Such a horrible business,' said Alba. 'And it was doubly painful for us, for we visited the lady and her orphans that very afternoon.'

Delphine stopped drawing. 'How so?' she said.

'My aunt is of a charitable bent,' said Alba, 'and she knew the lady through the many causes she is involved in. The lady had brought a whole houseful of the orphans to see the sea. They all seemed so very happy. To think one of them is now gone makes me very melancholy, though my aunt says she will be happier in heaven. I cannot quite picture the particular one, though.' She swatted at something in the grass. 'It could have been me,' she said.

Delphine continued drawing, trying not to show her disquiet, though the girl's words had set her mind racing.

'Mrs Beck,' said Alba, 'can I tell you a secret? Only, you must promise that you will not tell anyone.'

Delphine's mouth was dry; the charcoal slipped from her hand. She caught it, quickly but too tightly, and was glad that she was wearing her blackest mourning that day, so her dress would not be blemished. 'Of course,' she said, trying to sound unconcerned.

'I am not really Miss Waring's niece,' said Alba. She seemed childlike, mouthing the words in an exaggerated way, as though this somehow softened their impact. 'She is very good to say so, and of course it is better, for society, to think that I am. But really, I am an orphan, like that poor girl on the beach. Miss Waring's sister took me in when I was small, and now they pretend I am one of them, but really I am not.' She rushed on, 'When this summer is over, I must make my way in the world.'

'And how will you do that?' said Delphine.

The girl appeared to think, with an exaggerated kind of deliberateness that indicated she had previously imagined this conversation. 'The worst thing to do, would be to take a role as a governess,' she said. 'Altogether I think it better if I can marry, though when I say that to Miss Waring, she says nothing. Will you help me? You are so very elegant. I feel sure that you know the things I must say and do to be thought of – in that way. I have observed that Mr Hallam cannot take his eyes from you.'

She did not appear to hear Delphine's sharp intake of breath, nor notice that the widow was staring at her with a look of shock, her face pale against the black silk of her dress and the deep green grass.

Delphine took up her pad again, but the moment she put the charcoal to the white paper, it crumbled a little, and she set it down. 'You should perhaps consider,' she said, trying to ignore what had just been said about Theo, 'whether marriage is a step you truly wish to take. Would you not wish for more time? A little freedom?'

'What freedom?' asked Alba shakily, her smile fixed on her face. 'At present, I am kept at home, caring for the children of my guardian. They are growing older, and I have no place. You were married – surely it was not so terrible? You mourn so deeply – Miss Waring says it is a little self-indulgent, how deeply you mourn, and Mrs Quillian says *she* does not insist on wearing black rings and hair jewellery and such dark, cheerless clothes. But I think, if you mourn so deeply, then you must have loved very much, and I would wish for such a love.' She made this speech strongly, in a tone that Delphine had never heard from her before: with a sense of entitlement, as if the love she sought was some kind of prize, to be won by shying a ball at a coconut on the beach stall. 'You must help me, Mrs Beck,' she said pleadingly, observing Delphine's silence. 'I will do all that you tell me, I promise. I will persevere.'

'I am your good friend, in all things that are within my power,' said Delphine. 'But there is no help I can give you in this matter. I cannot create a marriage out of thin air for you, my dear girl – never mind love, which is far rarer.'

Alba was not peevish, but the words cracked her cheer, and it worried Delphine later when she returned that she might, unwittingly, have broken the girl's spirits. The front room of the cottage seemed full of shadows that afternoon. When Delphine turned her mind from the past, the present worried her just as much.

The Shell Grotto in Margate was a mysterious complex of underground caverns and tunnels, its walls decorated with shells, which had only been discovered some sixteen years before by two children playing in the grounds of a school. Mrs Quillian, in sending out notes to arrange an excursion, mentioned that it occupied a full page in Alba's guidebook. A full page, it was agreed, deserved a visit. Mr Benedict had returned to Broadstairs for a day or two, and so it was with full carriages that the little group set off to Margate.

Edmund found himself in a carriage with Theo, Alba, Miss Waring and Mrs Quillian. He was in a thoughtful mood, the reason being a letter in his breast pocket, from Charles Venning. He had written:

Mrs Craven is quite well, and you must forgive me for not assuring you of this. It was no 'line', Edmund, but natural delicacy which made me not mention her. The past should be left far behind. That is, in part, why I sent you to Broadstairs, such as you claim I did, though you are not of a character to be forced into anything; it is why you are my friend.

You asked me about Theo Hallam. I have known his family for many years. He went to Ceylon, as a very young man, and his naturally melancholy disposition has, I am told, yawned wider and deeper than ever since his return. His family is concerned for him, though he shuns their aid. I thought the sea air would do you good – and I also thought your natural facility, in matters of the mind, might prove helpful to this very dark and entangled case.

This very dark and entangled case, thought Edmund. How strange it was that, since coming here to holiday, his letters to his old friend were no longer full of small amusements and observations, the kind of chatter he would have enjoyed at his club. This morning he had stood outside Theo's study, that shrine he could not enter, and wondered, with an anxiety that seemed childlike to him, whether he should knock on the door. Then he had left the passageway, and when Theo had emerged, declaring himself ready for the Shell Grotto, his face was flushed with a faintly dangerous animation. It had startled Edmund, for the evening before, Theo had sunk into a gloomy silence, and when Edmund had asked him what was wrong, he only said: 'I see the face of that girl, with all the bruises there, dealt her by the sea and the driftwood, and it reminds me of the past.' But he would not say any more.

These worries displaced others. For days, when Edmund had picked up his pen, he only saw Julia, as she had stood in the doorway of the cottage parlour, so pale and tired in the lamplight, so utterly dear to him. It was her name he wished to write in the lines to his old friend, for in the last few days it was her he had thought of; even the poor dead girls on the beach had taken second place to her. He had never before felt so sickly over a woman, and he knew that a gentleman would not write this to another gentleman – especially not one of his advanced years – without expecting ridicule in return. But he also knew that he could be accused of fickleness, for his good friend had witnessed his apparent partiality for Mrs Craven, had been present at their conversations, which had shimmered with the suggestion of future plans. Even if Charles Venning did not say so, he could not bear for his friend to be disappointed in him; he even had the creeping feeling that Charles might begin to find him truly dishonourable.

The rocking of the carriage brought him to; Alba was speaking, her voice rising and falling, bubbling with enthusiasm. Edmund heard a gentleman laugh, and realized it was Theo. He laughed, and laughed again, and his face had that same flushed look, the kind of hard animation Edmund had only previously seen when Theo had spoken of his faith. He thought that he should write to Charles and tell him that Theo had not asked for help, and that he could make no inroads on his melancholy without knowing Theo's own thoughts, or speaking to him about it. He does not want to be helped but by God, Edmund decided.

Still, he brooded on the case, and during the journey to the Shell Grotto, whenever his awareness popped up to the surface of the conversation, he noted with surprise that Theo was conversing in an animated way with Alba and Miss Waring, negotiating the conversation with respect and even a certain amount of charm. It unsettled Edmund enough to keep him watching.

Delphine found herself seated alongside Mr Benedict. His appearance was as he had been the first day she had met him, as though it was a part he had chosen: dishevelled, the bejewelled skull pin placed securely in his lapel, his glossy black hair a little longer, and a touch of sunburn on the edge of his cheekbones. She had never been so close to him before. The rough road occasionally threw them together, and it was only this close that she noticed the faint grime in the pores of his skin, and the light occasional sighs which escaped from him. He was unusually taciturn, answering questions about painting politely enough, but without his usual gusto.

'How is Mrs Benedict?' asked Delphine eventually, thinking that if they stayed silent with each other it would be just as damning as over-enthusiastic conversation. 'I thought she might be one of our party today.'

'The good lady is occupied with our children,' said Benedict, in a detached tone. 'But she is well, thank you. Daisy, our youngest, has had a cold of late, and I have been a little worried about her – you must forgive my quietness. She is such a good girl; she never complains, and is always full of sweetness. My wife has told me, with her usual good sense, that I am of no use during

197

the child's sickness, and that she will send for me if there is any change in her condition. The best thing for me to do, she assures me, is to gather all my little sketches together and begin the next painting that I have promised her. I slipped to London for a day or two, also, and my dealer grows impatient. London, Mrs Beck, do you miss it?'

Delphine heard Julia's sharp intake of breath, and she knew that she had never mentioned their London house to the painter. 'It is a fine city, just as New York is,' she said, 'but I would not say I miss it. Paris has more of a pull on my heart.'

'How mysterious you ladies are,' he said. 'But I will not worry away at you. I am not like most men – I tire of a mystery, after a while.'

Delphine saw Julia's questioning glance, but could give her no answer.

It made Edmund suffer to see Julia handed down from the carriage by Mr Benedict, who was playing at being the perfect gentleman, one arm folded behind him, his fingers curling out to meet hers with elaborate affectation. But, to his relief, as the group merged and assembled, ready to descend into the Shell Grotto, it became clear that Mr Benedict only had eyes for Alba. To Edmund, he seemed to watch her with the same hungry stare that he had once displayed when he had spoken of Delphine, and he wondered at the young man's changeable nature.

The Shell Grotto was proudly announced in large letters on an arch over its gateway. They were greeted by a finely dressed and obsequious woman, who ushered them through a small parlour shop into the darkness of the grotto. They descended one flight of stairs, then another, into the dense cold of the underground passageway. 'The north passage,' the woman said, her voice echoing in the chamber.

For a moment Delphine felt as though the walls were closing in. They were rough, as yet undecorated – as far as she could see, a mix of dark rock and chalk, with patches of green where algae was growing, nourished by the dampness of the air. The path was uneven, the passage winding. She felt Julia's hand on her back. She was in the midst of the party, but in the sudden darkness, breathing in the unfamiliar scent of the saturated air, she felt alone.

In a matter of moments, they had reached the rotunda, announced by the woman as 'the place of birth', for its decorative scheme seemed to indicate a preoccupation with the beginnings of life, though the woman, with a polite cough, did not wish to indicate the exact images. It was, as promised, astonishing. The walls were studded with thousands of shells, formed into complex yet strangely naïve motifs: a heart, a shield with a central shell, or grotesques that seemed to make no sense other than in the mind of the person who had put them there. The shells offered texture to the eye – but it was still cold, and dark. In most areas the gaslight offered little relief, but there were also apertures from which pools of light fell and uncoiled, like white liquid, on the floor.

'Surely this is the work of a madwoman,' whispered Julia, and Delphine knew immediately the image her cousin held in her mind: a mad gentlewoman, fixing tiny shell after tiny shell to the wall in a mockery of the decoration that Alba would undertake on a little box with the shells she had gathered on the beach.

'It is very strange,' said Theo. Delphine heard his voice, soft and close. He moved past her, his eyes ranging over the walls. 'It seems a kind of hallucination.'

'It is a wonder,' said the guide, her rich voice trained, it seemed, to fill the caverns of the grotto. 'The shells are fixed with mortar; some of them are from the Indies.'

'The maker of this was no mere Broadstairs shell-picker like you, Miss Alba,' said Benedict.

They moved around the rotunda, and Delphine looked up at a great shell-pocked blister of daylight, bluish-white to her eyes. She blinked, suddenly disorientated, and took a faltering step back.

She felt someone's hands on the top of her arms, hesitant, steadying her. The touch was such a gesture of intimacy that she thought it must have been Julia. But glancing back, she found Theo there, his face barely two inches from hers. He should not have touched her; he should not have been standing so close, in the half-darkness. And she knew she should not have kept her face so close to his; she should have sprung back, exclaiming, curtseying, brushing him away with all the weapons in the armoury of convention. Yet she did not; and their eyes remained locked until the moment was broken.

'Do not be scared, Miss Alba,' cried Benedict, passing them, with a quick, cutting glance in the strange light. Miss Waring followed, chiding him strongly and holding on to her niece's hand, giving it the occasional strong jerk, as one would pull up a puppy on a lead. Neither of them noticed Theo and Delphine, for they had stepped apart immediately in the moment Benedict had passed them, and Theo turned and followed the group. Delphine let everyone pass, then walked on. Wrapped in her thoughts, she jumped and cried out when a skeleton of white and cream shells on a ground of black suddenly loomed out of the half-light at her. Regaining her composure, she hurried on.

'And now the altar chamber,' said the guide. 'We have moved from birth, through life, through to the afterlife: see the stars.'

It was a rectangular room, lit by gaslight, the walls again completely ornamented, a small decorative altar built into the back wall. 'Many spirits have been seen here,' said the guide, precipitating a few gasps. Theo shook his head disapprovingly.

A dark creature darted amongst them; Alba screamed.

'Some trickery,' said Miss Waring firmly. Delphine admired how the woman had not jumped; she kept her chin tilted up, but she had released her niece's arm.

'My cat,' said the guide with an embarrassed laugh. 'Please accept my apologies.'

'She likes to be scared,' said Benedict softly, watching as Alba, quickly recovered, moved along the walls of the altar room, running her hands along the shells, as though close inspection would reveal something more.

With a smile, and a nod that showed understanding, Mr Benedict took the lantern from the guide and drew closer to Alba. Then, acting so quickly Delphine hardly saw what he did, he snatched at Alba's hand. 'Come with me, Miss Peters!' he said, and Miss Waring cried out in fury as her niece was pulled away. He did not lead her far, only up to one of the walls, and trailed his lantern against it, watching the expression of fear on her face dissolve into wonder as the light lit up the shells at that particular place, forming a huge heart, surrounded by other lines of colour.

'A happy coincidence,' he said, watching her eyes take in the pattern, then settle on his own. Alba laughed, a laugh of embarrassment, her gaze flitting away from his onto the ground.

'Can she do nothing but giggle?' said Julia in a low voice. 'She is such a fool.'

'She can do nothing to please you, it seems,' whispered Delphine. 'Now she is too beautiful; now she laughs too much. She is merely young.'

'Have you done anything with your shells, Miss Mardell?' said Theo, approaching them, as Alba darted away from Mr Benedict and back to her aunt's side. The painter retaliated by placing his lantern on one of the altar room's niches, taking out a small sketchbook and beginning to draw. The guide cleared her throat, clearly wanting to conclude the tour.

'Nothing,' said Julia, 'and whilst I thought I might cover a box or two, it seems hopeless when I look around these walls.'

'This, though,' said Delphine, 'is a cathedral of shells – you would not wish to recreate this. It tells of a strange mind to make such a place. I think a box or two would be pretty, a keepsake of our days here.'

'And what will *you* have as a keepsake?' said Theo. There was no doubt that his words were directed at Delphine. His eyes had found her in the darkness, and his voice was freighted with some nameless emotion, as it was when he read from Scripture.

'I have my sketches,' she said, feeling that he was trying to voice some other question, but unable to decipher his meaning. 'That is all.'

Exhausted into silence by the emotional pitch of the visit and its strangeness, the group travelled back through the north passage. Before they left, Alba purchased a small sycamore box in the shape of a shell, against the advice of her aunt. To take the focus from her, Delphine did the same, despite Julia's evidently unimpressed roll of the eyes.

They came out into the daylight again, and it seemed to them all to be a hard climb out of the cold dark air of the grotto, into the sudden harshness of the summer light.

Mr Benedict approached Edmund and shook his hand. 'I haven't wished you good day yet, sir. I see the sea air has agreed with you.'

'And you,' said Edmund. 'I hope your family are all well.'

'Yes, well,' said Mr Benedict. 'But what of developments here? You will have noticed that I have changed my favour – from that dark widow to the haloed angel. I wonder where Mr Hallam's fancy will fall. He seems undecided at the moment.' He gave a low laugh.

Edmund said nothing, and tried to indicate through his expression that he had no intention of remarking on it.

'Everyone's spirits seem a little depressed since I was last here,' said Mr Benedict, unaffected by the silence. 'Even Mrs Beck has lost a little of her shine.'

'It is better that you do not mention it,' said Edmund, trying not to sound stiff, and failing. 'We have all been affected by the finding of another young girl's body on the beach.'

Benedict swung his gaze round to Edmund's face. 'Another? My God.'

'You have dropped your sketchbook,' said Edmund. He bent down and picked it up. Mr Benedict thanked him for it; his hands were trembling when he took it.

'I am worn to shreds,' said Julia.

They were standing outside the Grotto, waiting for their carriages to return. As Julia put her head against Delphine's shoulder, Delphine couldn't help but watch the group. Mr Benedict was trying to speak to Alba, but Miss Waring was manoeuvring herself like an outsized chess-piece, positioning her large, bonneted head between her niece and the painter until Benedict fell silent and glum. This only lasted for a moment or two, as he tried to catch Alba's eye, whilst simultaneously attempting to look penitent and careful for Miss Waring's sake. Eventually, he addressed the aunt herself, trying gallantry. 'Are you recovered, madam? My lady wife becomes faint when she first comes down to the coast. She says it is the ozone, and that her senses, used to the city, are overwhelmed by it.'

'I am quite well, thank you,' said Miss Waring. Delphine could see a little battle taking place on her face between her desire for respectable silence, and her curiosity. 'Pray, you were uncommonly busy with your sketchbook, even in the darkness,' she said. 'What were you drawing?' This last question she asked defiantly, as though it was a matter of morality, and that her guardianship of Alba gave her the right to know.

There was no sign of doubt on the painter's face. 'Sketches of light effects and the shells, that is all,' he said. 'There is a variety of subjects to catch my eye here. Why? Do you care for art, madam?'

'Some art,' she said stiffly.

'We – we went to the National Gallery,' said Alba, who had been listening, and seeking an opportunity to speak. 'My aunt likes paintings of the saints; she says they have the truth of holiness in them, unlike many of today's modern scenes. We saw the one where Our Saviour is praying, and there is a dove above His head.'

'*The Baptism of Christ*, my dear,' said Miss Waring.

'Piero della Francesca,' said Mr Benedict. 'A sublime image, indeed.'

'And what was the other one, Aunt?' said Alba. 'It is by Titian.' She sounded supremely excited to have remembered the name. 'The Magdalen is kneeling, and—'

'*Noli me tangere*,' said Miss Waring. 'I think that is the one you mean, my dear.'

'"Do not touch me",' declaimed Mr Benedict. 'Beautiful, beautiful.'

'I know what the title means.' Miss Waring's voice was soft, and it was this sudden softness that gave her words emphasis, so that Delphine found she was straining to hear. 'I know you think I am a foolish old woman, Mr Benedict, and perhaps I am, in some ways. But I know what the title of that painting means, and I do not need you to educate me, or to instruct me in what is beautiful.'

Silence fell. Mercifully, at that moment the carriages appeared from around the corner and were hailed by Theo.

'I am sorry to have offended you,' Benedict said, and Delphine saw the leaden white of shock on his face; the light suddenly drained away by the presence of disapproval.

'You have not offended me,' said Miss Waring.

'I am looking forward to the picnic Mrs Quillian has arranged for us tomorrow,' said Alba brightly, a slight quaver in her voice. 'How wonderful it is to always think there is something else to do, tomorrow and tomorrow. I would wish for this summer never to end.' She looked hard at Benedict. 'Surely, I do.'

'The carriages are ready for us, my dear,' said Miss Waring. 'Come now.' And her glance told Mr Benedict that he would go in the other carriage, and say no more words to her today.

CHAPTER SIXTEEN

The only person I saw with clear sight was Mr Steele. He was good, solid and true. He was a man of experience, and yet he had not been hardened by the world, though he tried to pretend he had. A hardened man would not have fallen in love as he did. No, it all showed on his face, and clearly; he sought Julia's look, he knew when she was tired and aided her; he brought her drink when she was thirsty. He did all of this politely, without weakness, and everything he gave, he gave freely. Amidst the complicated mass of my own feelings at this time – the memories of the past, my reawakened, violent bitterness, and the sense I had that relationships with others were nothing but poison – still, I believed in him. He was our rock when trouble came, again.

The next day was a fair, bright morning, with the promise of heat. Delphine wondered whether, after his exchange

with Miss Waring, the painter might renege on his promise to join the party, but he was on time at the Albion,
without a trace of discomfort on his handsome face,
though he had chosen to ride rather than take a place in
the carriage.

Mrs Quillian settled on a picnic spot a short walk from
Kingsgate. The lighthouse was in sight, and so was the
Captain Digby, a fine tavern and hotel which had had its
origins in a folly on Lord Holland's estate: a small gothic
castle near the edge of the cliff, faced with the local black
flint. It was near to the spot where Delphine had first met
Alba, and as the carriages followed the coast road, opening out on to the familiar view, Delphine saw Alba glance
at her shyly, a brief smile indicating their shared memory.
She understood implicitly that they would not talk about
that day, the day when the girl had run along the coast and
down the gap onto the beach, holding her skirts up, her
feet studding holes in the wet sand.

Delphine recognized with a brief shock that the girl was
a different Alba now. Aside from her nervous laughter,
which she used as a complement to her sunny nature, she
no longer allowed any gaucheness to slip through in her
behaviour; she was consciously delicate, and agreeable,
her gaze often flitting over the men in the party to gauge
whether they were attending to her. Delphine realized that
the long, bright days of her last summer as a young
woman must have focused her mind on the path ahead.
Delphine wondered whether she had chosen a suitable
beau, perhaps in one of the villas she and Miss Waring had

visited, and the thought set up a thread of misgiving in her mind.

She suddenly remembered her family's salon, on a hot day in New York. Her mother had said something – what was it? – about making a choice, the same choice that Alba now faced: marriage, or nothing, as though the young Delphine had been the pattern of Alba and of so many other women. They were a decorative chain of flat silhouettes, opening out one after the other, all cut from the same paper. Delphine remembered turning to watch her mother walk away, seeing her straight back, her finely corseted dress of pale blue silk, tight around her still-neat, disciplined figure. And she remembered that she, Delphine, was dressed in pink, in a gown displaying her fine young shoulders, her white skin almost translucent. And there were flowers in her hair; too many flowers.

She was only pulled from her thoughts when the carriages drew up. She saw that Mr Benedict had already tethered his horse and was making his way across the field, a wildflower meadow with deep grass. And she wondered why the past was intruding on her again, when she had worked so hard to dispatch it to a distant corner in her mind.

As the sun climbed in the sky the ladies opened their parasols and the men lay back on the picnic plaids, hot in their suits. Edmund noticed that Theo's gaze seemed to be fixed, as though he was struggling with some discomfort. He was wearing a straw hat to protect his head, but a fine sheen of sweat lay across his face, and he often closed his eyes. As Alba was distributing cold lemonade to the ladies, Edmund leaned towards him. 'Are you well?' he enquired. 'You seem to be suffering in the heat.'

A faint smile played over Theo's lips, but he kept his eyes closed. 'I am quite well, quite well,' he said softly. 'Remember, I have been in Ceylon.' He opened his eyes. 'Martha said she told you about my travels. Even here, in this English field deep in grass, sometimes the harsh sunlight takes me back to that time.' He smiled, and spoke a line from Psalm 32. 'For day and night Thy hand was heavy upon me: my moisture is turned into the drought of summer.'

Edmund sat back and accepted a glass of lemonade from Alba. She did not speak to Theo, only put a glass next to him then moved off to talk to Mrs Quillian, who was sitting on another rug, and setting up a place for herself. While Theo sipped the lemonade, his gaze rested on Alba, with the same marked intensity it had borne the day before in the carriage. The obvious, dramatic quality of his stare disturbed Edmund. It seemed to him that Theo had no real attraction to the girl; he had never seemed to have noticed her, or conversed with her beyond a word or two at the church door, until the last day or so. His changed attention to her had coincided with Catherine Walters's death, but also with Delphine's growing friendship with the girl, a kind of twisted synchronicity that Edmund could not fathom. He saw that Theo was drawn to Delphine, though he privately criticized her; he also saw that he was battling it, and markedly turning his attention to Alba. Behind Theo's studied politeness, and carefully thought-out topics of conversation, Edmund could see no trace of what his real feelings were, and Charles's letter had added to his uneasiness. *A very dark and entangled case.*

He could feel a headache beginning, lapping against his skull like the sea against the shore far below these white cliffs. If he was mulling over the possible marriage of the clergyman, it was because marriage was high in his mind. Every day he had gone out with Mrs Quillian's party, he had done so with the resolution not to speak to Julia, and yet every time he found himself at her side. He was sure now, that in his own way, he cared deeply for her – but he could never imagine broaching the subject with her. He was dedicated to the idea that he would return to London, to his old life and to his club, and was sure that his regard would fade with the effects of the sea air. But still, even now, as he sipped the tart lemonade, his eyes strained to catch a glimpse of her, over in the wild flowers with Delphine, their backs to him, looking at the view of the farmland.

'I saw you painting on the beach this morning.'

Delphine turned to see Ralph Benedict standing behind her. She had heard movement in the long grass, but had not expected him to come near her; his attention had been taken by Alba, and she had relinquished it without rancour. In the distance, Alba had left her lemonade and was collecting flowers under the supervision of Mrs Quillian and Miss Waring on their blanket.

'Make sure you pick a good selection,' called Miss

Waring. 'Not just the red and blue, but also some of the white, to balance them, my dear.'

Julia had gone a few yards ahead, to look at the view.

Delphine wondered what the heat was doing to the picnic, in its basket in the back of the carriage; imagined cheese melting and thinly-cut bread wilting.

'I am glad you did not come and disturb me,' she said. 'I was happy with my work today, but it depends on silence and solitude.'

'You are brave, going on to that beach alone,' said Benedict. 'It strikes me that Broadstairs is as deadly as any-where at the moment. It is a terrible thing.' The manner of his speaking made him sound as though everything was in jest, but when Delphine glanced at him she saw that he had that white-faced haggard look of distress. It struck her that he bore it in so many situations – when he was thwarted, when he was angry – and that his feelings moved through him swiftly, changing as quickly as the weather on this coast.

'You are right that it is a terrible thing,' she said. 'But my cousin and I are not fifteen. We are quite strong, and I trust I could defend myself with a parasol.'

He laughed unaffectedly. 'I am sure you could. But I am told there was no sign of a struggle on any of these girls, so we hardly know how they met their deaths. I do not like such a mystery.' He looked out over the field, and she saw an expression cross his face that she did not recognize. 'I am glad I have a moment to speak to you,' he said, and turning back, he held her gaze, his green eyes narrowed in the sun. 'I have recently returned to London, as you know, and as I mentioned, I had the chance to visit my picture dealer. I was explaining to him my latest concept of a picture – I can tell you what it is, since I am sure you will not tell my secret – a group of tourists in a place such as this, on the sands. All of them with their own stories, their own secrets, their own sets of high and mighty principles. Some of them young, some of them old.

'I talk frankly to my dealer, you see, and I was explaining – in confidence, of course – about some of the characters I had come across during my time here. Naturally I spoke of you, Mrs Beck, and of your cousin – for I do love an exotic character, and to me the American character is most appealing. And the strange thing was, Mrs Beck, he had heard of you. More than that, had had dealings with you. You sold him a painting, did you not? And to prove its provenance, you had to describe its history – and a little of yours, for it came from a distinguished collection. It seems that, in America, you were once another person.'

Delphine had turned her eyes away when he had started speaking, and though she felt the pulse of her blood beating in her throat, she kept her eyes fixed on the landscape: the green layers of the land, the blue of the sky, the torn cotton of the clouds. She tried to observe these things, and give weight to the observations. She saw horses in a distant field, one of them switching its tail.

'You must be mistaken,' she said, after a long pause. 'I have nothing to do with art dealers.'

214

'Oh, he was quite certain,' said Benedict. 'And I do not blame you for telling him too much. Like me, he is a persistent man, with a long memory, and you are fixed in it. He even described you, to make sure we spoke of the same person. But do not worry.' His expression switched from seriousness to gentleness. 'I will not speak of it – not to anyone here. I meant it, you know, when I said I wished to see your paintings. I am sure they will be of great power. You are no common lady, with mere technical proficiency. I know, just from watching you, that you have the character of an artist. I think you can see the life in everything. I know, for example, that you see the beauty in Alba.'

'One would be a fool not to see it,' she said.

'She would be the perfect subject for me,' he said. 'I cannot paint those who inspire strong emotion in me, you see – those I love, and those I hate. I must be detached, as I am with her. She is a beautiful stranger.'

'But Mrs Quillian has told me that you often paint your wife and children,' said Delphine. The answer to her words was all in his look – a glint of humour, a shrug – that truly chilled her.

'Yet you have such influence over Alba,' he said. 'Over all of us. I dearly wish to paint her. Perhaps you could put a word in for me – calm that rigid, fussy aunt of hers. I deplore that kind of narrow-minded conventionality.'

'Yet you seem to me to embrace it,' said Delphine, anger firing her words. 'A villa in Ramsgate for the summer, a wife and family, fine clothes and carriages. You could, perhaps, argue about the conventionality you seem to deplore and yet have embraced. There is no need to play-act sympathy with me; we are not the same. I don't know what you wish to entangle me in, but do not try it, I beg you, Mr Benedict, for your own sake. If you believe your art dealer, you will know that I am not a moral woman. If you make any move against me, or my cousin, I will not hesitate to destroy you. It would not be difficult for me.' She could not help it; her mouth trembled into a kind of smile, against her will.

'You are afraid,' he said. 'Such an extreme threat saddens me. I do not mean you any harm – I mean only to warn you that, even here, people are curious about strangers. In my character, I am closer to you than you think. I have my own secrets. I know what it is to live with them, to sleep, wrapped in them – to never be able to show my true face to the world. I warn you because I wish you well. You have created a desire in so many people, Mrs Beck, and when a desire is not satisfied, it is easy for it to turn into something else – something darker.'

Delphine turned away. As she did so, he took her wrist, a disrespectful gesture which showed, she thought, how far his opinion had fallen. 'I am your friend,' he said. 'In all that follows, pray remember that.'

The sunlight showed no sign of softening when, at last, the picnic hampers were opened.

'There are fine views across the fields,' said Julia. Edmund's hand met hers as they both reached for the jug of lemonade, and he flinched away, as bashful as a youth. He could have kicked himself for it.

'I shall have to set up my easel at last,' said Benedict. 'Or perhaps you can, Mrs Beck. I am sure you could make the most of that view.'

'It is certainly a lovely scene,' said Theo, who had taken out a tiny leather notebook and was sketching with a pencil. 'I might even be tempted away from recording the cliffside grasses. To record this view, and put it on my study wall, would refresh my senses every time I come to look at it.'

'I think you do not understand, Mr Hallam,' said Benedict, his hand stirring amongst the long grass, his lips wet with lemonade. 'I was not speaking of an amateur's enthusiasm. Mrs Beck sees things with a painter's eye.'

'I have painted,' said Theo. 'I think I know a little of what you mean.' His eyes met Delphine's and a smile flitted across his face, so swiftly that she wondered if she had imagined it.

'Forgive me,' said Benedict, 'but with respect, I must say that I do not think you do. You paint, I think, to record – to collect – with precision, yes, but not with,' he put his hand on his chest, 'this.'

Miss Waring gave an embarrassed laugh, shrugging at Theo, as though to proclaim her lack of understanding of the situation. 'This is,' she said, leaning in to Alba, 'perhaps not quite as it should be. It is a little improper. Listen to the birdsong, my dear.'

'For me,' Benedict went on, 'to live a passionate, full life is vital to a painter. Observation is essential, of course. I must feel – then I must stand back. Only when an emotion is past can I summon it in my pictures. But to paint human nature without being part of that great glorious medley would be an empty gesture, like trying to paint the sea from the shore.'

'It is possible,' said Delphine, 'to paint the sea from the shore.'

'But wouldn't you rather be lashed to the mast of a boat, as Mr Turner was? I would. The viewers of your painting would rather you were. You are their medium, you see: through you, they can feel, they can know. Everything.'

Delphine followed Theo's gaze. He was staring at the sudden, empty delight of Alba's expression, as though the painter had articulated something she felt. She saw a flash of anger in his eyes.

'We paint for different reasons, perhaps,' he said. Benedict inclined his head and tried to keep his expression agreeable, but Delphine could see the contempt there. And there was a definite sense, in the midst of the party, that some line had been crossed, and the day had turned.

After the picnic, the party dispersed. Miss Waring was the first to express a desire to return to the hotel; she was supported in this by Mrs Quillian. Alba, thwarted in an attempt to collect more shells, climbed into the carriage with the older ladies and waved from the window as it pulled away. After half an hour or so of wandering, and gathering flowers, Julia and Delphine decided they wished to walk on the beach; to their surprise, Theo, Edmund and Benedict stayed with them. Though the painter trailed some distance behind them, Delphine felt uncomfortable in his presence.

Joss Bay, along the coast from the busier Main Bay, was almost deserted, and everyone expressed their delight at having it nearly to themselves. They had not been on the beach long, moving slowly across the wide expanse of sand, when Delphine saw a figure approaching them. She put her parasol back and raised one lace-gloved hand over her eyes to shield them from the sun.

It was a child, running.

'Look,' she said.

'You know what children are, on the beach,' said Julia.

'No,' said Delphine. 'Something's wrong.'

It was she who set off towards the child, moving more quickly than propriety demanded; she who first saw the terror in his face, dropped her parasol, and held out her hands to him, as the small creature, not more than eight years old, ran into her arms then clung to her, pulling her, his hands entwined in her dress.

'You must come!' he shouted. 'Murder! My sister! My sister! She's dying!'

She hardly knew how it happened, for in an instant the boy had left her side, and she saw Edmund and Theo begin to run, then Benedict join them, following the child as he set his trail across the beach, his feet picking up sharply from the damp sand. Hobbled by their dresses, the women followed, Julia's hand in Delphine's, and Delphine found herself repeating the Lord's Prayer and heard the disjointed gasp of her cousin's weeping as they hurried around the curve of the cliff.

The girl lay, face down on the sand, but even as the first shock of the sight of her subsided, Delphine could see that she was moving, attempting to raise herself onto her wrists, then falling again, as though her limbs and body were too heavy to work properly.

'She's drunk something,' cried the little boy.

Edmund knelt down beside the girl and turned her over. Julia hurried to him, opened her smelling salts and held them to the girl's face. The child jerked awake.

'I'm sorry, little one,' said Edmund, 'but I have to do this.' And he pushed his fingers into her mouth, all the way back to her throat. Julia turned away and covered her eyes. The girl wrenched herself from Edmund's grasp, twisted round and vomited onto the sand.

Delphine gently manoeuvred Edmund aside, then rubbed her hand over the girl's back, holding her golden plaits out of her way. 'Get it all out,' she said and, as if on cue, the girl vomited again.

'Bessie,' sobbed the little boy. 'Bessie, get up. You can't die. Bessie, Bessie!'

'What's your name, boy?' said Theo, crouching down to be on a level with the child, and looking into his eyes. 'Where are your parents?'

'I'm Jack, Jack Dalton,' said the boy. 'Ma and Pa are up at the Digby. Said we weren't to disturb them, but just play here – and we did, we did.'

'I'm sure you did,' said Theo, still holding him firmly by the shoulders. 'Come now, Jack, I am sure your sister will be all right. What happened?'

The child sobbed, wiping one hand across his nose.

'Where are you, God damn you?' shouted Mr Benedict, turning wildly this way and that, surveying the coast – where they had come from, and what was ahead – but the natural bays and curves of the cliffs provided the perfect blind turns for whoever had been there, only moments before. As he turned, he caught sight of something in the sand.

'God,' he said. 'Oh, God, Steele – look. There is more to this.'

Edmund followed his gaze to the sand. 'What does it say?' he said, trying to keep his voice steady.

'It makes no sense,' said Benedict. 'It says MARY.'

'She must have did that when I came for you,' cried Jack, snatches of words between sobs. 'I broke away from her. She gave us sweets, but mine tasted funny and I spat it out without her seeing. She said I would feel sleepy, that I needed a rest, and I was to lie down and close my eyes. Bessie wouldn't have the sweets, as Ma always says she is too fat, but then the lady offered her a drink of ginger beer, and she took a mouthful. I'd done what she said, but when I saw she was going to drag Bessie away, I got up and ran. She tried to come after me, but I was too quick, and Bessie must have been too heavy for her to do it all.'

'Who did this?' cried Benedict, disbelief tearing across his face.

'A lady,' wept Jack. 'I didn't see her face. She had put a veil over her bonnet. A black veil.'

They all fell silent then, apart from the poor girl groaning on the sand. But it seemed to hit the painter the hardest. Before anyone could go to his aid, Benedict had turned away, and he, too, had vomited.

CHAPTER SEVENTEEN

Of Reculver, I remember the cold – the kind of cold you feel in your bones – the desolation of that spot, even in midsummer, though I do not know whether we found desolation there or brought it with us, this strange group of travellers.

The chill, deep blue of the sea, the grey of the flint towers, the clouds tracking above us, edged with light, hinting at the hidden radiance of the sun behind them ... it is all stamped into my memory. And it is not a dead thing, like pressed flowers, or a shell washed clean of its sand; it lives and scintillates, so that sometimes from my chair, I have watched it in my mind, a scene before me, on the canvas of the empty walls of the room.

'Jack,' said Theo, 'go and fetch your parents now – and quickly.'

Delphine could tell that the little boy's instinct was to obey. He had taken a step back at the words, as though ready to run, but then he looked around – at the other men, at Julia, at her. She realized, with a terrible despair, that he did not trust them.

'What if she comes back?' he said, in a small voice.

'Jack . . .' It was Bessie. She groaned, and coughed a little more.

'We will look after her,' said Theo. 'Go and get them, now. Go!'

Jack knelt beside his sister and put his face close to hers. 'I'll fetch Ma and Pa,' he said, 'I won't be long.' The look she gave him seemed to be enough to reassure him. He ran off across the beach.

Edmund went to Benedict. The painter had crawled a little way from where he had been sick. 'Someone must fetch the doctor for the child,' Edmund said. 'If I go, will you help Mr Hallam?'

'I will go,' said Benedict tightly. 'My horse is up on the cliff; I will be faster than you.' He stared at the wet sand for a moment as Edmund held his hand out to help him up. Benedict seemed to be trying to summon some strength, for his breathing was hard and ragged. And then a cry broke from him. 'What kind of woman?' It was picked up by the wind and cast across the beach, after the little boy.

'An unnatural one,' Theo said, kneeling on the sand beside the child. 'That is the kind.'

Edmund, Theo, Delphine and Julia all laboured to keep

Bessie awake, and succeeded. When her parents arrived, distressed, and led by Jack, still running as though the devil was behind him, they seemed awed – and displeased – to find a clergyman ministering to their daughter. Once they had ascertained that the girl was alive, and unlikely to die at that particular moment, they were more concerned with defending themselves against accusations of neglect.

'We only left them a few moments,' the mother said, straightening her bonnet. 'Are you sure it is that bad? Were you play-acting, Jack?'

'There is no acting of any type,' said Theo. 'Something very serious has happened here.'

'Well, if it has, it's not our fault,' said the father roughly. 'And I don't care to be lectured, sir.'

When Dr Crisp arrived he looked highly displeased to see the group he had met near the chalkpit a few weeks before. He gave curt greetings, and paused beside Delphine. 'I see you are here again, madam,' he said. 'I have hardly had time to forget your face.'

'The patient is over here,' said Theo sharply.

Dr Crisp knelt beside Bessie and began to examine her. Her eyelids were drooping again, and with startling efficiency he dealt her a swift slap around the side of her face, which made Delphine wince. 'Eyes open,' he commanded.

'Don't cause the doctor any trouble, Bessie,' said the mother, somewhat primly.

'The constable should be called,' said Benedict, who had

been walking up and down nearby. 'And as quickly as possible. The boy could give a description of the woman who did this.'

'I didn't see her face. She was wearing a very thick veil,' said Jack.

'Well, you're right, it's not just the sun,' said Dr Crisp, opening his bag and rummaging through it. 'She's been given a dose of something – an opiate, probably. It can't be so very much, otherwise she wouldn't be talking to us. She may recover well enough without anything, but to be safe I can give her an emetic.'

'Will that cost anything?' said the mother. She glanced, with something like shame, at Delphine.

'Allow me,' said Edmund, nodding to the doctor.

'And the constable?' said Benedict, standing with his hands on his hips.

'There's no need for that, sir,' said the father, in a tone that indicated he had endured quite enough orders for that day. 'We're respectable people. Bessie, get up. Show the man you can walk.'

Delphine had been calling Julia for some time, with no response, when she went into the front parlour. Julia was seated not in her normal attitude, with every limb positioned as though she had considered its aesthetic effect, but was bent over, her elbows resting on her lap, her head in her hands. There was something so full of hurt about that position, so like a beautiful flower, bent and crushed, that Delphine went cold for a moment, and – so alive to trauma as she was – wondered whether her cousin had collapsed, or was in some kind of fit brought on by the horror of what had happened on the beach that afternoon. At the idea of there being no law involved, Mr Benedict had begun shouting, and had sworn so harshly that Edmund had seen fit to escort Julia and Delphine home. They had been back an hour now.

'Julia?' she said sharply. There was no response. 'Are you well?' Delphine asked. 'Look at me.'

Julia moved her hands away, and her face was wet with tears. Delphine sat down beside her, staring at her dress, its crumpled black material, good quality, just catching the little light in the room. She waited.

'The children, today,' Julia said, and her voice twisted. The sound of it was terrible – that low, soft voice suddenly discordant. 'It was not just what had happened. It was that they had been left so alone. Their parents seemed hardly to trouble themselves.'

'They will live, at least,' said Delphine. 'It is a shock to think that a woman could do that.'

Julia shook her head. 'It is not just that,' she said. Her tears were still flowing. 'It is the old pain. No children.'

Delphine closed her eyes for a moment. She had prepared the usual arguments – the words she had spoken again and again over the years. Marriage was a prison, and who would wish, wantonly, for the pain and ruin of childbirth? Had she ever met a man she would risk that for, to bear his child? Delphine never had. Julia had said,

'Once, when I was young,' but Delphine had dismissed it, imagining a too-smart young swell with a thick cigar and a handlebar moustache.

'I thought we were past this,' she said. But as she spoke, she wished she could have breathed the words back in again, knowing that she had no right to question her cousin's feelings, and all the things she thought she had left behind. For she, too, felt the pull of the past, of New York, that emptiness in the pit of her stomach akin to homesickness. She felt like an instrument with its strings wound too tight. Mr Benedict's mention of the art dealer had drawn the walls in close to her again; she had no idea how much he knew, and raked her memory for the details she had given the dealer in London. She had given her family name; what else he had discovered, she did not know. Mr Benedict was the type to make something from nothing, and yet, if the dealer had contacts in New York society, who knew what he could have learned.

Thinking of the past made her feel trapped, and feeling trapped made her angry; it woke violence in her. Somehow, knowing that a woman had been behind an attempted murder on the beach made it worse, for it seemed that Mr Steele was right, and there *was* a pattern in the deaths. The authorities might not be interested – 'for who cared,' Mr Steele had muttered, 'for working-class children?' But now there was a woman, moving like vengeance through the brightness of a summer's day, seeking out something. But seeking out what? And

Delphine could not help but identify with the darkness, the bitterness, and the capability to wound.

She rubbed her face and held Julia's hand in the evening light, hearing the sea breeze stir through the cracks of the house like a lament. She remembered a friend of her grandfather's coming to stay in New York when she was a child. He liked telling Delphine stories, for she was his most appreciative listener. He came from the South, and when the others weren't listening he would tell her the stranger, darker stories he thought she could take. Where he came from, he said, the sun could burn so hard as to kill you, and the rain fall so hard as to raise you again. What did he mean? she asked. He had been to a funeral, he said, one day, when it had rained hard the night before: he had seen the coffin lowered into water. Delphine imagined it as he described it: the hot, humid air, the thick green of the moss in the trees, the sloshing as the casket hit the water. 'We were real hopeful,' he said, 'that the creek wouldn't burst its banks, and the water drive up the dead again.'

Could that happen? the little Delphine thought, and he saw the question in her eyes and nodded. 'The moral of the story is, little lady: bodies do not stay buried.'

And as she looked at Julia, she thought, Nothing does. Not the past, not the children we never had. Their ghosts follow us every step of the way.

After all that had happened, Edmund thought there would be no more excursions, or attempts at outings.

After Bessie Dalton, Theo locked himself in the study and only came out the next day for church services and to lead prayers at the local school. That evening, Martha, her eyes full of concern, placed a tray outside the study on the black and white tiled floor. Edmund passed it, and saw the steam rising from the soup as it cooled. He stood outside the door, his hand poised to knock, as Martha had knocked when she had placed it there, but there was something in the quality of that velvet silence, thick, impenetrable, which made him step back and return to the drawing room. Martha, he supposed, knew Theo's ways.

The next day, Theo appeared at breakfast, and as Edmund took his place and tucked in his napkin, he said: 'Do you remember that place we spoke of – Reculver? The ruined church, with a history going back to Roman times?'

Edmund speared the yolk of his egg with the tip of his knife, and watched the yellow seep over his plate. 'I believe so,' he replied. 'You said there was a new book on the archaeology of it?'

Theo smiled. 'I have been reading it, this last day or so. It is most comprehensive and – in truth – I almost envy the writer of it. Strange, when one glimpses the other lives one might have lived, if one were not called by God.'

Edmund opened his mouth to speak, but immediately realized there was little he could say without offending his host. He had thought that Theo was someone who did not care to dig too deep into anything, and he understood it – for surely faith was a matter of grace, not to be examined too closely, a glorious mystery. He knew that Theo collected sea grasses, and some butterflies, and he wondered at his contradictory desire to categorize and describe things, and how he could rejoice in finding something beautiful, and then cause its death. Though Theo often spoke of the glory of God's creation, Edmund somewhere deep inside could not reconcile this with the pinning of dead things to boards, for he viewed faith and love as things to be lived, rather than set down and described.

'I would like to go there,' said Theo. 'I am feeling weary, unwell. I could prevail upon the curate at St Peter's to take my services for two days. I believe the trip would do me good.'

Edmund's first mistake was to mention the possible journey to Mrs Quillian. He had felt sure that, as the trip was arduous in comparison to their other, short excursions, necessitating an overnight stay in Reculver, she would not feel any interest in it, but he was mistaken. She flew at the idea with even more enthusiasm than she had shown for the earlier trips. Soon a note was received: Miss Waring and Alba were eager, and Mrs Beck and Miss Mardell too, though Mr Benedict had gone to be with his family – understandable in the circumstances, it was agreed. Still, there were many more people now planning to visit Reculver than Theo had anticipated, and Edmund felt a little guilty about involving them. Although Theo was polite about it, Edmund had seen his face fall at the mention of others joining them.

On the morning of the trip a note was received; Mrs Quillian was unwell. So it was with a disconsolate Miss Waring at its head that the group set out.

Reculver sat on the coast. It had once been inland, but as the sea persuaded its way in on the soft cliffs of the coast, so it neared the place, which had first been a Roman out-post, then a monastery, then, at last, a decaying parish church, too grand for its purpose, its air struck through with echoes of the past – the cries of babies, the local people said – until being abandoned at the turn of the cen-tury. So it contained disparate elements; there were tombstones from its time as a parish church, and still the remains of what had once been a great abbey church.

There had been discussions about travelling to the ruins by sea, but these had been eschewed by Miss Waring, who resolutely refused to be in the water; she had seen the lights blinking on the Goodwin Sands, she said, and the hazard of it all was high in her mind. Therefore, the jour-ney was undertaken by carriage for the ladies, and horseback for the men. As they approached the coast, they travelled through farmland, passing a mill and a cottage here and there, until they were in narrow lanes bordered by high hedgerows.

Alba read to the ladies as they travelled, heedless of her travel sickness. She told them the story of the two sisters – Frances and Isabella – and of how they were shipwrecked. The elder, an Abbess, was saved. The younger was brought ashore and died, and so the towers were restored by the elder, with the purpose of warning shipping. She

was buried in the shadow of them with her sister. Ever
since, mariners had referred to the towers as the Twin
Sisters, or the Two Sisters. As Alba read this, slowly and
languorously, Delphine felt a shiver run the length of her
spine.

'It is all nonsense, of course,' said Miss Waring, not
unkindly.

'I do feel a little unwell, Aunt,' said Alba.

'Of course you do,' said Miss Waring. 'Another good
reason why I refused the idea of travelling in a boat –
imagine, my delicate Alba in a boat!'

'Have you travelled much, Miss Waring?' asked Julia.

'A little, here and there,' said Miss Waring vaguely. 'But
I spent much of my youth caring for my stepfather and
stepbrother, so my time was ordered by them.'

Delphine looked out of the window to see Theo, looking
forwards, his face impassive as he rode.

They disembarked at the King Ethelbert Inn, which
stood near to the towers, and made their way up the slope
to the promontory where the towers loomed over them.
The Isle of Thanet was visible just along the coast, but to
Delphine it seemed as distant as the sight of heaven from
the damned in a medieval church fresco; this was an
entirely different place. The two square towers were not
built of the black flint of Broadstairs, but of a solid, densely
packed grey flint, set with high spires to warn shipping.
The pointed stone section between them had a high circular aperture and two curved arched windows either side
of it, all empty of glass so that, standing there below it,

looking up, the clouds moved where the stained glass had once been. On that exposed spot, only the toughest grasses remained, thick and bushy and windswept; the pathway spotted with hard unyielding lichen, pale grey. Beneath them, the sea beat at the shore.

Delphine stood at the edge of the ruins and watched the choppy water; it was a hard blue, the colour of a bad sapphire. Its rise and fall, its network of small, sharp waves, the sheer violence of it as it drew against the cliff, all of these things made it seem entirely different from Broadstairs, even though the cliffs of Thanet could be seen from where she stood. The sea, and the hard cold air which blustered against this foremost point, seemed to be attacking the land, as though it had taken against the church and was eroding the ruins day by day, hour by hour, with the harsh sea winds shot through with salt. She drew her cloak around her, and imagined what it must have been like to live here, as a monk, with the wind and sea raging outside, trusting to God's providence; and even when Alba told her, reading from her guidebook, that the sea had been half a mile from the church at that time, she could not stave off the sense of isolation and fear that had settled over her.

The two steeples of the towers had come down, and been raised again, and now bore beacons to warn shipping, and as Alba wandered away, Delphine thought of the Goodwin Sands, of which the group had often spoken, and of the fear and misery of mariners caught in the violence of those seas.

'It is blowing a fearsome gale.' Theo's voice startled her. She had last seen him some yards away, as he pointed out aspects of the landscape and the Roman settlement to Edmund. He stood beside her on the edge of the cliff looking out to sea, his notebook and pencil clasped tightly in one hand, and she saw in his face some of the same haunted aspect that she had felt as she looked out there. She wanted to be able to laugh at him, this clergyman with his wide-brimmed hat and his neat black coat billowing in the strong wind, who always watched her so solemnly, but she could not. She realized that he had spent much of his time not wishing to be looked at; constantly in movement, or masked by politeness and discharging his duty as a priest. There were times when his face truly seemed to be carved in stone like the face on a crucifix. Now, he was just a man, and she observed the disturbing blue of his eyes, and the scarred texture of his face, as though she had never seen him before. He was a man, she thought, not the icon he perhaps wished to be.

'Have you recovered from the other day on the beach?' he said. 'I had no time to speak to you before you left.'

'As much as one can,' she said. 'It is a disgrace that Dr Crisp does not wish to look into the deaths further.'

Theo nodded. 'He is jaded, I am afraid. He is no stranger to the deaths of children. He told me that he has often seen parents refuse treatment for a child because they are enrolled in a burial club, and will receive money if the child dies. And he is encouraged – nay, pressed – into not pursuing expensive inquests, which the coroner has to cover from his own pocket, and which the magistrates will not pay back. He wishes to have his own life; he wishes to marry. He has seen many young children die in suspicious circumstances; he cannot pursue them all under his own purse.'

Delphine had a lump in her throat. 'I find it hard to believe,' she said. 'I cannot excuse him on the basis that he says the poor do not love their children.'

'Do you know anything of poverty, Mrs Beck?' he said. He did not accuse her with the words, but his gaze grew in intensity as he spoke. 'In the course of my work I have seen families with more children than they can count. I have seen squalor and despair, and the brutality that can cause. Many people do love their children; a few are so brutalized by loss and hardship that they dare not. I have not lost hope, but Dr Crisp has, and I do not think we should judge him for that.'

'This is a different kind of case, surely,' she objected.

'But the victims are not,' he said. 'Mr Benedict can scream and shout all he likes; there will be no investigation unless something more marked happens.' He finished with a nod that seemed to speak of finality, as though in agreement that they would bury the subject. They stood in silence for some time before he spoke again. 'Our painter friend would like this aspect, don't you think?' he said, without moving his eyes from the horizon. Delphine could not read him; his voice was completely neutral, but she was surprised that he would mention Mr Benedict to her again.

'I disagree, I'm afraid,' she said. 'I believe, for all his sketching of the cliffs and fields, his main object is to study people. I am told he excels at crowd scenes, at large compositions, sharpened by his attention to detail, textures and expressions.'

'Could he paint that spray, I wonder?' said Theo, as a wave hit the cliffs below them and sent a whip-curve of spray high into the air. 'Capture its real qualities? He would say that I should be in the water to see it properly – that is what he meant. He said I did not feel anything truly, or I believe that was his meaning.'

'I can hardly say,' said Delphine. 'I do not know what is in his mind.'

'I thought he was your good friend,' he said.

When he turned and looked her full in the eyes, the fierceness of his gaze silenced her. The sight of it not only surprised her, but made her fear for a moment, the true intensity of those eyes. She turned away, and they both faced the sea, standing alongside each other, buffeted by the wind. As the minutes passed, she felt something grow between them, like the threads of silk woven by a spider, a sense of communion, as though they were there alone. She did not want to move and break the threads, the voices of the others behind them lost in the strong sea wind. They were, for those few minutes, companions on the edge of something, as they had been on the day they had half-fallen down the slope at Dumpton Gap together, and the sea itself laid out in front of them with its threat and adventure.

'Mr Hallam! Mr Hallam?' It was Miss Waring. She was standing on the grass, in what had once been the great nave of the abbey, as solid and immovable as a standing stone. 'Miss Alba is becoming over-excited; this is a sombre place to spend so much time.' Beyond her, Edmund was reading the inscription on one of the eighteenth-century gravestones.

'If you wish, we can leave you here,' said Delphine softly to Theo. 'Mr Steele can accompany us to the inn.' She sensed that he did not want to leave; that coming here had been some kind of pilgrimage. She felt sorry that they had intruded upon it.

'No, I must see you all to the inn, and ensure the accommodation is comfortable,' he said. The familiar blankness had returned to his eyes, and she knew then that he had broken the threads between them. His words were not a rejection, but his expression and manner were. He straightened the collar of his coat, though it did not need meddling with, and began to walk through the grass towards Miss Waring, moving his limbs slowly, as though he was wading through water.

My dear Charles,

You will not expect this, but it is a letter from Reculver – a missive sent with the hope that your warm good cheer will be sent by return and be waiting for me at Broadstairs, so I may shake off the cold and melancholy of this place. We have come here on a trip which I thought would raise Theo's spirits, but in this dark little inn which, despite its warm fire and good food, is supported on all sides by the sounds of the sea and its attendant gales, those same spirits seem much depressed.

He had talked with enthusiasm of this place; of the archaeological explorations here, and its claiming from the Romans as a place of sanctity. But now we are here, he does not talk of those things at all, and if I mention them to him, he answers me with a politeness which, if not curt, is lifeless and without any of his previous warmth. He took dinner with the rest of the party, but did not eat; sat himself at the head of the table, at a distance from the others, and said Grace as sombrely as one in church on Ash Wednesday. The accommodation here is cramped. There are only a hundred or so souls in this whole place, and they are scattered to the lands, fearful of the incursions of the sea. As a result, Theo and I are sharing a room, and when I found him – for he retired early – he was on his knees, praying, and continued in a low voice. When at last I blew out my candle, I fancied he was still praying in the darkness, and I sensed the noiseless movement of his lips as he spoke to his God. It worries me, and worries me deeply.

I do not doubt that the events of the last weeks have affected him, though he is a man used, surely, to minister to the dead and the dying. The sight of that little girl struggling to live on the beach, and the awareness that some wretch of a woman had done this to her, affected us all greatly.

I spoke about this to Mrs Beck this evening. She and I are both greatly disturbed by the event, and she is dwelling on the *mystery that the words* MARY *and* WHITE, White as snow, *have been found near the bodies. Of course, you will have heard of the* Mary White *yourself, as she and her boatmen are of national fame, but connecting such a great blessing to these deaths feels wicked. We talked it through, and tried to decipher its meaning; and of course none of the lifeboatmen can be called into question, for they are beyond reproach, but the presence of those words haunts us, and talk as we did, we could go no further with it.*

Being here in this inn, as I looked around this afternoon at my companions, it struck me that we are all haunted, in our own ways. Perhaps it was the low light in the room – the way the shadows fell – but we all seemed burdened by things, the burdens usually hidden, but brought alive by the fatigue of the journey and the terrible events of the past weeks. The only countenance that was clear of these things – well, it was Alba's, as clean and fresh as a piece of parchment not yet written on. And it is for this reason that some of us love her, and in some of us her very innocence – which is not her fault – raises impatience. She alone does not seem troubled by the near-death of that girl on the beach.

And my burden – I have hesitated to tell you this over the past weeks, but now it is at such a pitch that I must share it with you. My burden is that I am in love; that a young woman here has come to mean more to me than anyone else ever has. How it has come about is a mystery, even to me. Love has its own form of witchcraft (forgive these dark words; this is a dark place), and if I feel this love as a regrettable thing, it is because I believe I have nothing to offer her, this lady, and I do not understand why she is still free, why every man who has ever met her has not bowed down before her.

If I have said too much, I am sorry. This place has affected me – as it has affected all of us – so I hope that when I next write, I will be in my right mind and no longer afflicted by this infectious melancholy.

I remain, your friend, Edmund Steele

That night in the parlour, with the logs crackling and spitting out their sap in the flames as though it was winter rather than summer, Edmund had said to Delphine, 'What of your husband?' It was a moment made for intimacies; everyone else had gone to their rooms, and he could tell she was on the brink of excusing herself, for it was not right that they should sit alone together. But they had been worn down by the day: the journey to this cold and blustery place, and the ruins of human lives all around them, the lights on the towers hinting at more ruins that might be to come, or might be avoided, and the wine drunk at dinner unlocking the fatigue in all of them.

She opened her mouth to tell him a well-practised lie; the lie she told everyone, that was now automatic and settled in her, part of the layers she had painted over herself, over the virgin drawing – chalk on board – that had once been her. Then she decided not to.

'I cannot tell you,' she said. And she saw him read something on her face.

It was in that moment, a moment too late, she thought, that she decided to leave him, to not speak any longer. She went into her room and watched the sleeping face of Julia before taking the pins out of her own hair. I have undone myself, she thought; I have undone us both. After a journey of a thousand miles, I have realized I cannot escape the past.

CHAPTER EIGHTEEN

On the trip to Reculver, Miss Waring was alone, without her usual friend Mrs Quillian. I was used to their good cheer; to hear them gossiping together, and occasionally advising Alba and correcting the faults in her behaviour. We saw them as a pair, these two older women, and yet they were quite different. Mrs Quillian saw everything with a warm, sunny eye, and cared for nothing much other than that her plans were not disturbed and that her dear nephew was well-fed. Miss Waring was a little different; she was stout, and strong, and dressed well, always with her cameo brooch fastened at her neck, always with her hair and dress so neat and perfect, as if every fold was thought about. But whilst she enjoyed her friend's good cheer, the visit to Reculver showed me that she was not naturally so. She chased Alba, as though Alba was a baby animal to be tamed, and it was with a kind of distress that she seemed to observe her; how often she *courted the good opinion of the clergyman in our midst, whilst looking at the other gentlemen with indifference. And her friendliness to me, once so evident, began to seem forced.*

When Delphine slept at last, the sleep was fitful and disturbed. She saw the dead girls in her mind, and the sight of Bessie Dalton, gulping for air on the sands, jerked her into wakefulness. A pale ribbon of light lay across her bed from the slit in the curtains, and she knew she would never sleep now. She climbed out of bed, moving slowly, by degrees, and dressed as well as she could in the dark room, with only the whispering of the fabric as she raised her painting dress to her shoulders. She let Julia sleep, and went quietly out, creeping down the winding staircase which creaked under her every step, her pale hands trailing down the smooth cold plaster of the white walls.

To her surprise she found Alba in the deserted saloon. She was wrapped in a cloak, but her slumped posture showed that she had no corset on. Delphine wondered whether she was still in her nightdress beneath her wrappings, and thought it was enough to send Miss Waring into a faint. Alba was seated by a small window facing the slope towards the Reculver, and the ruins itself, and her eyes were roaming over the view. When Delphine took a seat opposite her, Alba smiled, then turned back to the window. 'This is such a melancholy place,' she said. 'But beautiful, in its way, as all desolate places are. We must tell Mr Benedict about it.'

'Telling him will be no use,' said Delphine. 'He would

have to see it, to feel what you feel, to digest it in his mind.' The proprietorial tone of her voice surprised even her; she felt uncomfortable from it and decided she should probably stay silent until coffee was available. It had only just come to her, the vision of the painter eating all of his experiences, consuming life, carelessly. She never wanted to draw people, only places, but this was an image so strong that she itched to draw it, in that moment.

'Oh, but I think we could describe it vividly,' said Alba. 'You and I, if we tried, could make him understand its potency as a place.' She looked more like a work of art than a person, with her hair loose around her clear-skinned face, and, differently from usual, her violet eyes were not warm or cold, but bright with an animation that was somehow neutral, as though it depended on nothing – neither her happiness or sadness. Delphine envied her that.

'I do not intend to describe it to him,' said Delphine. 'He needs no encouragement.' She did not mean the warning in her voice to be harsh, but somehow it was. She had longed to take Alba under her wing, to protect her and warn her, but it seemed to her that Alba no longer wished for her protection, though she had originally made a bid for friendship. There was something innately confident and independent growing in the girl's gaze, a departure from her soft and yielding behaviour within the group. Delphine felt that her words were as ineffectual as throwing beach pebbles at a flint wall. Obscurely, this wounded her.

Suddenly Alba turned from the window, leaned across the table that sat between them, and clasped Delphine's hands. Her fingers were cold, and soft, and she held Delphine's hands so tightly that Delphine could feel the bones and joints. 'Please advise me,' said the girl in an urgent whisper, glancing around as though someone might be listening in the empty room.

'Go on,' said Delphine, slightly amused by the drama in her voice.

'It is Mr Benedict,' said Alba. She was talking quickly now, as though she feared they might be discovered at any moment. 'He – that is, he has led me to believe – that he admires me greatly.'

For some reason she could not articulate, Delphine wanted rid of her hands, cold paws clawing at her own. 'We all take delight in you,' she said. 'You are very beautiful – you do not understand how beautiful. The young have their own particular power over those who are tired of the world. If he admires you, then I am not surprised; and you should not take him too seriously, or give his words too much weight.'

'You do not understand,' said Alba. 'He has written to me. Secretly.'

'Written?' Delphine could not understand how this was possible. Miss Waring was so careful over Alba, so watchful.

'I received a note at the Albion,' said Alba, 'sent care of his servant, and given to me covertly. I always knew he looked upon me with favour. There were a few stolen

moments, when he spoke to me,' she lowered her eyelashes, 'at the almshouses, and when we were on the cliffs
the other day – but his letter is different. I believe he
wishes me to return to the city with him. He says if I sit for
him, Mrs Beck, I will be the most famous woman in
London.'

Delphine almost laughed out loud from shock. The only
thing that stopped her was the expression on Alba's face.
It seemed that the girl was deadly serious; her eyes wore
an expression of assessment. Delphine did not understand
why Alba – sensitive, curious, amused little Alba – was not
shocked to the core by this offer. In fact, she seemed to be
considering it, as a much more worldly woman would
have considered it, with a balance-sheet of profit and loss.
Delphine sat back.

'What have you done with the letter?' she said.

Alba lifted her chin. 'I have burned it, of course.'

'Good,' said Delphine. 'That is the first sensible thing
you have said. Do you understand what he is asking you?
You seem sanguine, so I assume you cannot.'

'I think I do understand,' said Alba, and her gaze was
suddenly level, unblinking, flat as the blue sea against the
horizon.

'Did you tell him you were adopted?' said Delphine.
'Did you tell him of your background?' She saw assent in
the girl's face, and pressed on. 'He only asks because he
knows this. He knows you are vulnerable. You should not
have told him. You should not have opened yourself to
such advances.' She was surprised at the strength of her

feeling. 'If it was even discovered that he had sent you that letter and you had received it and considered it, you would be ruined, utterly ruined, and Miss Waring's family, too. Their reputation, not just yours, would be destroyed. He is a charming man, but he has gone too far – to try and corrupt your innocence.' The sight of Alba's passive face maddened her. 'God, do you understand?'

'I do not know why you are speaking so harshly to me,' said Alba. 'It is you who have made me see beyond my narrow lot. You urged me to open my thoughts to ideas of freedom, you told me of women wearing pantaloons on Piccadilly, you shied from me when I asked you to help me marry, and now you reprimand me? I listened to you, Mrs Beck, you above everyone – even when Mr Hallam urged me not to.'

At Theo's name, Delphine felt a tightness in her chest, as though she had been laced too tight and could not breathe properly. 'Mr Hallam? What is he to do with this?'

'He warned me most strongly against listening to you. But I see beyond his simple morality – you must believe me when I say I do. He says you are a bad example, and yet he cannot keep his eyes from your face. They are drawn there each and every time you look away, like filings to a magnet in one of the sideshows.'

Delphine hardly knew what to think about first. She knew that time was ticking away, the moments of Alba's life where a decision might be made – a bad decision, the kind she had made on one distant night in New York. She tried to put thoughts of Theo Hallam aside.

'Alba,' she said, trying to make her voice gentle, 'it was never my intention for you to be convinced by rogues like Mr Benedict. You are young – please, make a sober judgement. I speak as someone who has made many errors. Do not – *do not* – make the mistakes I have made.'

Alba stared at her. 'You have never owned to any mistakes before. And you seem perfectly comfortable to me,' she said.

Delphine banged on the table, and felt pain sear through her clenched fist. 'He is asking of you what he would ask of a woman of ill-repute. He is seeking to take you from the respectable, safe life you have and ruin you. And once he is finished with you – where will you be? Dead, under a London bridge, within a year.' She broke off, knowing that her voice was beginning to crack, and her words and thoughts were beginning to break up from the pressure of sheer emotion. It was, perhaps, the first time she had faced her own desperate situation. There would be no more money from her grandfather, one day soon; she was fading in his mind, until one day he would think of her as dead, truly dead, a beautiful ghost that had once flitted through the rooms of his New York mansion. Replaced by other grandchildren, maybe great-grandchildren – had her brother married? All of this added to the vehemence of her voice and expression, the earnest hope that she could prevent another woman from her own particular type of ruin; from becoming invisible to every person who had ever known or loved her.

Alba looked amazed – not shocked, or thoroughly

warned, but simply startled, as though by a failure of manners. 'I know of whom you speak,' she said. 'I know about those women; my aunt talks of them all the time, in veiled ways. But I also know that there is a chance that Mr Benedict may be right. Once I end this season with my aunt, I will become a burden to the family. I have wished for marriage as the only route I may sensibly take. Now, I have an alternative, and I long for excitement and variation in routine.' She leaned forwards and whispered, 'As we all do, Mrs Beck. Is it not worth taking one risk, to leave such a life of dullness behind?'

Delphine could say nothing. She knew that she had once felt as Alba did; it was perfectly understandable, and could not be argued against. But she felt, knowing that she could not transfer her experience, filled with grief. 'If only,' she said, 'I could make you understand my life. If I could make you feel, for a moment, what it is to live with my heart. You will face such hardships if you follow this man, little Alba. There are no words that do justice to them.' She reached out and touched the girl's face. Alba did not move away, but nor did she yield to the touch. 'I fear I will be disappointing you,' said Delphine, 'but I must say that my honest advice is to make a marriage if you see that as the only alternative. Do not underestimate the value of safety, darling Alba, please do not.'

Alba was no longer looking out of the window; she had slumped against the wooden back of her chair. She looked younger than ever, her lower lip jutting out as she considered Delphine's words. Eventually, she spoke. 'You are right,' she said. 'I must have been mad to even think of it. But he is persuasive.'

Her face was passive in expression, but when she looked at Delphine, the other woman could see the glisten of tears in her eyes, and it reassured her.

'He is that,' Delphine said. 'Do not speak to him again, if you can help it.' She rose from the table, her limbs feeling stiff and cold, as though she had aged in those few minutes. 'We should both go, before the others come down. Remember what I have said to you. He is dangerous. I did not know how much.'

Alba reached out and pressed her hand. 'Thank you,' she said, then turned away, to look out again at the ruins above them on the slope. Delphine walked away, but an instinct made her turn round and look at the girl. Alba had untied the ribbon holding her hair back, and was running her fingers through her red-gold tresses.

After breakfast, the group decided to venture to the ruins again, as though they might make good their aborted trip from the day before. The decision was made on the basis of a suggestion from Edmund, who thought that the day before had been lost, and, in some way, felt obscurely responsible for it. There was no great agreement with this suggestion; rather it was that no one said 'no', but thought that it would be well enough. Delphine even said that it might be brighter, and the sea winds not so punishing. But as they climbed the slope she knew the folly of her words, felt the power of the wind, and looked around at the shivering women in their dresses, and envied the men their long coats, splashed with mud as they were.

She had been determined not to speak to Theo again. At Alba's words *I listened to you, Mrs Beck ... even when Mr Hallam urged me not to* she had felt the depth of her unknowing about Theo Hallam. It was as if a great hole in the earth had opened up before her feet, and she could not take a step forwards or trust even the evidence of her eyes. But when he passed her on the slope, she could not help but raise her eyes to his face. He smiled – a brief, shy smile – and against all her instincts to smile in return, she turned away, mustering as much of an expression of cold-ness as she could. He hurried on past her, the wind tugging at his black coat, and she watched him move away from her, walking quickly, into the ruins.

They found the ruins still torn by the wind, the sea even wilder below the cliffs, and Alba scampered in the long grass, calling for Theo. He stood beside her, leaning on his walking stick, deciphering an inscription for her, which she said she could not read.

Edmund saw Julia standing at the section of the nave fur-thest from the towers. She was looking over the weathered stones before her, and laid a gloved hand over the nearest stone. As Edmund approached, he saw the look on her face, as though the inert things were wounded animals that she might heal with her touch. He did not wish to sur-prise her, and coughed to show he was there; but he had not broken any meditative state, for she turned and smiled at him serenely, as though she had been aware of his presence and attention all the time.

'These stones,' she said, her veil pushed against her face by the wind, like a second skin. 'I was thinking about all the things they must have seen, and all the centuries they have spent here.'

He smiled, but said nothing; looked at the hat in his hands.

'I am glad we came with you,' she said, and her voice throbbed with emotion; the first time he had heard it in her, this refined, controlled creature. 'It is good to be away from Broadstairs, after all we have seen there in the last few days. And this is a fine view, all the countryside, laid out in swathes and patches, and our little home for the season somewhere along that coast. I had no idea there was such a place, this close, so set out on its own – so majestic, so lonely. All those souls who passed their lives here – what did they feel when they looked out on this? What did they see? Had I come here all those hundreds of years ago, like the two sisters, I would not have wanted to leave.'

Edmund smiled at her warmly. 'I am quite sure you will be glad to leave by the time we come to,' he said, glancing at her in her dress, shivering a little. 'May I give you my coat?'

She shook her head. 'I have borne far worse than this. A little sea breeze is nothing. But tell me.' She came closer to him, and the sight of her face seemed suddenly clearer to him, even beneath the veil; her lips red, her eyes blue – not the blue of the sea crashing against the cliffs below but with a warmth that told of candlelight and the sunlight she seemed to shelter herself from every day he had known her. 'What do you think of this view, Mr Steele? You said to me before that you came from London. How does this compare?'

He did not take his eyes from her face. 'It is beautiful,' he said. 'So beautiful it is almost painful to the eye, for to look upon it is to know you must leave it again.' He broke away from her gaze; the urge to embrace her was too strong. 'But I would not know how to live with these empty fields and ruins. My eye is accustomed to the throng, to narrow streets and the way of the crowd; my lungs to the scents of the city. I can appreciate this, but only as an onlooker.'

She inclined her head, and he could not tell if she approved or disapproved of his words. But her turn away, as slight as the movement was, was too much for him. He had thought of her in the night, and wondered if he would ever have a chance to speak to her. He had learned to take chances in life; it was something his parents had urged upon him, though he had thought it strange, these two quiet people with their contented isolation in a country cottage – yet there was a vividness in their eyes as they urged on his thoughts and ambitions, no matter how childish they had been. He thought of them now, even if it was only for a moment, as the woman he loved reached and touched the stones again.

'To be plain, the most agreeable view for me, is you,' he

said. The moment he said it, he knew it sounded wrong; for the first time in many years he had spoken with painful self-consciousness, and it sounded wrong to his ears.

Julia turned sharply, her hand still outstretched as though it might meet the rock.

'What do you mean?' she said, and her voice was full of emotion. He could not identify it, although there was fear, and pain, and he suddenly realized that she thought he was mocking her. He wanted to reach out to her and make her understand – but to touch her would be improper and wrong. He could only say it in words, as clearly as he could.

'You are beautiful,' he said, and he did not look around before he said it. He said it in a way which indicated that he did not care who heard.

She looked at him, then shook her head. 'I am not,' she said, and she sat down upon the remains of a stone wall and looked out at the sea.

'I disagree with you,' he said. 'I think you are one of the most beautiful women I have ever seen.'

He saw the bitter curl of her lip. She did not turn, but kept her eyes fixed on the horizon.

'You are kind, Mr Steele,' she said. 'And I am most grateful. I take it – for you cannot be dwelling on my blemished visage – that you detect something in me. A spiritual beauty, perhaps? I value you, sir, you are a kind gentleman, so I will spare you from keeping that illusion. There was a time when I did not feel ashamed of myself. But my deformity has not made me purer. Quite the contrary. I am all darkness, through and through.'

His mouth was dry; she had spoken with such certainty. He looked around him – at Alba and Theo, talking together, Miss Waring only a few steps behind; at Delphine, struggling to find a focus as she moved here and there. Everything seemed strange to him, suddenly, as though the world was changing before his eyes.

'I do not believe it,' he said, and he bowed, before turning away and walking across the nave where monks had once chanted, leaving her to look out at the sea, at the place where so many ships had foundered.

CHAPTER NINETEEN

When we arrived in Broadstairs, I had felt reconciled to my years of travel, and to our solitude. Julia and I took pleasure in food, in walking, in filling our long days with trivial things – in a way, it was a repeat of our younger days, but carried out in the shadow of the worry about money, and in much less luxury. I had once drawn because I loved it; now I drew because I thought that I might need to sell my pictures at some point. A room in our London house was waiting for me, to be my studio. And yet, that need dried up my desire to draw, and made every line from my charcoal dead and lifeless.

My connections with Mrs Quillian's salon by the sea, as Julia had predicted, made me vulnerable. In the evenings I would smoke a cigarette and watch my cousin read or rest, and wonder why I had chosen to be part of that group. Perhaps I was just tired of solitude. Perhaps I saw in them the model of my own *family, a new group to reconcile with, as though I could remake the connections I had once lost. These connections made me weaker – so, when I could have spoken up more strongly for Polly, I stayed silent. I regret it, for it was my silence that had damned me in New York. I speak up now – these words to you are a form of shouting, even – but they come a little too late. Too late for me, for her . . . and for Alba.*

'Stay away from the beach early in the mornings, madam,' said Martha one day in late August, her rough voice filled with apprehension. The phrase was not a suggestion; it was a command.

Delphine stared at the butter, deep yellow, seeping into the toasted crumpet she was about to bite into. The silence in the room was leaden and charged. Julia stared, mystified, at the maid.

'I know I shouldn't say such a thing,' continued Martha bravely, 'but I say it for you, as much as me. There's talk, madam. They say you've brought bad luck to the town.'

'Me?' said Delphine, hearing the crack of Julia's astonished laugh.

'What with the loss of those girls,' said Martha, struggling on, 'and all these summer storms. One of the luggers was almost lost the other night. There's been rumours of the smugglers' ghosts being seen up at Lanthorne, too. It's stirred up things.' She lowered her eyes. 'There's talk about it in the taverns. They say you go walking on the beach too early, and are dressed all in black, and with all your mourning jewellery. They say you talk to the weather, and that you've put a curse on the town. It's stirred up the memories of my niece.' She broke off.

'And what do you think, Martha?' asked Delphine.

Martha held her gaze. 'I'm a good Christian,' she said, 'and I have no truck with superstition. But I think you're exposing yourself to the talk. You've marked yourself out.'

'That's enough,' said Julia, pale with fury. 'If Mrs Beck's behaviour troubles you so much, perhaps we should engage someone else to char for us.'

Only now did confusion filter into Martha's expression. 'I said I would stay for the season, and so I will,' she said. She placed the teapot down on the table with a decided clunk, and went back into the kitchen.

'I'll put her out of this house,' snapped Julia, rising, but Delphine stopped her.

'Come now,' she said. 'She is overwrought, that is all.'

She sat back in her chair and wondered if Mr Hallam had contributed to the rumours about her. On Sunday she had spoken to him at the church door, briefly and coldly, and there was something in his expression which disturbed her. She sensed he was beginning to hate her. Hate was the word that came into her mind, extreme as it seemed; but she could not, would not, ignore it. She had learned to trust her instincts, to seek out the stealthiest, most hidden voice in the back of her mind, for she knew that it was often whispering the truth, so softly it was beneath the level of human hearing. Alba had also seemed distant at church; her face guarded, and Delphine believed Theo had warned her again. The only thing that gave her gladness was that Mr Benedict was not at church, but spending more time in Ramsgate with his family.

'It is time for us to leave here,' said Delphine quietly. 'I will write to Mr Lock and say that we will need the house in London reclaimed from its tenants. We can leave as soon as he has done so.' She passed a hand over her brow; she would think of the money later.

'They will think us guilty of all their strange charges,' said Julia, with a half-hearted laugh, 'if we go now.'

'From what Martha is saying, they think me guilty of it already. Why would you want to stay?' said Delphine sharply. 'Is it Mr Steele? If you wished to encourage him, Julia, I think it is too late now. You should have brought it to a conclusion sooner.' And she raised her voice on the last words, for Julia had got up from the table and left the room.

Theo found it was harder than he had anticipated to approach Mr Benedict on the beach. He had been summoned early to the Albion Hotel by Mr Gorsey, had listened gravely to the hotelkeeper's grievances and assured him that he would act on his behalf, as it was his duty so to do. Then, standing in the empty terrace, the tables not set by the absent Polly, he had seen his target: Mr Benedict, cloaked and hatted, with his watercolour sketchbook on his knees. Still, Theo paused before going out there, and watched him until Mr Gorsey came up behind him and cleared his throat. At that moment he saw a little girl approach the painter, and the man strike up a conversation. Theo then went swiftly out of the door of the terrace, down the steps into the garden, and through the garden gate on to the promenade.

As he passed from the promenade to Harbour Street, Theo almost broke into a run, suddenly frightened that Mr Benedict might have gone by the time he reached him. But he was still there, the sea wind unsettling the folds of his cloak; and the child had disappeared, small footprints leading off in the direction of the Tartar Frigate. Out of danger, Theo thought, and his relief surprised him.

Benedict looked up at his approach, frowning in the sunlight. His gaze swooped around Theo, as though he thought someone else should be with him, for surely the clergyman would never willingly seek him out? 'Good morning,' he said, with a note of insolent surprise, turning his eyes back to his sketchbook and dipping his brush into a jar of water he had set into the sand.

Theo returned his good morning, disconcerted that the other man had not risen to his feet, or was even holding his gaze, making the kind of conversation he was planning to have difficult.

'I am here on a commission,' he said eventually. This caught Benedict's attention, as Theo had hoped it would. He planted the brush in its pot and shut his box of colours. But he did not get to his feet.

'From whom?' he said.

'Mr Gorsey,' said Theo. 'You may guess what the subject is.'

'May I?' Benedict spoke as if he was savouring the

words, and leaned back on to his hands, leaving his sketch – lines of colour to Theo – open and drying on his lap.

'Since you are determined to make this difficult,' said Theo, 'I see I must speak plainly.'

'It seems so,' said Benedict.

'You must leave Broadstairs,' said Theo, 'and as soon as possible. Mr Gorsey says you have paid unwelcome attentions to his daughter, Polly.'

A cry of laughter emerged from the painter's mouth. 'Unwelcome!' he said.

Theo sighed. 'You must go, or there will be consequences. You may have misunderstood the nature of this place. You are used to London. Feelings run high here, and when a local girl is dallied with,' he said, observing Benedict's mocking smile, 'believe me, you do not wish to stay here. Some act of violence may even befall you.'

'This is all nonsense,' said Benedict, tenderly placing his sketchbook on the sand and rising to his feet. 'I will speak to Gorsey about it.'

'I would urge you not to,' said Theo. 'He has asked me to act on his behalf. You may return to the hotel to instruct your man to pack, but that is all. He will not let you stay here another night.' He looked in the direction of the hotel and Benedict's gaze followed his own. Gorsey stood in the glass gallery of his hotel, looking out. Even from a distance, his expression was grim.

'Well,' said Benedict, 'this is bad.' He hurried to tidy his things. 'At least you have had the chance to enjoy it.'

'Believe me,' said Theo, 'I do not enjoy this duty.'

'Really?' Benedict turned with sudden violence and looked at him. 'Do not think I have not noticed your jealousy. Who has been talking of me and Polly Gorsey? Did Gorsey come to you, or have you drawn this out of him, or her? I had no doubt that you would be seeking out some evil to be used against me. We are enemies simply by our natures, Mr Hallam; I can acknowledge the beauty in this world, whilst you simply run to box it in; I can speak to women as if they are human beings, whereas you hide in a corner, behind the plate-glass of piety.'

'I have carried out my commission,' said Theo. 'I will walk you to the hotel. There is no need for further conversation between us.'

Benedict made a mock-bow to him. 'How it must hurt you to be so honourable,' he said. 'I will make my own way; I will not move an inch until you are gone. Oh, do not worry, I will not cause a scene with Gorsey. I shall go to Ramsgate. Now leave me to shift for myself, like a gentleman.'

The letter had been despatched to Mr Lock telling him of Delphine and Julia's planned return to London. There was the slightest chill of autumn in the air when Delphine and Julia walked to the Albion Hotel, where they had agreed to take tea with Mrs Quillian. They went to the gallery, to watch the waves rolling into the bay and the agitated seagulls calling to each other in the wind. A remark Mrs Quillian made indicated that she knew of the rumours about Delphine. Delphine thought, if this lady knew, then it was definitely time to be gone, and she almost hired a carriage in that moment. She glanced at Julia alongside her, pale and sad since she had said they were to leave, and thought, We are all beginning to be estranged from each other.

At that moment, she saw Mr Benedict coming towards them. He was moving swiftly, and Mr Gorsey was following him. The landlord's face was glistening with sweat.

'I am on my way,' said Benedict to Gorsey, over his shoulder. 'The carriage is being packed at this moment, as you have seen. Will you let me bid farewell to my friends, at least?' He was pale and haggard-looking, but there was a vicious turn to his mouth. His lips were moving slightly, as though he was having an imaginary conversation with someone.

'Very well,' said Gorsey, acknowledging the ladies, and then moving away.

'Forgive me,' said Benedict, bowing to kiss Mrs Quillian's hand. He was speaking softly, and his gaze swept their faces. 'Urgent business forces me to leave for Ramsgate.'

'Mr Benedict,' said Mrs Quillian, with some concern for her favourite. 'You seem to have lost your composure. Perhaps you are unwell.'

A kind of tenderness came into the painter's eyes. 'Dear Mrs Quillian,' he said, 'you are right, as always. A walk is what I need – a brief promenade in the fresh air. Will you join me?' He offered her his arm.

She took it, clearly not knowing what to do, and Delphine and Julia rose to go with them, a glance of mutual confidence indicating that they wished to protect the poor lady. Emerging on to the pavement of Albion Street, where Benedict's carriage was being packed, they met Theo and Edmund.

'Aunt,' said Theo, but Mrs Quillian had already passed him, Mr Benedict casting a glance behind as they did so.

'What is going on?' said Theo. His eyes met Delphine's but jumped away. She felt a rush of anger at his reaction.

'He is leaving,' she said, 'but he is behaving erratically.' She looked at Edmund, who was bidding good day to Julia. 'Please come with us. Benedict's wildness worries me.'

It was an ordinary day, the street a little quieter than usual. No one looked at Benedict, other than the occasional person who noticed his grim expression, but Delphine's sense of foreboding would not die down. They turned down Harbour Street, and as they walked under the shadow of York Gate, a man stepped out from a doorway. His hands were in his pockets, but his expression was clearly hostile; large and solid, he turned, and caught Benedict's shoulder with his own, knocking him. The jolt was enough for Mrs Quillian to stop, and step away from Benedict. Theo hurried forwards and offered her his arm.

'Call y'self a gentleman, do you?' said the man. He brought his face close to Benedict's. A foot away, Delphine saw the anger burning there: plain, true, unhidden. And also a kind of vacancy, a blankness. From that blankness, she sensed, violence would come.

Benedict said nothing, which surprised Delphine. It was the first time she had seen him lost for words.

'What is wrong here?' said Edmund softly. His interjection startled the man, who had obviously thought he was alone with the object of his disgust. His gaze flickered to Edmund's face then back to Benedict.

'I've no quarrel with you,' he said, 'other than your association with him.' He turned back to Benedict. 'Do you know half the havoc you've caused? For all your fancy ways you are nothing but a crook. Were there not enough girls here for you, that you had to meddle with another man's wife? Her husband's gone, you know, has said she can no longer use his name, nor can he trust that her children are his.'

'You are mistaken,' said Benedict, and Delphine heard the sound of his dry tongue breaking away from the roof of his mouth. 'There has been some misunderstanding about Polly Gorsey; there is no man's wife involved.'

'No man's wife?' The incredulity of the man's expression was extreme. 'Who told you she was still Polly Gorsey? Her old man, eh? Always saying my Polly this and my Polly that. She might have been born that, but she was Polly Dean until an hour ago, mother to a little one, for all that she leaves the girl with her ma so much. You have ruined another man's marriage, and now I'll ruin you.'

He stepped forwards, then stopped and looked at him. 'She didn't tell you, did she?' He shook his head. 'Oh, he is not like you, he is a man to keep his word, and she will not see him again. And in a few months, sir, isn't it true, she will bear your child?'

The frozen little group in the street, all behind Benedict, watched the painter step back. When he turned, Delphine had no doubt that the news had shocked him profoundly. She sensed it was not the pregnancy which had disturbed him so deeply, despite Mrs Quillian's audible cry. Was it not true that men of his sort had women all over London? It was news of the husband.

He rocked back on his heels, and sat down in the middle of the road. It was this action, Delphine thought, which saved him from the violence of the other man, who looked down on him uncomprehendingly for a long moment, then turned and walked away in the direction of the Dolphin. She noticed there were more people on the street now; a couple of children, staring, aping the expressions of their mothers, who stood in doorways, their arms crossed, their eyes hard, watching.

'Where is my man?' said Benedict, to no one in particular. 'Send to the hotel. I need my medicine. Someone fetch him.'

They all stood there, a frozen little tableau in the middle of Harbour Street. It was Theo who broke it, and as he passed Edmund, he unfroze too. They went either side of the painter and lifted him, the man struggling to his feet. 'I had hoped to spare you and the town this, Mr Benedict,' said Theo.

Benedict shook his hands away, muttering a curse under his breath. 'Leave me,' he said. He began to walk away towards the Albion Hotel.

'Come now, Aunt,' said Theo. 'Do you wish to go back?'

'Not just for the moment,' said Mrs Quillian unsteadily. 'I believe the air will do me good.' She attempted a smile for some of the locals who were still watching.

The sands were busy, and the group moved easily in amongst the people on Main Bay. As Edmund walked alongside them, Delphine saw Julia's hand twitch, and she wondered what her cousin was thinking of.

'We haven't seen you much these past few days,' said Julia. 'We have felt the lack of your companionship.'

Delphine saw the astonishment on Edmund's face, the emotion stealing over his kind expression. Ahead, Theo walked with Mrs Quillian. She wondered if Mr Benedict had found his way safely back to the hotel.

The clouds were moving fast in the sky, and a sudden shadow made its way over the beach, casting the promenaders and playing children, the bathing machines and line of donkeys, into lower light.

'We cannot depend on the sunshine any more,' said Julia brightly. 'Autumn is coming, Mr Steele. When will you be returning to London?'

At the edge of the water, Delphine saw a woman holding a child on her hip. She appeared to be paddling.

'It's Polly,' she said, and she heard Edmund and Julia cease their conversation. She was trying to work out why Polly would be doing such a thing with all the calamities that had happened – and then she realized that the girl was not just paddling.

She was walking into the sea.

'Mr Steele!' cried Delphine, and she started weaving her way through the other people, hoping that he was following her.

By the time she reached the water's edge, Polly was waist-deep in water. It was clear her dress was weighing her down. Her daughter could not have been more than a year old and was silent in her mother's arms, looking bemused.

'Oh my goodness,' gasped Mrs Quillian. The group had come to the water's edge, and Delphine was aware that Theo stood beside her. 'The poor dear girl.'

'What are you doing, Polly?' shouted Delphine.

At that moment, Polly dipped suddenly, and Delphine thought that the sand she had been on must have shelved off, as it often did; for the sand was moved here and there by the sea, a new landscape every time a tide came in. Suddenly she was in the water nearly up to her shoulders and her daughter's hair was floating in the sea.

The cry tore itself from Delphine's throat and she ran forwards; she was already knee-deep in the sea when she felt hands on her shoulders.

It was Theo. 'Do not,' he said, glancing at her heavy skirts. 'You will sink like a stone.' He let go of her and tore off his jacket; beside him, Edmund had already done so and was wading and splashing through the water towards the girl, her head still high, facing the sun and the horizon. Theo reached out for the child first; struggled with Polly, and tore the girl from her arms, lifting her clear from the water as Edmund reached for Polly.

Polly fought them; Edmund had had no idea she would

do so. There was saltwater in his eyes and his mouth, and he wondered for a moment, such was her ferocity, whether she might push him down and drown him. He remembered the faces of Amy Phelps and Catherine Walters, and the thought crossed his mind – quick as a pulse – whether Polly had had some part in their deaths. *A lady, with a veil across her face.*

Standing on the shore, never had Delphine felt more constricted by her unwieldy dress. Her bonnet had fallen back, and she found her hands were in her hair, untangling it from its pins. Her cousin held her close, and Delphine heard her fast breathing, knowing that she too was waiting to see the drama unfold.

As she watched Theo wade back, the tiny girl in his arms, Delphine saw the distress in his eyes, and in the moment that he looked at her, it was as though they were on the cliffs at Reculver again, the connection between them suddenly present, the cobweb threads clear in the sunlight, if only for that moment. He dropped to his knees when he reached the beach, put the girl gently down, and Delphine knelt beside her. The little girl was shocked; choking, but alive, and Delphine lifted her and placed her over her shoulder, patting her on her back so she could spit out the last of the seawater.

'Bravely done,' she said to Theo, but her words were lost in the turn of the last wave, and Theo had gone back into the sea to help Edmund with Polly. Delphine put the child down on the sand, stroking her hair and saying, 'All is well, all is well, all is well.'

Polly was still struggling and fighting, but silently –
saying nothing. There was only the pant of her breath and
the dull plash of her arms against the surface of the sea.
Eventually both men dragged her, one arm each, back-
wards; no respecters of her status as a woman, but as
though they were hauling some wild fish from the sea.
When they finally released her she lay on the sand, beside
her daughter, her breathing laboured, her dress dark with
water. A small crowd had gathered nearby, and Delphine
glimpsed Martha at the front, an expression of distress on
her face.

Polly turned to look at her daughter, then reached out
towards the little girl. They all thought it would be a touch
of tenderness, but instead her hand formed a claw, and it
was as though she sought to dole out her sentence of death
on the child, even now. But her hand would not reach; she
was too far, and Julia snatched the little girl up. 'I will take
her to our cottage,' she said. 'She will be safe there.' And
she looked at Edmund, soaked through, picking his coat
up from the sand, and some kind of understanding passed
between them, for he came to join her.

'Let me carry her,' he said, and they set off across the
sand together.

Delphine sat down beside Polly, Theo standing over
them both. Polly was looking around now, lying on her
back, her eyes darting this way and that. She saw Martha.
'Come to triumph over me?' she said. 'Get away! Get
away!'

Delphine saw the puzzlement in Theo's eyes. 'They've

known each other since they were children,' she said, getting to her feet and brushing a little of the wet sand off her
ruined dress. 'Martha,' she said, 'take Mrs Quillian back to
the Albion.' For the old lady, standing on the edge of it all,
looked deeply shocked.

'Don't worry, Aunt,' said Theo. 'Mrs Beck and I will see
to Polly. Please go back, I will call for you tomorrow.'

Polly had begun to cry – Delphine sensed that tears
seemed easier than speaking – and her first, tight little sobs
began to run into cries, terrible shrieking cries, that
reminded Delphine of the gulls. Theo leaned over her and
put his hand under her elbow. It was a kind of physicality
Delphine had never seen in him before; she had the sense
that no power on earth could shake that slim, strong hand
from the girl's elbow. 'Get up,' he said, in Polly's ear. 'Get
up now, and we will take you to the parsonage. You do not
have to go home yet.'

'Home?' said Polly. 'I have no home.'

'We'll see,' said Theo.

Delphine did not want to touch the girl. She had seen
how the petal-sweetness of her beauty had a dangerous
edge. It was as if Polly was all sharp edges now, and one
could wound oneself even by her touching her. But she
knew it was what Theo needed, so she took the girl's other
elbow and they hauled her, almost a dead weight, to her
feet. Across the sand they went, with their burden, Theo
casting kindly but grave nods to anyone who crossed their
path, strangers and locals alike. One of the women who
had stood on the doorstep to see Mr Benedict berated had

come down, without her own child, and as they neared her, Delphine saw malice cross her face, the muscles around her mouth tensed as though she would say something, spit something, make clear the disgust she had for Polly. But instead, she stood back and crossed her arms, and looked down at the sand. She was a good-looking woman, with tight blonde curls and a tortoiseshell comb in her hair, and Delphine allowed herself to wonder whether she and Polly had once been friends, and had their pick of the young men of Broadstairs together. Would Polly's failure mean she would now be cast out from such companionship? Was her real sin her failure to remain a winner in all the local games?

Just as swiftly came the thought: Was that her only sin? Was her own child the first person she had tried to kill?

'Quickly now,' said Theo, and they walked up the middle of Harbour Street, their heads bowed, up the short slope like shire horses dragging their plough behind them. Polly began to sob again, as though her sorrow might earn her the pity of her neighbours, might draw them from their houses and lead her mother to take her in her arms, and say: 'It's all right, my girl. Things will be mended.' But no such mercy happened, and Delphine thought to herself that they must send a message to Mr Gorsey. She wondered if the painter was sitting in a carriage, Ramsgate-bound, blaming others for his misfortune.

Julia and Edmund had long since gone before them with the child; the door of Victory Cottage was closed. Without discussion Theo and Delphine turned up the driveway to the parsonage, their charge now silent, submitting to their guidance without any protest.

Theo ushered them into the hallway and Delphine saw him glance at their state; covered in seawater and sand. 'Into the kitchen,' he said, and Polly gave a low, bitter laugh.

They sat in silence for several minutes around the kitchen table. It was Theo who spoke first.

'Do you remember your Bible study, Polly?' he said. 'Luke, chapter seven, verse forty-seven: Her sins, which are many, are forgiven; for she loved much: but to whom little is forgiven, the same loveth little.'

Polly watched him sullenly. 'Is that all you have to say?' she said.

'All?' said Theo. 'It is everything, Polly, if you would but realize it. Can you see that your Saviour offers you hope? Offers you forgiveness from your sins?' He paused. 'No matter how numerous they are.' And Delphine saw the doubt in his eyes, and wondered if he too was thinking of the girls washed up on the beach, of Polly's frequent presence on the pier, scanning the horizon with her cutting gaze.

'Not sins,' said Polly in a low but defiant tone. 'Mistakes.'

'The two are often confused,' said Delphine.

Theo looked at her. 'I'd say it was a sin,' he said, 'to try and take your own life, and that of your child. What did you hope for, Polly? The muddy corner of Mockett's field, past the wall of the churchyard? A forgotten grave beyond the reach of prayers?'

Polly's mouth twisted in distress and her tears began to fall again. 'I did not think of anything,' she said, 'other than the terrible things that Michael said to me. They were not true. Jessie is his, and I meant to be a true and good wife to him. If this,' she placed her hand on her stomach, 'is true, then it was an error only; one mistake. I have been Michael's sweetheart since I was fourteen years old. The others admired me, but I kept eyes only for him.'

Delphine saw Theo's gaze flick down to the surface of the kitchen table. She sensed he doubted Polly's words, and she wanted to say: 'Just because she is aware of the effect she has on men, it does not mean that she was untrue to him.'

'Fourteen years old,' said Polly again. 'I was good at my lessons, but no one cared for that. I am twenty-four now. It is a lifetime, to be in this place. And he gives me no word of praise, except now and then. All his warmth he saves for his evenings in the Tartar Frigate, for his old mates on the boat. If I am there it is to be sweet little Polly. He does not care what I say, or think, as long as I do not interfere in the singing of their sea shanties.'

Theo's eyes were blank as she spoke, and Delphine wondered how many times he had heard this story. She glimpsed in Polly's eyes the truth of it all, and knew that she herself would rather have anything than the stultifying boredom of the fireside with someone who did not understand her or know her.

'I have spent my life trying to think what to say to him,' said Polly sadly, 'but I do love him. Mr Benedict was so fine – like a bird with exotic plumage. He made me laugh. He saw me as they used to see me – as unreachable Polly, as beautiful Polly; when I was a prize to be wanted and sought for. He saw all of that in me. It was a little wrong of me to spend time with him. But Michael – he has kissed other girls, I have seen him. When the *Mary White* happened, his friends told me he went to Ranelagh, and said he pretended he had been one of the lifeboatmen, just to be with a girl – a slip of a girl. All of those friends of his wanted me once; now I am a joke to them. If he has done that, then why is what I have done a sin? He was wrong to leave me, wrong to leave me. I am so angry sometimes, it builds in me like a fire, and I hardly know what to do with it.'

At the words *Mary White*, Theo and Delphine's eyes had met. Theo seemed to be searching for something to say.

'Marriage is a sacred bond,' he said. Delphine wanted to say, 'No, no it is not. Not that kind of marriage.'

'You are shivering, both of you. I will get some blankets.'

He went out and they heard him ascending the stairs.

Polly turned her gaze to Delphine's face. 'How does he know what marriage is?' she said.

Delphine sensed spite behind her words. 'He means to help you,' she said, 'but I know it is hard to hear his words. Polly, you may tell me – has there been more to this? Were the bodies on the beach anything to do with you?'

Polly frowned, but kept her eyes on Delphine's. 'No,' she said. 'Now you wish to pile every sin on my head. Is that convenient for you? It hardly surprises me. Mr

Benedict took me to the Ranelagh Gardens. We drank champagne as he told me all about you as a little group – how amusing he was. And you sit here all grave and pious, as though you are a true lady and I am dirt.'

'You are mistaken,' said Delphine. 'I am not judging you. I do not like you, it is true. But I would have dragged you out of the water myself, if I had to. I understand the damage a man can do to a woman.'

'Yet you do not defend me,' said Polly. 'Instead, you ask me if I am a murderer. Such a fine lady, you are.'

'I am talking to you,' said Delphine. 'I am trying to talk to you, Polly. We should speak openly with each other. Why are you not listening?'

'Mr Benedict knows who you are,' said Polly, and for the first time a smile seared its way across her red lips. 'What would happen if I told *him*?' She nodded towards the door, at the distant sounds of Theo returning.

It was like the day she had met Benedict, Delphine thought; the day the carriage had come hurtling down the hill towards her. *So this is how it ends.* She had no idea exactly how much Benedict knew, and what he had told Polly, but she knew it was enough to lay waste to the façade she had carefully built around her. She held Polly's gaze. 'Tell him,' she said.

It was strange, the relief that flooded her, now that the moment had come. And in that kitchen, soaked to the skin, the thought hit her like the revelation she had spent so many years hoping for, staring at stained-glass windows. *I have already lost everything. There is no need to be afraid.*

She rose as Theo entered the room, blankets in his arms. 'Polly has something to say to you,' she said. 'Go on,' she prompted Polly. 'Say what you have to say. Tell him.'

The girl looked at her mutely.

'Very well. Shall I begin?' Delphine turned to Theo and looked directly at him. 'I am not a widow, Mr Hallam. I have never been married.'

CHAPTER TWENTY

Unbeknownst to me, Julia had begun to make her own quiet bid for freedom. She, who had been so against our making connections in the town, who had so often kept her face veiled. When I heard what had happened I worried for her, and even more so for Mr Steele. I wondered if my comments about money had burrowed deep into her mind, and made her risk a marriage she would not normally have wished for. Our family had allowed us an income, as long as we stayed away; they had never increased it, even as the years passed. It was enough for us to live decently, though not well, but its unchanging nature worried me. I thought that one day, when the memory of us had faded enough, it would stop altogether. But now I see it was not the dwindling of the money that terrified me, so much as the proof it offered: that the love they had for me, hidden beneath convention and anger, had dwindled, too, wasting away to nothing.

I should not have worried for Julia when I learned what had happened. That I did worry shows me how little we knew each other, even after all those years.

They had come into Victory Cottage in a hurry, knocking things off the hallstand, Edmund holding the dripping child in his arms and thinking, It is so small, so dark in here. It no longer felt like the comfortable cottage he had taken refuge in on the night of the mist. In the parlour, he laid the girl down on the sofa and saw how threadbare its embroidery was, unsoftened by the evening firelight and candlelight. He looked around and became aware that the books and ornaments which had been present before had all been removed, and the suspicion that Delphine and Julia were packing up to leave entered his mind. There was a chill stealing over him, the chill of autumn, and he realized, warmed as he had been by his terror and excitement, that he was now cold, cold to the bone, from the seawater soaking his clothes.

Julia put a hand on his arm, and her unexpected touch sent shivers through him.

'Dear Mr Steele,' she said, 'will you put the kettle on the range? It should have water in it.' He went silently, without replying, but feeling the sensation of her hand on his arm as though it was still placed there.

He moved around awkwardly in the kitchen, hearing the wail of the little girl in her unfamiliar surroundings. The kettle was on the side, but it had no water in it, and he carried it back into the parlour, befuddled, and thinking that all he wanted was a good strong brandy. What he saw there pulled him up on the threshold.

Julia had taken off her cloak and had wrapped the little girl in it. She had pulled the veil back from her face, and her profile was haloed by the light from the window. The little girl was silent, her hands moving, her expression absorbed, for Julia was singing to her, her American accent giving the words a kind of lilt that was, to Edmund, both exotic and comforting: this new voice imparting a deeper meaning to the words she sang, a resonance that echoed through him.

> *Hush, little baby, don't you cry,*
> *Mama will sing you a lullaby.*
>
> *Hush, little baby, don't say a word,*
> *Mama's gonna buy you a mockingbird.*
>
> *And if that mockingbird won't sing,*
> *Mama's gonna buy you a diamond ring.*
>
> *And if that diamond ring turns brass,*
> *Mama's gonna buy you a looking glass.*

Suddenly aware of Edmund's presence, Julia broke off and looked at him, her face flushed. 'Mr Steele,' she said. 'Is all well?'

Edmund was holding the kettle in one hand and the lid in the other. 'Miss Mardell,' he said. He leaned back against the doorway, stared at her, and at the little girl who turned to look at him in babyish wonder. 'If I live long enough, will you consent to be my wife?'

'Martha,' said Theo, to the astonished girl who stood in his kitchen doorway. 'Take Polly upstairs to the second guest room. See that she gets warm and dry, and that she sleeps. You are to stay with her. On no account are you to leave her alone.'

The two girls glanced at each other, wariness in Martha's eyes, a tired enmity in Polly's.

'But the dinner, Mr Hallam,' said Martha.

Theo sighed. 'I do not want dinner,' he said.

Martha gave Delphine one long look. 'Madam?' she said. Delphine nodded.

'Mrs Beck is here because she helped me with Polly,' said Theo. He sounded weary. 'Please, leave us.'

'Yes, sir,' she said, and curtseyed before shuffling out and going up the stairs, followed by Polly.

Delphine looked around the kitchen – at the red and black tiles on the floor, and the blue and white tiles on the wall. Beyond the small window she saw the movement of the evergreens, their waxen leaves shining in the sun. The smell of this room was of mouldering bread, and of beer, and it was small to service such a large house. She supposed this would be the last time she saw it, and she tried to fix it in her memory. At Theo, too, she looked – hungrily, without reservation or embarrassment. Unlike her, he was sitting forwards, bent over the table, slightly hunched, his hands clasped together in front of him. She wondered if he was praying; whether almost every activity he did was a form of prayer. She looked over his head, the hair neatly shorn, the summer light showing the gold in every strand. She did not know what it was that made her want to stay in this room, with him, for as long as she could.

At last he spoke, his eyes fixed on his hands, on the table. 'Is it true?' he said. 'Did Polly really speak the truth?'

Delphine's first impulse was to speak tartly about the confessional, to say that he was at last showing the true Catholic spirit Mr Benedict had suspected. But even as the words rose in her mind, they only had a dull kind of shine to them, and she doubted that she had the energy to carry them off.

'In part, it is true,' she said. 'Benedict has spun stories from a few scraps of information. I have lived as I am for so long, because people do not know what is true and what is false. They know only that I am a lost woman. I cannot dispute that.'

He raised his eyes to her face. They were the piercing blue of the sky; there was nothing veiled about them, and his gaze had an intensity which, though she had seen it before, still had the power to astonish her. 'What is true and what is false?' he said.

I still have a choice, she thought. But she knew she would speak to him; that she could not help but speak to him, and that there was no longer anything to be gained by staying silent.

'It is true that I was – am – disgraced,' she said, 'and

through a connection with a man. What the world supposes to be that connection, is false.' She did not like the note of justification she heard in her voice, and paused to consider her words. 'Mr Benedict heard of it because I sold a painting in London, and I considered it mine to sell. It was necessary for me to do so, to support myself and my cousin. She knows nothing of this, and I would ask you not to mention it to her. It was an Old Master, and the dealer was suspicious of me – a woman, not apparently wealthy, owning such a thing. I told him its provenance, in the strictest confidence, which he has broken. If my father finds out I have sold the painting, he will be disappointed, but as for stealing it . . . that is not the case. It is from my family; it was given to me by my aunt, when I left. If they wished to seek it they would have done so, long ago. They have always had track of me, through my agent in London. I am given a small income, but as the years pass, it is not always enough, for they will not increase it. I have broken no law. They have always known where I was.' Her voice cracked on the last word and she bit her lip; she had not expected emotion to creep up on her, to overtake her so quickly, choking up her voice. Her distant family, the people she had tried to think of as dead, were suddenly so real that they seemed to stand in the corners of the room. I have gone from stone to sand in a moment, she thought. She willed herself not to cry.

'You were never married,' he said, with a finality that indicated it was not a question. 'Did you live with a man, as though you were?'

'No. But why that should matter to you, I do not know.'

'You have lived a lie. What is your real name? I presume the one you have given me is false?'

She met his gaze with her own. 'I will not tell you. You speak to me as though you are my judge, but you have no such exalted place. Look to your own soul.'

She saw the flicker of doubt in his eyes, and knew she had hit some inner nerve; knew also that she had pressed on that point of doubt she had always seen in him. She had not wished to wound him, but she had tired of his merciless questioning, seeing in it one weak individual finding strength in pushing down another. Once, they had been equal adversaries, over Alba – though she had not known, at the time, that he was battling for the young woman's soul. But now he had seen a way of triumphing over her, and had taken it, and she despised him for it.

He pushed his chair away from the table, but did not stand. 'When I think,' he said, 'of the way in which you singled out Miss Albertine, and spent so much time with her, trying to influence her.'

'Do you suspect me of trying to drag her into some kind of wickedness?' she said. She was angry, but she did not believe it wholly; saw the strain in his countenance, the movement of his lips pressed together. He was unsure and uncertain. He was, she thought, trying to play a part; following the urgings of the God he had read of and been schooled in – a God that, she guessed, had no direct words with his heart.

'If you intend only to insult me then I will not speak to

you of it any more,' she said. She got up, quickly, and he sprang up, too; stood in the doorway. She took a step back, astonished.

'Tell me your name,' he said hoarsely.

'No,' she said. 'Not under duress.'

'Do you not understand?' he said. 'The truth is important, it is central to everything. I must know the truth about you. What is that, even?' He gestured to the choker of woven hair she wore. He shook his head angrily. 'It is the same colour—'

'—as Alba's,' she said. 'Yes. But it is not Alba's hair. It is mine. As it was when I was a woman of twenty. I wear it because I mourn for myself, for what I once was, and for every part of the life I left behind.'

She picked up her bonnet. Felt, beneath her fingers, the tight weaving of the Parisian bonnet-makers, the smoothness that money can buy. It was an old bonnet, growing frayed through use. 'You know the truth of me,' she said. 'If I did not tell everything about me, that is not a lie. Is it really Alba you are angry about? Is it really my effect on her, or on someone else? I have never played a part – not like you, no. Not like you.'

She moved to go past him; he put his arm up to bar the door. She touched it; sprang back from it as though it was charged. 'Let me through,' she said. 'Let me out.'

'I will not,' he said. 'You have ruined everything. You are an agent of corruption. The devil lives in your words.' The quiet certainty of his voice cut through her. Their summer seemed to splinter like a mirror hit with a hammer. There was, it seemed, no way of escaping the darkness of New York and its judgement. Their sunlit days here had been merely an illusion.

'Nothing has been the same since you came here,' said Theo. 'This quiet place, where I thought I would be safe – you have turned everything upside down. I have tortured myself over a whore.'

There was no way past him, and the noise grew loud in Delphine's mind. She took a step back. The thought crossed her mind that she would take a knife, and run it through him, as though he was that first man and every man since who had judged her and taken away her free-dom. For the silence of her mother, and the complicity of every friend and relation she had known in her whole life. One ring for each of them, worn on her fingers, fingers loaded with gold enamelled over with black. But she felt tired; and she knew there was only one way out of the room without violence. It was the truth.

'Very well,' she said. 'If you must know it. Despite it all, Mr Hallam, I am a virgin. As pure as every one of those little girls found on the beach. My name is Amy.'

She had shocked him; he dropped his arm. She went past him, quickly, down the hall, out of the front door into the bright, cruel sunshine that blinded her, pulling the door shut behind her with all her strength. The door slammed shut so hard that the knocker rattled against it, but she did not look back; she had broken into a run towards Victory Cottage, running as if he might follow her.

Theo stood in the darkness of the hallway, a few steps from the door, now shut. His left hand hung at his side, but his right was raised slightly, the fingers curved round. He stared at it for a moment, this hand which seemingly did not belong to him. The hand that had reached out as she left, reached out to take her right arm and turn her round to him, and take her face, so that he might kiss her.

CHAPTER TWENTY-ONE

Let me tell you what I wore, each day, apart from my dresses: grey, lavender, black – all of hard-wearing, itchy stuff. Neither full mourning nor half-mourning, but in flux day by day.

On the little finger of my right hand, a ring bearing a monogram of my grandfather's initials.

On the third finger of my right hand, a ring enclosing beneath rock crystal the entwined hair of my grandfather and grandmother.

On the second finger of my left hand, a black enamelled mourning ring enclosing the hair of my parents, tied in a love knot.

On the third finger of my left hand, a gold band enamelled in white, with forget-me-nots picked out in gold. The interior engraved with my real name. A mourning ring for a virgin, or one unmarried.

Around my neck, a choker made of woven hair, the last remnant of who I once was.

Alba had said that Miss Waring thought me over-indulgent in my mourning. Perhaps she saw my face, and thought it too should have been plain and unornamented, that my gaze should not have been searching for something, as clearly it was – though at the time I thought myself stringent in my carriage and expressions. It was a fair question, though. Why did I still mourn? Why did I still wear those rings, that choker, those dark uncomfortable dresses? Because I was driven to remember. I thought, I must keep the wound open. It was only by grieving, and hating, and memorializing, that I remembered who I was. And I could do it in a way that the world did not question. For all of my coolness, I wore my wounds openly, I showed the world that I had known suffering. And I built my walls, hopeful that no one would ever break them down.

Now? Now I wish to be happy. And to be happy, one must choose to live with the past. I must find a place inside my mind for it; a dark corner, where it can sleep.

Victory Cottage was silent as Delphine entered; in her fumbling urgency it took her more than one turn of the handle to get the front door open.

She went first to the parlour and found Edmund and Julia there, with Polly's child sleeping in Julia's arms. The light was already greying in the room; Julia placed a finger to her lips as Delphine sank into the chair. Her face was white, and as Edmund approached her he saw the shock there. He leaned over her.

'Something has happened,' she said in a whisper.

They heard the front door rattle in its frame – someone clumsily trying to open it. Delphine covered her face and turned away. 'Not him,' she said. It was such a gesture of vulnerability that Edmund stepped out into the hallway swiftly, wondering what he would face. He went to the door and yanked it open.

A woman stood there; her face was faintly familiar. 'I've come for the little one,' she said, and curtseyed belatedly. 'Martha sent word that she was here. I'm Mrs Gorsey, Polly's mother.'

'One moment,' he said, and went back into the parlour. Julia was already on her feet, carrying the little girl out into the hallway. The child held her arms out at the sight of her grandmother.

'We can keep her here for a while, if you wish,' said Julia, with such a note of pleading in her voice that it pained Edmund.

The woman shook her head. 'Best with family,' she said, and received the child into her arms. The little girl looked over her grandmother's shoulder as the woman walked down the path, and raised a chubby little hand as though to say goodbye. Edmund watched Julia – but she only smiled and waved back, as one would to a child on the beach. She had done it in a practised manner; turned away and smiled brightly. From what she had told him, he guessed that she had known many goodbyes, and become accustomed to it.

Delphine was still sitting in the same place. Julia sat

down beside her and Edmund went to stand by the empty fireplace, feeling that he was intruding as he watched Delphine wipe a tear away with her thumb.

'Dearest,' said Julia after a moment, 'what has happened?'

Delphine looked at her. 'He knows,' she said, 'Mr Hallam.' Her eyes glanced regretfully at Edmund. 'There is no need to go, Mr Steele. I am sure he will tell you everything. You need only cross the street and walk up the drive, and you will have a full and colourful version of my character painted for you.'

'I think I may make my own judgement,' said Edmund and, alarmed at her pallor, he went quietly from the room to find something for her to drink.

Julia leaned towards Delphine, took her face in her hands. 'You look terrible, my darling – worse even than *that* day.' They sat in pregnant silence as Edmund returned with Madeira, neither he nor Julia wanting to ask what had happened, only knowing that it must have been something of great violence.

'We must leave this place,' Delphine said. 'I never want to see him – or anyone else from our party – again.'

'I do not believe that,' said Julia bravely.

'Then you must learn to listen better.' Delphine took the glass Edmund offered her, drinking it down in one mouthful. She caught his gaze with her own as she put it on the table beside her. 'He has insulted me,' she said. The clock ticked in the silence she let fall. 'I never thought to hear such words from his lips. I think I held him sacred, until this moment.' She wiped another tear away. 'I have been a fool.' She looked at Julia. 'You must forgive me for letting you down,' she said. 'He knows who we are – and he is wild with anger. I do not know what he will do – who he will tell. I am sorry, but we must begin again.'

'Do not say you are sorry,' said Julia. 'I cannot bear it.'

'He has hurt me,' whispered Delphine, and she caught Edmund's glance again. 'I felt it so much I almost wanted to kill him.'

Julia looked from one to the other. 'Do not speak so intemperately. There is a man here who will defend you,' she said, 'who will be family to you, as soon as God allows.' She had one arm wrapped around her body, the other hand pressed to the mark on her face. She looked at Edmund.

Delphine's gaze flickered between them. 'Oh,' she said, a gentle smile flaring up on her face, in such contrast to the grief that it was almost ghoulish. 'Tell me.'

Edmund swallowed; he would not have chosen this moment to tell her. It seemed insensitive, and yet Julia's strained gaze was unwavering. 'Your cousin has done me the honour of agreeing to become my wife,' he said.

Delphine nodded. 'I am glad,' she said.

Julia sprang to her, held her tightly. 'So you see,' she said, 'Edmund will defend you. He will right all the wrongs Mr Hallam has done – won't you, dear?'

Edmund was shaken by the novelty of the word. He nodded.

Delphine pulled away from her. 'There is nothing Mr Steele can do,' she said.

'But there must be,' said Julia, a scratch of vulnerability in her voice.

Delphine shook her head. 'Whatever connection lay between Mr Hallam and me,' and her face showed her astonishment, that her mind had been a stranger even to herself, in this sudden recognition of the store of feeling which lay beneath the surface of each 'good morning' and 'good evening' exchanged between her and Theo. 'Whatever that connection,' she went on, 'though we were hardly aware of it, either of us, it is now broken.' She looked up at Edmund, and he saw in the shadows beginning under her eyes, the exhaustion of extreme emotion. 'You do not need to defend me. I do not doubt that you are a gentleman, and loyal to my cousin – but you have no debt to me. There is nothing to be done.' She reached across and poured herself another glass of Madeira. 'I have fought worse battles than this,' she said, and at her words Julia picked up the decanter and hurried from the room. Delphine watched her. 'You should go after her,' she said.

Edmund followed his fiancée to the kitchen. She had put the bottle down, and was leaning on the counter with a stricken look on her face.

He placed his hands on her shoulders. 'My dear girl,' he said, then paused, for he did not know what to call her. She had confided her real name to him, but the information was so new that he could not say it, for he knew it would sound wrong to his ears.

She turned to him and rested her head against his shoulder. Edmund hardly knew what to do with this closeness;

the scent of her, and warmth of her, was so far from what he had yet experienced that he had to check himself.

'I thought,' she said in a low voice, 'that we might both be happy, my cousin and I. After all these years of resignation.'

Edmund hesitantly allowed his arms to slip around her. He listened, but he could not hear Delphine crying; he could not bear to think she had been left alone to struggle with her trouble.

'I am glad you know my name,' she said. 'There is more I have to tell, but not tonight. Not now.'

She clung to him, then raised her face to his, and he knew not whether their kiss had been begun by her, or by him; only that it was not chaste, but fierce, and that he held her bodily against him in a way which he had not anticipated. Her sudden intensity was surprising – almost, the word came to him later – dangerous. But he did not feel any misgiving in that moment; only love and tenderness, sharpening into hunger.

CHAPTER TWENTY-TWO

Mr Clare was the man who ruined me. A little older than me, rich, and passionate about me. I was told he was handsome too, but I never quite believed it, even if my opinion did not match the crowd's. There was dissolution in those features, I thought – but what I had really seen was cruelty. I was from a strict household, also rich, but climbing, and I was rebelling – just with words, of course, the only weapon I had. When Mr Clare sent me a note asking me to meet him (most improper) I saw another way to rebel. Out on a New York sidewalk, I saw in an instant that I had made a mistake, heard the heated, champagne-fuelled words of offer: an elopement. He believed I loved him, was dazzled by him, wanted him. I did not; I fled. But I had been seen, and I had no idea what his hurt pride and the malice of my enemies would do to my life. I had never even known I had enemies.

Edmund wondered whether he had waited too long. He walked the last stretch of the parsonage drive with a sense of foreboding in his heart, as one would approach an empty and haunted house. The light was fading, the trees were still – and then he saw a faint glow in the drawing-room window.

As Edmund knocked on the front door of the parsonage, it reminded him of that first day, arriving in the blazing sun. Now the sights and sounds were familiar to him; the softness of the summer warmth fading as night descended; the distant sound of the sea, wild tonight, and its ceaseless turning over of the waves on the beach. He could smell the sea in the air; hear the sounds of people returning to their lodgings for the evening, a few fretful children's voices. There would be an assembly tonight at the rooms on the front, but he was far from clapping and cheering, or wanting to hear music and merriment. He knocked on the door, and he was fearful of what he might find. Unbeknownst to Julia and Delphine, he had kept his eye on the window, and had seen that the lamps of Holy Trinity had not been lit for Evening Prayer. He had wondered if one or two worshippers might have waited on the steps of the church, but knew that none of them would have gone up to the parsonage, probably thinking that the priest had been called away on urgent business, and was perhaps attending a dying person's bedside.

The door opened. The hall was dark, and he saw only the shape of someone, a little sliver of a white face in the shadows. 'Theo?' he said.

'Ah, Mr Edmund Steele,' said Theo, and Edmund smelled at once the brandy on his breath. 'Come in.' He stumbled ahead of Edmund, reaching out to touch the walls, until he came to the drawing-room door and opened it.

'Did Mrs Gorsey come and get Polly?' asked Edmund, entering and looking around the room. There was no sign of disturbance. Two oil lamps burned, companionably, their buttery flames giving the room a soft glow.

'Yes,' said Theo. 'And I told Martha to go too. Then I took your advice; a drink or two hardly hurts a man.' He sat down heavily in the chair by the fire, where no fire burned. He was talking precisely; without the fumes of the brandy, and his erratic movements, Edmund would have assumed he was sober.

'You did change?' said Edmund. 'That seawater chilled me through.'

'Of course I did,' said Theo impatiently. Then he looked at Edmund. 'But you did not. My dear sir, please go and put dry clothes on. You place your life at risk to wait so long with,' he paused, 'the ladies.'

Edmund did what he said. When he returned, Theo had got another glass out, and had filled both his and Edmund's with a good measure of brandy. Then he sat back in his chair, and though he raised his glass at Edmund's bidding, he had lost the slightly forced good cheer he had been manifesting when Edmund arrived. Instead, he sat, drink in hand, lost in his thoughts.

'I should tell you,' said Edmund. 'I am engaged.'

A frown crossed Theo's brow. 'Engaged?' he said. 'To whom?'

Edmund almost smiled; wondered if he had really been so opaque when, internally, his whole world had been shifting, and knew in that moment that he had inherited his father's ability to mask his thoughts. 'Miss Mardell,' he said, using her assumed name, as the most familiar.

'Oh.' The perplexed expression faded from Theo's face; the hardness of panic that had entered his eyes, briefly, softened back into thoughtfulness. He took a draw from his glass then. 'Is she who she says she is?' he said.

Edmund was disturbed by the tone of his voice; barely veiled violence hung behind his words. 'She has travelled under that name. Her real name is De Witt. When one is escaping trials, it is understandable that one would not wish to carry that name and move under its shadow everywhere,' he said.

Theo made a sound – half-cough, half-*hah*. 'I see,' he said. 'She has tricked you too.'

'No one is tricked,' said Edmund brusquely. Theo blinked; he looked hurt. Edmund leaned forwards, and put his glass down. 'Theo,' he said, trying to make his voice even, 'what is wrong? Will you speak to me? You can, if you wish, or I will sit here with you.'

'Matthew twenty-four,' said Theo. 'Watch therefore: for ye know not what hour your Lord doth come. But know this, that if the goodman of the house had known in what watch the thief would come, he would have watched, and would not have suffered his house to be broken up.'

'Theo,' said Edmund.

Theo slammed his glass down onto the table which such force that Edmund was sure he had broken it, but it stood there, in the gloom, still whole.

They sat in silence for what seemed to be an eternity to Edmund. Misery hung in the very air. He felt it soak into him and depress his spirits, spirits which despite everything had been high, for he had the expectation that he would marry, and the subject of marriage now seemed a thing of joy. At length, he thought he would try one last time.

'I may be wrong,' he started, 'but I suspect that you may also have thought of marriage. And, I must claim some secret knowledge here, I do know that it was once a possibility for you, a long time ago, in Ceylon.'

Theo blinked, but said nothing.

'I know what end it came to,' said Edmund, 'that the poor lady died on her way here, and that you have mourned her, with the grace that I would expect from a man of your honourable character. But, if I was to say one thing to you, my dear Hallam, it would be that you cannot mourn forever. That God, in all His mysteries, does grant us other chances – to be of use, as you have found with your vocation here – but also to love. Surely if we are offered such a chance, we should take it.'

There was perplexity, again, on Theo's face.

'Perhaps I am not making myself clear,' said Edmund, with a sigh. 'I am poor with words, as Charles will tell you. But what I mean to say is – you are not tied to the remembrance of that good lady, unless you wish to be. You have done her memory honour, and may begin again, and make an honest marriage, blessed by God. Do you think our Maker would begrudge you that?'

Theo's frown had faded. He was breathing slowly; every breath was a sigh, as though he was near sleep. 'You are kind, to speak to me so,' he said eventually. 'I thank you for it. But you do not understand, Mr Steele. That lady you speak of – she was a virtuous girl. I heap blessings on her in my prayers. She was a local girl in Colombo, whom I saw one day when I was leaving church; hardly sixteen when I met her ... Ah, yes, you see, that puts a different complexion on things. I see that even in this poor light, your expression has changed.'

'Not at all,' said Edmund gravely.

'Well.' Theo waved one hand in the air. 'I was young too – just out of Cambridge, flushed with my purpose. I saw her, and felt the most powerful emotion I had ever felt; thought I heard the voice of God Himself speak to me. *He* had chosen my wife, not I – that is what I told myself. I pursued her; her family saw a chance in me. I was granted the liberty to become engaged to her – and I con-sidered myself quite a pilgrim, I can tell you. I came back here, as promised, to prepare a place for her and now,' he said, smiling at Edmund, 'now, here comes it, Mr Steele. All those feelings, the voice of God – they all faded. I had her likeness, which I had drawn myself. I had a lock of her hair. She had been taught to write, so I even had her words before me. But when I read those letters, I knew that our souls did not correspond at any point. When I asked questions, she did not know how to reply; and I was the same. Her words seemed hollow to me. They were the words of a stranger. And she was coming to me. I was to honour my promise. But the truth is, the worst of it is . . .' He looked down, as though his head was suddenly heavy on his neck. 'I did not want her to come. All of those feelings, so potent in the hot sun, had vanished. And I realized – on my knees, in this church – that all I had felt was lust. I! Always so pure, always so quick to examine my own heart. And when her ship foundered, and I knew she was dead, do you know what I felt?'

He leaned forwards, his eyes glinting in the light from the oil lamp.

'Relief,' he said. 'Just that – pure relief. Relief that she was dead, and that I would not have to live out a lifetime with her.' He curved his hand around the empty glass; Edmund did not reach for the decanter to refill it. 'Now, man of the world as you are, tell me what I deserve.'

Edmund wondered if Theo really did expect words of punishment. It seemed the man was punishing himself enough already. Edmund thought he could only speak to him in the language he would understand. 'Forgiveness,' he said. 'That is what you deserve, and if you ask for it, you will receive it – is that not what you tell your flock every day?'

Theo shook his head. Edmund saw the distress as it came into his face, pushing out the exasperation and frustration written across his features.

'I am in the darkness,' he said. 'I have prayed on it, these past few weeks. I have meditated on the storm within me. And there is no light, Edmund.' He looked up, and there was a shine to his eyes. 'I am guilty. I can almost touch the fires of hell. God will not speak to me. I cannot make the wrong decision, again. I have seen the hurt that it causes. I cannot step further away from God and His purpose for me. But He has not deserted me. I must wait. I must wait – and word will come, I know.'

He stayed still. They sat together in silence. At length, Edmund rose and took up one of the lamps. 'I wish you good night,' he said, and walked towards the door. He was reaching for the handle when he heard Theo say his name.

'I have lost her, haven't I?' he said.

Edmund knew he was asking for the truth. 'I think so,' he said.

He went out of the door and closed it quietly behind him, holding up the lamp as he looked down the hallway. By its dull light, he saw the closed study door and decided that its mystery had troubled him too long. He walked silently down the tiled hall, then opened the door, turning the doorknob slowly so as to make his entrance as quiet as possible. He saw first on the wall the drawing of Saint Sebastian, an image of holy suffering, which had alerted him to Theo's particular melancholy. He took a breath, preparing himself for what he imagined: neatness, order, sterility. Perhaps walls full of pinned butterflies, or collected sea grasses. A place where Theo could nurture the coldness he felt was necessary to deal with others.

In that moment, the door hit an obstruction and refused to move any further. Alert to every sound, Edmund edged his way around it and angled the lamp to cast some light on the room. It was then he saw how wrong he had been.

He could barely see Theo's desk. It was obscured with piles of paper and newspapers. The whole room was filled to its corners and half its height with books, newspapers and religious tracts. Piles had been made, and fallen over; the only space on the floor was a small pathway to the desk. There was no order; only clutter and chaos. The sickly-sweet smell of rotting food assailed Edmund; he stepped back out of the room and closed the door. As he turned, he caught sight of Theo, standing in the hallway, in the light from the drawing-room doorway.

'I didn't want you to see that,' he said.

Edmund caught his breath; felt his heart pounding in his chest. 'I am your friend,' he said. 'There has been a crisis, but you will come through it. Believe me, Theo.'

Theo leaned against the door. 'They sent you for me, didn't they?' he said. 'That's why Mr Venning sent you here. My family think I am mad, don't they?'

'No,' said Edmund. 'No, they do not. But you are struggling with some great weight on your soul.' He came forwards. 'We are all of us haunted in our way, Theo.'

Theo looked at him, a glassy quality to his gaze. 'You should be here on a winter's night,' he said, 'when the weather is all around, so it feels as though it has the house in its grip. I can hear the sea from here, its roar and its fury, hear the rain hard against the windowpane, the gale in the trees. I almost imagine myself at sea – with *her*.'

'Some believe,' said Edmund, 'that if you speak of such things, it offers the mind relief. That you can relearn how to think of the past. I have seen it. Will you speak to me of it?'

Theo nodded, his head low. 'Very well,' he said.

CHAPTER TWENTY-THREE

I often think of the conversation in the parsonage kitchen, when all the strength I had built over a decade dissolved in an instant; an illusion. I felt desolation – and I saw it in the eyes of he who spoke with me, too. I took no pride in it. I saw that he could only think of me as someone wicked; that it was his way of defending himself from whatever, unnameable feeling he had for me. Mr Steele said it was love; I do not think it was, not then. We were so far from loving each other in that moment, that I cannot think of what it would have taken to bring us together; an act of God, perhaps. Our clash, that day, was like the warning reverberation of the cannon they fired from the lightships at the Sands when a ship foundered, causing everyone to spring up and look at each other, and say: 'Is it a wreck? Is it a wreck?' In his goodness, Mr Steele saw that as the precursor to love. But I believed, in that moment, that we would have made each other miserable; that whatever tied us together would have destroyed our peace. It was why we drew together then sprang apart so often during that summer. We were frightened of our desires, and of what their consequences might be.

As a child, Delphine had been told of the curative properties of sleep by her governess. Often, she had allowed herself to succumb to sleep simply out of this long-engrained lesson; that the mind would be washed clean of all its cares in beautiful oblivion. This morning there was only a moment before the events of the day before tumbled over in her mind – and the remembrance of them was like a flame approaching paper, and drying everything up in its path the moment before it burned.

She heard movement downstairs, went down quickly and discovered Julia at the window of the parlour, her hair loose around her shoulders. When Delphine came in she turned, and looked a little ashamed.

'Mr Steele won't call just yet,' said Delphine, with a faint smile.

'Martha has not come this morning,' Julia replied.

'I wouldn't expect to see her again,' said Delphine. 'I think, perhaps, she believes that we have brought bad luck with us. We had a good few months here, my dear. We will be gone soon.'

They decided to stay in that morning. Delphine built up the fire and Julia made the breakfast. It was half past eleven, and they were both reading when they heard the sound of the gate opening. However, before Julia could even look out of the window, there was a sharp rapping at the door. She ran and opened it.

'My dear,' said Edmund. 'May I come in, briefly?' He was in the parlour in two steps, and both women fell silent at the signs of strain on his face.

'You must excuse me this morning,' he said. 'I cannot stay. I came to tell you why Martha has not come to you. Her niece – Sarah – she cannot be found.'

'Has anyone been to Polly?' said Julia.

'Polly has been with her family all night,' said Edmund. 'They gave her laudanum so that she might sleep; it is nothing to do with her. I doubted it anyway, but now it is certain.'

'Oh, dear God,' said Delphine, sitting down suddenly. 'Can we do anything?'

'Stay in,' said Edmund. 'I am sorry to say it, but there is bad feeling in the town at the moment – very bad feeling. Towards Dr Crisp for not noting the other deaths as suspicious, and towards the strangers in the town – especially you, I regret to say, though it is best you know. I will be searching for the girl with Mr Hallam.' His eyes dipped at the mention of the priest's name. 'We do not have time to speak of it now, but I hope that the breach between you can be healed. I must go, now. We will head towards Kingsgate. I have hope that she may be found; that this is not a case like the others. But stay in. Do not answer the door.' The tenderness in his eyes as he looked at Julia filled Delphine with joy, even in that dark moment.

'I am not afraid,' said Delphine.

'Put aside your courage, just for today,' he said, and, with a bow, departed.

Delphine waited for people to halt outside their front gate, for carts and carriages to slow. In the end it became too much for Julia, who went to her room, saying she wanted to be quiet. So when a knock came at the door, it was Delphine who went to answer it, without hesitation despite Edmund's words.

On the step she found Mr Benedict, his gloves in his hand, dressed more neatly than she had ever seen him; in his black coat and grey waistcoat he looked more like a clerk than an artist. He raised his hat. She did not open the door any wider, but looked at him warily, allowing all the dislike she felt for him to stain her expression.

'A word,' he said. 'That is all – about the missing girl. I had come back to see Gorsey, to try and make amends – of course he will not see me. I went to the beach and one of the boatmen told me.'

'You should have left when you were told to,' Delphine said. 'I would not have opened the door, had I known it was you.' She moved to close it, but he put his foot in the door: one shining black boot. She wondered who had shone it – some maid in a Ramsgate villa?

'I am aware of what you think of me,' he said, 'but I believe I know who is behind this all. While the others are busy shunning me, you may be able to do something about this. Please.'

Glancing around, she let him in. As he walked into the

parlour, she regretted it; found even the curve of his shoulders, and the glossy length of black hair, repulsive. She did not want him to breathe the air of her cottage; he ate the oxygen. She stood by the small fireplace, her arms folded.

'Speak, then,' she said.

'I speak to you as a fellow painter,' he said, but she waved her hand in the air to indicate that he must move on, and quickly. 'Very well,' he said. 'The words were always what troubled me – MARY, and WHITE, *White as snow* – they were so precisely drawn into the sand, with such care. I did not know what it was that disturbed me so much about it, only that there was something which kept troubling my mind. It came to me this morning, as clear as the bell at Ramsgate which announces the arrival of the London newspapers. Whoever did this was *signing their name*. They are an artist, and they were signing their picture. The "white as snow" is merely a play on that.'

Delphine felt cold. 'I hardly see how,' she said. 'The *Mary White* is the lifeboat; before that it was a ship. Are you saying someone from the crew is involved?'

'No,' said Benedict. 'That is, I might have thought so – but Bessie Dalton said it was a lady who had done this, and all along these crimes seemed strange – committed with softness rather than brute force. The *Mary White* is coincidence, that is all. It was this morning when I remembered a conversation I had with Miss Peters some weeks ago. If you remember, she always said she liked word games. I asked her about her name, Albertine, and said what a fine coincidence it was that it resembled that of the

Prince Consort. She laughed in a very forced way and said that she had been rechristened by the family who had taken her in; renamed entirely, to escape her past – and her parentage.'

'And much capital you made out of it,' said Delphine. 'I know of the offer you made her – that you did it in such a way disgusts me.'

'What offer?' he said, and his face was full of astonishment.

'She said that you wished her to model for you. That you would paint her, and make her the toast of London.'

He shook his head. 'I may have said something of that sort, in jest. I wrote her a stupid note, once – under the influence of too much claret, mixed with medicine – and told her she was beautiful and would be fêted if the world ever recognized it. But I never made her an offer.'

Delphine tried to reconcile the certainty of Alba's words during their discussion in Reculver with the artist's astonished expression. 'She is an innocent young woman, with a strong imagination,' she said. 'With your loose tongue it is not surprising that she misunderstood.'

'Let us return to my point, Mrs Beck,' said Benedict. 'I was astonished that she should admit to the adoption, to point out, so cheerfully, her lower status and class, and make it clear she was not from a respectable background. I had a kind of feeling she was trying to draw my attention, and my pity – and this, combined with her evident effort to attract Mr Hallam also, gave me a slight suspicion of her. It was that which remained in my memory, and then I remembered this morning how she said: "I was but plain Mary, and I was found here. I used to pretend I was secretly from a rich local family."' He looked at Delphine, then continued urgently: 'I would warrant she wished her second name was White. It may be that she was an illegitimate child of the White family, who have built ships here for generations. Either way, that does not matter. What does matter is who she is now. Search your memory, Mrs Beck. She would have been free to see those girls; she even met one of them. Have you seen her, this morning? I went to the Albion Hotel, and though Gorsey would not speak to me I heard from one of his servants that she was not at breakfast. It is her we should be looking for.'

Delphine stood there and stared at him. He seemed agitated, and in earnest. But her reticence showed in her face, and she turned away, trying to think clearly, beyond his gaze.

'We are running out of time,' he said impatiently, rising to his feet.

'You can hardly blame me for giving a second thought to such a wild accusation,' she said.

'I know what it is,' he said. 'After everything with that wretched Polly girl, you think I am not to be trusted; not a single word of mine is to be given any weight.'

'That wretched girl?' said Delphine. 'You may be the father of her child. You trusted her enough to tell her everything you knew of me.'

He flinched. 'I had drunk too much champagne that

night,' he said. 'I apologize, unreservedly. My judgement is poor sometimes. I do not wish you to think ill of me.'

'Too late,' she said.

'You should still listen to me,' he said. 'Whatever else has passed between us, a child is in danger and Miss Peters is behind it all.'

She doubted almost everything he had said, but she knew she could not take the risk. She nodded at him, then went to the hallway and called for her cousin, tying on her bonnet as she did so.

CHAPTER TWENTY-FOUR

If I had my way, I would have been gone, never to see my summer companions again. I longed for the rattle of the coach on the road, for the looking-forward to our London house, for new scenery and sounds, and a way of forgetting. It was the search for Sarah that drew us all together again. And in those last days of summer I see, now, the seeds of the knowledge of what I wanted. I can confess it now: despite everything, I wanted you.

Delphine, Julia and Benedict found Edmund and Theo at Stone Bay. They had hailed a cart to take them along the coast road, and it was Julia who had spotted their horses tethered at the gap in the cliffs.

The two men were on the sands, walking fast, calling Sarah's name disconsolately. There had been no sighting of the girl, no glimpse of the checked blue and white dress she was wearing. There was no trace of her.

It was Delphine who explained the painter's thoughts, whilst Mr Benedict waited silently, pale, his hands clasped together, his head lowered in penitence. Julia stood beside him, and Delphine knew her cousin's presence added a gravitas to their small group, even in the eyes of Theo, who never met her gaze with his own, only kept it on the horizon, the wide brim of his straw hat pulled low.

'There may be something in it,' said Edmund, when Delphine had finished. 'Either way, we have no other route of enquiry. And it has a certain terrible logic to it.' He plucked at Theo's sleeve. 'Theo? What do you think?'

'I don't believe it. But I think we must find Miss Albertine,' said Theo. 'That will end our suspicions. Meanwhile, you should stay here and carry on looking for Sarah, in case you are wrong. We should not waste any time. Have you tried at the Albion?'

'Of course,' said Delphine, trying to stay calm. 'We went there to check, before coming to find you. She is not there; we went with one of Mr Gorsey's servants and he knocked on the door. Miss Waring was resting in the room, but said that Alba had gone out early and that she hadn't seen her since. She seemed disorientated, as though she had been drugged.'

'You did not trouble Mrs Quillian with all of this?' Theo demanded, pulling on his riding gloves.

'Credit me with some sense,' said Delphine.

'Very well,' said Theo. 'Then I must look for her else-where.'

'You should go to Northdown House first,' said Julia. Everyone turned and looked at her. She was wearing her veil, close to her face. 'Do you not remember, Della? When we were first introduced, Miss Waring said they had vis-ited there, and that Alba loved it. I would try there first.'

Theo nodded to Julia, and the company; he seemed unable to speak and Delphine itched to say to him that he should unstick his tongue and voice his opinions, if he wished. She watched him as he strode away, his riding whip swinging in one hand.

'That was well done, Mrs Beck,' said Benedict. 'I knew you would make him listen.'

'God help that child,' said Delphine. She left them there, the little circle of Benedict, Edmund and Julia, and she fol-lowed Theo, gathering her dress in her hands, striding after him, up through the gap in the cliffs. Behind her she heard Edmund calling for Sarah again, and she blessed him for leading his followers on in a search. Try as she might, she could not keep up with Theo. He seemed to be moving with a fury, as though he knew he was pursued. Yet he did not look back. He untethered his horse, and it was in this moment that she caught up with him – but something drew her up, six yards or so before she reached him. She had nothing to say to him, she realized: nothing that could matter in this moment, when they were search-ing for poor Martha's niece, the little girl Delphine had drawn out of the road on some distant Sunday.

She stepped back as he put one foot in the stirrup of his saddle, and drew himself up and on to the horse's back in one smooth, athletic movement. He, who had always seemed so confined, so drawn in and contained by his prayer and stillness, was a man of flesh and blood; had limbs with a strange, wiry strength which seemed foreign to her knowledge of him. He drew the horse's head round strongly but without savagery; as it turned he turned too and met her eyes for the first time that day.

'Forgive me,' he said. Then he rode on.

The horse crossed the road at a trot, Theo looking this way and that, went past the lighthouse and as soon as the horse's hooves hit farmland he loosened his reins and drove it on with his heels, his right hand raised so the horse could see the whip in it. A trot, a canter – and then he was galloping, galloping away from her. Straight across the shorn field, the horse's chestnut flanks glistening in the pale light of the dying summer.

As he rode, the thunder of hooves in his ears, the land passing by in a blur, Theo tried to focus on the task in hand and not allow his mind to dwell on Delphine. It would be in such a moment, he knew, that he would let his horse catch its foot in a rabbit-hole; be caught unawares when it was spooked by something . . . and then he would take a fall, and hit his head, and end his life. Because of a lack of discipline; because he did not trust his Lord.

He rode partly across the farmland, partly along the road, and when he came to Northdown House and turned down its long drive, bordered by dense foliage, he noted that the house seemed unkempt. It was often rented out, he knew, and he was aware that the family Albertine had visited had left suddenly a few weeks before, so might still be paying for the place, but without interest in its upkeep. He rode into the courtyard; no one appeared from the stables to take his horse.

'Hello?' he called, and the words reverberated around the courtyard. He dismounted, led his horse to the wall and tethered it. He then went to the front door and, polite as always, pulled the bell. He heard it jangling in the depths of the house; no one came. Something drew him on; the certainty that she was in there somewhere crept over him. He pushed the front door, and it opened.

The entrance hall was clean, but empty of furniture. There was a picture or two on the walls, but the place seemed uninhabited, and there was an oval on the wall where the papers were more intensely coloured, as though a painting or mirror had been removed. 'Hello?' he called again; went to the first door, and opened it.

The room was swathed in dust sheets, apart from two chairs, covered in striped silk. Theo froze in the doorway, his hand still on the doorknob. Alba had clearly been sitting in one of the chairs; she had risen to her feet at the sight of him.

'Mr Hallam?' she said. She seemed surprised, but not afraid. 'What are you doing here?'

'Looking for you,' he said. When he saw joy dawn on her face, he knew he had been misunderstood. 'Another child is missing,' he said, then stopped. How was he to tell her that she was suspected of taking her?

'I am just visiting Mrs Appleton, the housekeeper,' said Alba. 'The gardener brought me here in his cart. She is in the kitchen, making tea. She is a little deaf, I'm afraid, and will be surprised to see you. I like to look in on her while the family is away. I did tell my aunt – is she worried? Mr Hallam – are you well? You look pale.'

'I am perfectly well,' he said.

Edmund was still calling for Sarah, trailed by Delphine, Julia and Benedict, when they saw a figure appear from the direction of Main Bay. In a few moments they picked out the shape of Dr Crisp, and saw that he was waving his arms.

'They've found her,' he said, when he eventually reached them. He had taken his jacket off, and his shirt was soaked through with sweat, his neckcloth undone at his throat. 'She is safe and well. After everything that has happened, I almost believed ...' His expression cracked with the strain, fear breaking through.

Edmund went to him and patted him hard on the shoulder. 'She is safe?' he asked.

The doctor nodded. 'Yes.' He looked at Edmund, narrowing his eyes in the sun. 'I am so relieved. I was shying at shadows when I was searching, so terrified was I that I would find her, and not ...' He seemed to suddenly become aware of the ladies present. His eyes met Edmund's again, and they settled on the word between them: *alive.*

The only difference in Sarah from when her mother had seen her that morning was that her face was now freckled, for she had declared that she wished to be as brown as a hoveller and had long cast her hat aside. It was Solomon who had found her, curled up in the shade of an unused bathing machine. He had woken her, then carried her, sleepy and rubbing her eyes, out to Mr Gorsey, at which point her mother had been sent for. When Anna ran to her, sobbing, her breath catching in her throat, the little girl said petulantly, still rubbing sleep from her eyes, 'You are crying again, Mama. I wish you had let me sleep longer. You are always watching me. I wished to be on my own.'

Anna could say nothing; she only wept. It was Sarah's aunt, Martha, who crouched down beside her, touched her face with her large, workworn hand and said, with all the tenderness of those who would die for the ones they love, 'Oh, my dearest, we were so worried about you. Please don't do that again.'

'Very well, Auntie,' said Sarah.

When Theo appeared, bringing news of Alba and her innocence, Mr Benedict insisted that questions be asked about the earlier deaths.

'We have had enough trouble for today,' Theo said firmly. 'You have been reading too many novels, Mr Benedict. I abhor you for even mentioning Miss Peters's background. I do not intend to question her any further. You are lucky that I did not explain the accusations you had made against her. At the sight of her, I knew how unfounded they were. I can hardly fathom, Mrs Beck, how you could have encouraged him in this malicious suggestion.'

'Theo.' Edmund's voice warned him. The clergyman whipped his boot.

'I thank you for defending me, Mr Steele,' said Delphine, 'but I lost Mr Hallam's good opinion long ago.'

'Let us thank our God that we can put these ridiculous thoughts behind us,' said Theo.

Delphine looked at Mr Benedict, and he at her. 'I was trying to make amends,' he said. 'Perhaps I went too far – I have been accused of it before. Do not blame Mrs Beck.' He raised his hat. Across the expanse of wet sand he went.

The group took tea in the Albion, speaking little, drained of their energy and conversation, which was kept buoyed up by Mrs Quillian. She looked noticeably relieved at the sight of Miss Waring and Alba crossing the floor to join them.

'Good afternoon,' said Miss Waring. 'Heroes, I understand – Mr Steele, Mr Hallam.' Alba followed shyly behind. Delphine, sipping her cold tea, noticed that marked shyness, as though Alba had regressed to her earlier role, and wondered whether the girl had really grasped the implications of what had happened that day. She guessed not, for she looked happy, and was blushing. She was dressed in a gown Delphine had never seen before, pale pink, edged with lace; her face framed by a dark blue bonnet. For the first time, she was groomed in a particular, layered way, as though her youth had been tied up and bound. Still, she looked happy, and her eyes darted skittishly over the group.

'Miss Alba,' said Delphine, as the gentlemen rose and Edmund moved to bring extra chairs. 'Why do you not come and sit with me?'

Alba looked over them all, glanced at her aunt, at Theo, then laughed. Still, when Mr Steele put the chair down she did draw it near to Delphine.

Miss Waring took a seat too, giving the company a tender smile. Edmund signalled for more tea.

'I am glad this day has ended well,' Miss Waring said, 'indeed I am. I would not wish such a beautiful day to be overshadowed by terrible tragedy, but as all is well, so I said to Alba, let us come and see our friends, and be glad.'

'I am thankful that the little one is home,' said Mrs Quillian. 'I cannot help but think that those other deaths were accidental – but you can hardly wonder that the town is on edge.'

Delphine turned to look out of the window. Her spirits were too dull to disagree and remind Mrs Quillian that she had not been on the beach the day that Bessie Dalton had nearly died, and seen the terror in the faces of the Dalton children.

'As I say, we are grateful for the happy conclusion of events,' said Miss Waring, and there was a slight sense of reproof in her voice, for she had been interrupted. 'And Alba is grateful that Mr Hallam came to bring her from Northdown.'

Delphine's gaze darted to Miss Waring's face. Her little eyes were shining, and her lips were curved upwards in a bright smile, so that Delphine for the first time could almost see the young woman Miss Waring had once been. Then she followed the woman's gaze. She was looking at Theo's face.

He was, she thought, the same Theo, the clergyman, though his eyes were not alight. Then he licked his lips, and she noted that his hand had frozen, in the handle of his teacup, but he was not raising it. She sensed his nerves, saw the slight crease in the centre of his brow and looked closely at him, as closely as he would study one of his grass samples under magnification, her mind suddenly trying to describe him, as he was, in this one moment.

As she looked at him Delphine felt Alba's cold hand enclose her own, and she was reminded of that morning in the inn at Reculver, that cloying, cold, babyish hand which refused to let go of hers. She looked at Alba, at the beautiful face, the unalloyed cheer of her expression, and wondered why she had ever thought they were alike. But she fought this feeling, recognizing even in that moment that it was only jealousy; an emotion she had thought dead in her.

'He was so gentlemanly,' Alba whispered to her as the others conversed, 'when he came to Northdown, when he found me. He waited with me, and rode alongside the cart all the way back, and saw me into the hotel with many gentle words. I see now, all along, how he has wished to protect me, to shield me from difficulties. He has not yet declared himself, but – I believe, all will be well, Mrs Beck, as you told me it would be. His words were almost a declaration.'

Delphine did not blush or faint, or do anything other than sit where she was, straight-backed, her black dress spread out around her. Julia joined in the conversation in an animated fashion and, as she spoke, briefly touched her cousin's hand. Delphine was grateful. She knew that Julia had heard, and was shielding her, but in a moment she too found her voice and was able to say, with perfect feeling and correctness, what was right, what was expected of her.

CHAPTER TWENTY-FIVE

How the English amuse me, with their great gift of politeness. Their smoothing over, with silence. I had thought politeness a tyranny, another bar in the cage that kept us confined, but in fact it served to heal. Mr Steele begged that we might stay a few weeks, saying that things would calm down if I would only stay off the beach in the mornings. He did not wish to be parted from Julia, and he felt an obligation to stay at the parsonage a while longer. What the content of that obligation was, I did not know. Word came that Mr Benedict had settled a cottage and a pension on Polly Gorsey; no one mentioned the matter again, and though Miss Waring expressed, with great conviction, her low opinion of him, Mrs Quillian received him one day for tea – though not at the Albion – so it appeared he was forgiven.

Like the sand-sifters in the evening, searching for valuables left on the beach, so we scoured the landscape for some pleasure in our last days there.

'I haven't seen you for a good long time,' Solomon said.

Delphine smiled, and drew on her cigarette. It was early morning, and the bay lay, peaceful and calm, beneath the cool white of an autumn sky.

'I have come to say farewell,' she said. 'We are engaged to watch you all sail, at the Ramsgate Regatta, and then we will be leaving immediately afterwards.'

'It's best for you,' he said. 'I'm sorry you've had trouble. You only need to be a little different here, madam, and for one voice to pick you out, and then . . .' He gave an expansive gesture.

'There is no need to worry for me, Solomon. I wanted to bid you farewell, and see the bay one more time.'

'But not to paint it?' he said, kicking at a piece of seaweed with his booted foot.

'No,' she said. 'Not to paint it.'

The trunks were packed, the house in London empty and waiting for them. Mrs Quillian had arranged the trip to the Regatta, mentioning cheerfully that they would meet Mr Benedict and his wife there, as though the Gorsey incident had never happened. Delphine wished to leave, but she could not deny Julia one last day with Edmund, for he had promised to stay with Theo until the end of October, when he would return to London for the wedding.

It was like old times. Mr Hallam and Mr Steele rode

alongside the carriage which carried the ladies. Delphine could not help but notice that Alba did not look at Mr Hallam as he rode; her eyes were not drawn to him at all. She was the same old Alba, her face against the window, staring out at everything and nothing, occasionally responding to her aunt. But there was no more reading from guidebooks. It seemed certain that the clergyman would ask for her hand before the end of the season, so her great effort was over.

It was with some misgiving that Delphine looked from the window down the long sweep of the road to the harbour, at the grand marina of Ramsgate below, crowded with ships, their coloured flags flying in celebration, and the light sparkling on the water.

'It is very different from Broadstairs,' said Julia. 'How fine it looks, how crowded and busy, almost as though it is ready for a carnival.'

'Perhaps we should have come here for the season,' said Delphine, earning hurt looks from Mrs Quillian and, briefly, Alba.

Perhaps, she thought, I would have been friends with poor Mrs Benedict, herding her children along the beach. Perhaps I would have painted different scenes. Those girls' deaths would have been distant things; I would not have even heard of them.

Mr Benedict greeted them at the Custom House, and Delphine wondered how long he had been waiting for them. Mrs Quillian went to him first, and shook his hand.

He looked dapper and neat, clerkish in the way he had that last time she had seen him, and he was not wearing any of the jewels or flamboyant scarves he had favoured at Broadstairs. His hair was still long, of course, but other than that he was simply a respectable wealthy gentleman. His wife, her hand resting lightly on his arm, received each person graciously. She was, Delphine thought, painfully beautiful, with blonde hair, pale blue eyes and a delicate, aquiline nose – but her features held their beauty because they had a certain sweetness and other-worldliness.

She longed all at once to pay obeisance to Mrs Benedict, and to punish Mr Benedict, who had always cast his family to be such a burden – if not directly, then with many implied words and looks. But despite the children that crowded around her, Mrs Benedict was slim, graceful, and had nothing but kind words for the people to whom she was introduced. Five years before, Delphine thought, she would have put Alba into the shade, and indeed the girl seemed suddenly shy in the presence of this elegant woman, who let no shadow of suspicion fall across her beautiful features when Mr Benedict greeted Alba with wariness.

They walked along the harbour arm, remarking on the beauty of the boats and the stillness of the water, and Delphine found herself suddenly alongside Mr Benedict, who offered her his arm. She took it, because in that moment she could think of no way to refuse it. As they walked she saw him tip his chin up to the sun, luxuriating in it like a sunflower, this sensual man, and she felt the sadness of envy curl in her stomach. The ribbons on her bonnet caught in the breeze and rippled and danced like the sails of the boats in the harbour.

'I am not forgiven, even now?' he said softly.

She said nothing.

'I am sorry for speaking to Polly about your past,' he said. 'It was an error in judgement, but you have misunderstood me if you ever think I meant to cause you harm. I am a little over-dramatic, when I am spurned. You and I are alike – no, I do not jest with you. There is something of the same spirit about us, I think, and we both express it through painting. I said as much to Emma last night.' He glanced over his shoulder at his wife, caught her eye and smiled. Delphine turned and saw his wife smiling back at him – not innocently, but with a kind of knowing that spoke of the intimacy of marriage. Benedict continued.

'I thought, from that first moment, that you and I are both looking for purity in a world which is not pure. When I discovered, as a very young child, that I had a rare facility with the pencil and the brush, do you think in that same moment of joy, I learned how to flatter and charm? I did not. I pursued only my gift at drawing and painting, and with a wolf-like energy which, even now, I still wonder at. Like you, I did it for the joy of it. The moments when I saw something – a turn in the light, an expression on someone's face – I became enfolded in the curiosity of that moment, and sought to capture it.

'I have made compromises to become what I am now. I paint what the public wishes to see, and I am mocked for it – but one must live, mustn't one? And one must have money to live. I have taken this route, and there is nothing I can do now. "Conventional" – how you wounded me when you said that, perhaps all the more so because it is true, and refers to my painting as well as my life. I have tamed my art, to make it palatable. Despite my mocking of Mr Hallam, I am no more a true follower of Turner than he is. Yet when I remember leaning over my sketchbook as a child, a piece of chalk clutched in my chubby fingers, it turns something like a key in my breast. Nothing in my life has ever come close to those moments. I still seek it, though, and sometimes in the worst places – seeking sensation after sensation, as though that might surprise me again.'

They drew up. Ahead, Alba was remarking on a colourful craft, pointing the details out to Mr Hallam and her aunt.

'I do not want to listen to your excuses for ruining people,' Delphine said. 'You repeated rumours about me, when you did not know the truth.'

'Oh, I am past excuses, Miss Sears,' he said, and the use of her real name made Delphine's heart jump in her chest. 'I think Amy is a pretty name,' he went on. 'I remember that day, long ago, when Miss De Witt fainted at the sound of it – the name of the dead girl, Amy Phelps. Did she think you had been found out?'

Delphine looked at him coolly.

'I wish I did know your story,' he said. 'I will not harm you, for not telling me. I am only trying to get your attention, to make you see the truth. For all my courting of convention, the truth is I will never be accepted, not really. When I went to the Royal Academy, saw all the grand gentlemen grouped together – did you believe that was easy? You think me a proper swell now, don't you? Easy in my words and manners. But then it was forced. And the real Ralph Benedict remains within me – an outsider, like you. I am sorry for wounding you. My darling!'

A child had come barrelling out of the group, a little girl in a white dress, running at him, her arms outstretched. Mr Benedict caught her up and swung her around. They were both laughing, and Delphine saw that some of the onlookers thought them vulgar.

'This is my best girl,' said Mr Benedict to Delphine. 'This is my Daisy. Does she not look like her mother?'

Delphine managed a weak smile for the little girl. 'She does,' she said. And Daisy smiled at her with perfect confidence, utterly secure in her father's arms.

Only a week before, Mr Benedict told them, the boatmen had been dragging in the carcasses of over a hundred dead sheep, drowned in a wreck, for which they had the right of salvage. But now such a scene was unimaginable, the sea glittering with sunlight as the boats bobbed in the harbour, the boatmen brown-faced and smart in their best clothes. There was the smell of burnt sugar and the salty sea breeze; there was colour all around, and talk of fireworks, later.

The group took lemonade on the harbour arm, a long,

picturesque walk built of grey stone, and when Julia tucked her hand in the crook of her cousin's arm and bade her stop, Delphine framed the view with her hand. 'It is so beautiful,' she said, 'but I will not be sorry to leave, I admit. And neither will you, my dear – for you have your new life ahead of you.'

She could see Julia's pensive expression beneath her veil, and continued, wanting to rouse her into happiness. 'I am so glad for you,' she said. 'I cannot tell you how full my heart is at the thought that you have found joy. You should never think otherwise, you know. I am truly happy for you.'

'I must ask something of you,' said Julia, so softly that her words were almost carried away by the sea breeze.

'Anything,' said Delphine, savouring the bitter sweetness of the lemonade on her tongue.

'That you listen to what I have to say, and once I have said it, you let me return to Mr Steele's table; and that you will think on what I have said before you make any judgement, for it will have a bearing on our future relations with each other,' said Julia.

The smile faded a little on Delphine's face.

'I did not wish to spoil today,' said Julia, 'but I cannot bear to speak to you in the cottage, where we have been so happy in our quiet moments together, and I have, for weeks, been trying to find a way to tell you what I have to say. I have spoken to Mr Steele of it, and he agrees with me that I can only begin my new life with my old one quite clear of all its debts. I have lived in the shadow of this too long. Now I must speak to you, before my courage fails me.'

She tugged on Delphine's arm and led her a little way from the group, to a bench where they sat down together. Julia pulled the veil back from her face. She was wearing lilac, a colour that usually suited her and brought out her golden hair and blue eyes, but today it made her look drawn and ill, her pallor alarming once the veil had been lifted. Delphine almost exclaimed at it, but something in her cousin's expression stopped her.

'You used to ask me why I travelled with you,' Julia said. 'In truth, it was not because I was bored of life as a New York old maid, nor was I merely being dutiful to my parents. You said – when you were disgraced in New York, that night – you thought it was one of your parents' enemies who saw you speaking with that man, from their carriage, and spread the gossip. The truth is, it was not. It was me.'

Delphine let go of Julia's gloved hands. Julia continued, the words crowding from her lips.

'I had been to the theatre with Aunt Rose and I saw you from the window of her carriage, walking alone with Mr Clare. I told Mrs Moulin, the next day, when I visited her for tea, knowing full well that it would damage you.' Her voice failed; she put one hand over her mouth, as though to stifle a sob. 'I am sorry,' she whispered.

Delphine kept her gaze on the wooden slats of the bench. She felt sweat glisten on the back of her legs; it had only been a few moments, but now the sun seemed unbearably hot, the contrast of the cold sea breeze sickening to her, as though the juxtaposition of heat and cold had been designed to torture her.

'Why?' she said.

Julia took a breath, a deep, conscious breath, as though she wished to take in enough air to say all of her words in one go. 'I was jealous of you. You were fêted your whole life, sure to make one of the finest matches. Beautiful, elegant, clever. Thoughtless. And you had him – Edward Clare – hanging from your every word. I told you once I had known someone I thought I could marry. It was him. I would watch him at the parties and breakfasts; handsome, gifted, so full of confidence in the world. If I had the love of such a man, I thought it would save me. But he wanted you.

'So I told Mrs Moulin when I took tea with her the next day, and made her swear never to tell it was me. But even as I walked out of her house, I regretted it. There was no taking it back, however. I would ask you to believe me when I say that I had no real idea of how bad it would be; how comprehensively you would be disgraced. I did not know that Clare would turn against you, too.'

'I rejected him that night,' said Delphine.

'I know,' said Julia.

'That is why he said what he did. Telling our family that I had asked for the meeting, that I had begged for an elopement. And the gossip spread fast; the number of callers dwindled to nothing. My mother would sit and wait, the tea-table set, and no one would come. Father kept himself to the office, but our grandfather – he could not look at me; he would not listen. He said that I had disgraced the family, that it would have been better if I had died.'

'I know,' Julia said again.

'Of course you do,' said Delphine. 'Because I have told you it again and again as we travelled – on mountain ranges, high seas, across continents – and yet you never thought to say – to mention – that you helped to destroy my life?'

'I truly did not know what the consequences would be,' said Julia, her voice wavering a little. 'There was a whole storehouse of jealousy towards you in our New York circle which was waiting to be ignited like gunpowder. A woman can be clever, or elegant, or beautiful: she cannot be all three. And you were; you were. I made a mistake that could never be undone. When you made arrangements to go, when that became necessary, I knew then that I should go with you, to serve you and protect you as best I could. I owed you that.'

Delphine raised her hand to silence her. She felt numb, and was grateful for it. The two women sat in silence, side by side, the whole world of the seaside moving around them, the sights and smells and sounds a world away from where they were in their minds; the large rooms of a New York mansion.

After a few moments, Delphine could bear it no more. 'Please go,' she said.

'I am sorry,' said Julia. She leaned over and kissed

Delphine lightly on the cheek. Then she quietly rose, flattened down her skirts and walked back to where Edmund Steele was sitting, watching them.

That afternoon, the hovellers raced each other in their luggers, in a sailing match that was watched with much joy by the spectators, excepting Delphine, who managed to keep herself a little way apart from them. Whenever Alba tapped her, and pointed out one of the boats – 'Look, Mrs Beck, it's the *Petrel* from Broadstairs!' – she would nod, and she soon learned that was enough to satisfy Alba, or anyone else who spoke. Julia kept away, leaning on Mr Steele's arm, and if Delphine ever looked, she saw that her cousin's head was lowered and her gaze bent downwards, so different from her normal, graceful carriage.

The boats were abreast for many miles, so that the crowd whipped itself up into a high pitch of excitement – those who cared, who were not looking about for different entertainment – and Mr Benedict remarked that the Broadstairs hovellers were doing so well on account of all the butter they had salvaged from another recent wreck, earning a reproving look from his wife. In the end the *Petrel*, sailed by Joseph Miller, came third and the *Fame* came fifth, its yellow flag fluttering in the wind.

As the cheers rose in the crowd, Delphine walked away, weaving through some of those standing at the harbourside, and found a bench where there was a space to sit down. Her head was weighted with a heavy ache, as though the air itself was pressing down on her skull. She tried not to draw attention to herself but sat upright, with a fixed expression, attempting to look pleased at the outcome of the race. After a moment the pain was too much and she pressed her fingers to her brow. When she looked up, Theo was standing there, having emerged from the crowd. He looked awkward, leaning on his stick, as though he was actively thinking how to stand. 'Miss Alba said you looked unwell,' he announced, a little too loudly and formally. 'But she wanted you to know the *Little Western* will be arriving soon.'

'You may go back to the group,' she said. She glanced at the couple next to her on the bench – a gaily dressed local girl with her swain. They had been laughing and talking about the race, but Theo's appearance had silenced them.

'Go,' repeated Delphine. 'I will return directly.' She made to rise, and he looked as though he might turn away, when there was an immense noise – the firing of one of the cannons on the harbour. It drew cries of delight from the crowds, but neither Delphine nor Theo acted so. She flinched, violently, and sat back down suddenly on the bench, overwhelmed with a burst of pain in her head, and he moved to her side in a moment, dropping his cane as he did so. The girl and her swain giggled, glancing at each other.

'Are you ill?' He did not pick up the cane, only stood over her, his shadow over the back of her neck. 'Mrs Beck?' he said hesitantly. Delphine, sheltering her face with her hands, did not see his hand rise, then fall away without touching her shoulder.

She did not look up at him. 'Do not speak to me as though you are making a recitation. I have a headache, and if you come here to be Alba's envoy I would rather you did not come to me at all.'

He moved closer to her, crouched down so when she looked up, his face was improperly close, his eyes level with hers. She met his gaze; breathed in sharply, as though in pain. He could not stop himself; he reached out and took her hand. His skin was cool, hers burning hot. 'What is wrong?' he said, his voice so low only she could hear. 'Tell me.'

She looked at him. 'I do not want to see the ship,' she said. 'I sailed here from New York on the *Great Western*.' She saw her distress mirrored in his eyes. She did not take her hand from his, nor could she explain the magnitude of the memory, emphasized by Julia's words. 'It took fourteen days,' she whispered, and a single tear fell from her lashes.

'Don't lose your cane, Vicar,' dared the girl beside Delphine. Theo shook his head, as though batting away an irritant, his eyes never leaving Delphine's face.

There was the distant sound of a ship's horn; the bubbling excitement of the crowd rose. The cry went up: 'It's the *Little Western*!' and the girl beside Delphine stood up, pulling at her man's arm.

'I'd kiss her, if I were you,' called the man over his shoulder to Theo as he was led away, and Delphine heard the burst of their laughter as they merged into the crowd. She leaned back on the bench and looked up at Theo, for he had stood up again at the man's words, and picked his cane up from the ground.

'You wouldn't dare, would you?' she said, and she felt the sickly smile cross her face.

He did not look at her as he replied. 'If I began,' he said, 'I would not be able to stop. I do not know what would become of us.'

There was no time to say any more. Alba was coming for him, wanting to bring him to the edge of the harbour so that dear Mr Hallam might see the arrival of the *Little Western*, belonging to the General Steam Navigation Company. He went with her, Delphine following at a few steps' distance, and Alba, with a touch of pique in her voice, described how it had sailed from London, its decks laden with passengers and its colours flying. Salutes were fired, the great roar of gunfire thrilling the crowd.

Standing near Theo, Alba and Miss Waring, Delphine saw Alba tilt her head and smile at Theo. 'There will be fireworks this evening,' she said. 'I am so excited.'

Delphine could not bring herself to speak to anyone, to keep up the pretence of good manners any more. She prayed only that she could stay, standing upright, and that the day would soon be over.

CHAPTER TWENTY-SIX

I was unprepared for betrayal when it came, on that summer afternoon. I could have heard dark words from anyone and brushed them away – apart from she who said them. Julia, my poor Julia, carrying the weight of her guilt all those years, the knowledge that she had set fire to my life and watched it burn. As I moved through the crowds, I thought of Amy Phelps and Catherine Walters, their bodies washed clean by the sea, and I wondered if they had fought, as Bessie Dalton did, as Martha's eldest niece surely did. When I saw a woman in a veil I would examine her closely, but no one looked as though they could kill. Then I realized how hopeless it all was. Because, for those ten years we had travelled, when I looked at Julia I had seen only innocence.

We write stories for other people and yet we are blind to the truth until it hits us, as suddenly as a stranger's hand on our neck, pushing us into dark water, holding our heads under until we are finally free from the reach of cruelty.

It was past five o'clock when Delphine saw Julia's fair head bent towards Mr Steele's, and she knew her cousin was speaking to her beau with some urgency. Sure enough, Edmund came to Delphine.

'She wishes to go home to the cottage,' he said. 'She is insistent. Will you go with her? She does not wish for me.'

'No,' said Delphine. Though she had longed to go home, she knew that to be alone with Julia would be unbearable.

He returned; she heard Julia's soft voice raised anxiously, telling Edmund she wished to be alone. Felt Mr Benedict's eyes on her as she went to the front and held on to the metal railing which prevented her from falling into the harbour. Edmund spoke to the driver, asking him to return once he had taken Julia home.

The gaiety of the day had deepened. Some of the merrymakers were drunk; others tired. Squalling children were carried away to sleep off the heat and excitement. But as the daylight filtered from the sky and it darkened into night, there was a growing sense of expectation at the idea of fireworks.

'Papa,' said Daisy, 'please let me stay with you.'

She twined her hands into Mr Benedict's coat, giving the strong impression that she would hold onto her father and not let go, not at all, until he gave way to her. She insisted that she was grown up and that, this evening, everyone should call her Marguerite, her given name. She was no longer Daisy, she said.

Mrs Benedict, the children and their governess were all preparing to go; the children were tired and over-excited. Mr Benedict, of course, had to see the fireworks. He used the painter's prerogative, brushed his breast-pocket with his hand to indicate that he would be taking drawings with his pencil and sketchbook. His wife smiled faintly, indulgently.

'Please, Papa,' said Daisy again. 'I will be a good girl.'

It was clear that Mr Benedict's resistance was melting away; as with a pretty serving girl, so with his daughters, thought Delphine, the strength of her irritation surprising her. So it was that Mrs Benedict and her little troupe went off into the dusk, without a glance behind her. How strange it was to see Mr Benedict, who had often bemoaned the burden of family, watching his wife go, keeping his eyes on her until she was out of sight.

They moved through the crowds to find the best vantage point. The fireworks were to be set off from the *Little Western* in the harbour, and there was a rising sense of anticipation all along the front.

'There are so many people,' said Alba, sounding a little peevish. 'Can we not find a place to sit?' But of course Mr Benedict would have none of it; the right vantage point had to be found, and he would keep looking until it was found, so they walked until the first rocket flamed into the sky and blistered the darkness with its explosion, and Miss Waring said she would walk no longer.

Delphine looked at the sky at first, but she could find no pleasure in the sprays of light. She watched her fellow tourists, their faces lit up in the darkness by yellow then peach-coloured light, and she saw in no one an unthinking delight, save Mr Benedict, who had lifted Daisy onto his shoulders, and Mrs Quillian. These three, in tandem, oohed and aaahed; Alba did the same, but self-consciously, glancing now and then at Theo, who was feigning pleasure – a polite smile, as if he did not trust himself to let his face rest. Mr Steele enjoyed it too, but Delphine saw that he was worrying about Julia. Poor Julia, she thought sourly, who had confessed her sins but had not shed her guilt – and she felt no desire to go home and to speak to her, now that everything was changed.

Miss Waring was not enjoying it at all. 'Such a crush,' she said, after five minutes or so. 'I must find a place to sit and rest. I must also have a drink – no, do not bother yourself, Mr Hallam, I can see that you are relishing the spectacle. Mrs Quillian, will you come with me?'

Poor Mrs Quillian did not want to go, but she did. More light and sparkle flew through the air, more eruptions and cracks like gunfire. Daisy bounced and cheered, until her father lifted her down, declaring himself tired.

'You have been very quiet,' he said to Delphine. 'Are you well?'

'Perfectly,' she said. 'I've just thought, this will be the last evening we all spend together. I am trying to observe, to remember.'

He looked at her quizzically, then became aware that Daisy was not tugging at his hand or his coat.

'Daisy?' he said. A firework exploded with a spray of light. He glanced, not panicking yet, at the people around him, then looked low, trying to make out his daughter's golden head.

'Daisy? Where are you? Daisy!'

He began to push through the crowds, searching, his voice drowned out by the noise of the fireworks and the crowd's reaction.

It was Delphine who told the others; Delphine who calmed the immediate worry in Benedict's face, walking alongside him, looking too.

'All will be well,' she said, but she could see the sweat on his brow. 'She is adventurous and wilful, but a good girl – she will find the muster point.'

'Yes! The Clock House!' he said. 'We will go there. That is where she will be.'

There were rooms set up at the Clock House, for anyone who was taken unwell; and when they arrived Mr Benedict told one of the local women, who had been assisting there, what had happened.

'She is this high,' he said, 'and she has long, very long golden hair, and she is dressed in green, with a high lace bow in her hair.'

'I think I saw her,' the woman said. 'She was with a lady who said she needed to lie down.'

'Where?'

She directed them to the room. As they walked down

the hallway, they heard the delighted cries of the crowd as another firework exploded. Mr Benedict tried the door.

'It is locked,' he said. 'Daisy? Daisy!'

'It should not be locked,' said the woman. 'I will find the doctor.'

It was then that panic overtook Mr Benedict. There was no answer to the calls he made, and he began to bang on the door with his fist, then kick it. And when the woman returned and said they could not find the key, he began in earnest, working at it with his shoulder, Mr Steele and Mr Hallam with him.

When they finally broke the door open, the room was silent. The sight that met their eyes was puzzling in its domesticity. The room was lit by a single oil-lamp, flickering behind its cranberry-coloured glass shade. In the far left-hand corner of the tiny room, Daisy lay on a bed, her hair neatly combed around her face, her arms relaxed by her side. She was quite still; not the struggling, vital little presence she had been earlier. She was watched by a woman who sat with her back to the door; it was obvious that she knew they were there, for their entrance had been violent, but she did not turn. She was a familiar figure, dressed in a pale brown dress with tiny pink roses on it; tall, broad, her hands clasped in her lap, her hair drawn back neatly.

Delphine did not know how long they stood there; it seemed an eternity, but it must have been only seconds. She felt as if her mind was playing tricks on her, jumping around in this room of pink shadows, her gaze dwelling on the flickering lashes of the sleeping child; then that familiar figure. It dwelled on, and circled the question of who this woman was, for what her eyes were telling her could not be true.

It was Benedict, of course, who broke this daze that had fallen over them all. Benedict who stampeded forwards and pulled the woman round by her shoulder. And as the woman turned, Delphine saw, as though every tiny movement lasted many seconds, that she was like a puppet in one of the seafront shows the children loved. The face, lit by the pink light, was working; the lips moving in some grotesque incantation – not a prayer, she thought. Oh, God, not a prayer. Then the lips stopped moving and the woman stared hard into Benedict's face, rage blazing in her eyes.

'Do not touch me,' said Miss Waring to Mr Benedict.

The familiar face was unfamiliar; the usual softness of feature, the air of gentility – all gone, replaced by hardness, and ugliness. Even the set of the mouth at rest was different; the eyes cold, unknowable. Delphine knew, suddenly, that this was the natural face, the natural expression, of Miss Waring. She had seen hints of it, flashes of it, merely; in the moment when she had spoken of painting with Mr Benedict; in the moment she had urged purity on her niece. Tiny flashes of the disgust that now worked the features, disgust so concentrated it was painful to look upon. Even then, she thought, Why did I not see? I am a person who prides themselves on seeing everything, even secrets, even those things below the sur-

346

face. As when the sand is blown over the beach, laying a skin over it, the ghost of the real beach lies below, just visible, and the ghost outline of the real Miss Waring had been there all the time.

Benedict had passed her, had seized his daughter by the shoulders, raising her from the bed, saying her name repeatedly. Delphine was aware of Edmund turning and running into the next room, calling for a doctor.

'Oh, do not disturb her,' said Miss Waring, and she gave a little tut below her breath. 'It is too late. She has taken her medicine.' She moved forwards to look at the girl's face over Benedict's shoulder, and there was a strange kind of gentleness, even of love, in her eyes; not the social affection she had feigned on their trips and excursions for her niece and the others, but something true and felt.

'What have you done?' roared Benedict. 'What have you done to her?'

The disgust returned. 'I do not expect *you* to understand,' she said.

Delphine had dropped her reticule without realizing; she turned in horror and met Theo's eyes – and saw the same horror mirrored there.

Alba screamed, a scream such as ladies give when they are going to faint, and Theo caught her just as she fell, Delphine going to her other side. A doctor came running in, and Benedict spoke quickly of what had happened, his voice racing over what Miss Waring had said.

'An emetic,' shouted the doctor. 'Bring me Ipecac.'

As she held Alba, supporting her shoulders in her lap as

she sank to the floor, Delphine noticed that the young woman's gown smelled strongly of violet. She saw Theo relinquish Alba and glance at Daisy on the bed, as though he did not know who he should be praying for first. The doctor slapped the child and shook her, and her eyelashes began to blink. Delphine sought Theo with her eyes, and he held her gaze, held it as though he took succour from her sympathy, and they looked at each other in the reddish-darkness, looked at each other with sympathy, as though for the first time they were companions, and the past meant nothing.

Miss Waring, ignored, had stepped back, looking around her in a slightly bemused, even amused way. Alba had returned to consciousness and was sobbing, glancing at her aunt and then shielding her face with her hands.

'Oh, hush, you wretch,' said Miss Waring. 'Hush, hush.'

She turned, as though to go; but Theo barred her way.

'Why have you done this?' he said.

She tilted her head, and her expression softened. Delphine saw regard there; perhaps that was the only thing she had not faked. Her regard for the clergyman; her belief in the efficacy of prayers.

'To protect them,' she said. 'In their moment of best happiness. Before men forced themselves upon them. Before every piece of their innocence was washed away.' She was rubbing at her wrist, where Benedict had seized her.

'Why not me?' shrieked Alba. 'Why hurt them?'

'I was not hurting them,' said Miss Waring slowly, as though she was speaking to a simpleton. 'I was saving them. And I saved them because they were pure. There is nothing pure in you, Alba.' She addressed Theo. 'You astonish me, taking to her,' she said. 'Oh, it was too late for her – much too late. She is mine, you know, my daughter – and as for her father . . .' Disgust shivered across her face, and she could barely get the next words out. With another glance at Alba: 'Oh, look at you! Does that surprise you? Do you want to faint again? My daughter was born sinful, Mr Hallam, and no holy water could ever wash that away.'

It was Theo who, with a gesture only, showed Miss Waring that she was to go, to be taken to another room to await the constable. She only smiled, and looked behind her towards Daisy and said: 'You have taken your medicine well, my lamb. Taken it well.'

A few minutes later they found Mrs Quillian outside, disorientated and distressed. She had lost Miss Waring in the crowds, she said, did anyone know where she was? By that time, little Daisy had been borne from that place in her father's arms, followed by the doctor, so that her mother might hold her. She was still alive, they were told, but the next few hours would be critical. The fireworks had long since ceased, and the crowds had already ebbed away.

Alba clung to Theo's arm; she had not ceased weeping since the revelation that Miss Waring was her mother. 'I cannot believe it,' she said, her voice trembling as he spoke gently to her. Mrs Quillian, told the news by Edmund, went to the girl's other side to try and comfort her, the shock clear on her face.

'You must try to compose yourself,' Theo said. 'I know it is difficult. Would you prefer to be with Mrs Beck? She may comfort you as I cannot.'

'No,' said Alba, the tears still pouring down her face. 'I wish to be with you.'

Theo looked up; he saw the concern in Edmund's face and the desolation in Delphine's.

'The carriage will be waiting for us,' said Edmund. 'Come now, Miss Alba, it is best if we get you home. You need to rest.'

The nurse from the Clock House was coming towards them. She touched Theo's arm.

'The constable asks if you would come, sir,' said the nurse. 'He is awaiting the wagon so that he might take her away, but she says she wishes to speak to you.'

'What can she have to say to you?' cried Alba. Theo shook his head.

'You should go,' said Edmund. 'I will see the ladies home.' He caught Theo's eye. 'And I, an expert on the mind,' he said. 'I never suspected her.'

CHAPTER TWENTY-SEVEN

Miss Waring, the purest of us all, had taken those girls, the first one being Martha's niece. 'When I was younger and stronger,' so she said. 'When I did not have to give them laudanum.' And I thought of the large bag she carried, and how we always joked about her: this stern, proper woman.

Death strips every trivial thing away. That night, I went into the cottage and told Julia. I embraced her as she wept, and the thoughts I had been thinking on that endless journey home crystallized in my mind. I held her face in my hands. 'Did you only travel with me from guilt?'

'At first,' she said. 'But not now. You are as a sister to me.' And I knew that the bitterness I had tasted on the harbour arm that day should be dropped into the depths of that harbour like the other, wretched memories of that day.

We stayed only to hear that Daisy lived; then Julia and I left

*for London. Julia asked if I wished to see Theo again. I said no.
But he had cut a scar in my heart, and I only knew this when I
kept seeing him: a stranger's back on a London street, the shape
of a hat across a crowded shop. Once or twice a day, I thought I
saw him. It was as when I first left New York. I thought I saw
my mother everywhere.*

*I say 'him', but I do not know why. I have only been able to
write about that summer, about us, without admitting you are
the reader. So let me write it. Once or twice a day, I thought I
saw you, Theo.*

The constable had locked Miss Waring in a room, but she
was not trying to get out. She had sat down in a chair and
was waiting patiently when he unlocked the door and let
Theo in. Her harsh expression unbent at the sight of him.
The constable did not go. 'I'll hear what she has to say to
you,' he said, and locked the door from the inside.

Theo pulled a chair across the room and sat down opposite the woman, but a distance away. He did not want to
be near her. He did not want to look at her. His eyes had
seen many things, and his faith had strengthened him in
times of fear, but this was one thing he could not look
upon. Still, she sought him with her eyes, tilting her head
until she caught his gaze.

'I believe in God, Mr Hallam,' she said eventually, her
voice swollen with emotion. 'I thought you might pray
with me, but I can see it would pain you to do so.'

Theo felt ashamed. It was his duty to pray with whoever requested it; that she had seen so clearly and

immediately in his face that he did not wish to help her, distressed him.

'Will you listen to me?' she said. 'You mean a good deal to me, Mr Hallam. You are, perhaps, the first good man I have ever known, with the exception of my own parish priest.'

'Did you kill Martha's niece?' he said.

She nodded, and he saw the constable taking notes. 'And the others,' she said. 'Amy, Catherine, and the other girl – I tried. Sweets and drinks.' She leaned down and tapped the large, leather bag on the floor by her feet. 'I was always prepared. I would drown them, if I had the strength. Or, if not, I knew the sea would take them. I always waited for them to fall asleep. Apart from that last girl; her brother got away from me.' She smiled, gently, and Theo felt sick with it, sick and at the same time, tears pricked at the corners of his eyes.

She sought his gaze once more, but he could only look at her for a moment before looking away again.

'Do you not see it?' she said. 'It was my mission to protect them. It was noble, it was pure. Like them, I was a happy little girl until my mother died. Before long, my stepfather, my stepbrother – I was never safe from them. So when I saw beauty, and innocence, I had to protect it from the lusts of men. I would never have had the strength to kill the men – and how would I ever do it? How could I empty the world of these beasts who had destroyed the me that had once lived? How would I know who was good and who was not? No, I sought only to save a few beautiful girls, who in their heaven will surely thank me for my custody of their souls.' She looked at Theo sadly. 'I wish someone had drowned me at ten, so that I could have gone to heaven, and been at peace.'

Theo shook his head; he could not speak.

'It was on the beach at Broadstairs,' Miss Waring said, 'that my stepfather emptied my world of all its hope. It was the summer after my mother had died, and I had spent the day gathering shells. How I treasured it: the beauty shell I found. I was sitting, looking at it, the first time he touched me.'

Theo remembered the day of shell-gathering on the beach; how Miss Waring had fainted at the sight of the beauty shell.

Her face crumpled to the look of disgust she had shown at the sight of Benedict. 'I became a repository for all his darkness, all his filth. My stepbrother, too, who was led by his example. When I returned to Broadstairs, as a grown woman, I thought I would lay the past to rest. I only meant to walk on the beach. But I went to that spot, and there was a little girl looking into a rock pool, all alone – it overcame me. But the little girl on the beach was not the first one.

'The first was my cousin. He had joined in with ... the others. I still loved them, at least a little – a child loves, is meant to love. My stepfather had been the only father I had ever known; my stepbrother, away at school, had seemed like a god to me, before it all began. But not my cousin. I always hated him. I was walking into the dining room one day, and he was sitting with his back to me: lumpen, oblivious. So I stabbed him with my scissors. Oh, the feeling – it was horrible, Mr Hallam. Like pushing a blunt knife into cold butter. I could not have done that again.

'We were alone in the house, that day. When my step-father and brother saw what had happened, they did their best to cover it up, and they did, they did so very well. They moved his body to another place, and when he was found it was decided that he had been killed by a person unknown, for he had many enemies, and many debts. They didn't wish to lose me, you see.

'I went to Broadstairs after that; because I was with child. Alba looks like my stepfather. She has that same, unreadable expression.' She blinked, as though coming out of a daze. 'Years later, when I saw the first little girl on the beach, she looked so beautiful. So happy. That uncaring, innocent, absorbed happiness.'

'And you envied her?' said Theo, trying to recover his composure.

'Oh, a little, but that was not why I killed her. I simply watched her playing, and watched the expressions stirring on her face, and the sunlight in her golden curls and new skin, and I knew that she would never again be so happy in her life. All that was to follow was disappointment. Her beauty would be bruised and, finally, ruined completely – by the stifling qualities of life; by men. It was best to send her to heaven as she was; for her to have had a completely happy life. Complete happiness – what I would have given, to have had that. To always have had hope.

'I was strong enough to do it then, and quickly; though

the gorge rose in my throat, it was better than that horrible stabbing feeling. She did struggle, and that grieved me, for I told her that I was trying to help her, and I blessed her as she died. When I came back this summer, I knew I would never be able to do something so simple, and brutality was beyond me. So I simply took opportunities when I could. I always had the laudanum with me, for ease of use. And I let them sleep, and let the sea wash them clean. Clean, white, pure as Mary, Mother of God, Our Lady of Sorrows. I always said a prayer over them.' She leaned forwards, tried to pluck at his hand, but he pulled it away. 'I always prayed for their purity. I left them a token always – did you see? Shells for the pilgrim, and a word in the sand. I always blessed them for dying clean, white, pure as Mary. As I wished I had died.'

Theo emerged from the Clock House after the constable had led Miss Waring into the wagon and it had been driven away; he waited until the sound of the horses' hooves on the cobbles had faded. His mind was dark with a headache that had descended suddenly – a signal of the ordeal he had just gone through. The harbour was deserted, the boats still, apart from the slight rise and fall of the water, the sea dull and slick as oil. He looked around him. He had half-hoped – desperately – that Delphine might have waited for him, that he could at least speak to her and take some comfort from her presence. This night had stripped away all pretence; he loved her. But there was no one waiting for him.

He walked a little way along the harbour arm, found the seat that she had been sitting on in the sunshine, before any of this had come to them. He sat down where she had sat, looked out at the night, and began to pray.

CHAPTER TWENTY-EIGHT

I truly believe that I have only really begun to live again in the last year. Until Broadstairs I was simply the ghost of what I had been. I felt my life had been ended at twenty, as surely as if a street robber had stuck a knife clean into my young red heart. I told you I am a virgin; and I want you to know also that I never even kissed the man who took my life from me with his words.

Mine, you see, is a confession of innocence. I make it to show you that innocence does not always appear to be innocent. It does not glow in its own particular, holy light – not always. Sometimes that innocence can still be shrouded in shame, in accusation and in guilt. And sometimes it is the darkest heart that appears to be the purest, and the purest heart that appears to be the most corrupt.

My soul was like the uncut pages of a book. I had no idea of what lay within; and no instrument to cut them free. The summer of 1851 I set the knife to those pages, and only now have I begun to read them. We are alike in that way, you and I.

It is the same for Alba. She writes to me occasionally. She is married now – I hope you do not mind to hear that? She only had to bear a few months working as a companion to an old lady, before the lady's heir was so overcome by her beauty that he proposed. I fully expect her letters to stop soon. She was always practical, dear little Alba, and for all that she suffered, I believe that she has the character to break with the past, completely.

I do not know how to close this letter, Theo. Part of me does not wish to, because it closes our conversation, and I must wait for another letter, or nothing.

After Julia married, I went to the western tip of Britain on my own. There, the rocks are hard, mud-coloured honeycombs, not soft, crumbling white cliffs, with their slight upper layer of earth and grass. I stood high on the cliffs, as high as the gulls, who screamed at me. Below me, the sea weaved and roared, grey, brown and white, a net of light over it. From that height it seemed to have its own pattern, its own logic. There was something mathematical there; if I had the right mind, I could have pinned it down, and turned it into an equation.

I thought long on it, but in the end I realized that I did not want to pin it down, just as I do not need to understand fully what lies between us.

I write to you now as Delphine Beck, not Amy Sears. And it is this new name that I will keep, for I have chosen it, as I am choosing to take the path towards you. We can only know what our story is by living it.

May, 1852

As he travelled, Theo imagined Delphine on the train jour-
neys she had taken over the years. He thought of her past,
and of his own, and he turned his face to the window. As
the train jolted through the countryside, he imagined her
sitting beside him, her bonnet tied neatly under her chin,
the ends of the bow of even length; her gloved hands
folded in her lap, gloves that fitted so perfectly it was as
though they had been sewn on to her hands. Yet he knew
for all her stillness that her eyes would watch as keenly as
he watched, drinking in the details of the landscape, the
sunlight of spring, and the sharp outline of the train's
shadow on the track.

Have you ever seen a sky so blue? he thought. Have
you ever seen the grass so green? Each tree – a bright mystery, connection after connection in its branches. The dense
acidic yellow of the rapeseed flower; a tree standing there,
the circumference of its shadow forming a perfect circle in
the middle of the yellow field, where its shadow had
fallen, and the flowers had not grown.

His hand moved to touch his breast-pocket, and he felt
the shape of her last letter there. He could not take it out
and read it again; that would be too much. As if he did not
know it off by heart already.

The companions in his carriage were a middle-aged
woman and her daughter. The mother talked effusively
whilst the daughter, dull-eyed with misery, glanced apolo-

getically at Theo now and then, and licked her lips in the heat.

After the woman enquired of his wife and learned he was unmarried, Theo saw faint embarrassment in the girl's face – embarrassment, yes, and was that – actually – *hope*? He stifled a sigh, turned back to the window and braced himself for whatever delicate enquiries might be coming next.

The next thing he knew, he was waking in full sunlight. On opening his eyes, he knew his gift of falling asleep in any situation – though bad-mannered – had saved him. The light was so bright, so warm on his skin, that he thought for a moment he was in Ceylon again, jogged awake by the movement of the cart taking him to Colombo.

The first sight that greeted him was the blue sky, its slowly moving clouds tangling and untangling – the same sky as in Ceylon, he thought; he could be there. Then the focus of his gaze changed direction and he saw the mother, her face fixed in an expression of proud displeasure. The daughter risked a slight smile in his direction.

Did I speak in my sleep? was his first thought. He wanted to ask them. He wondered, with a pang, what he had said. Or maybe it was just the mother's unhappiness at being thwarted in her marital intentions that so stiffened her expression. Then it occurred to him that soon, perhaps, he would be able to ask his wife if he spoke in his sleep. What would she say? He rehearsed her name in his mind: said it again, and again, and again. He had never spoken her first name out loud. He would not say it now; he would speak it when he met her, so that she would hear it as he did: anew. Saying it in his mind gave it a soft kind of vibration, a resonance that moved through his body.

Delphine sat on the edge of the park, watching those who walked through it, listening to snatches of conversation. It was one of her favourite occupations, though normally she brought Julia, for the sake of respectability.

Walking down a street in the City a few weeks before, she had caught the scent of it: incense. Even in that London street it sent her nerves tingling with so many sensations that for a while she was no longer there, but in the solemn, flint-fronted church on the Kent coast. Smells, sounds and sights came upon her: dust, the pages of prayer books, the hardness of the wooden pews darkened by thick varnish, every single coloured cell of light from the windows cast on the wood of the floor. She thought about the vast sunny spaces of that church; how Theo had to close them in with incense – of how he sought to make mysteries out of clear space. She remembered his voice, the voice that had reminded her of the faith of her childhood: resonant yet tender, pure and precise. It was unwise to love him, yet she did.

His first letter had come on a bright, clear March day. It lay on the breakfast table, on the silver tray their maid used for the letters, Delphine's name written clearly on the front.

Edmund saw it first. 'It's Theo's writing,' he said, and

passed it across to Delphine. 'In his last letter, he said he would be writing to you.' They looked at each other across the table, as Julia poured the tea. 'He has been examining his thoughts,' she said. 'We have conversed in our letters about the deep melancholy that ailed him, and how he may live with it in future. But it is up to you, my dear sister, whether you wish to hear what he has to say.'

Delphine took the letter, and went up to her room.

My dear Mrs Beck, the letter began, *forgive me.* She still remembered the first shock she had felt at seeing his hand-writing form her name. The delight that crept over her as she read his words, densely packed into each page, sur-prised her too. He had asked her if she wished to know of him, truly. She had thought about it for days, sitting on the edge of the park, as she did now. She had thought it would be better to tell him not to write, to learn to live quietly, to be peaceful, at last. Then, when she sat to compose the letter, she had found herself writing the word, *yes.*

Since then, Edmund and Julia had watched with amaze-ment as a dense cream envelope arrived on the silver tray every day. The penultimate letter was a declaration of love, a declaration that had made Delphine catch her breath, for they had never been in each other's presence since that dreadful night when Miss Waring, now com-mitted as insane, had sought to kill Daisy Benedict. Then the last letter came.

Please, tell me, he had written, the same words he said to her on the harbour arm at Ramsgate. *Write to me openly, and honestly. Let me see that summer through your eyes. Let me hear your apprehensions, your impressions. I cannot make you do this, I know. But I cannot forget that summer, until I know the truth of it all, from you.*

The clouds were moving fast across the sky. She watched the colour of the grass, dark then light, from those clouds moving above. She had written her letter, and waited, never expecting a reply. But it had come, three days later. *I will arrive in London on the 25th.*

The shadowline of the trees sharpened as the sun came out from behind the cloud then, just as suddenly, shadow unfurled itself across the park, a darkness moving at walking pace, just as it had on the day when they had pulled Polly Dean and her child from the sea.

The wind shook the trees above her and a few stray leaves fell, floating in the breeze, a diagonal line to the ground. She would go home now, leave the serenity of the park and venture through the London streets. When I see him, she thought, then will I know.

The house Delphine shared with Julia and Edmund was in the City; it was comfortable, and as she approached it, she thought of the contentment she had found there, watching Edmund and Julia in their happiness. A child was to be born to them, very soon, and at the moment Delphine had learned of it, the final vestiges of the anger she felt at Julia's betrayal had disappeared, like mist broken up by the morning sunlight.

That house was now her home. Knowing that Theo was sitting in its parlour made her nervous, and she wondered again if she had been wrong to encourage him.

The maid let her in; she opened the parlour door.

'Theo is taking tea with us,' said Julia. 'Will you take a cup?'

Delphine sat down. How strange the conversation was, how stilted, until Edmund at last found a reason for Julia and himself to go out for a moment, leaving Delphine and Theo sitting, side by side, neither eating nor drinking, until Theo set his cup down with a clatter and she saw that he was shaking.

He turned, and they looked at each other.

'Is there a way to begin again?' he said.

EPILOGUE

London, 1854

The couple, a lady and a gentleman, were the first to enter the Great Room of the Royal Academy for the Summer Exhibition. It did not take them long to find the picture they were looking for, having sought advice from the porter – and it was in a prominent position. The canvas was several yards in length, and the couple regarded it with deep concentration, standing apart, he in a black coat and top hat, she in a pale blue dress and bonnet.

'Do you like it?' she said, at last. 'The newspapers say they will likely have to put a rail up, to keep the crowds away, as they did with his painting last year.'

'It is finely executed,' said Theo. 'But you are the artist, my love. Your opinion counts more than mine.'

Delphine glanced at him and smiled.

'He is very clever,' she said. 'There are some critics who will sneer, of course, but his grasp of detail and composition is unrivalled.' She moved to the corner and looked at the signature – neat, with a swirl on each capital: *R. Benedict.*

'Another triumph,' Theo said, without rancour.

Already more people were approaching, and the sound of voices was growing louder in the room. Delphine set to examining the painting again, as though she hoped to grasp every detail before other people came alongside her, expressing their opinions. The picture was of the sands at Broadstairs, and it was painted from the viewpoint of the sea. It depicted the mass of visitors on the sands of Main Bay: a gentleman reading the paper; two women gossiping; another woman lifting a child into the water so that she might paddle. In the distance there were bathing machines. One of the men was clearly Edmund Steele. A young girl, with a gaily beribboned bonnet, was Alba, and the lady sitting on the sand, dressed in white, bore a resemblance to Julia, but with no birthmark.

'Is it ethical,' said Theo, 'for him to paint people without asking?'

She sighed. 'No. Alba knew – she said so in her last letter – and I suppose Edmund and Julia will not be so troubled by it. Perhaps. As long as their names are never mentioned. I don't think he would – do you?'

'One can never know,' said Theo. 'But I think not. He wishes to forget that summer, I'm sure.' He brushed at her waist with his hand. 'I am astonished that he did not paint *you*,' he said.

Delphine remembered the wildflower meadow on the cliffs near Kingsgate, that blistering day. Remembered Benedict's cold and hazy gaze: 'There are some people I cannot paint,' he had said. She wondered if he had loved, or hated her; and she shook off the thought.

'Let us go, shall we?' she said, tucking her hand into the crook of her husband's arm. 'It is such a crush, now.'

The Hallams' visit to the Academy was at the beginning of a short holiday for them. Their parish in London took up a good deal of their time. At the end of that day they took the train to Margate, then travelled by hired carriage to Broadstairs, where they had rented a small house for a fortnight. They came via the coast road. The light was fading, the sea mist rolling in, setting its thin veil over the sea and cliffs. The light of the North Foreland lighthouse pressed out its insistent beam into the mist, and at the sight of it Delphine took her husband's hand, for she knew it would remind him of his past.

The rented house was on the road to Stone. The front doorway had a Gothic point to it, as did the latticed windows. The sharp sea-winds set off little draughts here and there, through the house, their whistling seeming to call to the gulls.

'Perhaps we should not have come back,' said Delphine

that evening. She was sitting before the dressing table, in her nightdress, brushing her hair. 'I did wonder.' In the mirror, she saw her husband, sitting on the bed, misgiving written plain across his face. 'I know you wished to see the place again, with me at your side, but some things should be left in the past.' He said nothing, and she put the brush down. 'My dear?'

'Mr Benedict never approved of me,' he said. 'He would say I have taken something beautiful and imprisoned it.' He looked at her. 'Have I?'

'Am I a *something*?' she said archly, catching his gaze in the reflection of the mirror. 'I made my decision. It is true, I never saw myself as a clergyman's wife, but now I am, and it is the first decision I have ever made for myself, freely.'

'I can still hardly believe it,' he said.

'Nor I,' she said, and laughed. 'It is a mystery, Mr Hallam.' And she tied her hair back with a ribbon.

There was a boom, like distant thunder.

'There's a wreck,' he said.

Delphine rose and tiptoed across the bare boards of the room, over the bedside rug with its flowering rose pattern. She climbed up on to the bed, knelt beside him and untied the stock around his starched collar. He watched her, and there was a quality to his watching as though he was observing her for the first time. When she had finished untying it, he kissed her.

She drew away. 'Do not think of melancholy things,' she said. 'You told me you were longing for a respite from

London; that you were going to pick me up and twirl me around the moment you could breathe clean air again.'

His mouth twitched. He guided her hands around his neck, set them firm there, then encircled her waist with one arm and put the other beneath her, as though he was about to lift her. His gaze was no longer opaque to her. She saw the emotions that crossed his face: his faith, his doubt, his devotion and his passion. And through it all, with her gaze, she drew a smile from him.

'Will you promise me something?' he said.

She nodded.

'You won't let go,' he said.

She raised her hand and looked at the single gold ring on her finger, the only piece of jewellery she now wore. They heard another boom roar out over the sea, its angry lament echoing in the darkness alongside the warning of the lighthouse beam over the crashing sea.

'The promise is already made,' she said.

AUTHOR'S NOTE

The inspiration for this book was William Powell Frith's painting *Ramsgate Sands (Life at the Seaside)*, which depicts Victorian holidaymakers on the beach. Frith holidayed in Ramsgate with his family every year, and would have been working on preparatory sketches for the picture in the summer of 1851; Mr Benedict was inspired by the idea of an artist on holiday. *Ramsgate Sands (Life at the Seaside)* was shown at the Royal Academy in 1854, becoming an instant hit, and was bought by Queen Victoria and Prince Albert. It remains in the Royal Collection today.

Some eagle-eyed readers will have spotted that, whilst it is perfectly possibly that Miss Waring and Alba viewed paintings at the National Gallery, they would not have seen the particular paintings discussed with Mr Benedict. *The Baptism of Christ* by Piero della Francesco and *Noli Me*

Tangere by Titian were acquired by the Gallery in 1861 and 1856 respectively.

I have only ever been to the Goodwin Sands in my imagination. My vision of it owes much to the many excellent books on the subject, especially *Memorials of the Goodwin Sands* by George Byng Gattie, and *The Goodwin Sands* by George Goldwin Carter, in addition to the advice of my father and Tim Seward.

I have chosen not to use the names of the real residents of Broadstairs in 1851, apart from Solomon Holbourn, the lifeboatman who played a pivotal role in the famous *Mary White* rescue, and who is immortalized in the song of the same name.

Main Bay, Broadstairs, was renamed Viking Bay in 1949.

ACKNOWLEDGEMENTS

I am grateful to my editor Clare Hey, not only for her excellent judgement in the editing process, but for being the most tactful and good-humoured of editors. I am also grateful for the support of a fantastic team at Simon & Schuster: Carla Josephson for her editing skills, Joan Deitch for her superb and sensitive copy-editing, and the wonderful Helen Mockridge, Dawn Burnett, Jamie Groves, Gill Richardson, Rumana Haider, Dominic Brendon, Mel Four, Glen Holmes and Nico Poilblanc, and many others.

Grateful thanks as always to my brilliant and support-ive agent, Jane Finigan, and to all at Lutyens & Rubinstein. I am so thankful to be represented by such a fantastic team of people.

My father and Tim Seward answered my sea-related

questions, and I am grateful to both of them for their local knowledge.

As always, the staff of the London Library have been extremely helpful.

My thanks to my friends and colleagues for cheering me on: your support means a great deal.

I am immensely grateful to my family for their loyalty and encouragement: thank you Mum, Dad, Lisa, Samuel and Harrison. Love also to my sister Angela and her family. Last but not least, I owe so much to my husband, who makes everything possible. This book is dedicated to him, with love and gratitude.